# SQUIRE & KNIGHT

## SCOTT CHANTLER

For the late Ronald Jacob, school librarian,
and for everyone else who keeps the lanterns lit.

# SQUIRE
# & KNIGHT

## SCOTT CHANTLER

First Second
New York

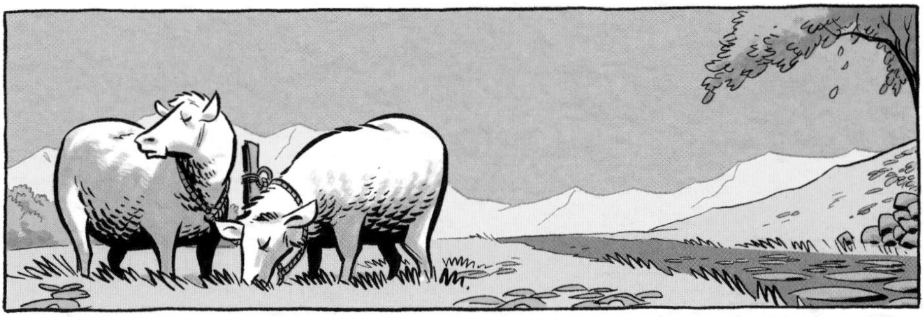

# CHAPTER ONE

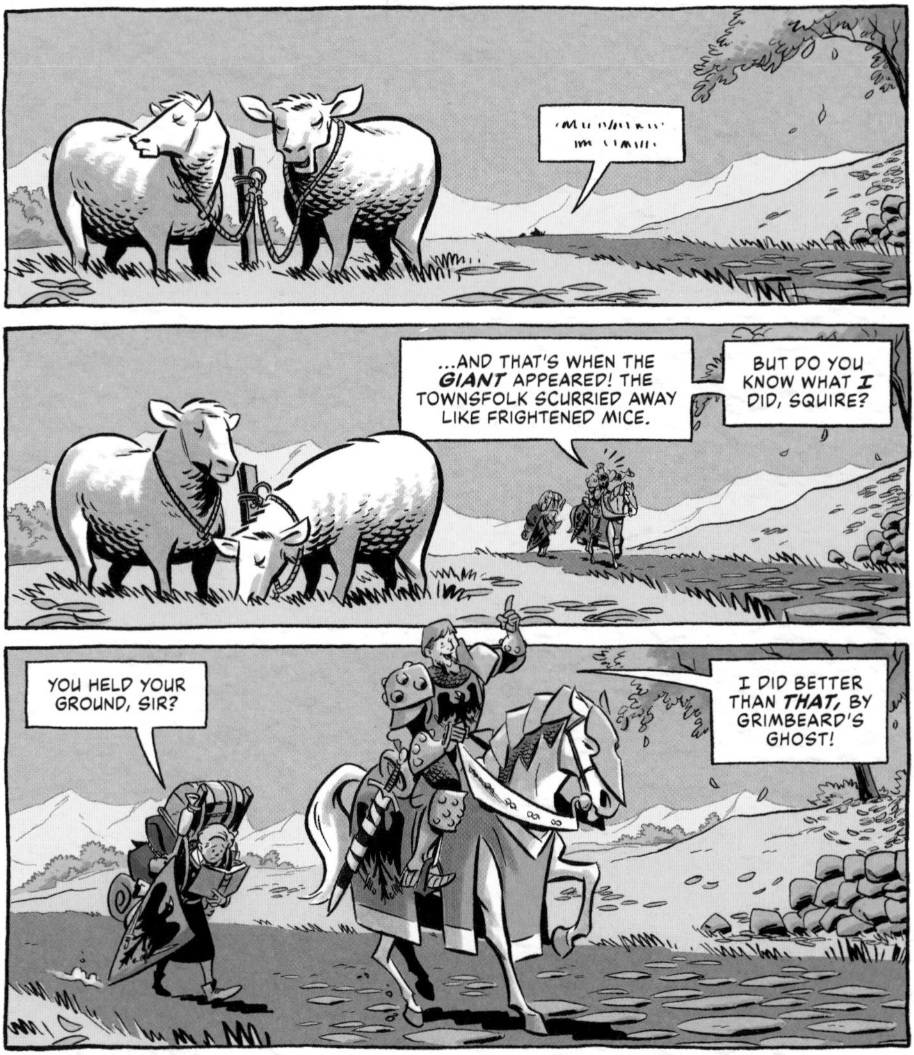
...AND THAT'S WHEN THE GIANT APPEARED! THE TOWNSFOLK SCURRIED AWAY LIKE FRIGHTENED MICE.
BUT DO YOU KNOW WHAT I DID, SQUIRE?
YOU HELD YOUR GROUND, SIR?
I DID BETTER THAN THAT, BY GRIMBEARD'S GHOST!

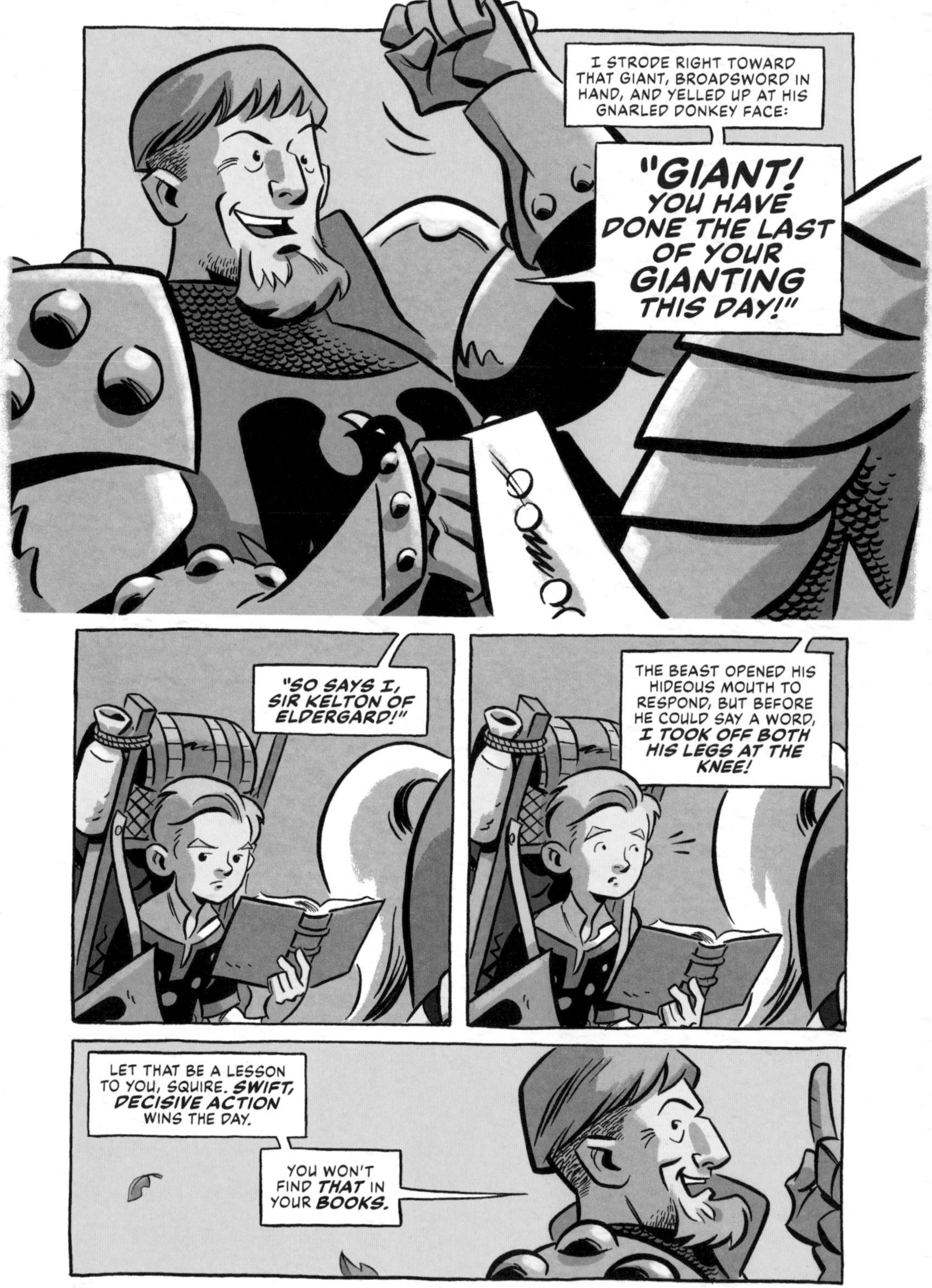
I STRODE RIGHT TOWARD THAT GIANT, BROADSWORD IN HAND, AND YELLED UP AT HIS GNARLED DONKEY FACE:
"GIANT! YOU HAVE DONE THE LAST OF YOUR GIANTING THIS DAY!"
"SO SAYS I, SIR KELTON OF ELDERGARD!"
THE BEAST OPENED HIS HIDEOUS MOUTH TO RESPOND, BUT BEFORE HE COULD SAY A WORD, I TOOK OFF BOTH HIS LEGS AT THE KNEE!
LET THAT BE A LESSON TO YOU, SQUIRE. SWIFT, DECISIVE ACTION WINS THE DAY.
YOU WON'T FIND THAT IN YOUR BOOKS.

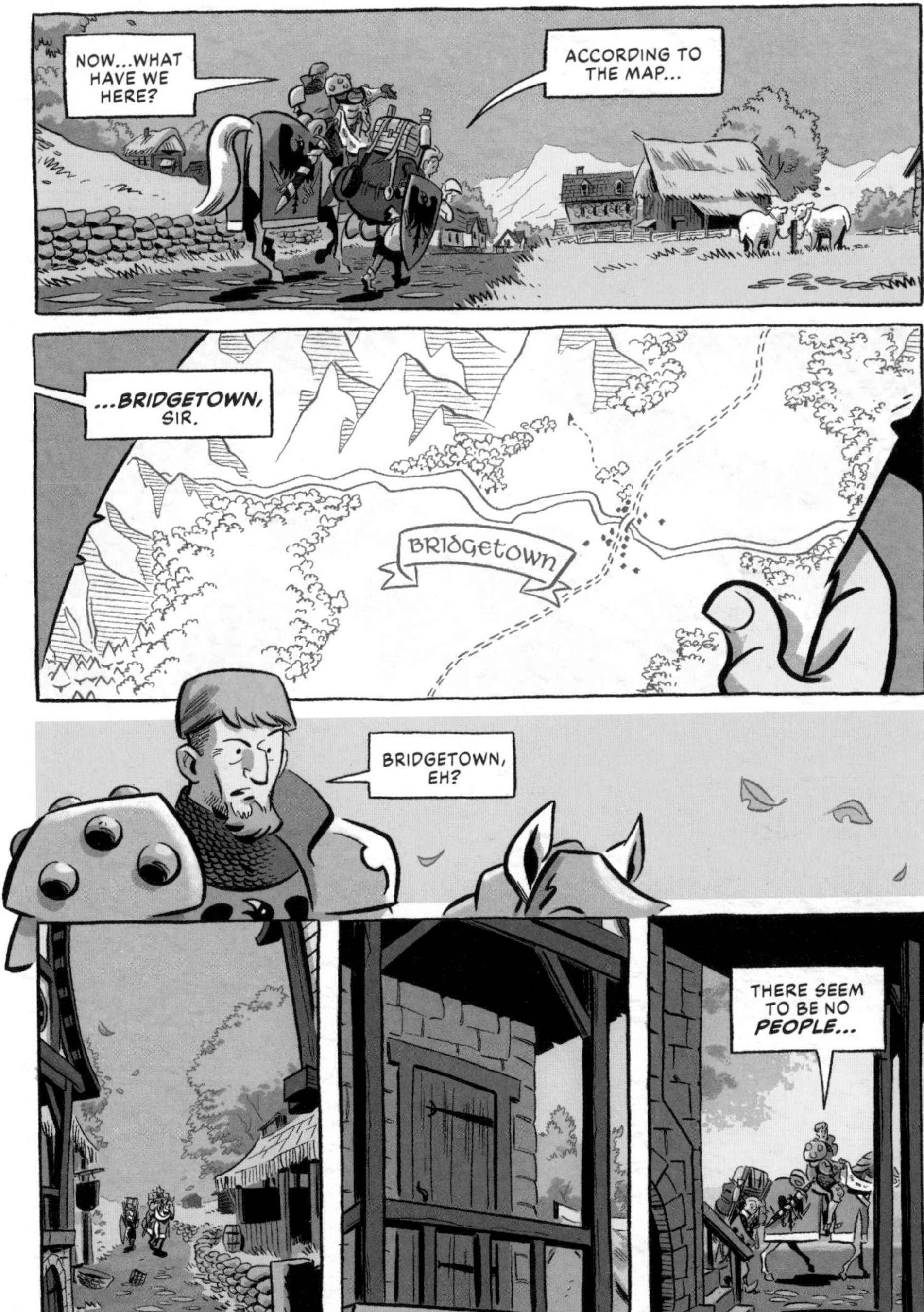
NOW...WHAT HAVE WE HERE?
ACCORDING TO THE MAP...
...BRIDGETOWN, SIR.
BRIDGETOWN
BRIDGETOWN, EH?
THERE SEEM TO BE NO PEOPLE...

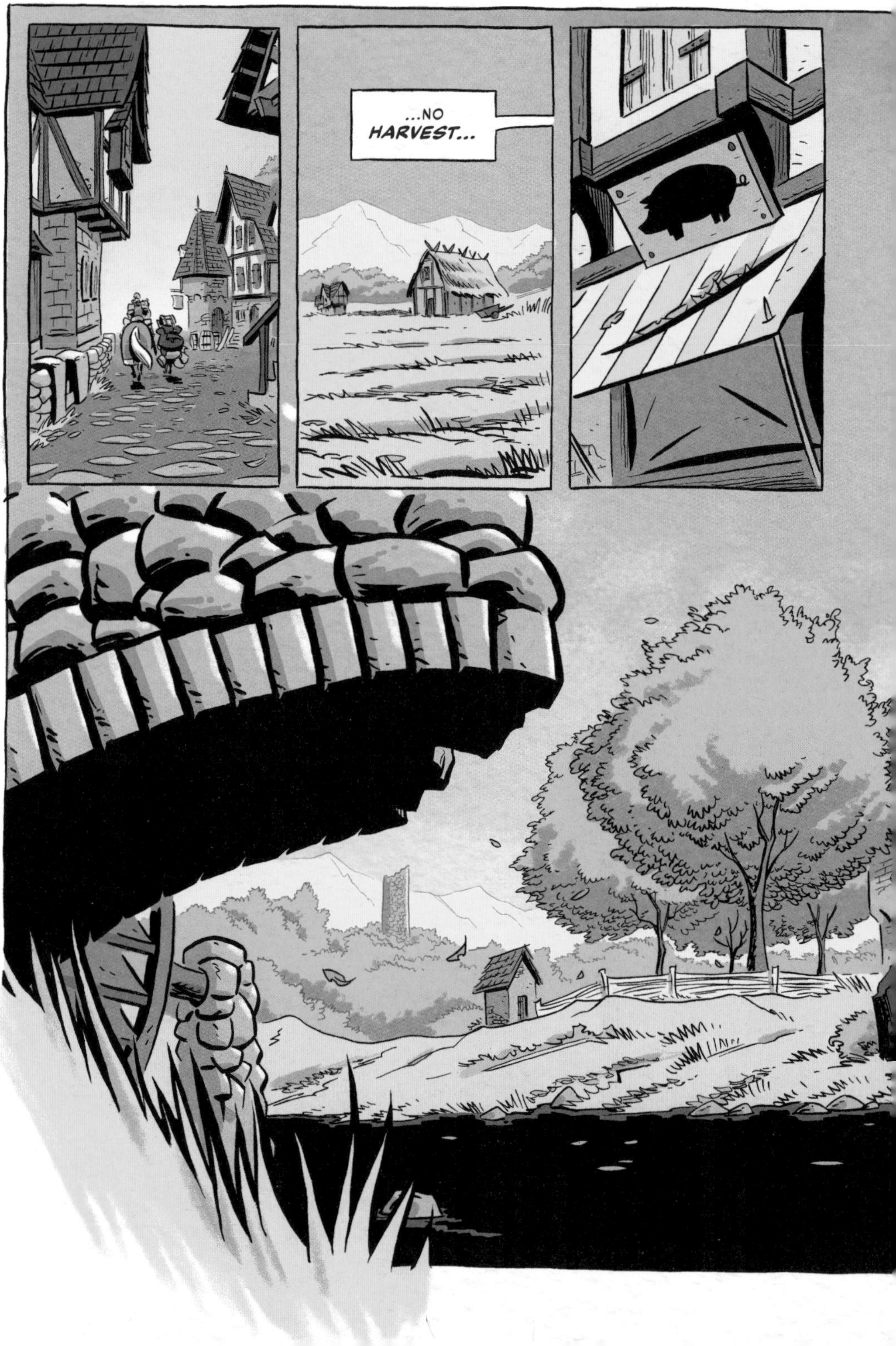
...NO HARVEST...

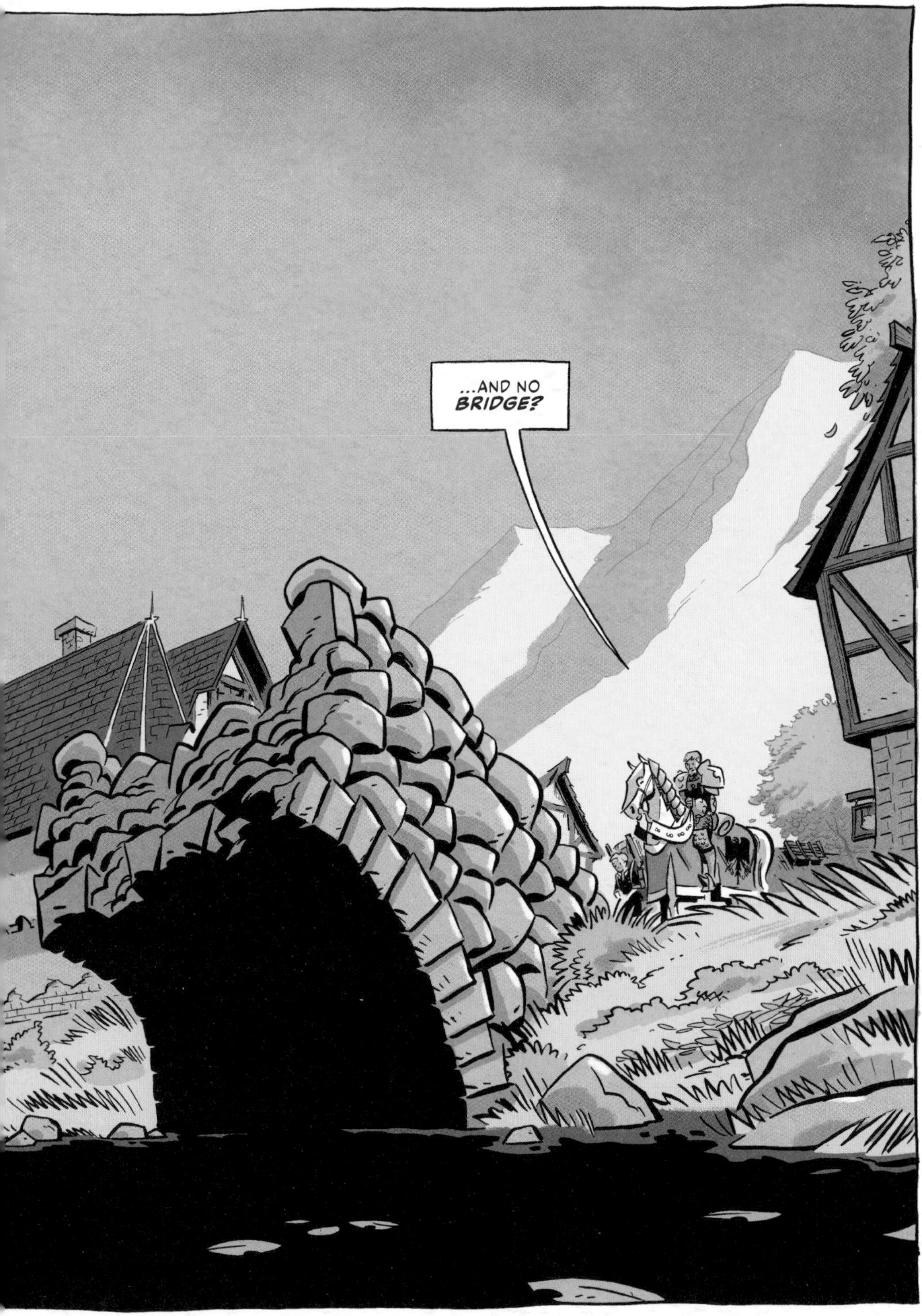
...AND NO BRIDGE?

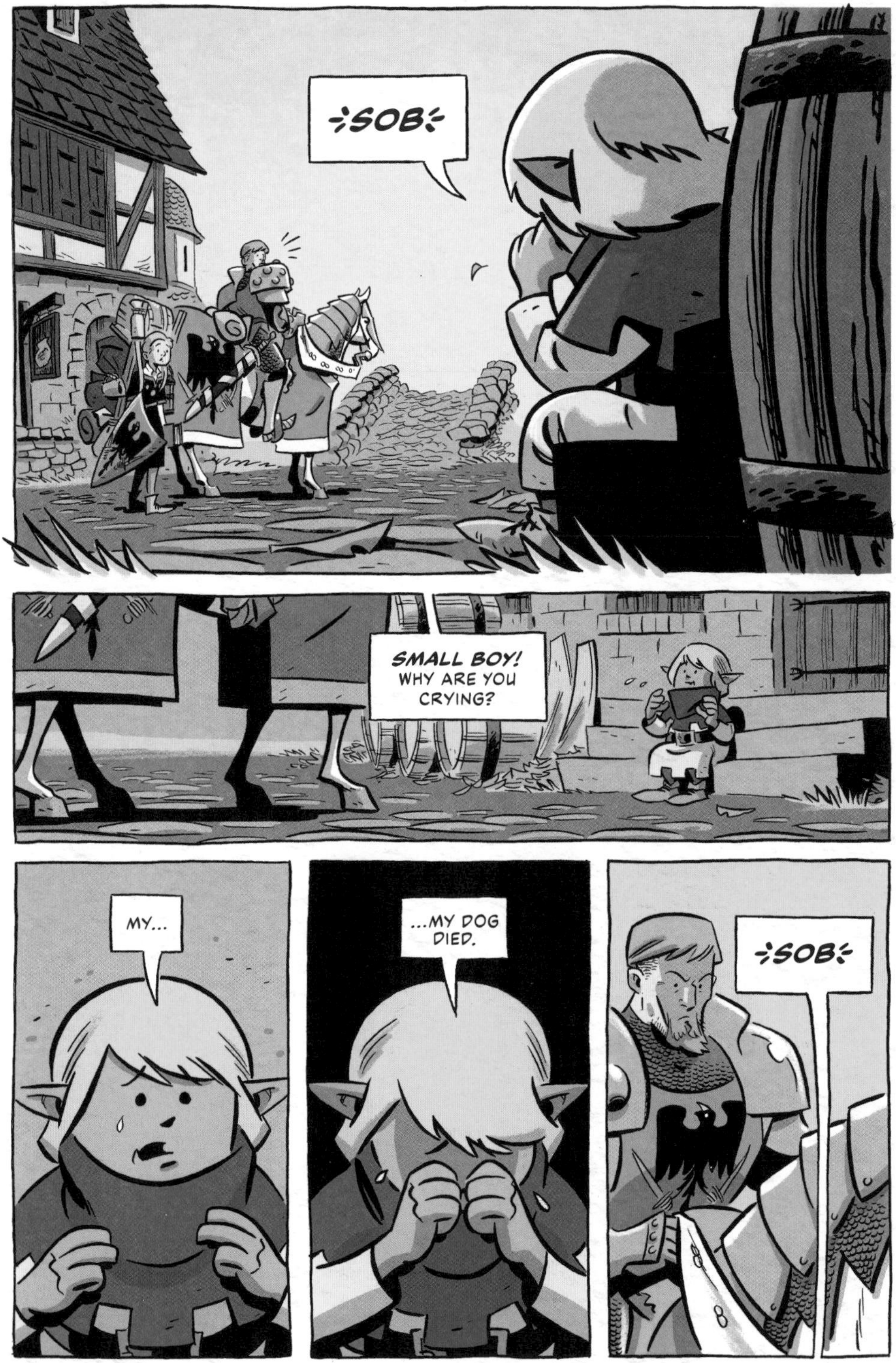

SOB
SMALL BOY! WHY ARE YOU CRYING?
MY...
...MY DOG DIED.
SOB

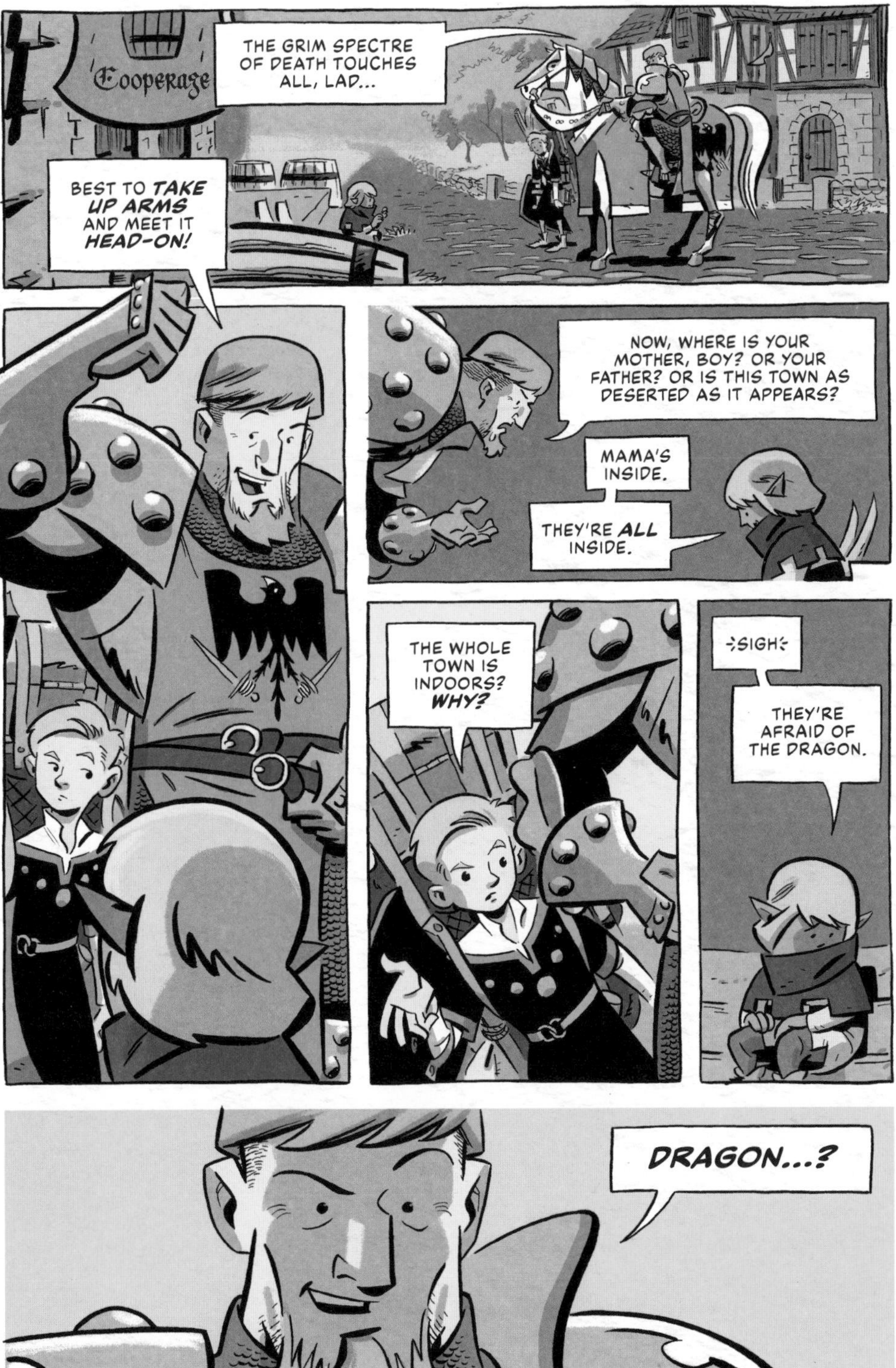
Cooperage
THE GRIM SPECTRE OF DEATH TOUCHES ALL, LAD...
BEST TO TAKE UP ARMS AND MEET IT HEAD-ON!
NOW, WHERE IS YOUR MOTHER, BOY? OR YOUR FATHER? OR IS THIS TOWN AS DESERTED AS IT APPEARS?
MAMA'S INSIDE.
THEY'RE ALL INSIDE.
THE WHOLE TOWN IS INDOORS? WHY?
SIGH
THEY'RE AFRAID OF THE DRAGON.
DRAGON...?

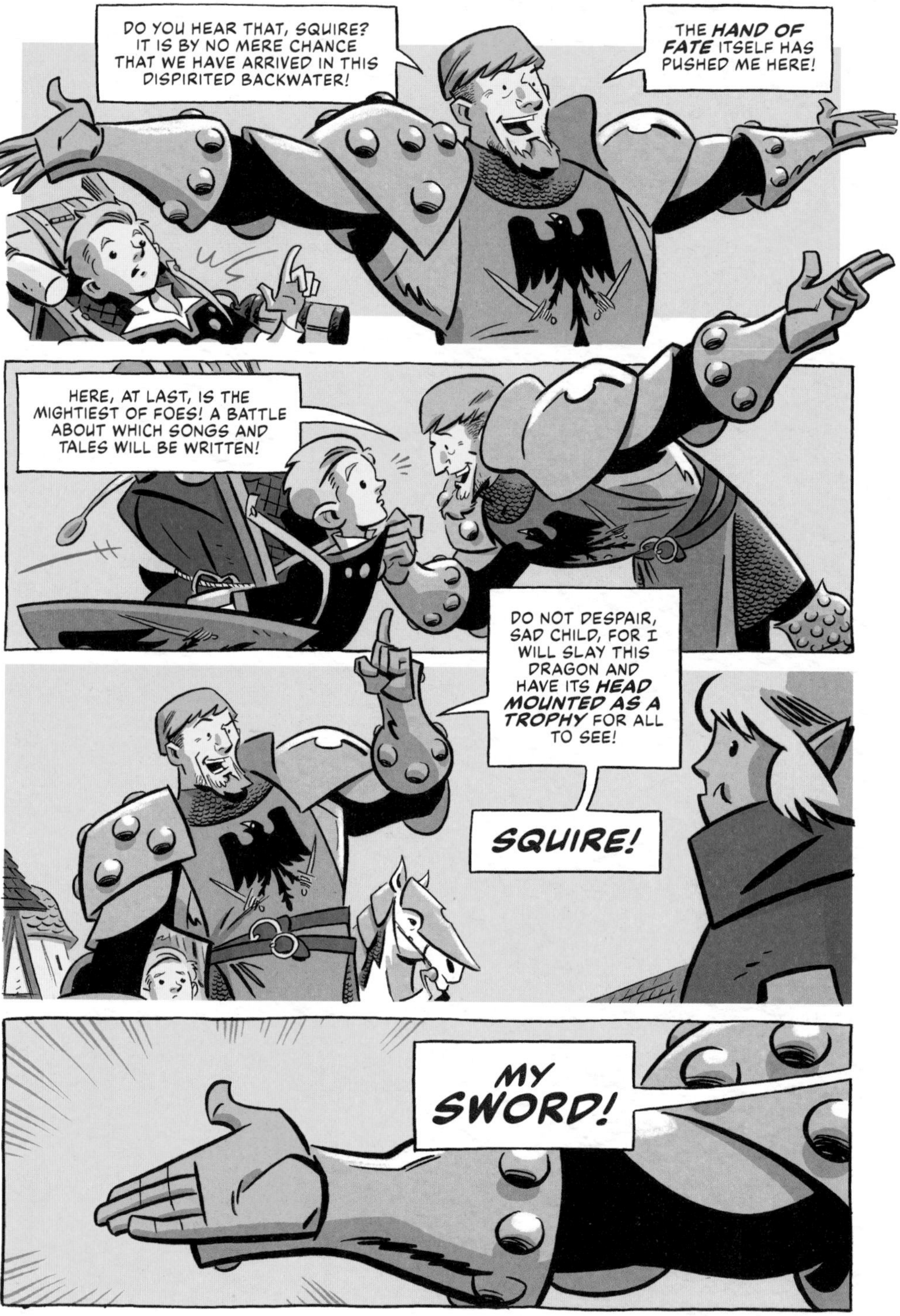
DO YOU HEAR THAT, SQUIRE? IT IS BY NO MERE CHANCE THAT WE HAVE ARRIVED IN THIS DISPIRITED BACKWATER!
THE ***HAND OF FATE*** ITSELF HAS PUSHED ME HERE!
HERE, AT LAST, IS THE MIGHTIEST OF FOES! A BATTLE ABOUT WHICH SONGS AND TALES WILL BE WRITTEN!
DO NOT DESPAIR, SAD CHILD, FOR I WILL SLAY THIS DRAGON AND HAVE ITS ***HEAD MOUNTED AS A TROPHY*** FOR ALL TO SEE!
***SQUIRE!***
***MY SWORD!***

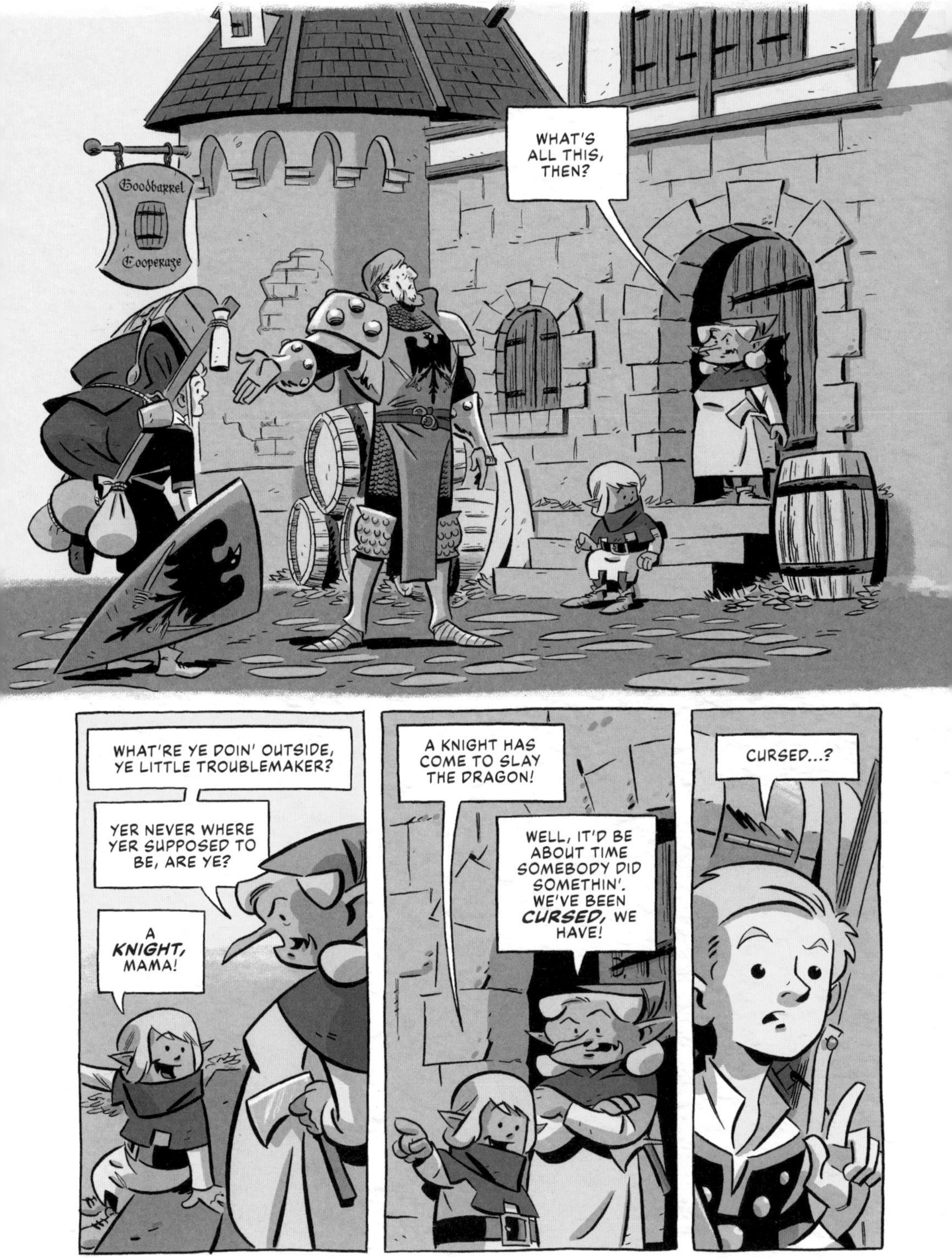
Goodbarrel
Cooperage
WHAT'S ALL THIS, THEN?
WHAT'RE YE DOIN' OUTSIDE, YE LITTLE TROUBLEMAKER?
YER NEVER WHERE YER SUPPOSED TO BE, ARE YE?
A *KNIGHT,* MAMA!
A KNIGHT HAS COME TO SLAY THE DRAGON!
WELL, IT'D BE ABOUT TIME SOMEBODY DID SOMETHIN'. WE'VE BEEN *CURSED,* WE HAVE!
CURSED...?

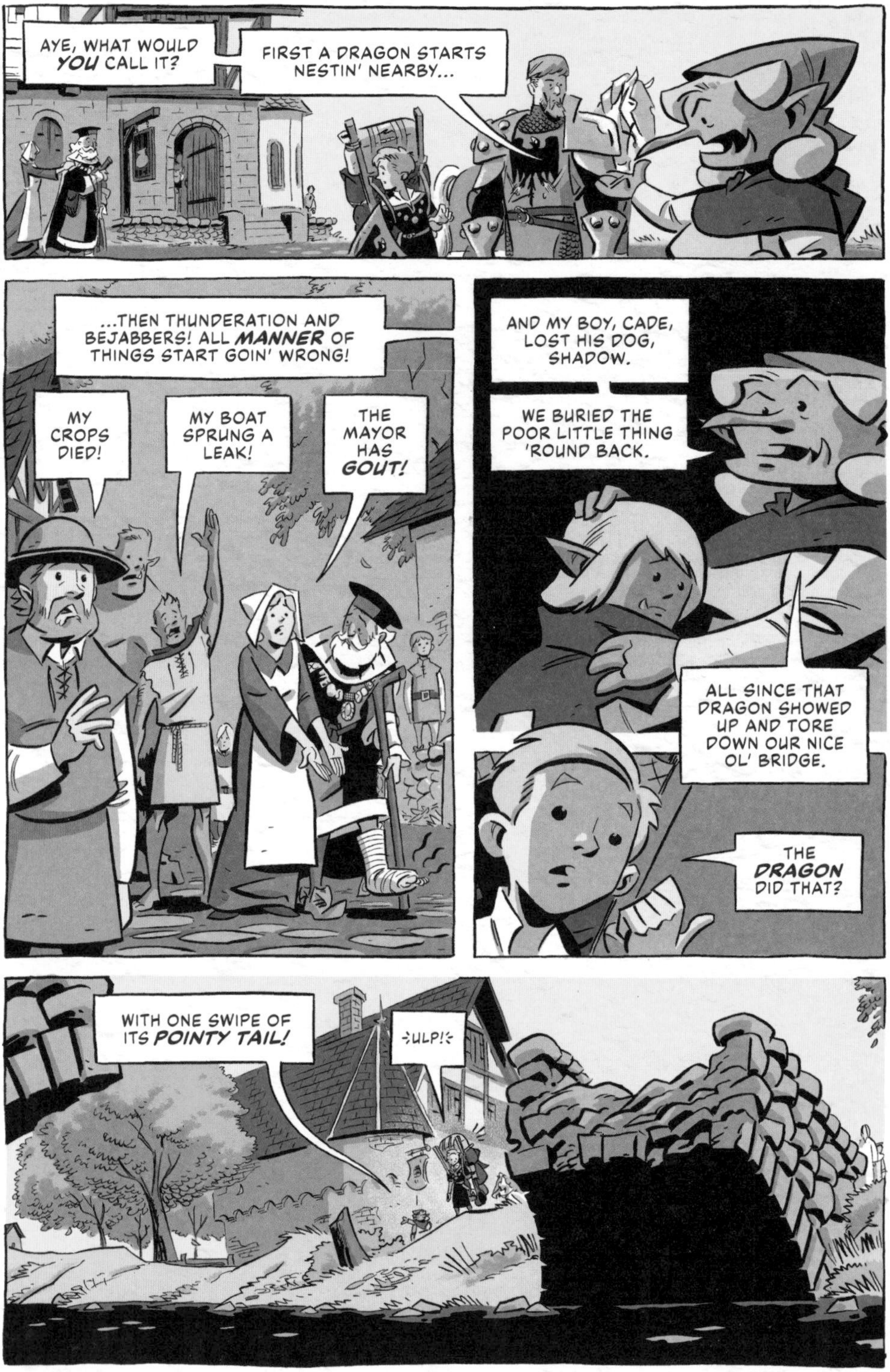
AYE, WHAT WOULD YOU CALL IT?
FIRST A DRAGON STARTS NESTIN' NEARBY...
...THEN THUNDERATION AND BEJABBERS! ALL MANNER OF THINGS START GOIN' WRONG!
MY CROPS DIED!
MY BOAT SPRUNG A LEAK!
THE MAYOR HAS GOUT!
AND MY BOY, CADE, LOST HIS DOG, SHADOW.
WE BURIED THE POOR LITTLE THING 'ROUND BACK.
ALL SINCE THAT DRAGON SHOWED UP AND TORE DOWN OUR NICE OL' BRIDGE.
THE DRAGON DID THAT?
WITH ONE SWIPE OF ITS POINTY TAIL!
ULP!

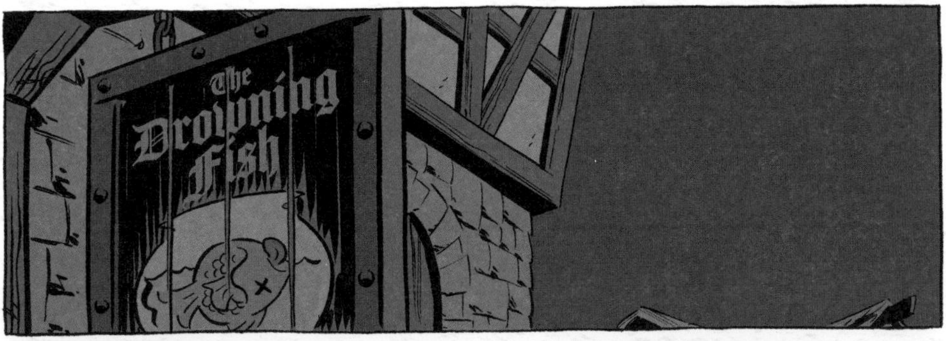
The Drowning Fish

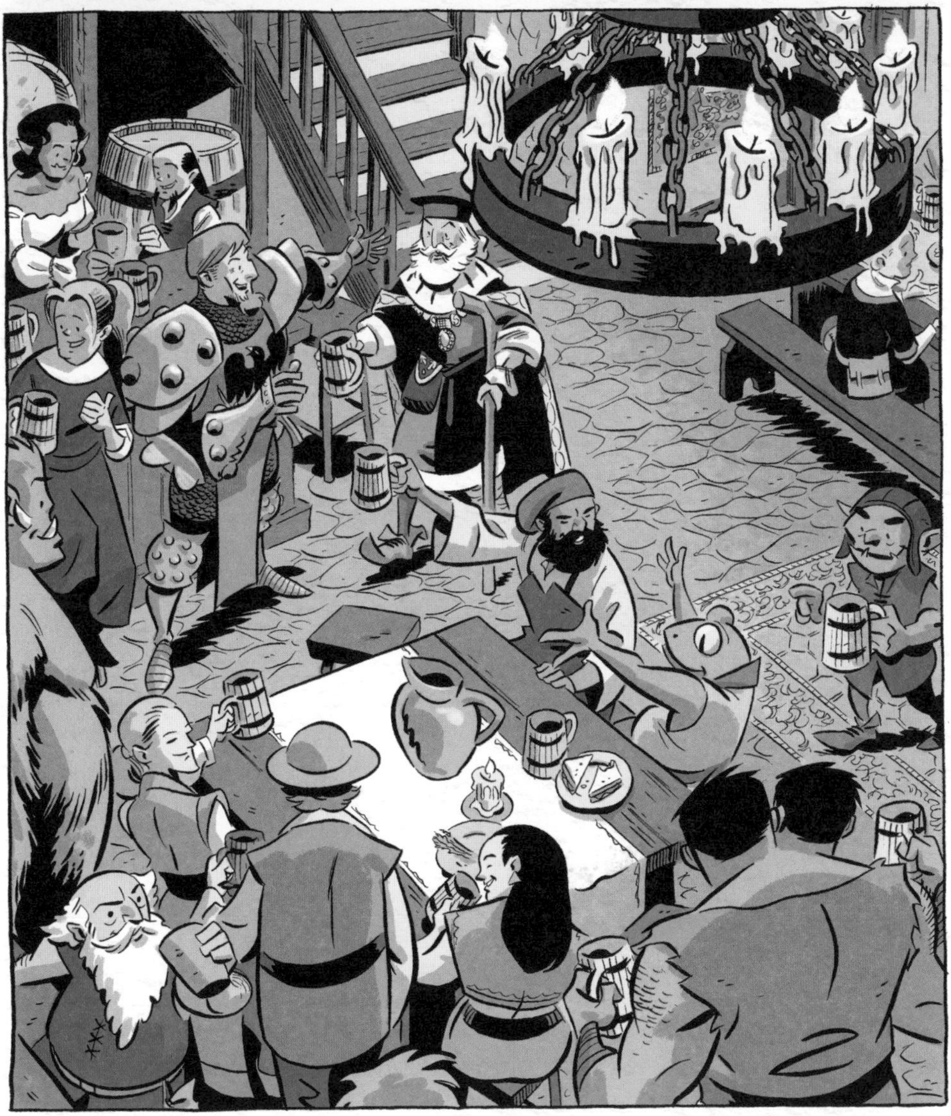

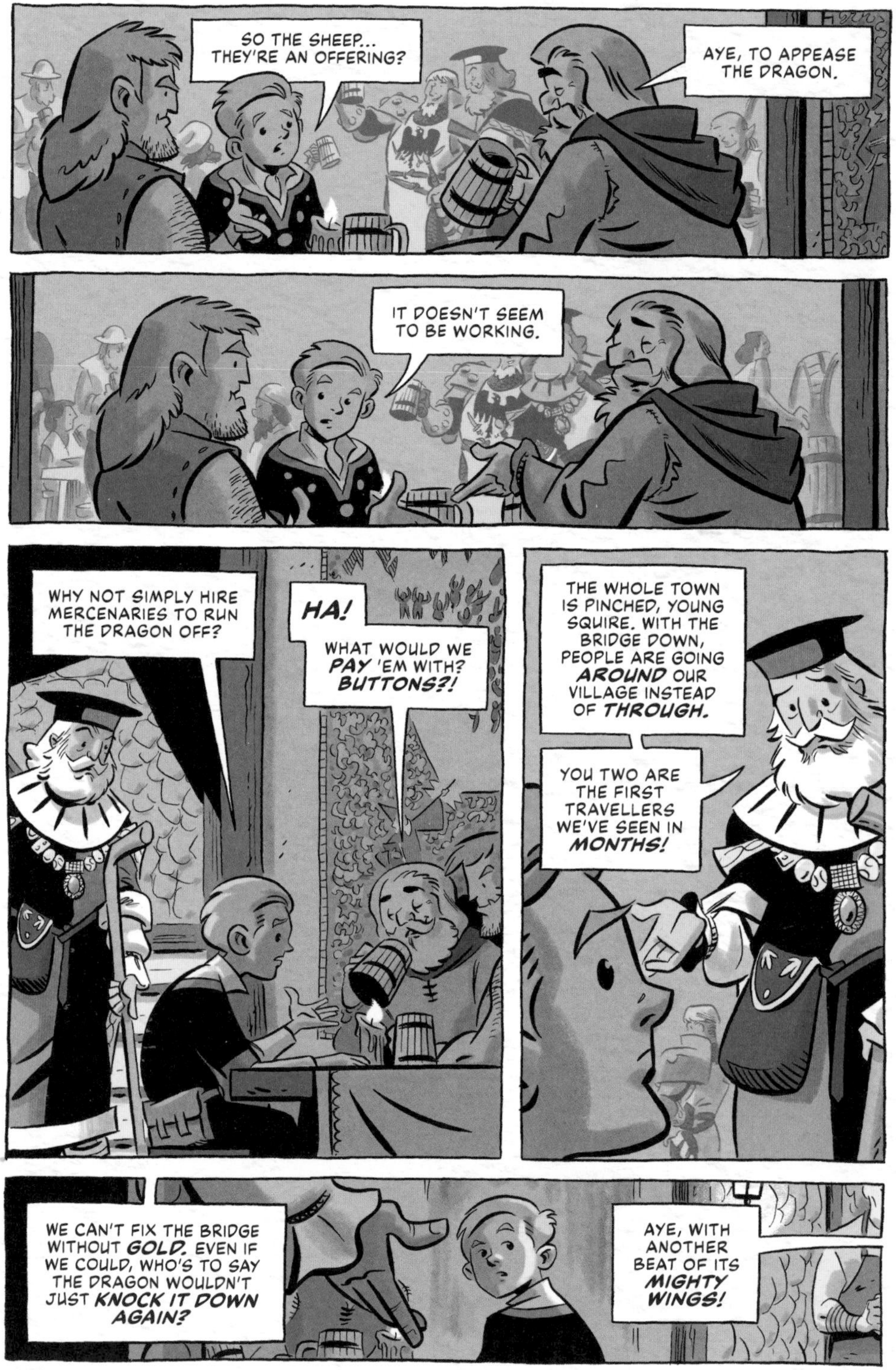
SO THE SHEEP... THEY'RE AN OFFERING?
AYE, TO APPEASE THE DRAGON.
IT DOESN'T SEEM TO BE WORKING.
WHY NOT SIMPLY HIRE MERCENARIES TO RUN THE DRAGON OFF?
HA!
WHAT WOULD WE PAY 'EM WITH? BUTTONS?!
THE WHOLE TOWN IS PINCHED, YOUNG SQUIRE. WITH THE BRIDGE DOWN, PEOPLE ARE GOING AROUND OUR VILLAGE INSTEAD OF THROUGH.
YOU TWO ARE THE FIRST TRAVELLERS WE'VE SEEN IN MONTHS!
WE CAN'T FIX THE BRIDGE WITHOUT GOLD. EVEN IF WE COULD, WHO'S TO SAY THE DRAGON WOULDN'T JUST KNOCK IT DOWN AGAIN?
AYE, WITH ANOTHER BEAT OF ITS MIGHTY WINGS!

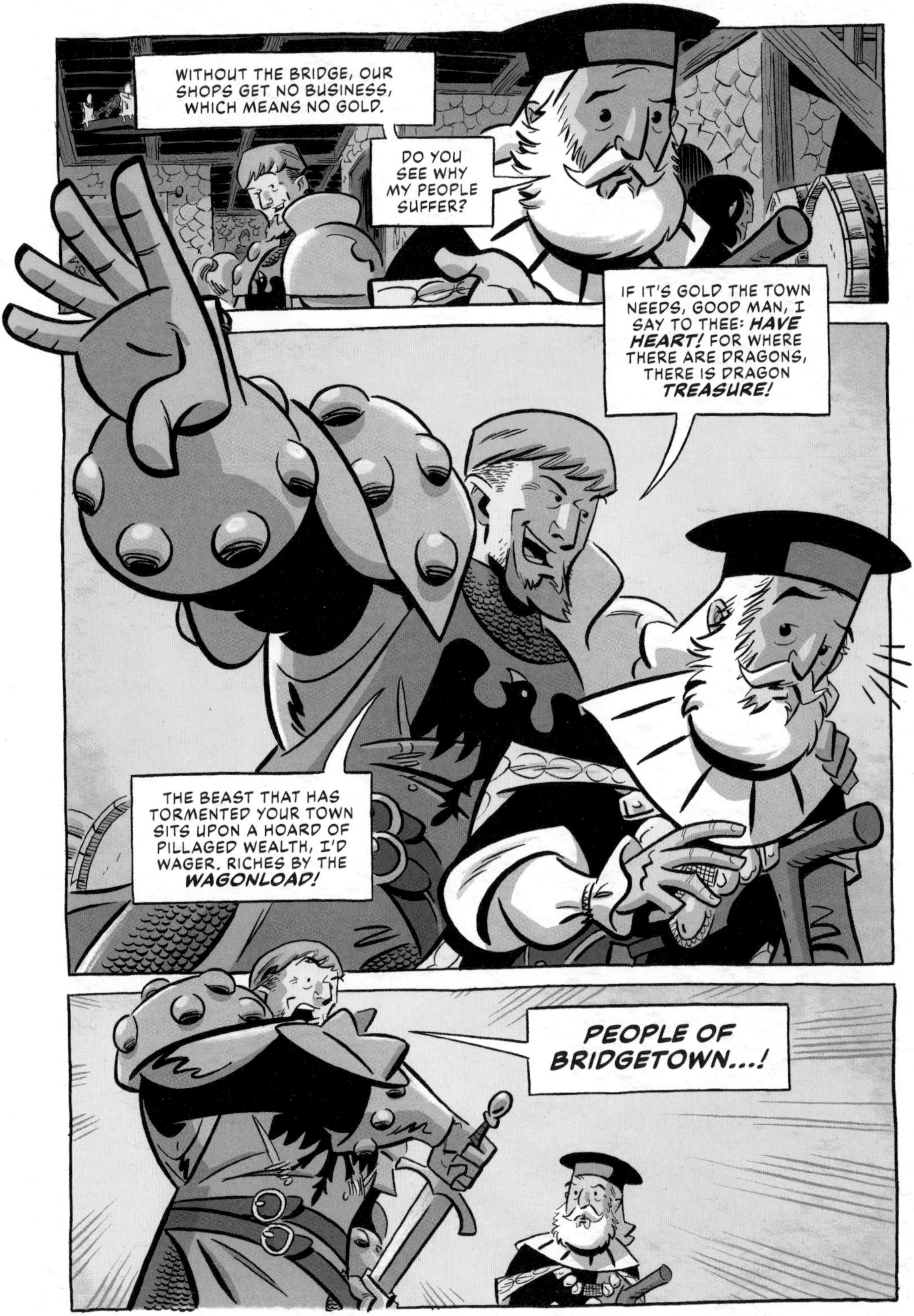
WITHOUT THE BRIDGE, OUR SHOPS GET NO BUSINESS, WHICH MEANS NO GOLD.
DO YOU SEE WHY MY PEOPLE SUFFER?
IF IT'S GOLD THE TOWN NEEDS, GOOD MAN, I SAY TO THEE: *HAVE HEART!* FOR WHERE THERE ARE DRAGONS, THERE IS DRAGON *TREASURE!*
THE BEAST THAT HAS TORMENTED YOUR TOWN SITS UPON A HOARD OF PILLAGED WEALTH, I'D WAGER. RICHES BY THE *WAGONLOAD!*
*PEOPLE OF BRIDGETOWN...!*

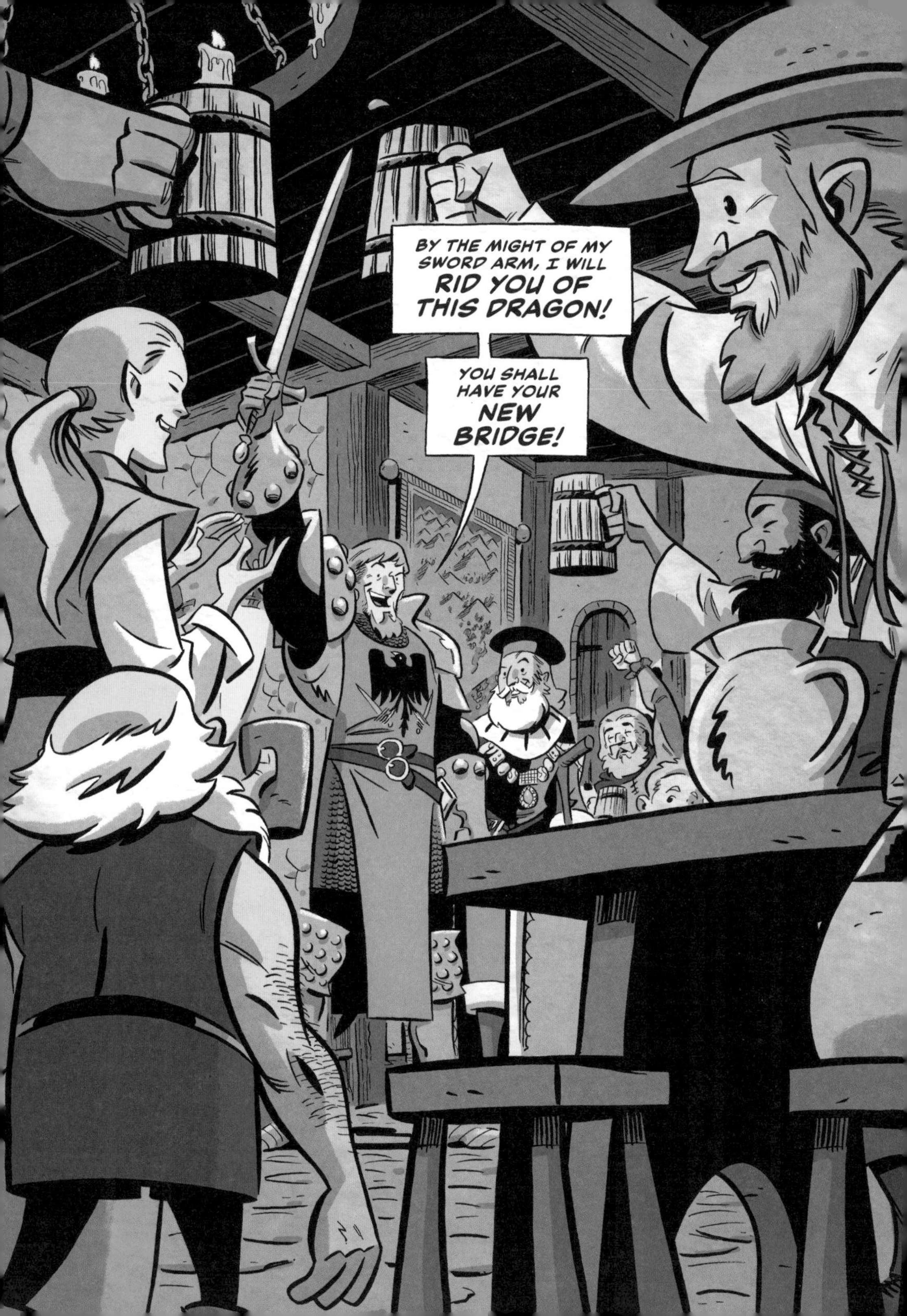
BY THE MIGHT OF MY SWORD ARM, I WILL RID YOU OF THIS DRAGON!
YOU SHALL HAVE YOUR NEW BRIDGE!

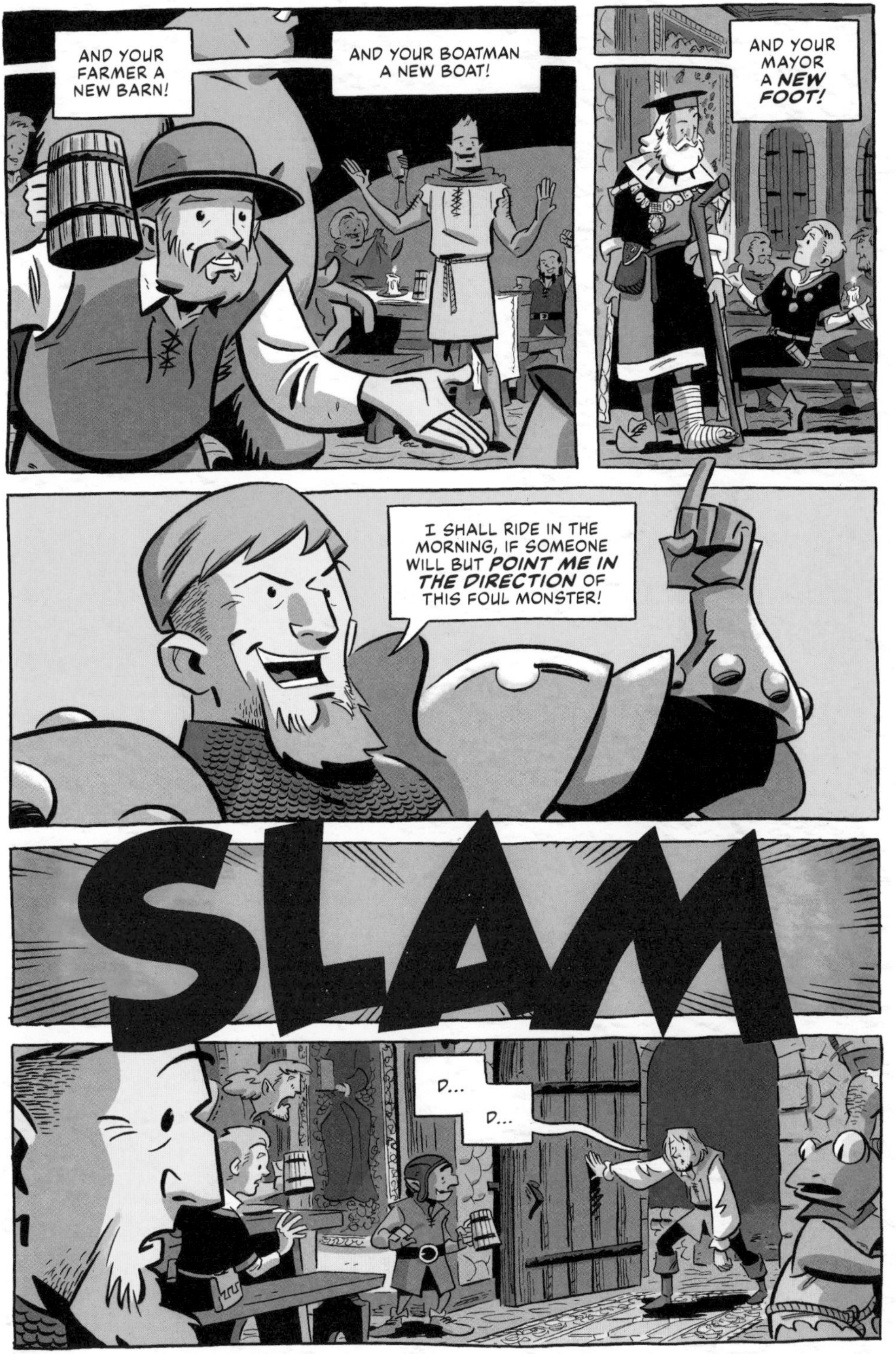
AND YOUR FARMER A NEW BARN!
AND YOUR BOATMAN A NEW BOAT!
AND YOUR MAYOR A ***NEW FOOT!***
I SHALL RIDE IN THE MORNING, IF SOMEONE WILL BUT ***POINT ME IN THE DIRECTION*** OF THIS FOUL MONSTER!
SLAM
D...
D...

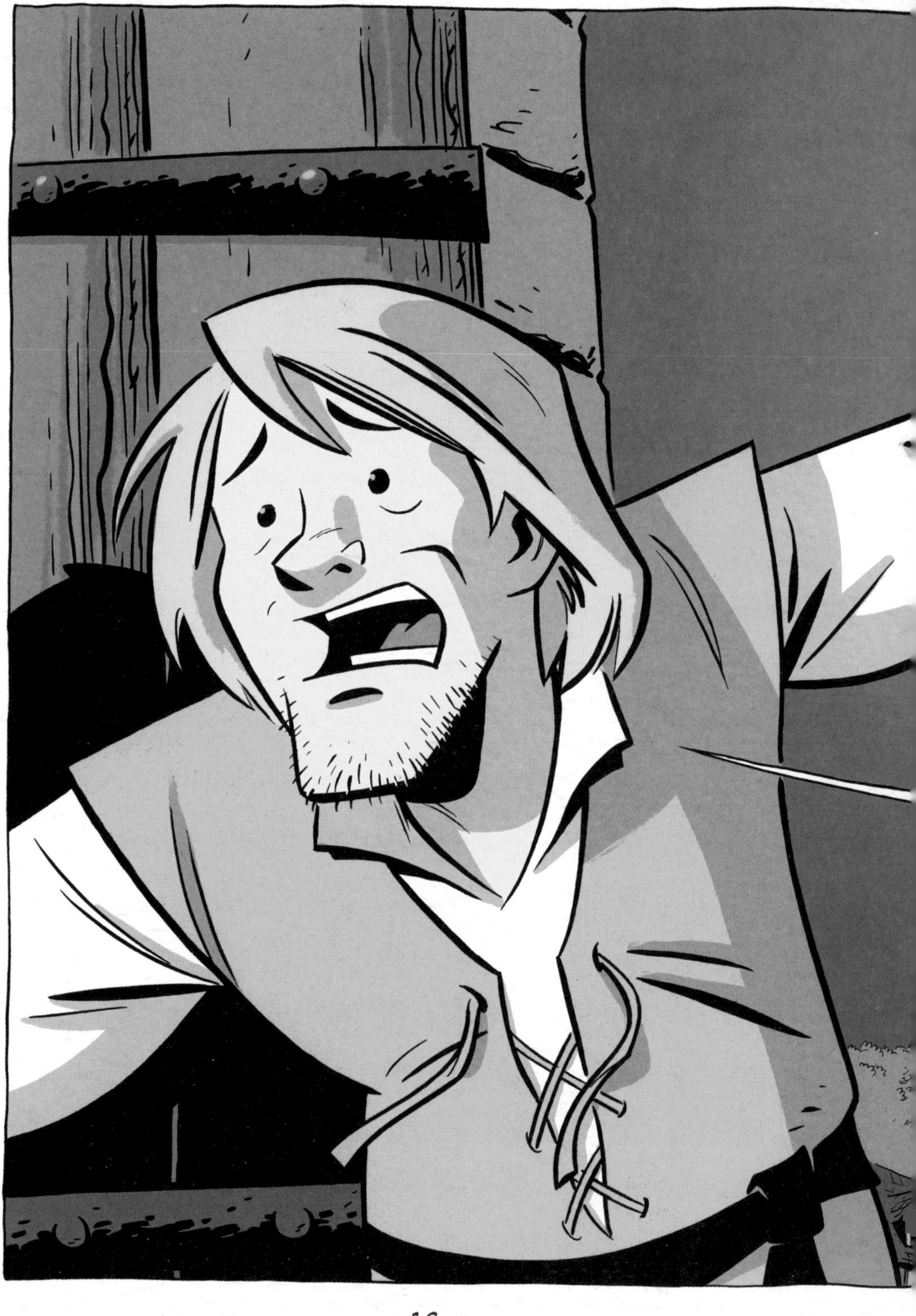

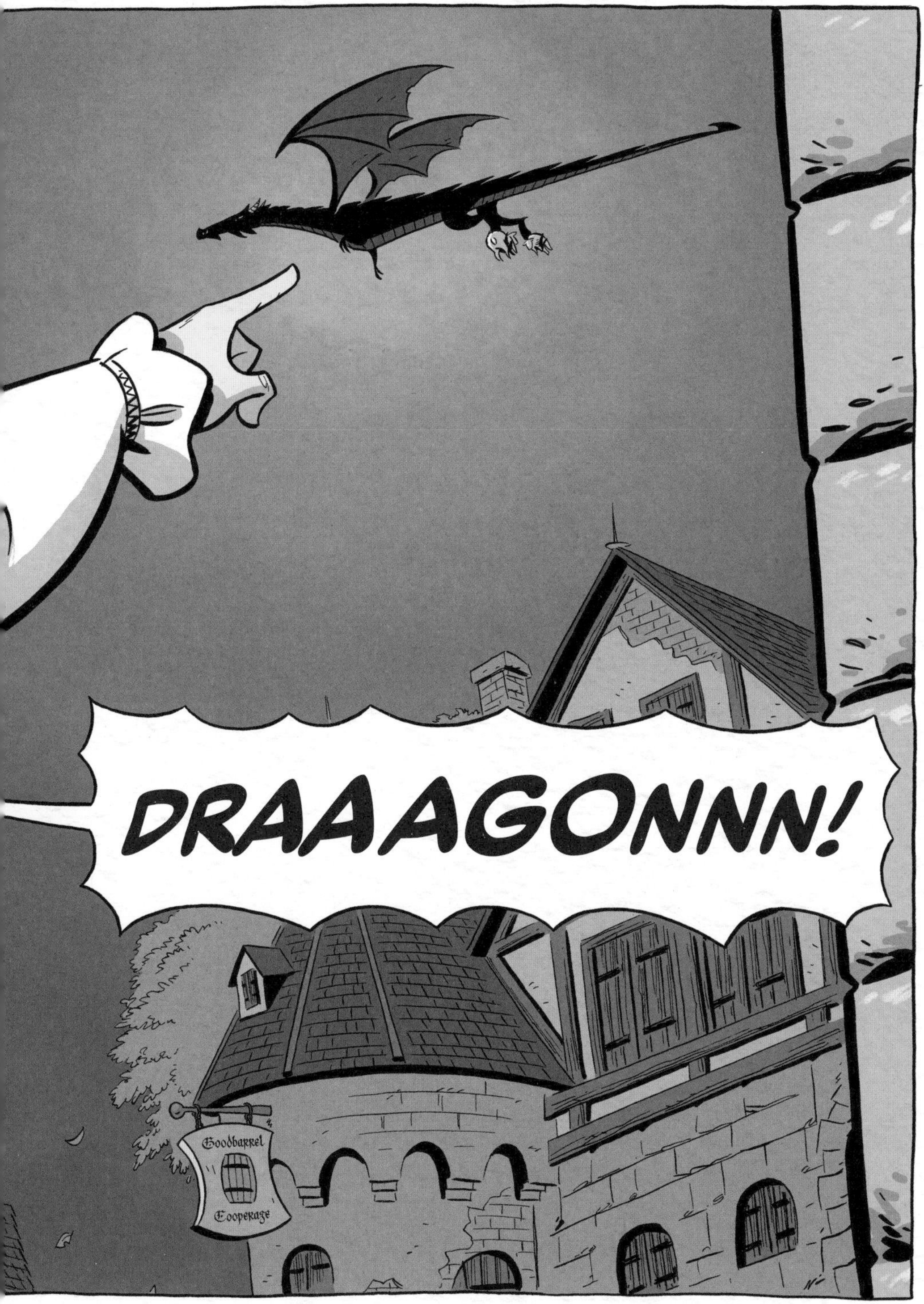
DRAAAGONNN!
Goodbarrel
Cooperage

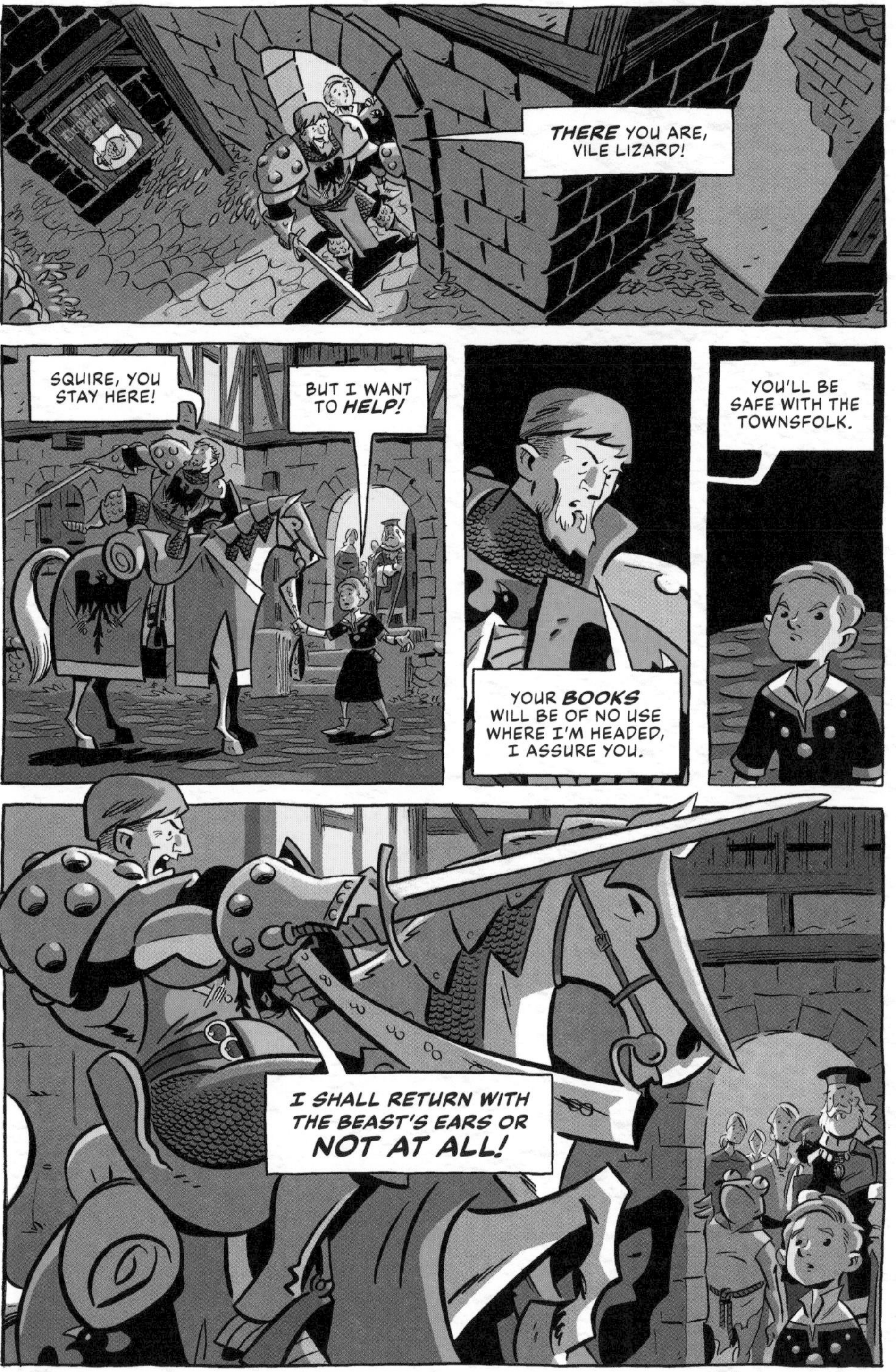
THERE YOU ARE, VILE LIZARD!
SQUIRE, YOU STAY HERE!
BUT I WANT TO HELP!
YOUR BOOKS WILL BE OF NO USE WHERE I'M HEADED, I ASSURE YOU.
YOU'LL BE SAFE WITH THE TOWNSFOLK.
I SHALL RETURN WITH THE BEAST'S EARS OR NOT AT ALL!

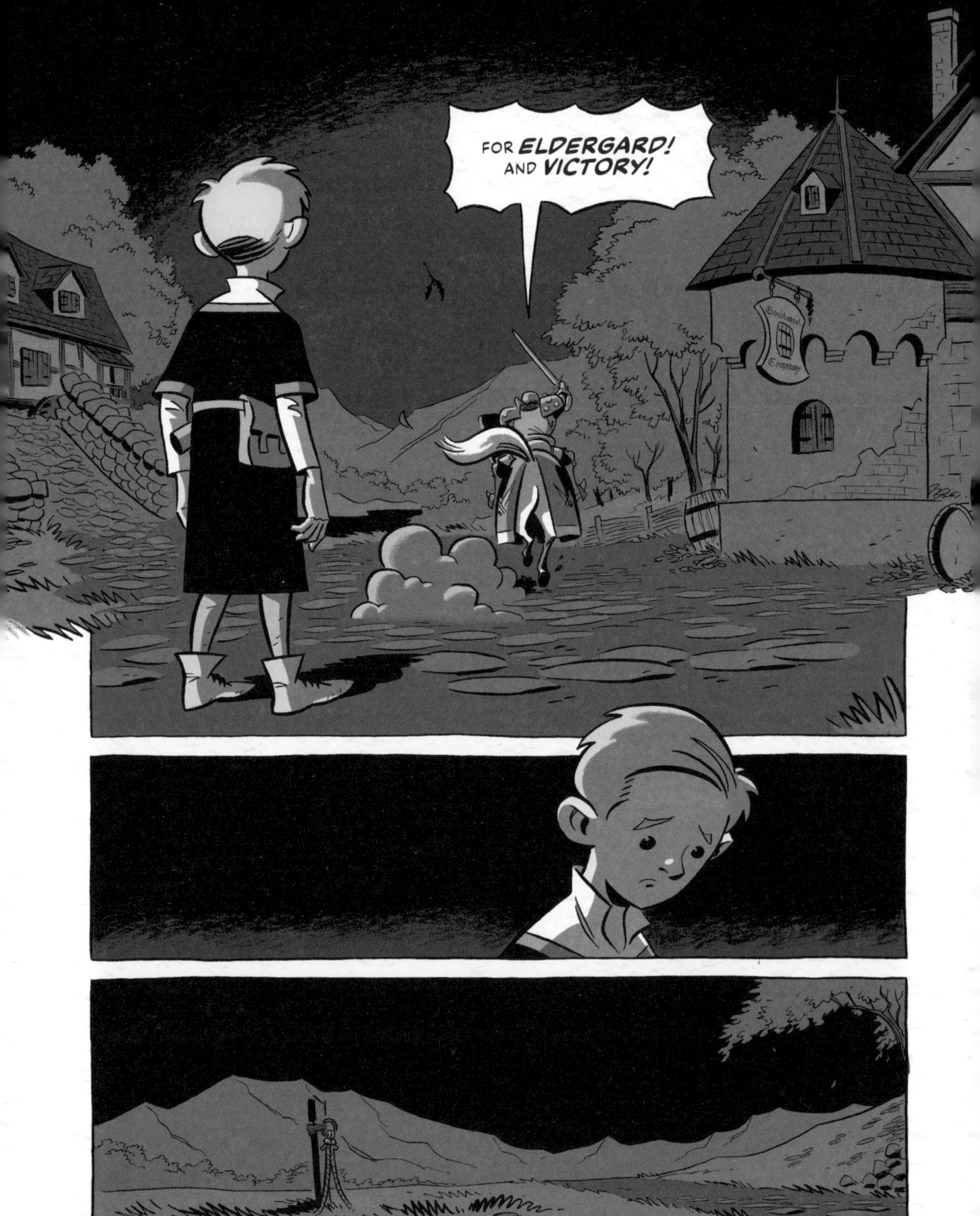
FOR ELDERGARD! AND VICTORY!

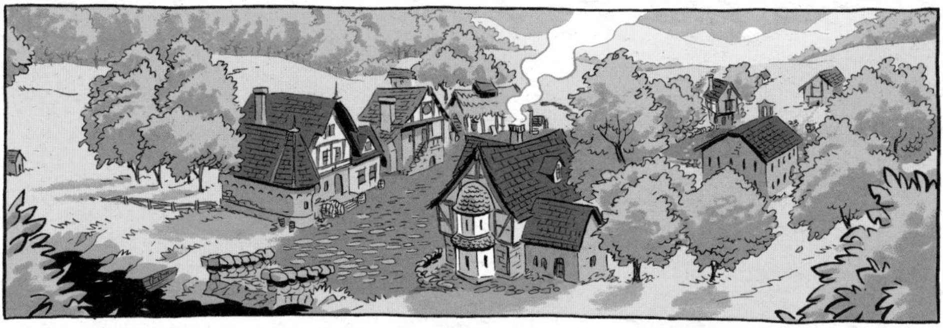

# CHAPTER TWO

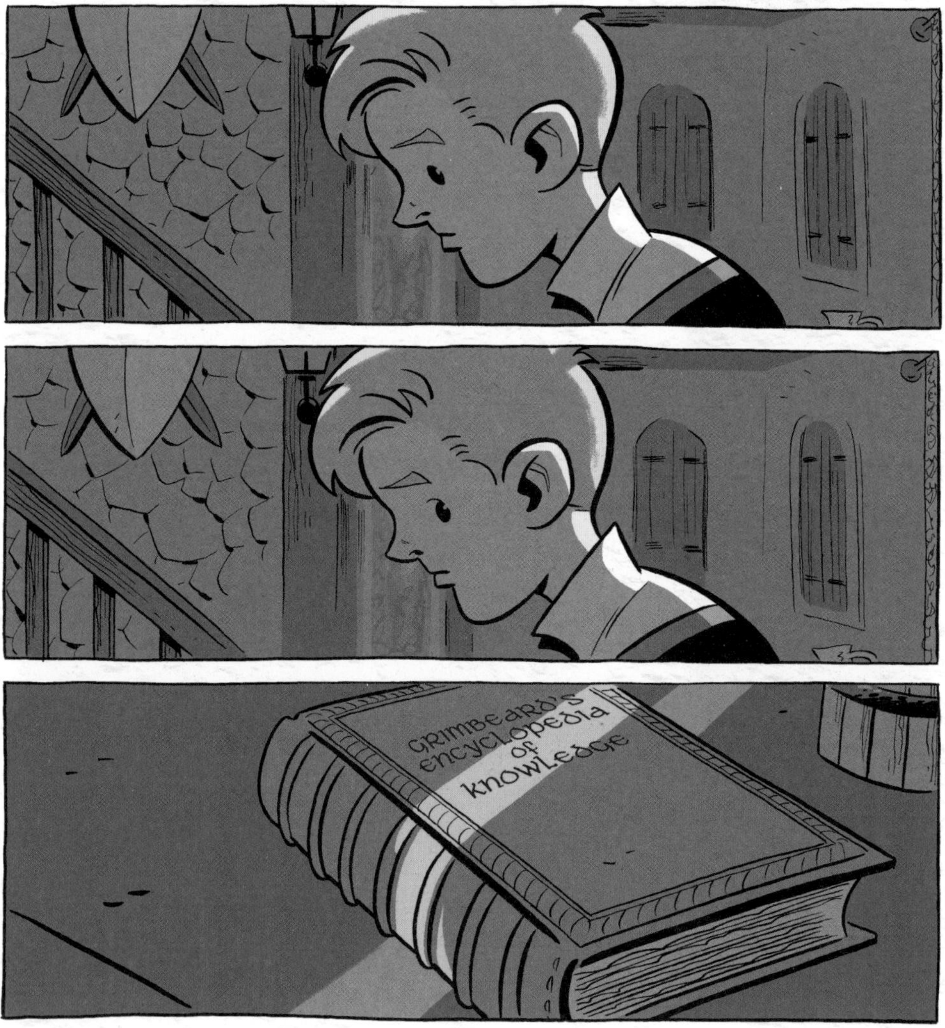
GRIMBEARD'S ENCYCLOPEDIA OF KNOWLEDGE

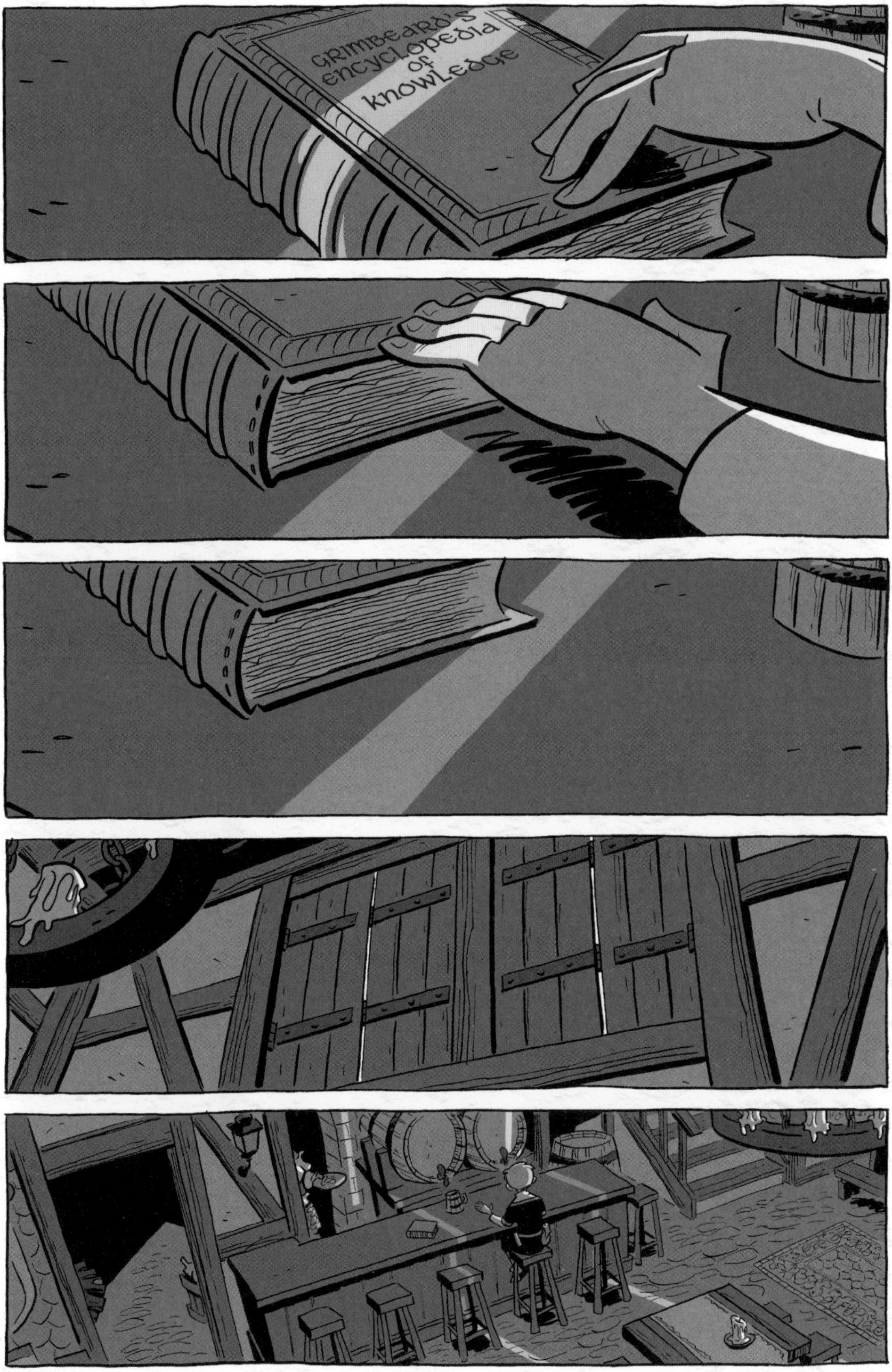
GRIMBEARD'S ENCYCLOPEDIA OF KNOWLEDGE

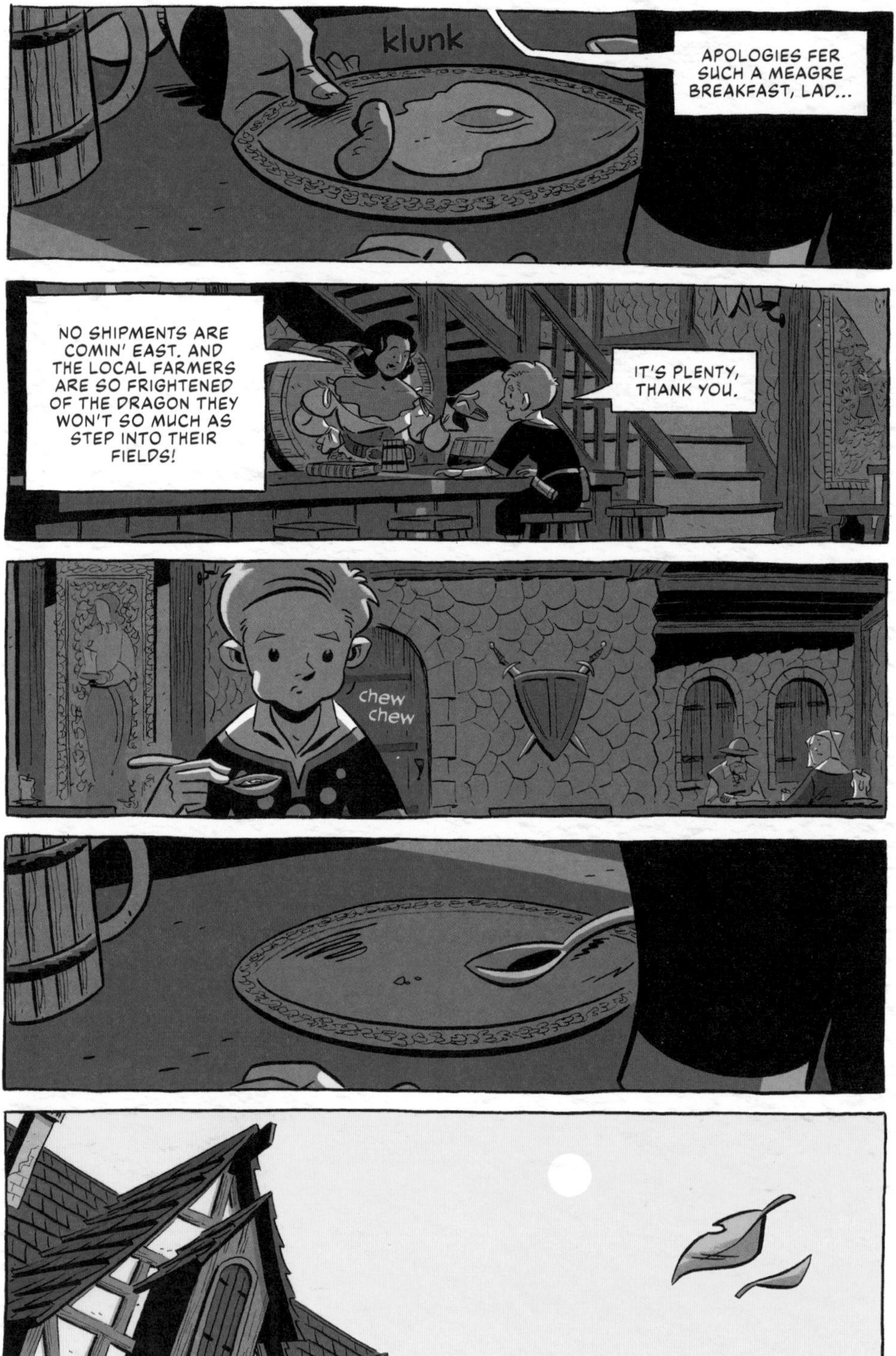
klunk
APOLOGIES FER SUCH A MEAGRE BREAKFAST, LAD...
NO SHIPMENTS ARE COMIN' EAST. AND THE LOCAL FARMERS ARE SO FRIGHTENED OF THE DRAGON THEY WON'T SO MUCH AS STEP INTO THEIR FIELDS!
IT'S PLENTY, THANK YOU.
chew chew

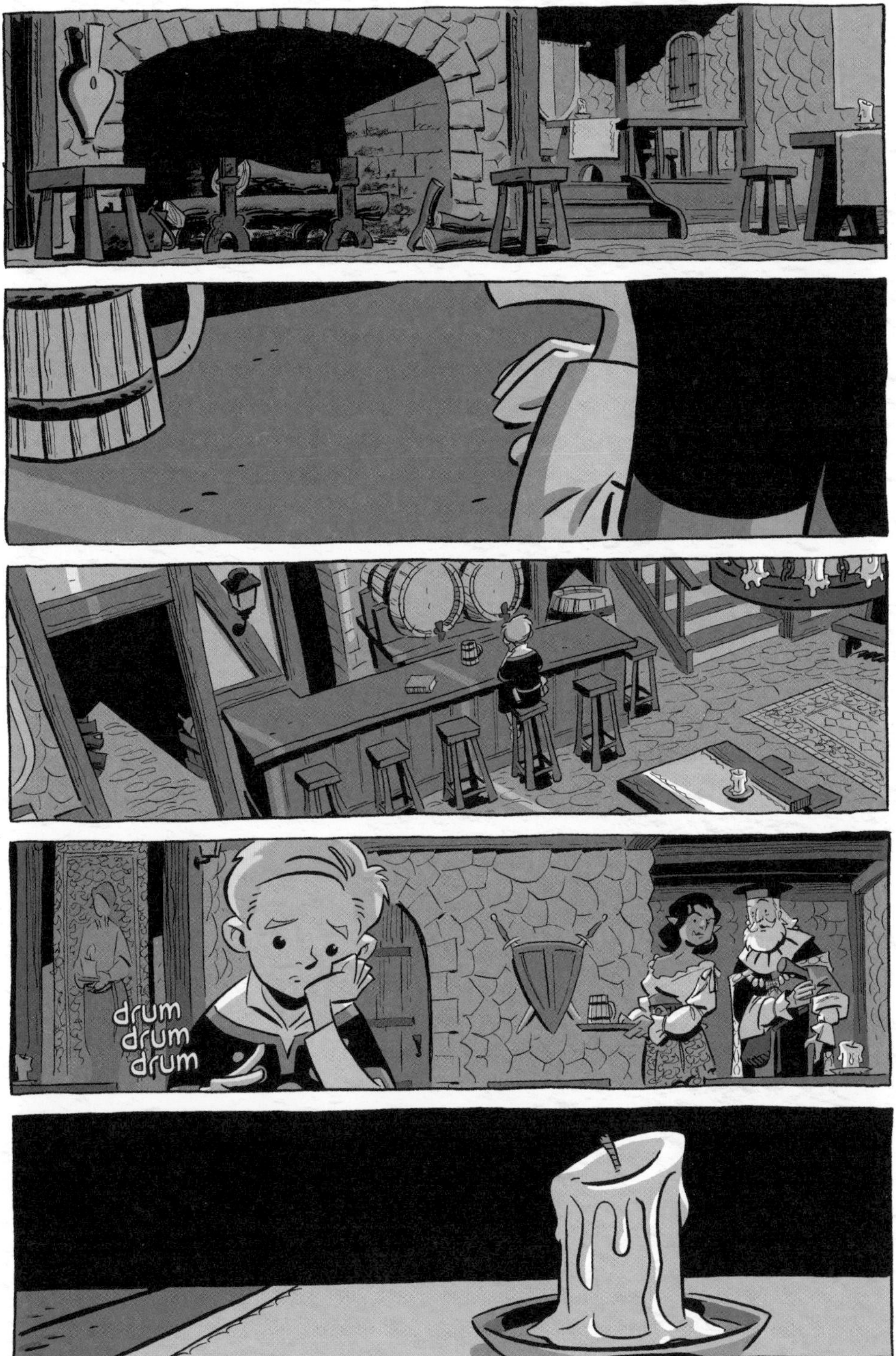
drum
drum
drum

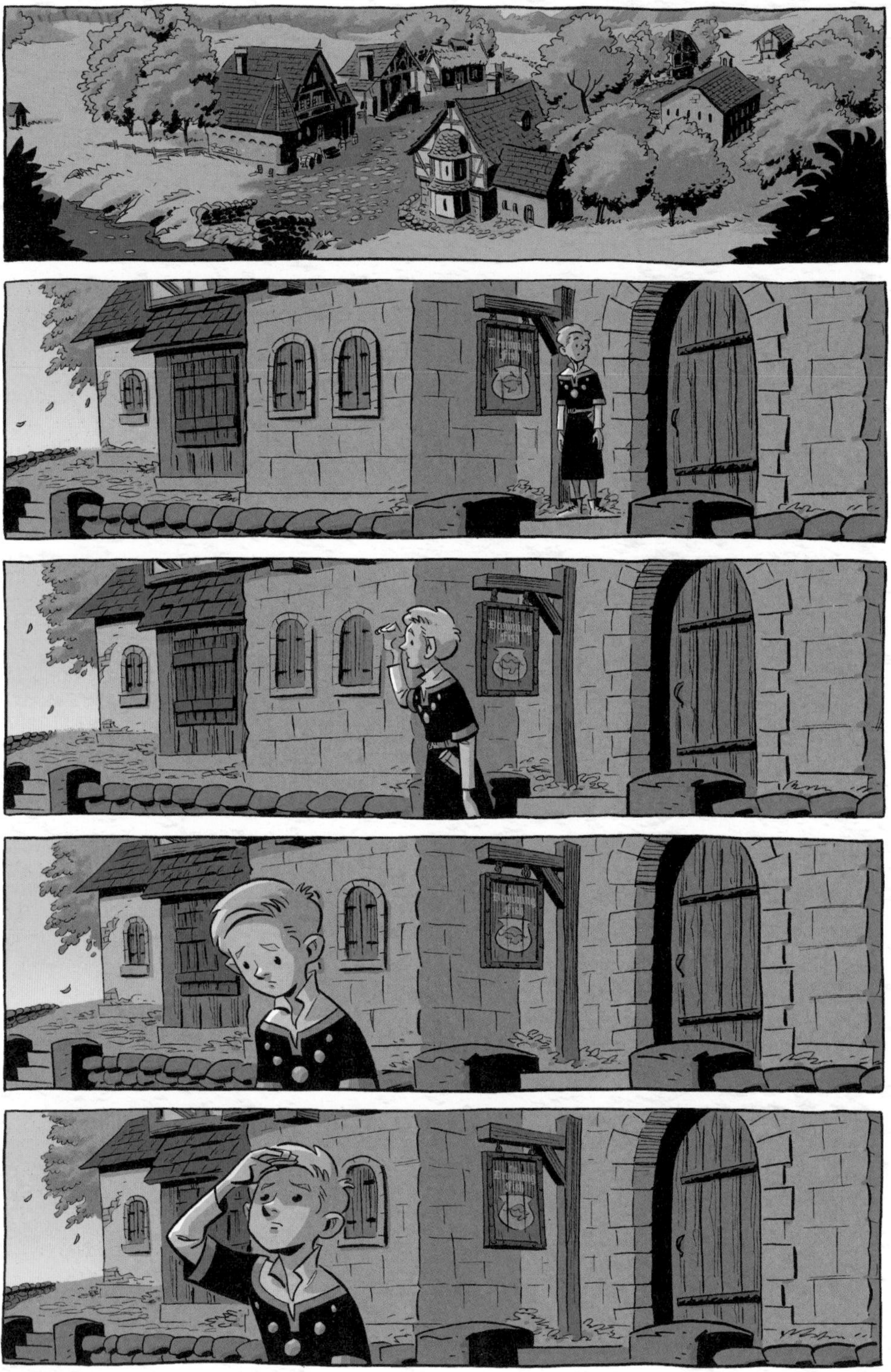

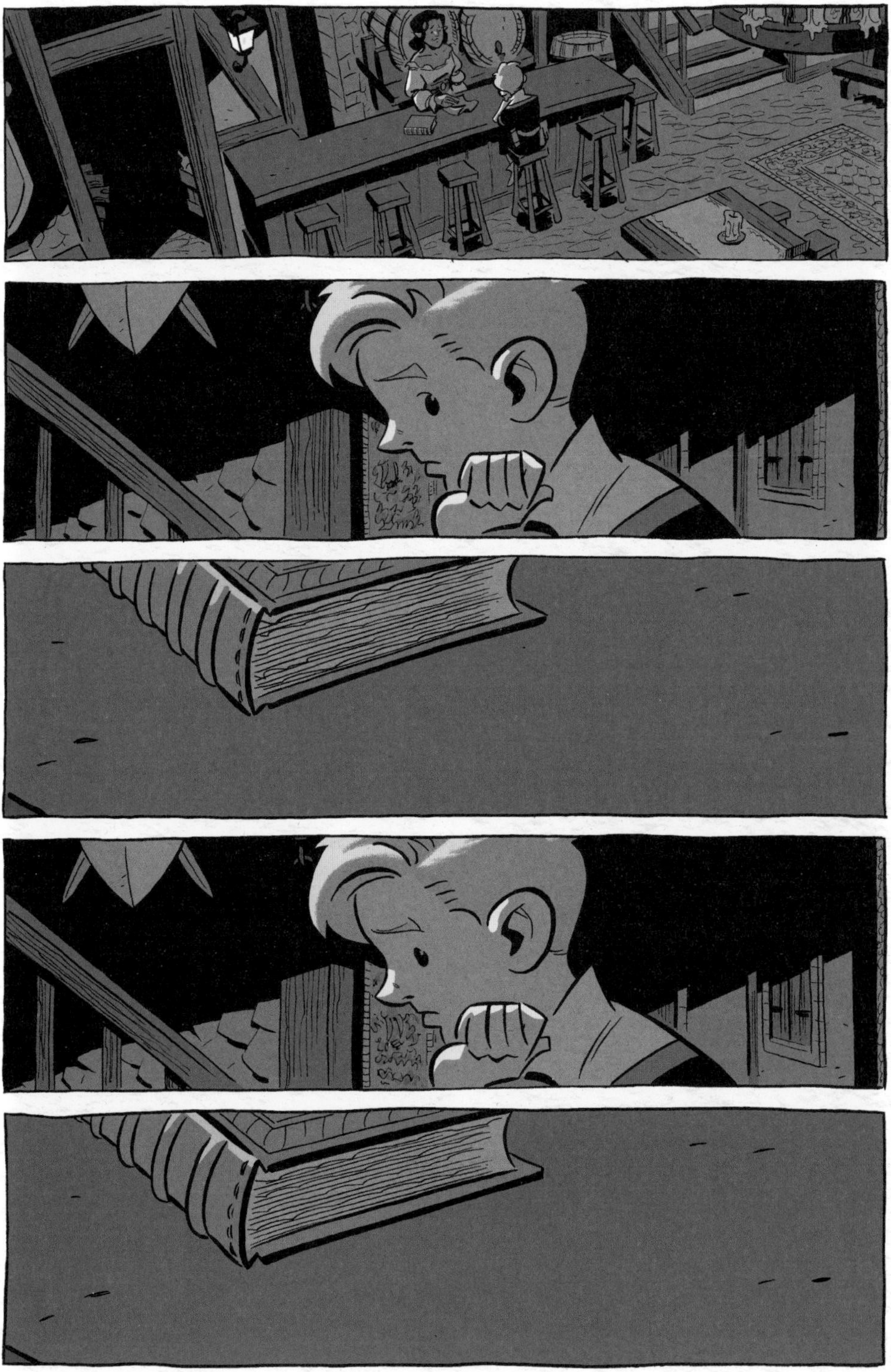

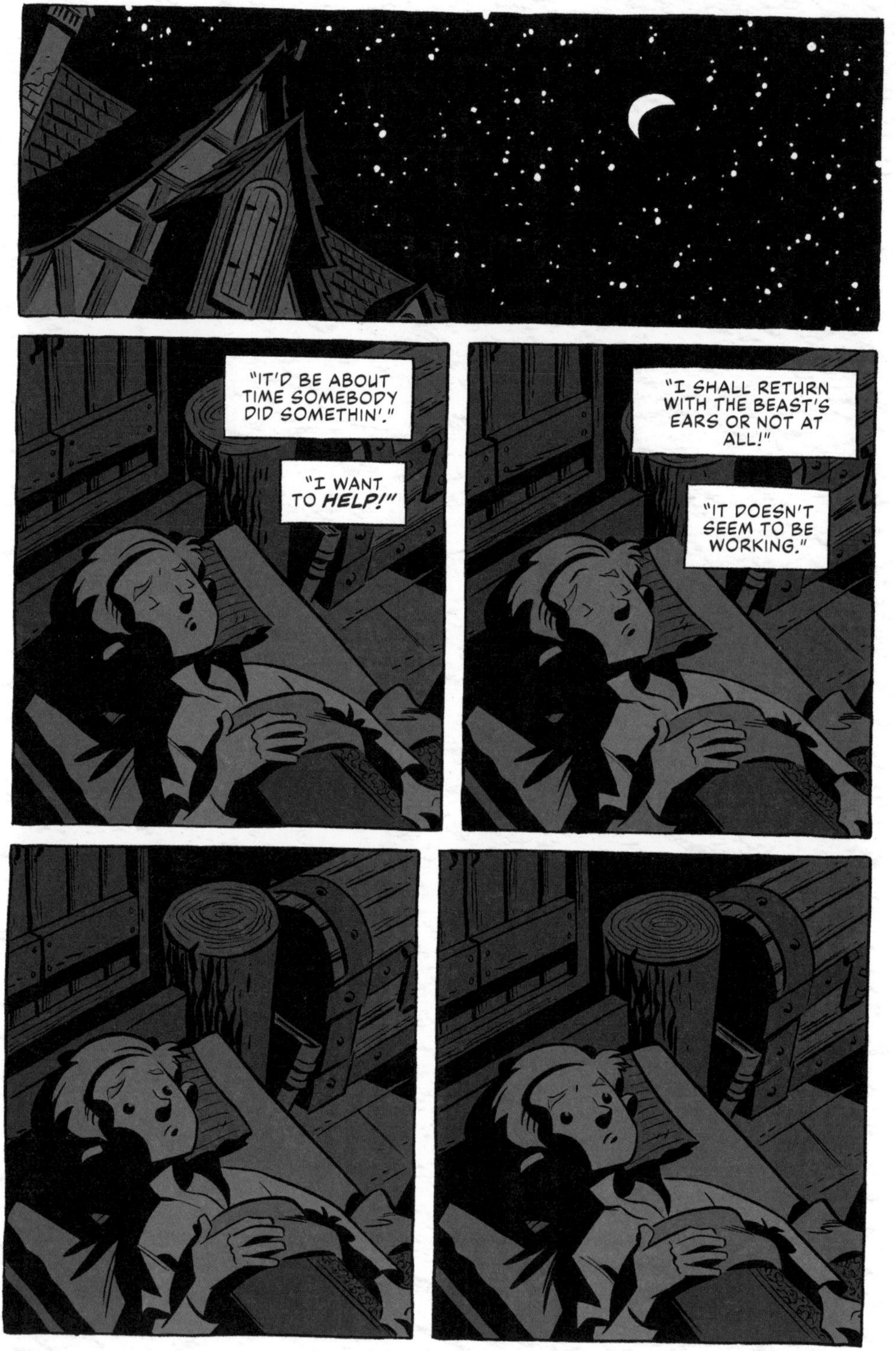
"IT'D BE ABOUT TIME SOMEBODY DID SOMETHIN'."
"I WANT TO HELP!"
"I SHALL RETURN WITH THE BEAST'S EARS OR NOT AT ALL!"
"IT DOESN'T SEEM TO BE WORKING."

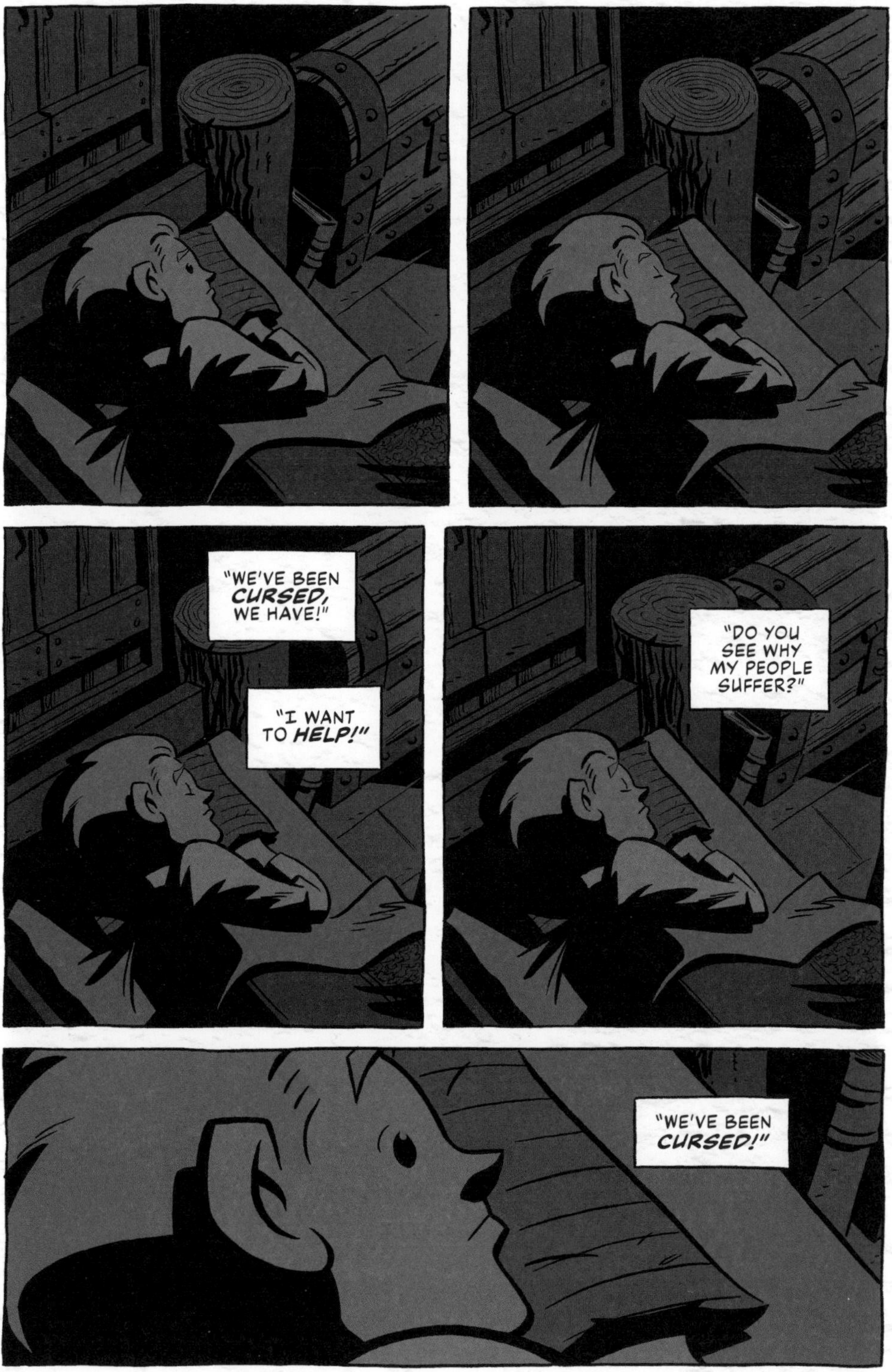
"WE'VE BEEN *CURSED,* WE HAVE!"
"I WANT TO *HELP!*"
"DO YOU SEE WHY MY PEOPLE SUFFER?"
"WE'VE BEEN *CURSED!*"

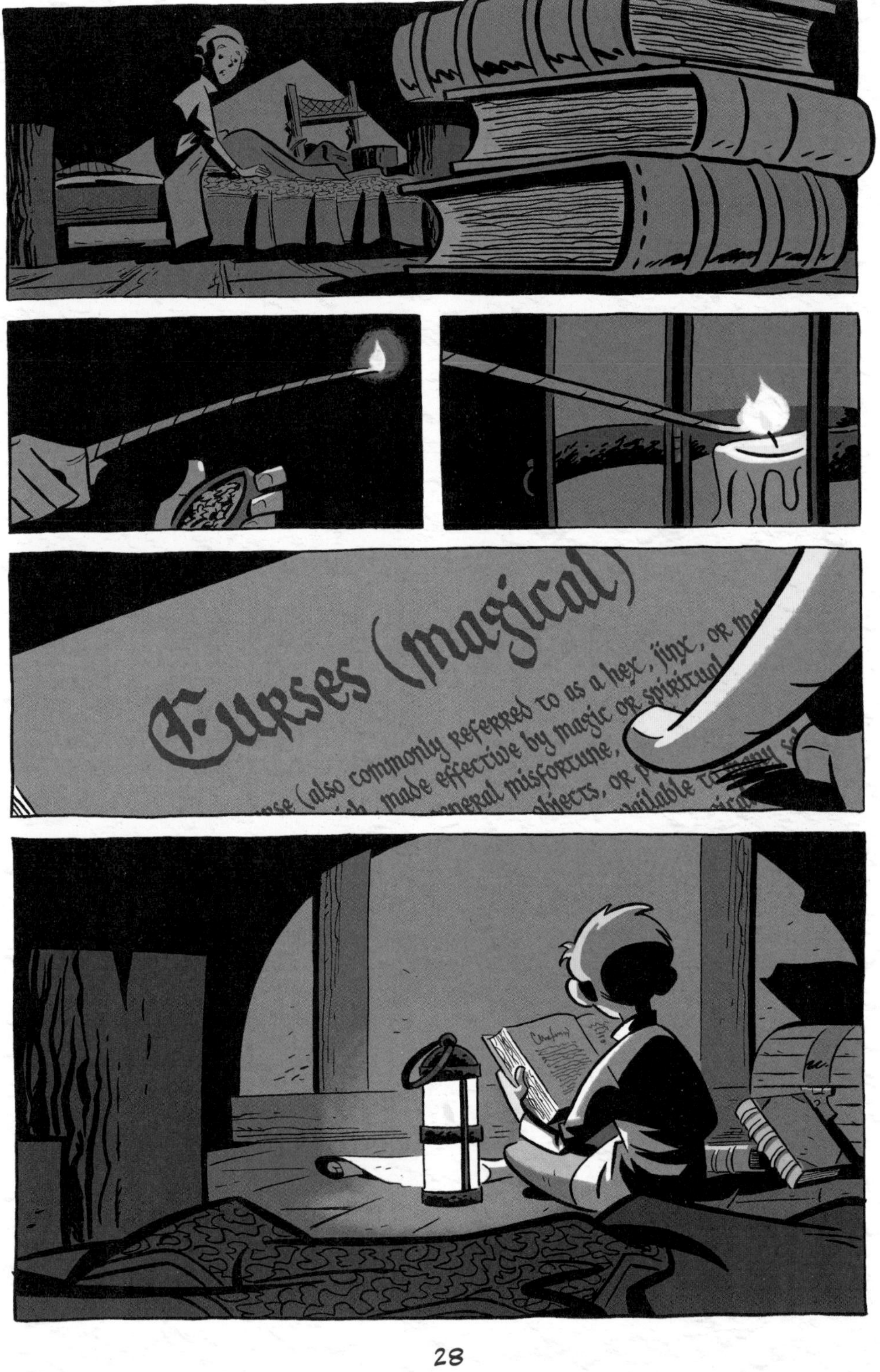

Curses (magical)
(also commonly referred to as a hex, jinx, or
made effective by magic or spiritual
general misfortune,
objects, or
available to

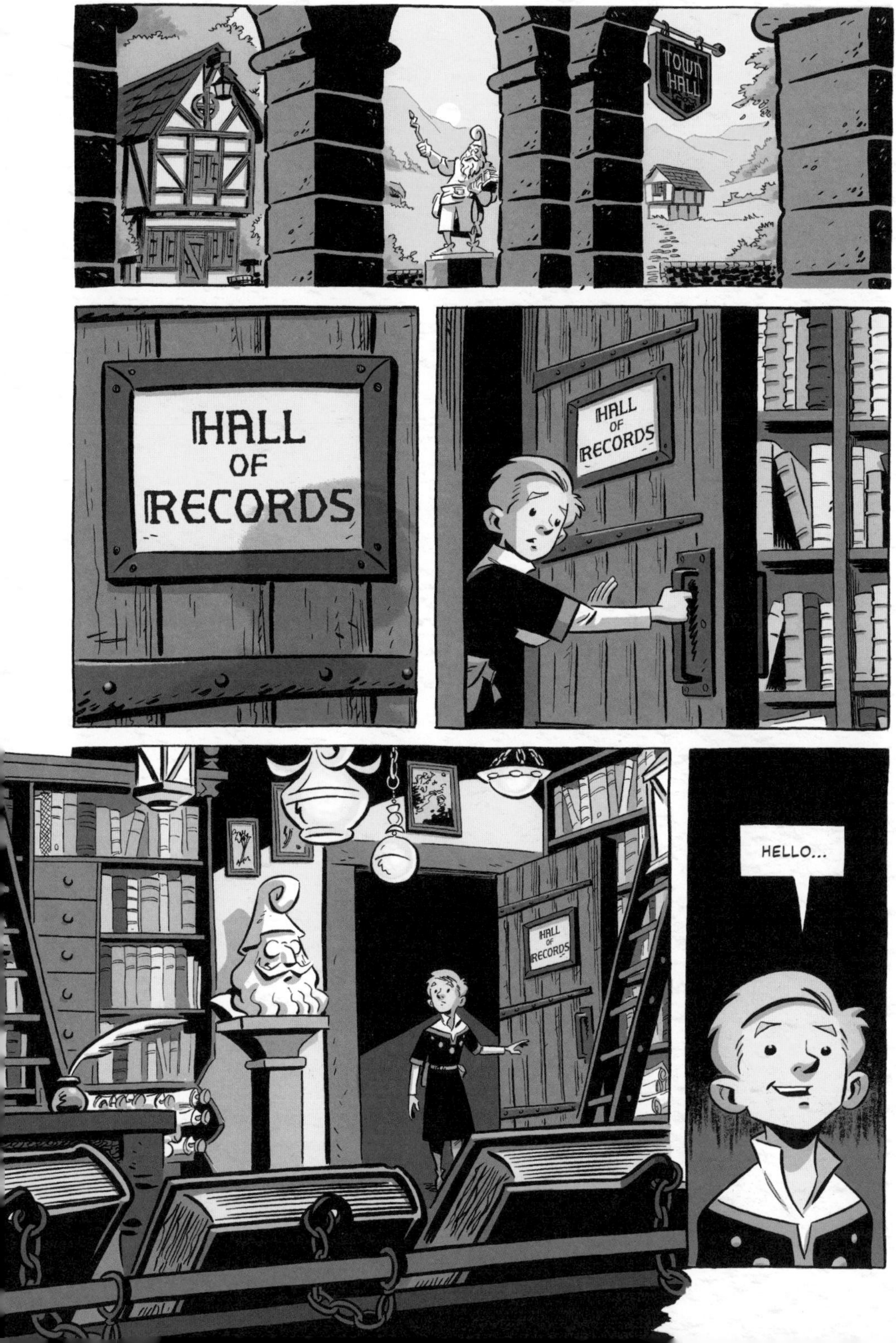
TOWN HALL
HALL OF RECORDS
HALL OF RECORDS
HALL OF RECORDS
HELLO...

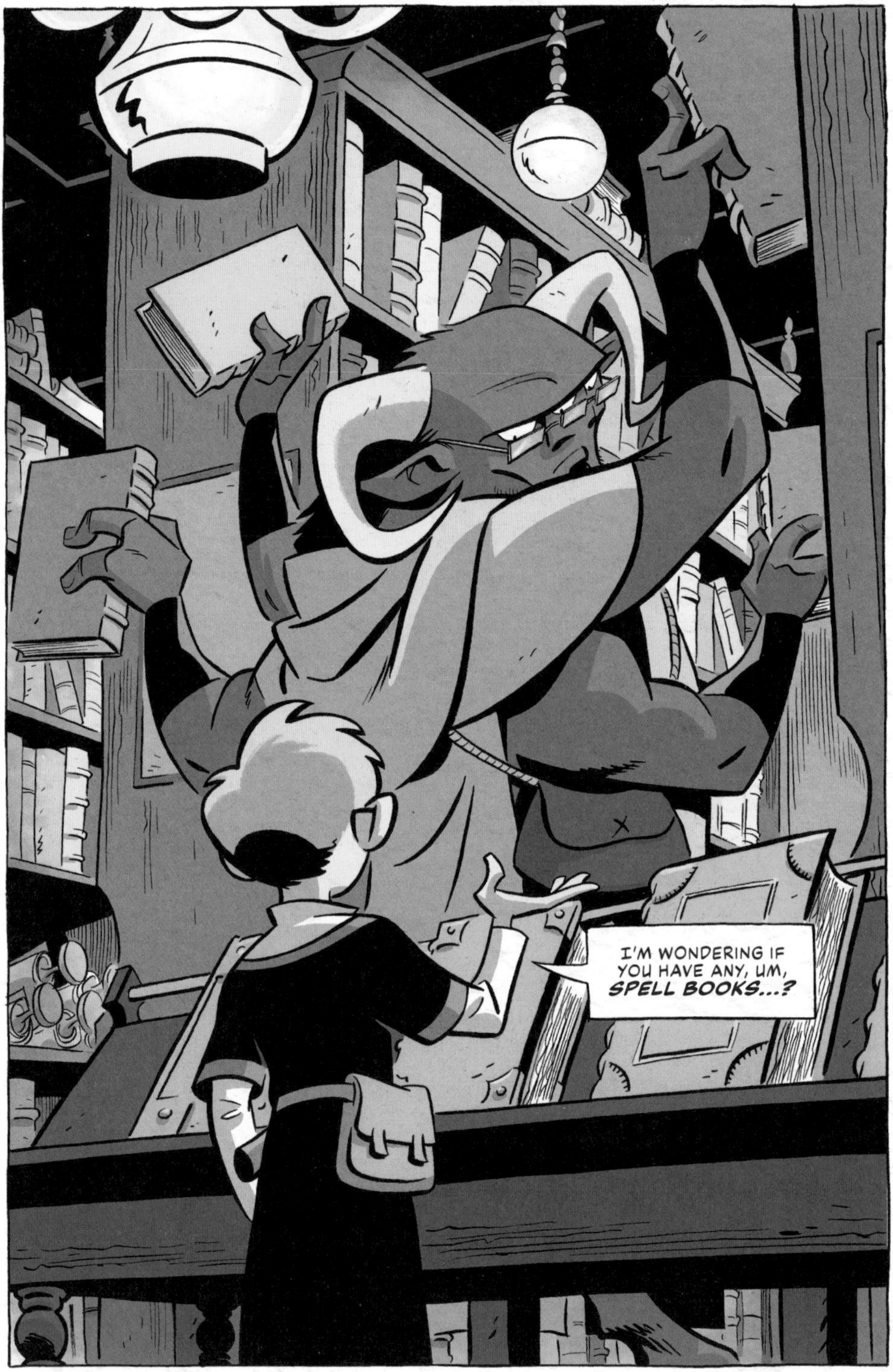
I'M WONDERING IF YOU HAVE ANY, UM, ***SPELL BOOKS...?***

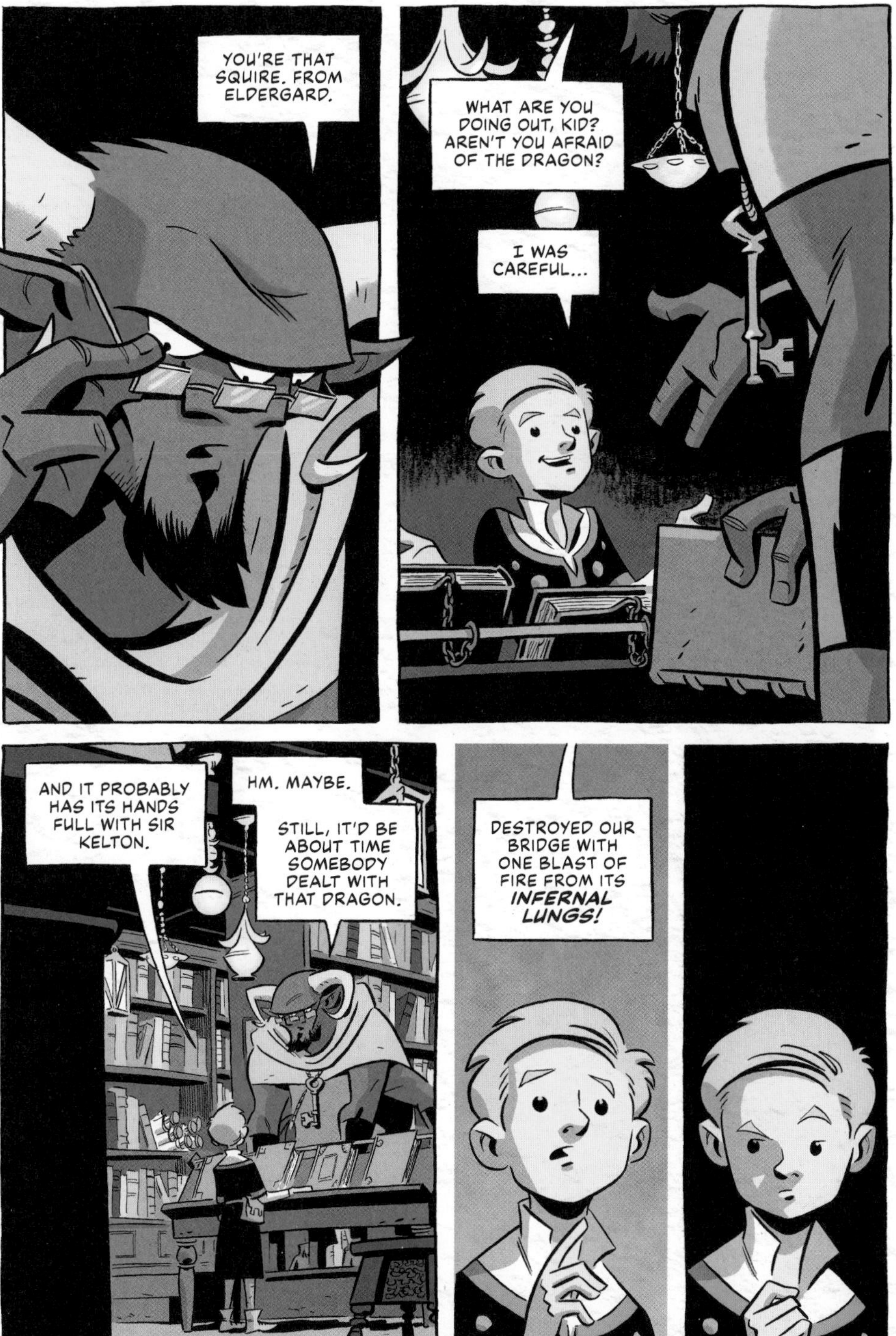
YOU'RE THAT SQUIRE. FROM ELDERGARD.
WHAT ARE YOU DOING OUT, KID? AREN'T YOU AFRAID OF THE DRAGON?
I WAS CAREFUL...
AND IT PROBABLY HAS ITS HANDS FULL WITH SIR KELTON.
HM. MAYBE.
STILL, IT'D BE ABOUT TIME SOMEBODY DEALT WITH THAT DRAGON.
DESTROYED OUR BRIDGE WITH ONE BLAST OF FIRE FROM ITS ***INFERNAL LUNGS!***

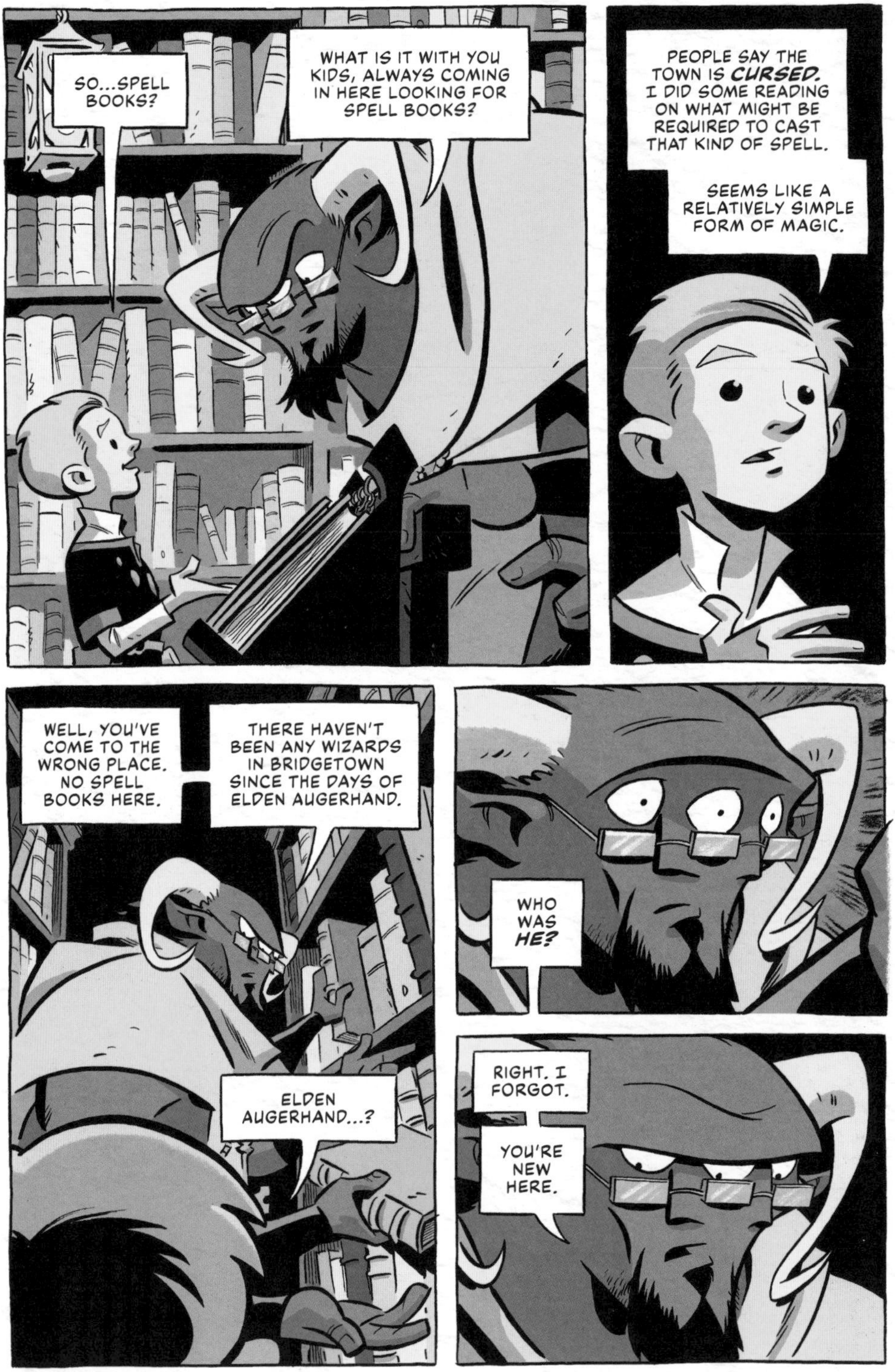
SO...SPELL BOOKS?
WHAT IS IT WITH YOU KIDS, ALWAYS COMING IN HERE LOOKING FOR SPELL BOOKS?
PEOPLE SAY THE TOWN IS *CURSED.* I DID SOME READING ON WHAT MIGHT BE REQUIRED TO CAST THAT KIND OF SPELL.
SEEMS LIKE A RELATIVELY SIMPLE FORM OF MAGIC.
WELL, YOU'VE COME TO THE WRONG PLACE. NO SPELL BOOKS HERE.
THERE HAVEN'T BEEN ANY WIZARDS IN BRIDGETOWN SINCE THE DAYS OF ELDEN AUGERHAND.
ELDEN AUGERHAND...?
WHO WAS *HE?*
RIGHT. I FORGOT.
YOU'RE NEW HERE.

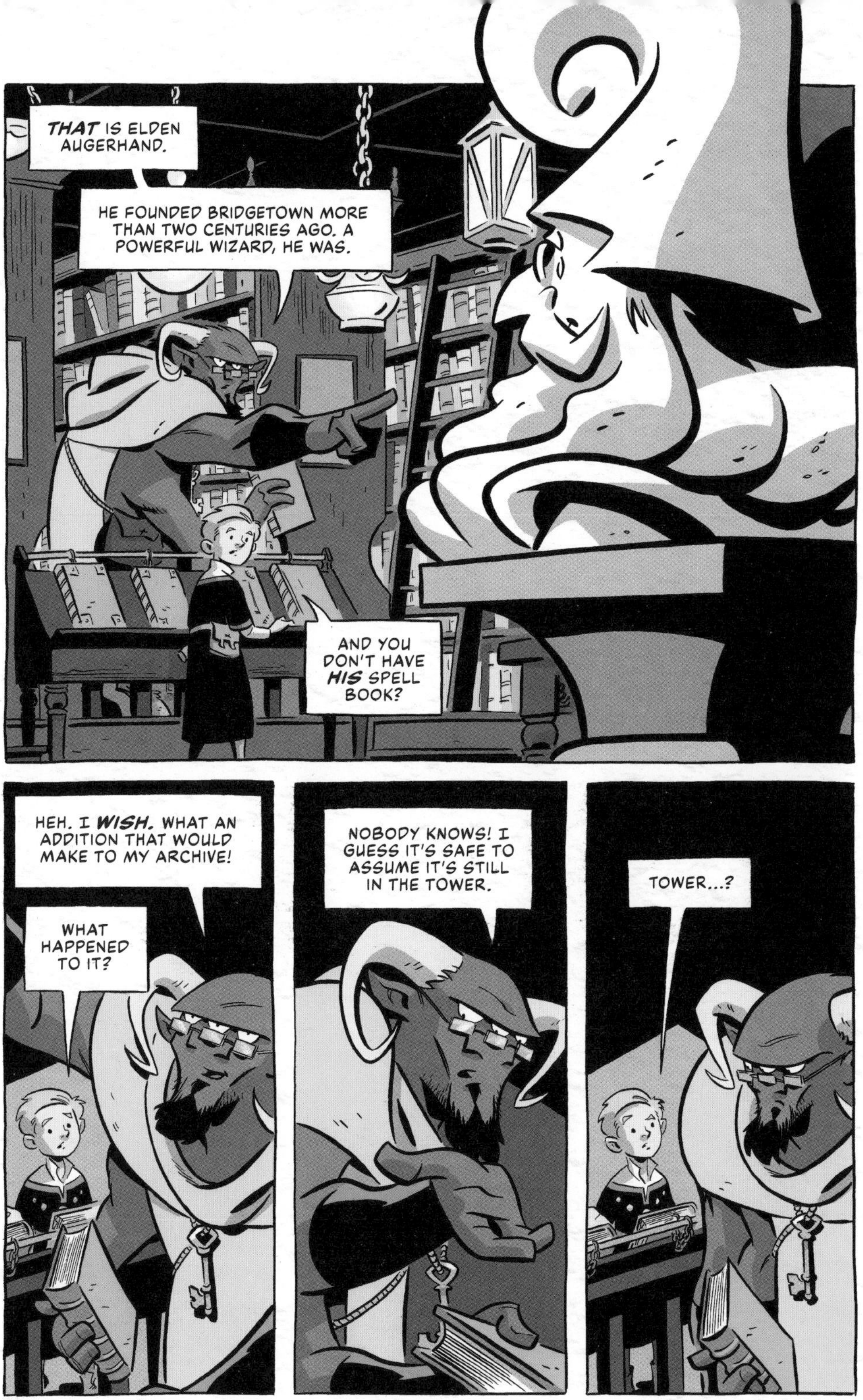
THAT IS ELDEN AUGERHAND.
HE FOUNDED BRIDGETOWN MORE THAN TWO CENTURIES AGO. A POWERFUL WIZARD, HE WAS.
AND YOU DON'T HAVE HIS SPELL BOOK?
HEH. I WISH. WHAT AN ADDITION THAT WOULD MAKE TO MY ARCHIVE!
WHAT HAPPENED TO IT?
NOBODY KNOWS! I GUESS IT'S SAFE TO ASSUME IT'S STILL IN THE TOWER.
TOWER...?

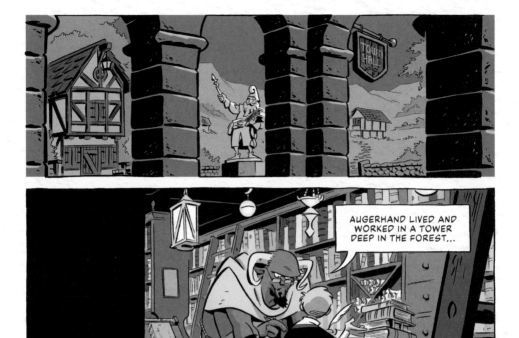

AUGERHAND LIVED AND WORKED IN A TOWER DEEP IN THE FOREST...

HERE.

HAVE YOU EVER BEEN IN THERE?

NOBODY HAS.

PEOPLE AREN'T CURIOUS?

EVERYONE'S CURIOUS. BUT THERE'S NO WAY INSIDE.

WHY NOT?

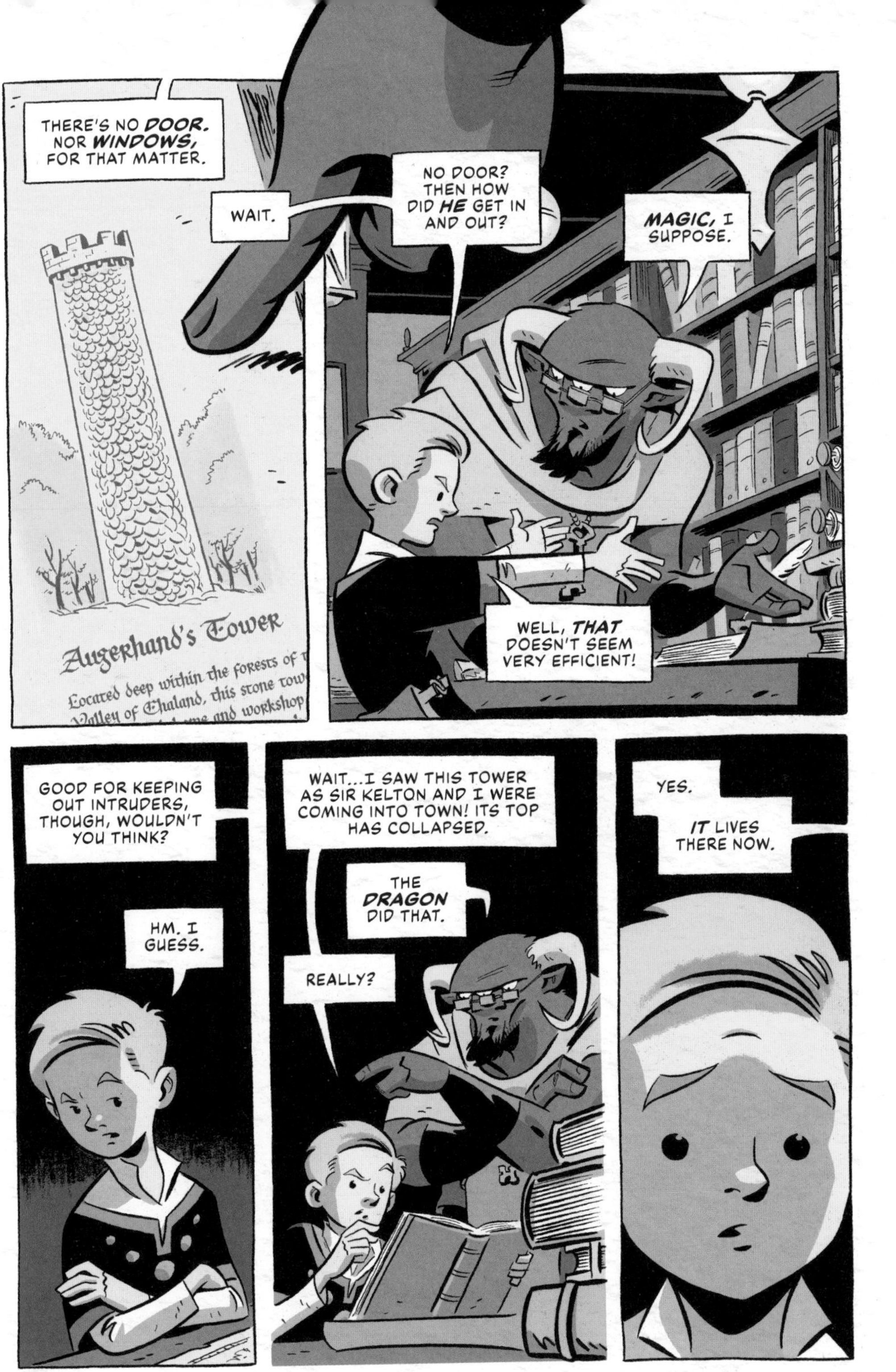
THERE'S NO DOOR. NOR WINDOWS, FOR THAT MATTER.
WAIT.
NO DOOR? THEN HOW DID HE GET IN AND OUT?
MAGIC, I SUPPOSE.
Augerhand's Tower
Located deep within the forests of
Valley of Chaland, this stone
and workshop
WELL, THAT DOESN'T SEEM VERY EFFICIENT!
GOOD FOR KEEPING OUT INTRUDERS, THOUGH, WOULDN'T YOU THINK?
HM. I GUESS.
WAIT...I SAW THIS TOWER AS SIR KELTON AND I WERE COMING INTO TOWN! ITS TOP HAS COLLAPSED.
THE DRAGON DID THAT.
REALLY?
YES.
IT LIVES THERE NOW.

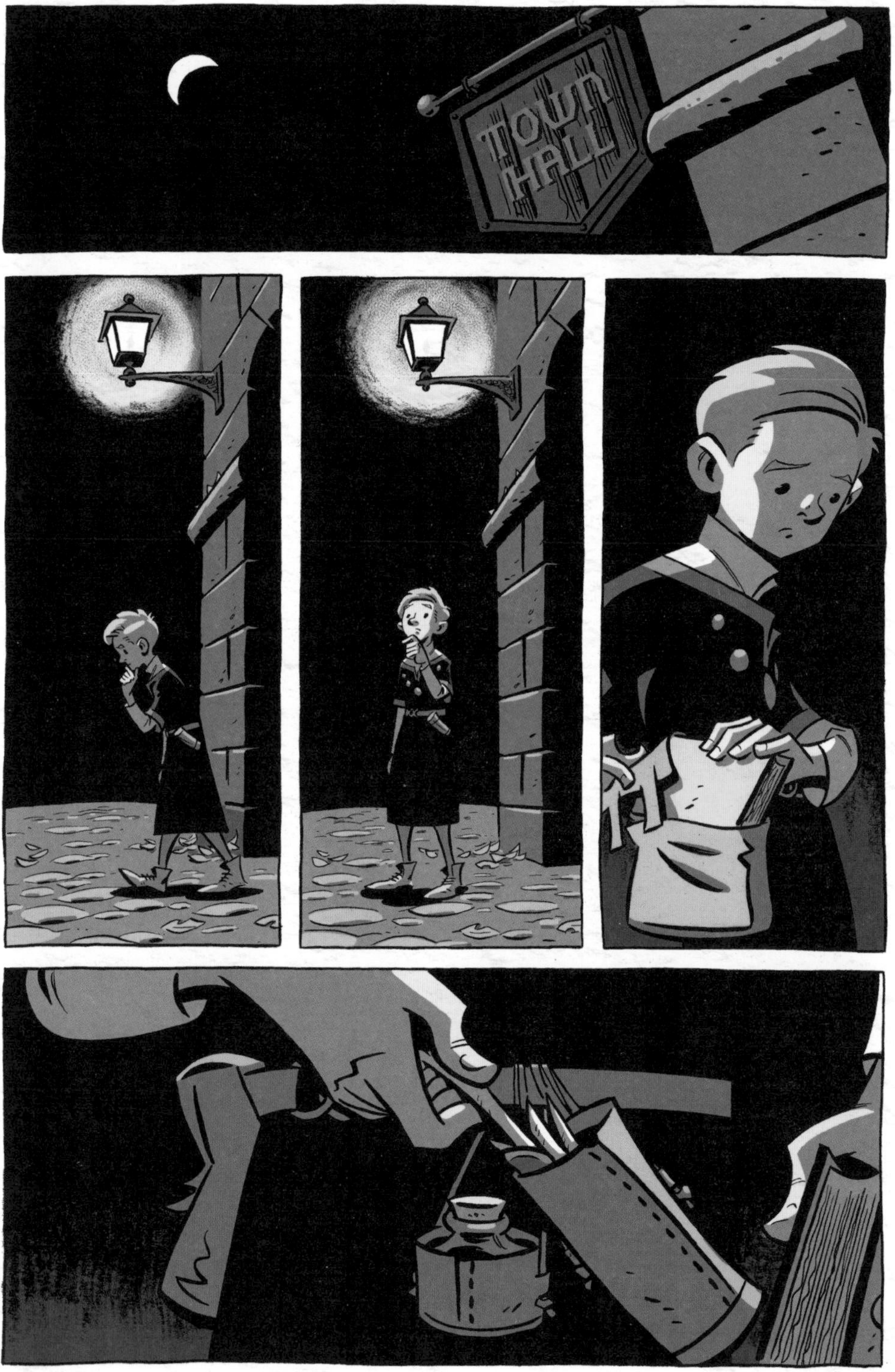
TOWN HALL

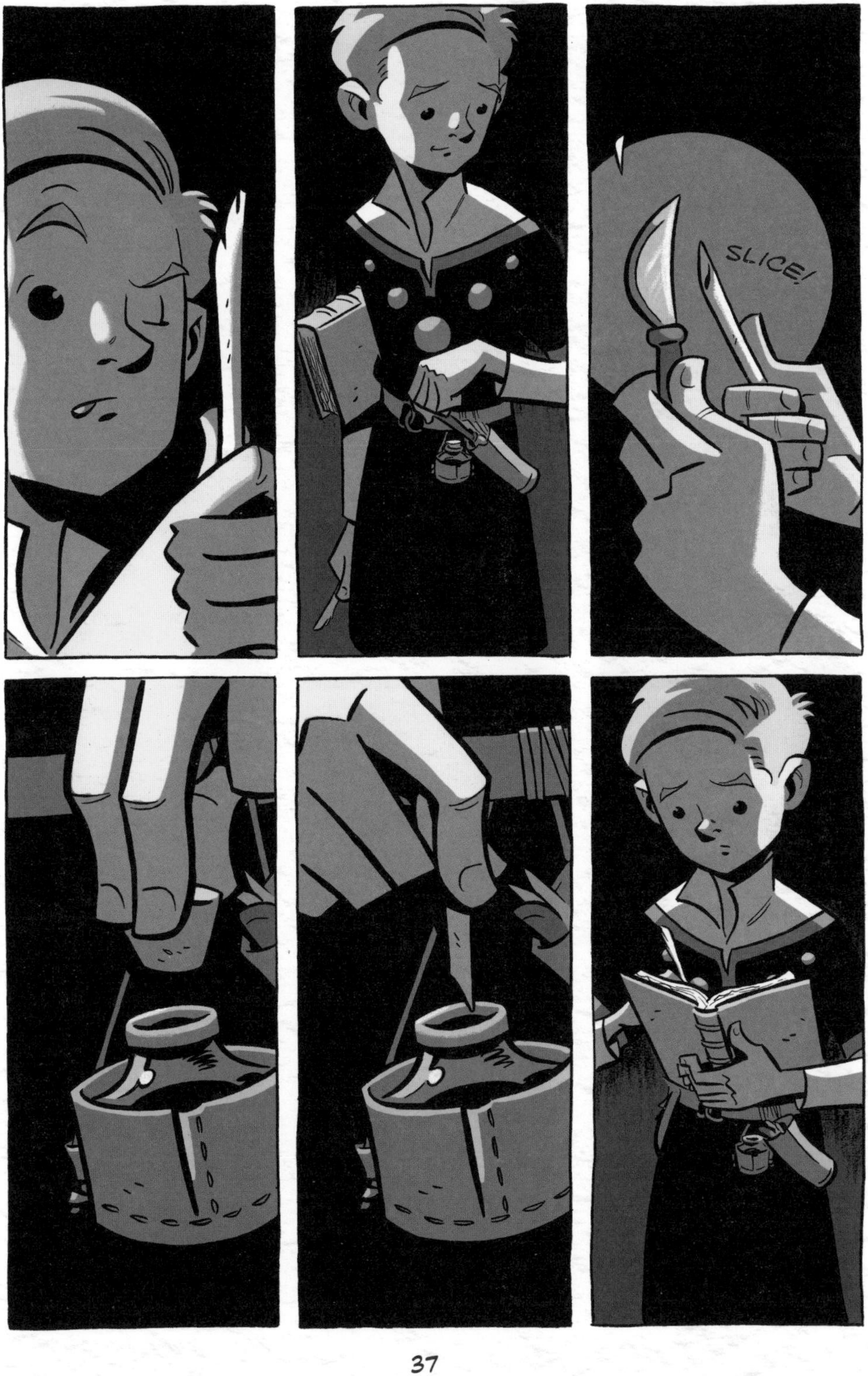
SLICE!

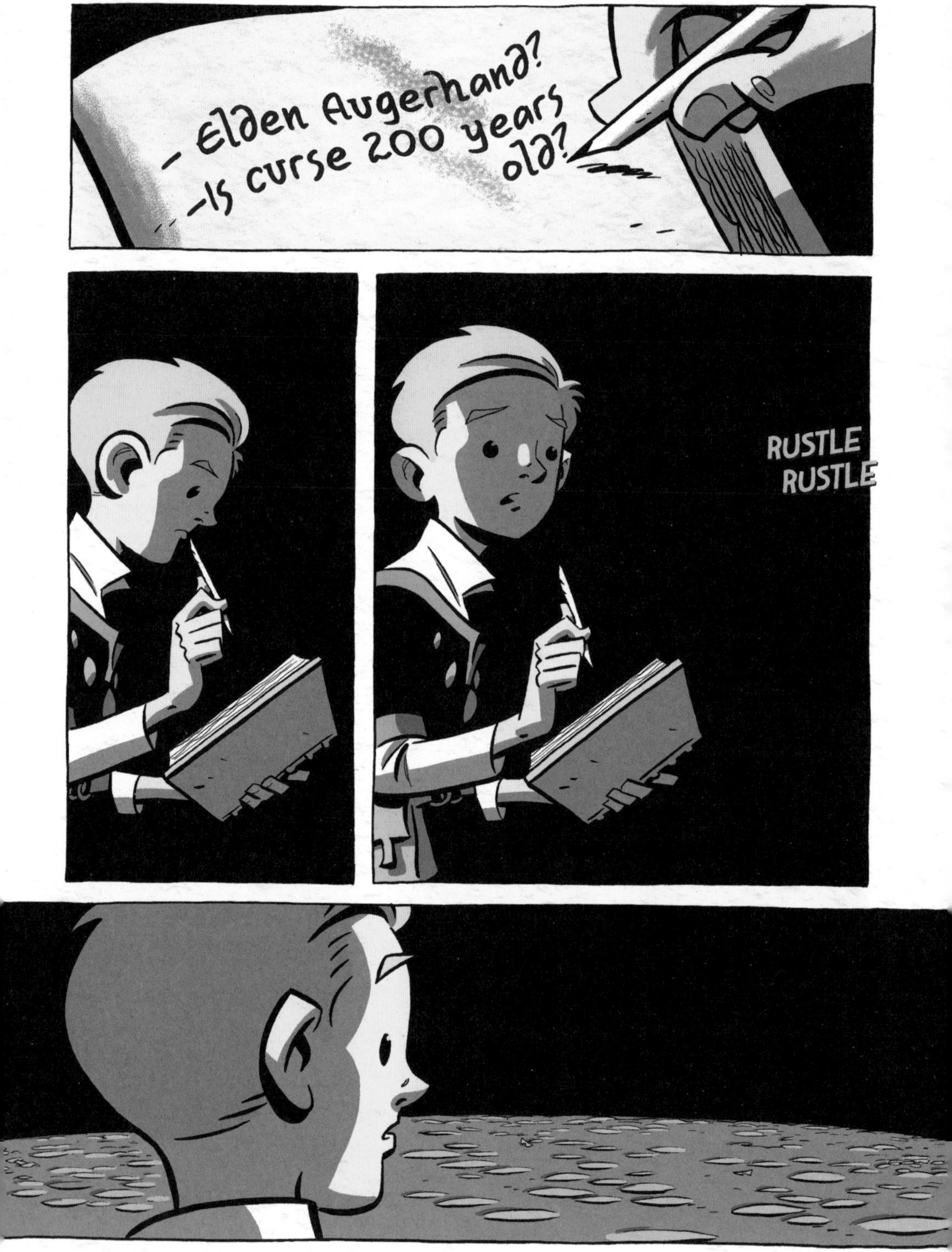
- Elden Augerhand?
-Is curse 200 years old?
RUSTLE
RUSTLE

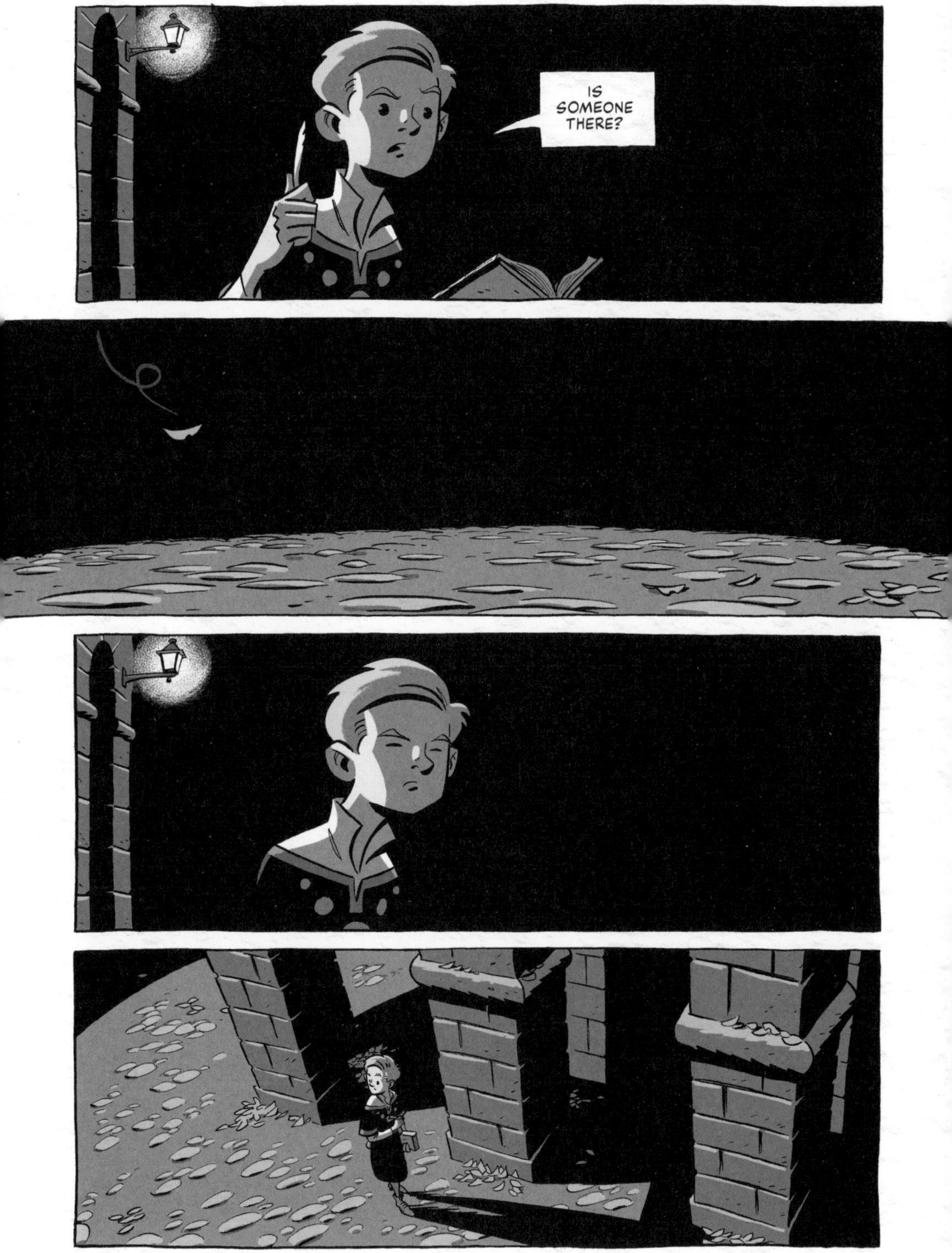
IS SOMEONE THERE?

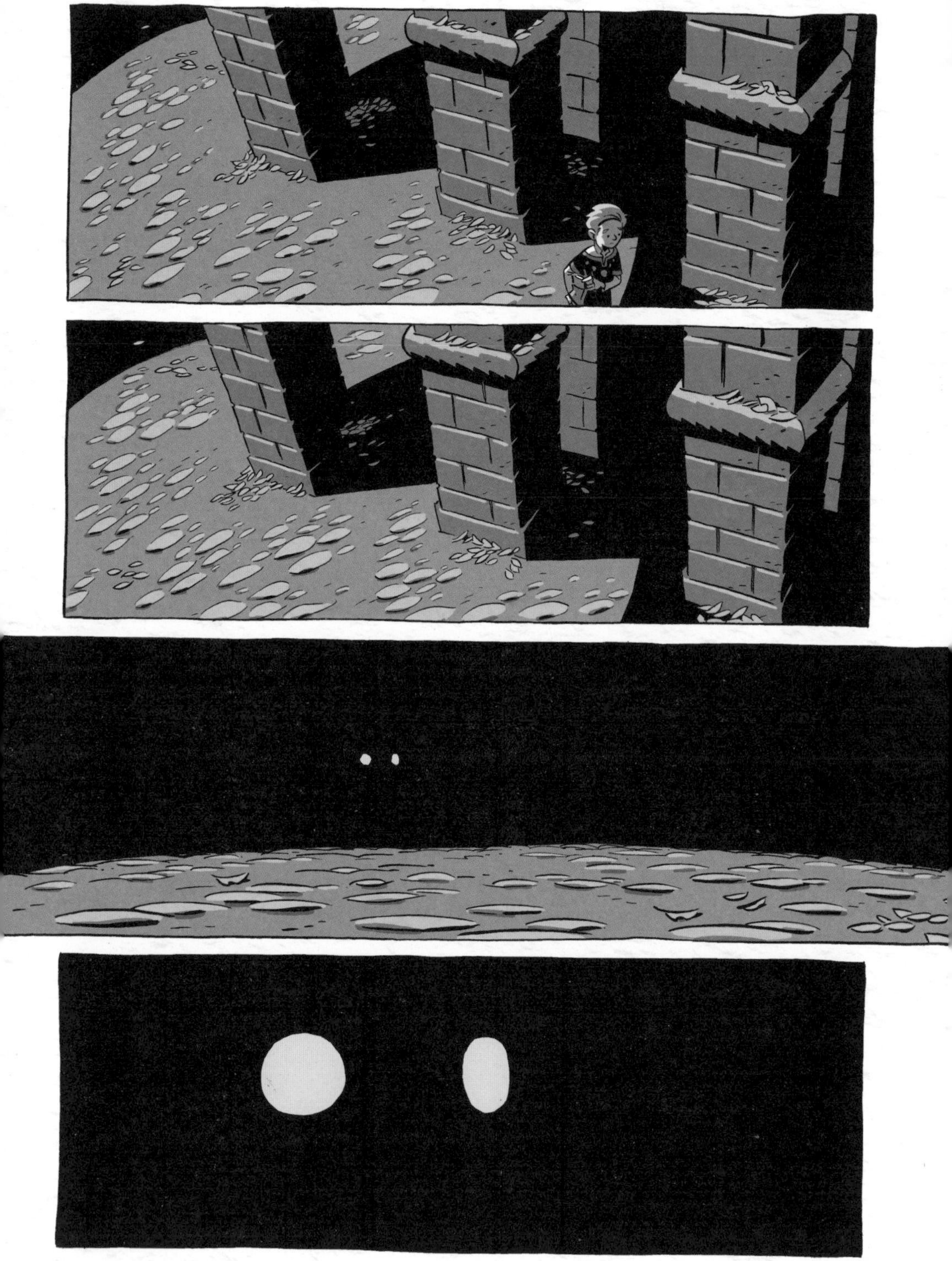

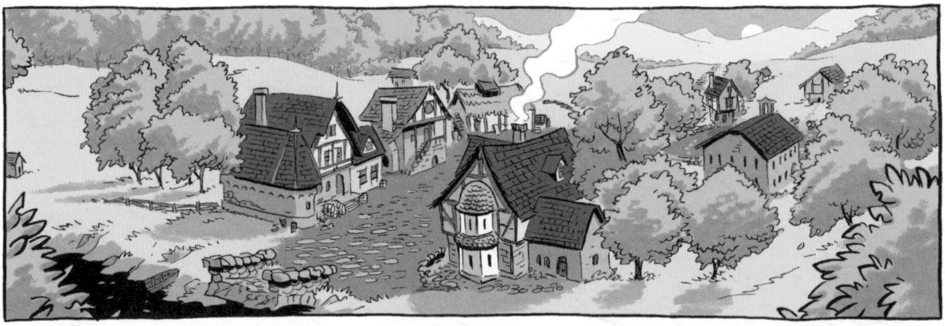

# CHAPTER THREE

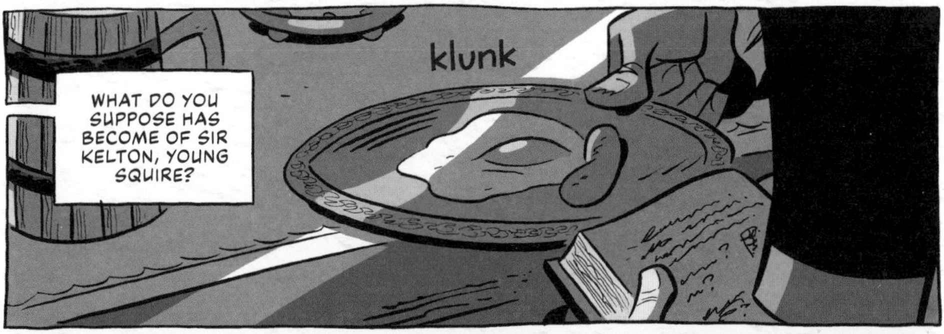
klunk
WHAT DO YOU SUPPOSE HAS BECOME OF SIR KELTON, YOUNG SQUIRE?

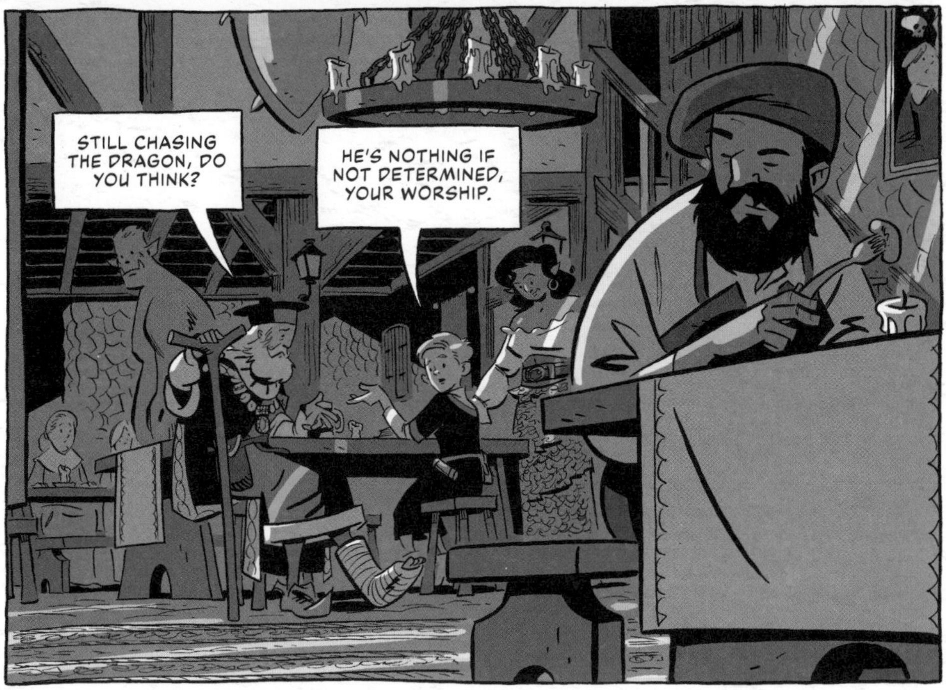
STILL CHASING THE DRAGON, DO YOU THINK?
HE'S NOTHING IF NOT DETERMINED, YOUR WORSHIP.

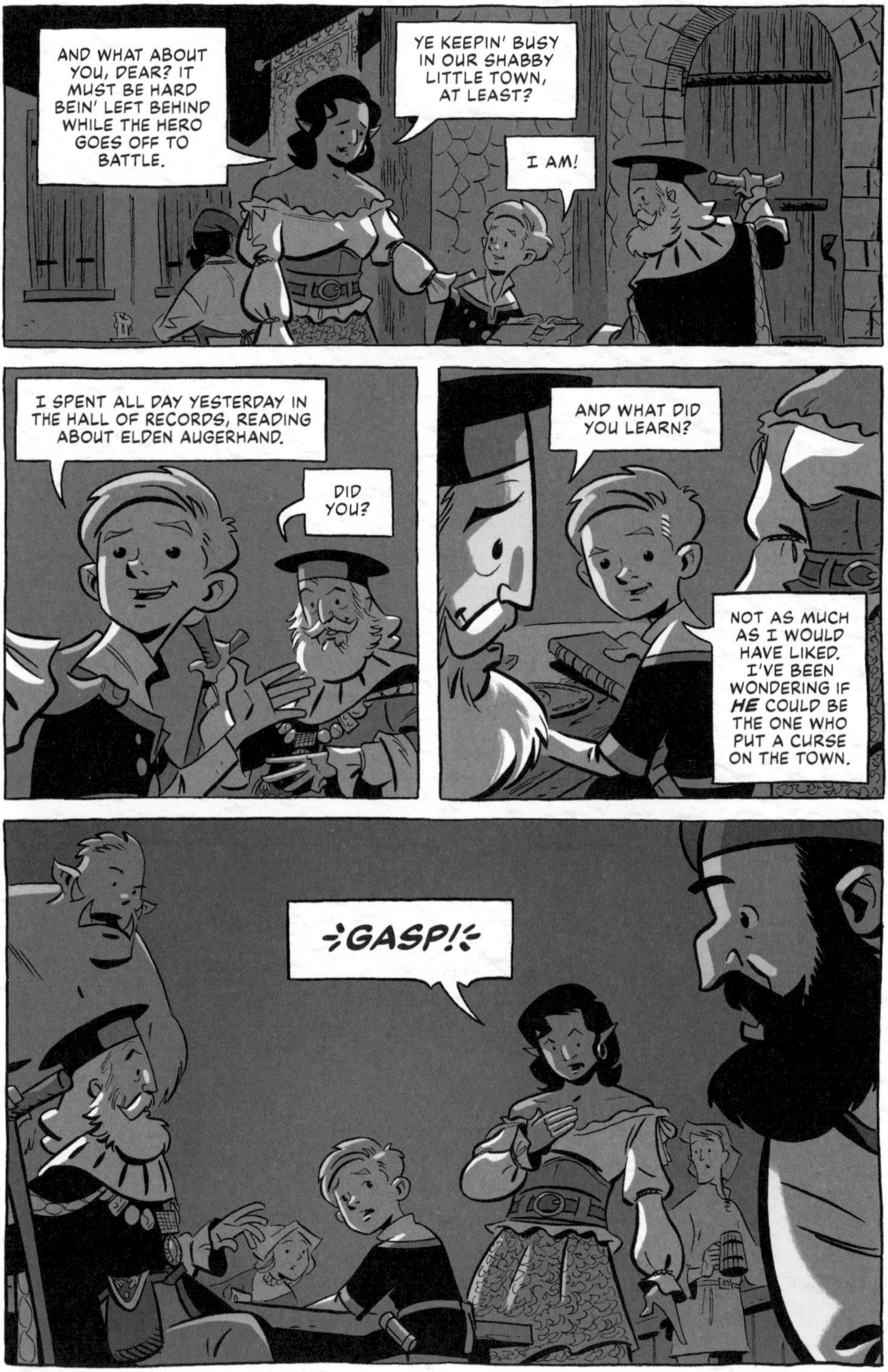
AND WHAT ABOUT YOU, DEAR? IT MUST BE HARD BEIN' LEFT BEHIND WHILE THE HERO GOES OFF TO BATTLE.
YE KEEPIN' BUSY IN OUR SHABBY LITTLE TOWN, AT LEAST?
I AM!
I SPENT ALL DAY YESTERDAY IN THE HALL OF RECORDS, READING ABOUT ELDEN AUGERHAND.
DID YOU?
AND WHAT DID YOU LEARN?
NOT AS MUCH AS I WOULD HAVE LIKED. I'VE BEEN WONDERING IF ***HE*** COULD BE THE ONE WHO PUT A CURSE ON THE TOWN.
GASP!

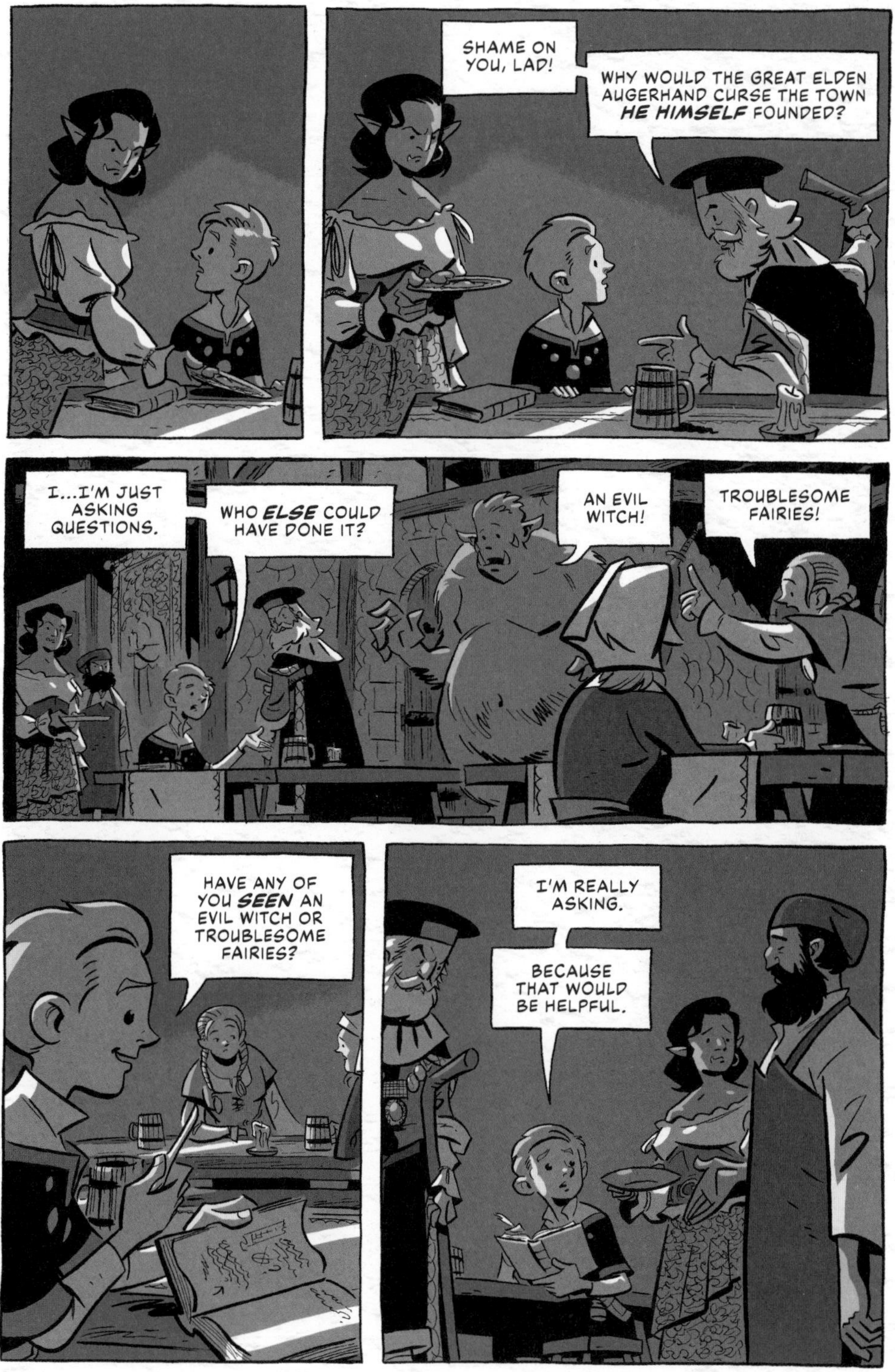
SHAME ON YOU, LAD!
WHY WOULD THE GREAT ELDEN AUGERHAND CURSE THE TOWN ***HE HIMSELF*** FOUNDED?
I...I'M JUST ASKING QUESTIONS.
WHO ***ELSE*** COULD HAVE DONE IT?
AN EVIL WITCH!
TROUBLESOME FAIRIES!
HAVE ANY OF YOU ***SEEN*** AN EVIL WITCH OR TROUBLESOME FAIRIES?
I'M REALLY ASKING.
BECAUSE THAT WOULD BE HELPFUL.

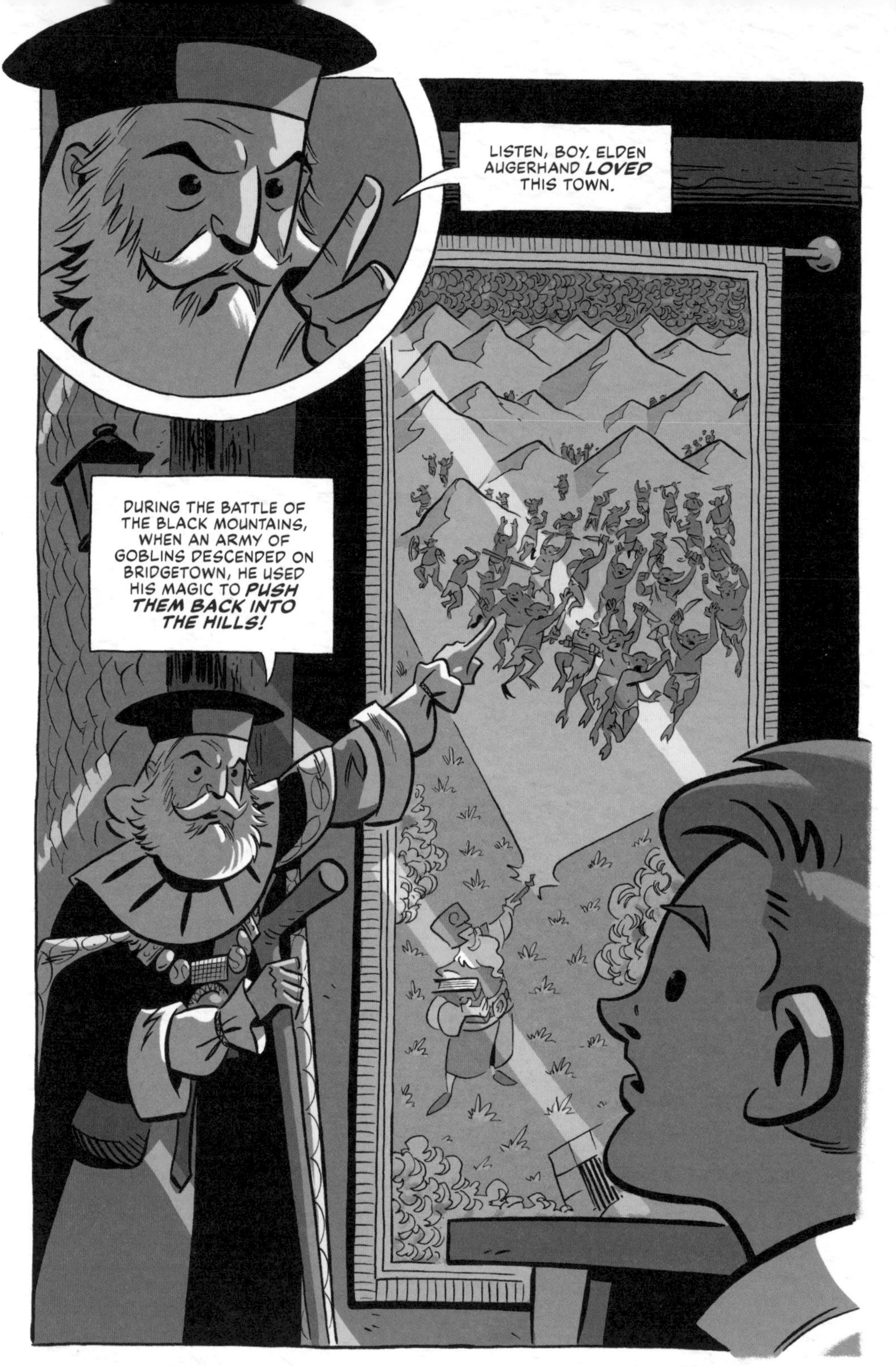
LISTEN, BOY. ELDEN AUGERHAND *LOVED* THIS TOWN.
DURING THE BATTLE OF THE BLACK MOUNTAINS, WHEN AN ARMY OF GOBLINS DESCENDED ON BRIDGETOWN, HE USED HIS MAGIC TO *PUSH THEM BACK INTO THE HILLS!*

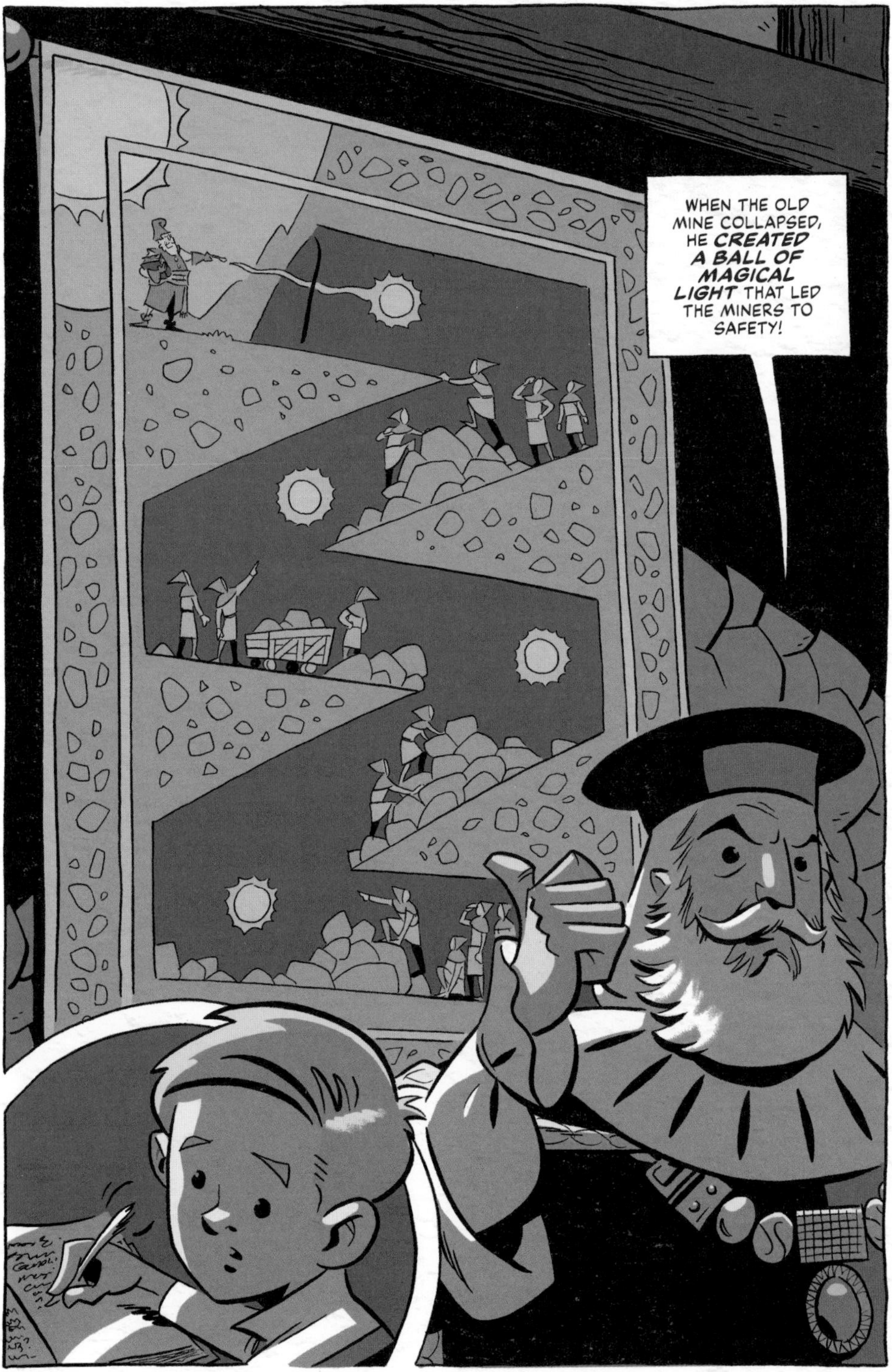
WHEN THE OLD MINE COLLAPSED, HE **CREATED A BALL OF MAGICAL LIGHT** THAT LED THE MINERS TO SAFETY!

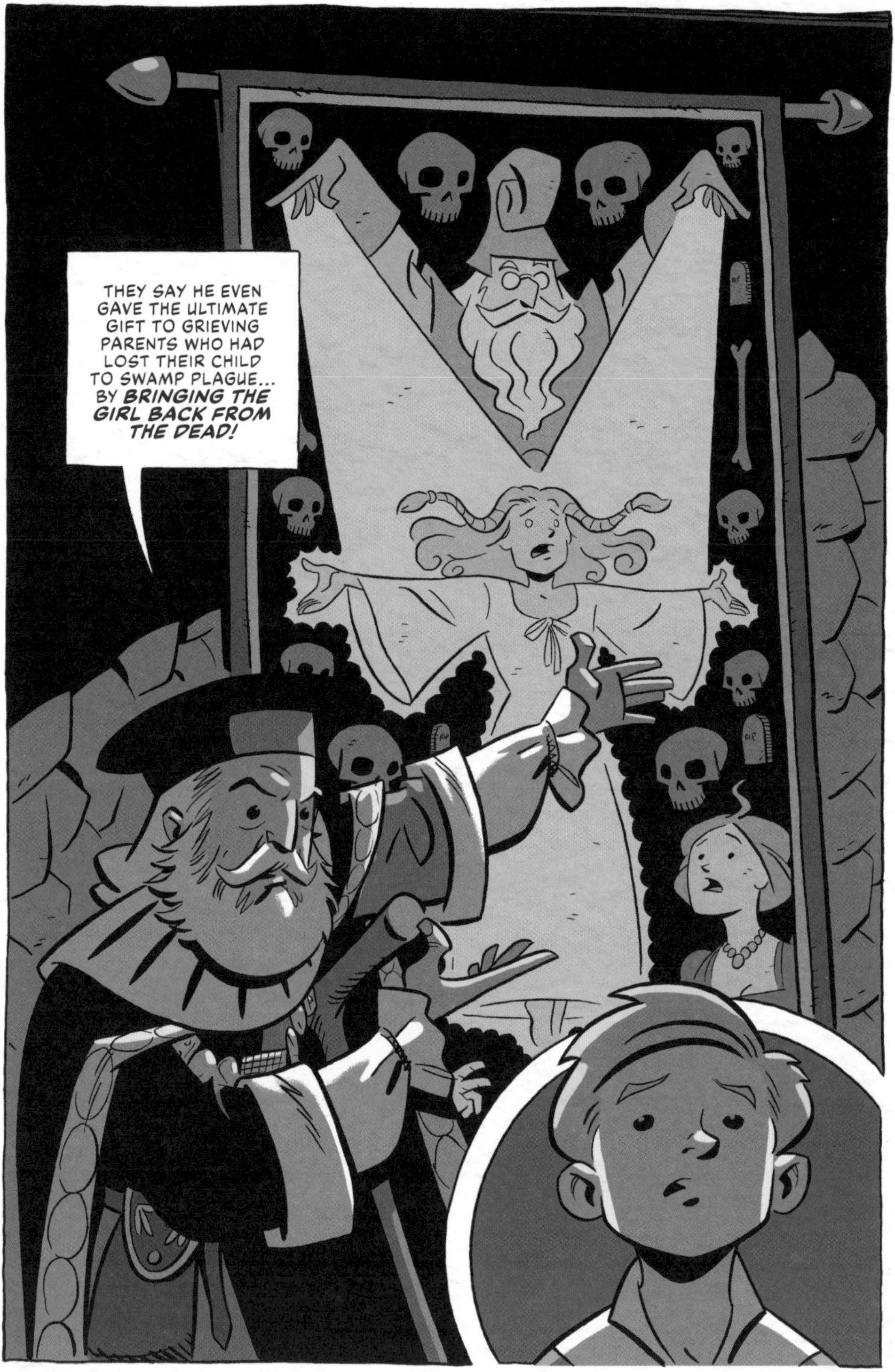
THEY SAY HE EVEN GAVE THE ULTIMATE GIFT TO GRIEVING PARENTS WHO HAD LOST THEIR CHILD TO SWAMP PLAGUE... BY ***BRINGING THE GIRL BACK FROM THE DEAD!***

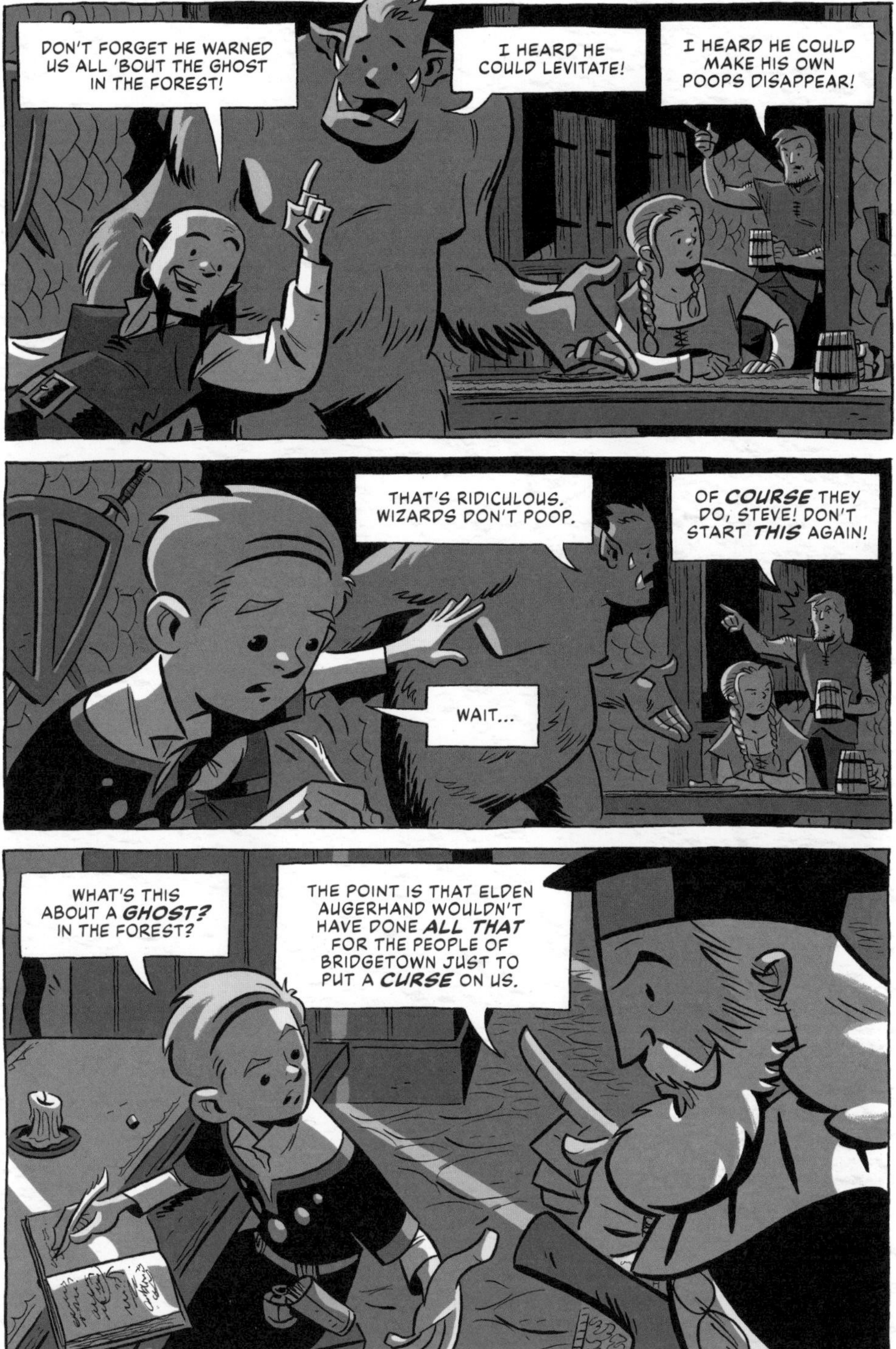
DON'T FORGET HE WARNED US ALL 'BOUT THE GHOST IN THE FOREST!
I HEARD HE COULD LEVITATE!
I HEARD HE COULD MAKE HIS OWN POOPS DISAPPEAR!
THAT'S RIDICULOUS. WIZARDS DON'T POOP.
OF **COURSE** THEY DO, STEVE! DON'T START **THIS** AGAIN!
WAIT...
WHAT'S THIS ABOUT A **GHOST?** IN THE FOREST?
THE POINT IS THAT ELDEN AUGERHAND WOULDN'T HAVE DONE **ALL THAT** FOR THE PEOPLE OF BRIDGETOWN JUST TO PUT A **CURSE** ON US.

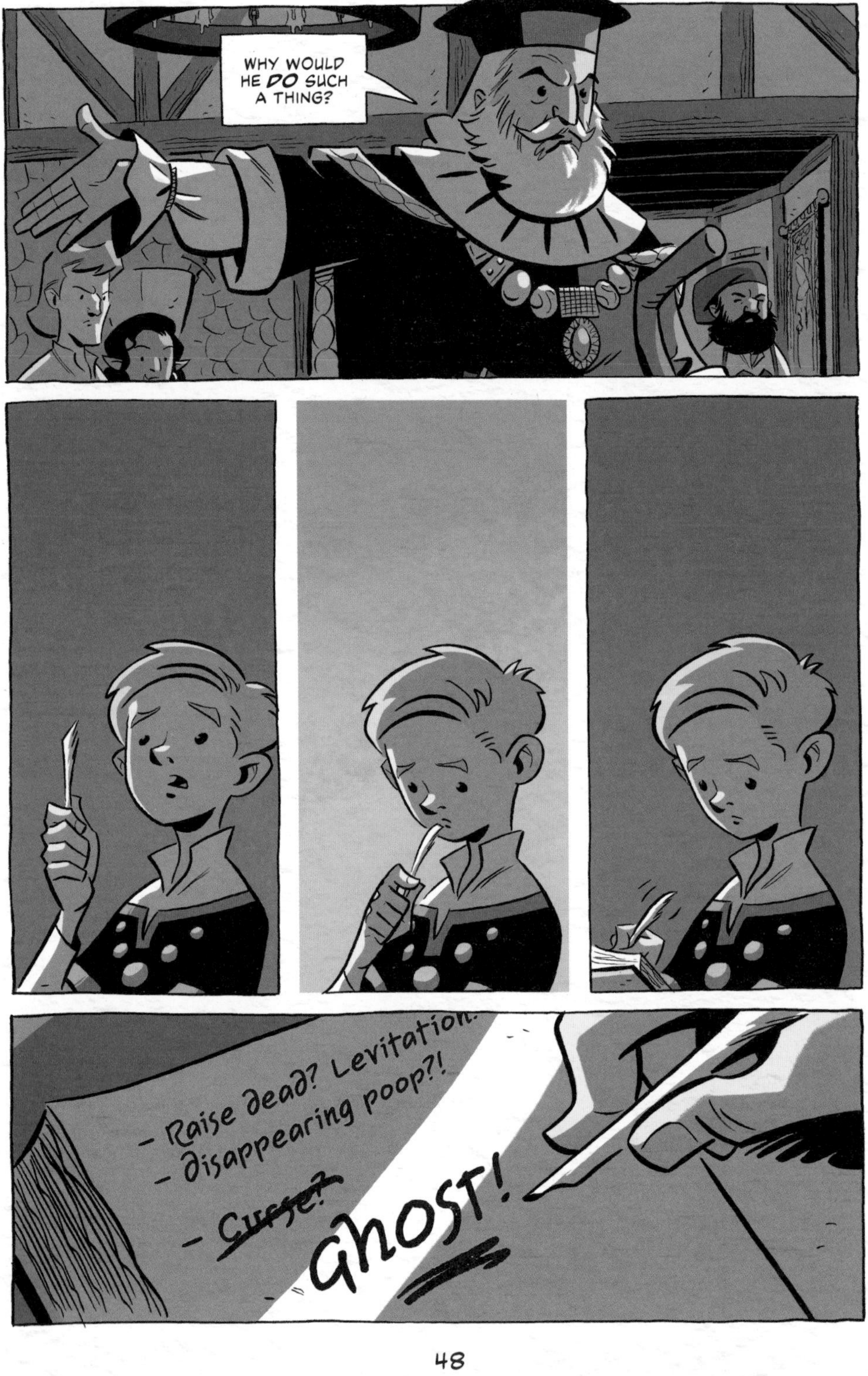
WHY WOULD HE **DO** SUCH A THING?
- Raise dead? Levitation
- disappearing poop?!
- ~~Curse?~~
GHOST!

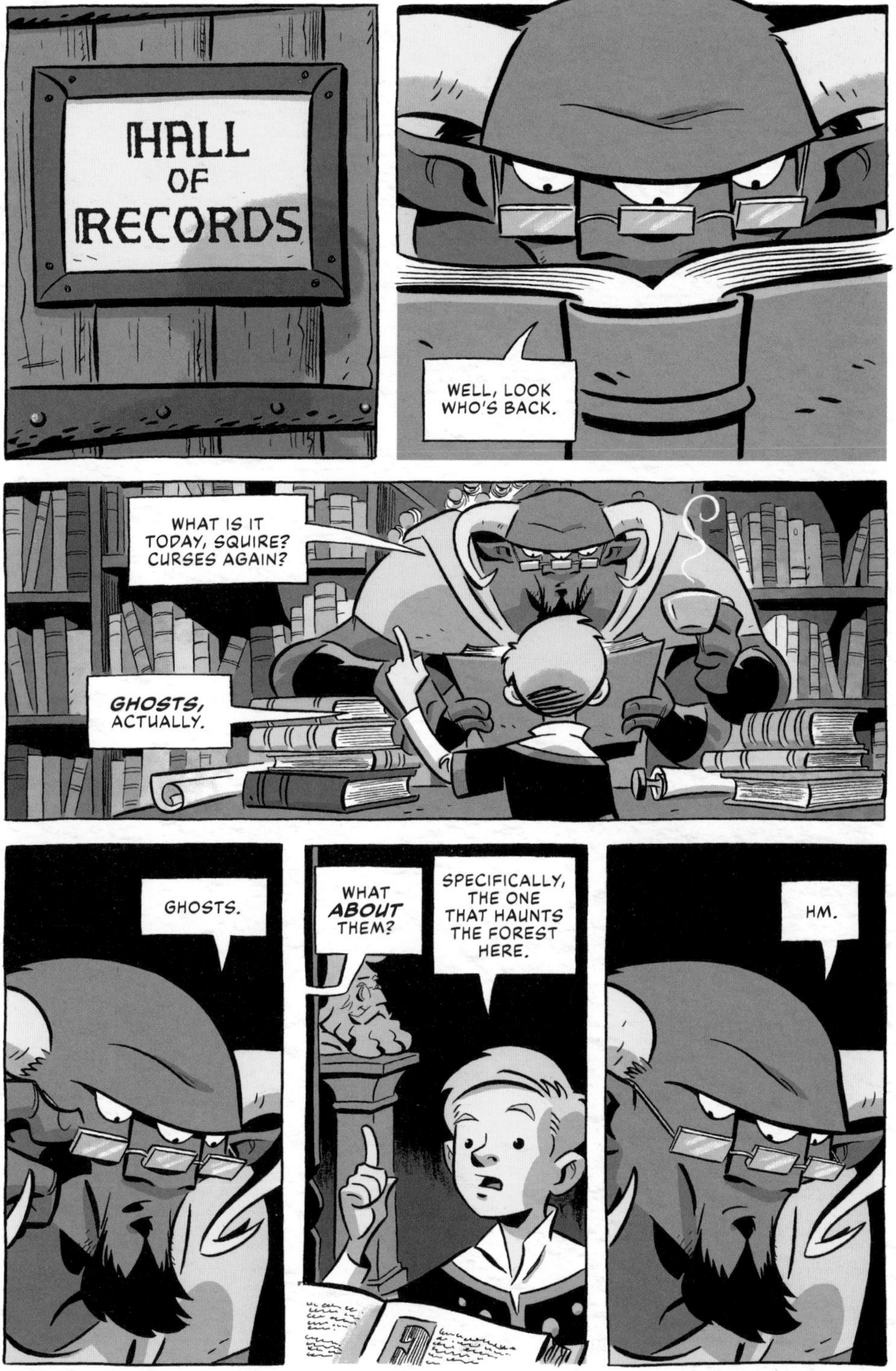
HALL OF RECORDS
WELL, LOOK WHO'S BACK.
WHAT IS IT TODAY, SQUIRE? CURSES AGAIN?
*GHOSTS,* ACTUALLY.
GHOSTS.
WHAT *ABOUT* THEM?
SPECIFICALLY, THE ONE THAT HAUNTS THE FOREST HERE.
HM.

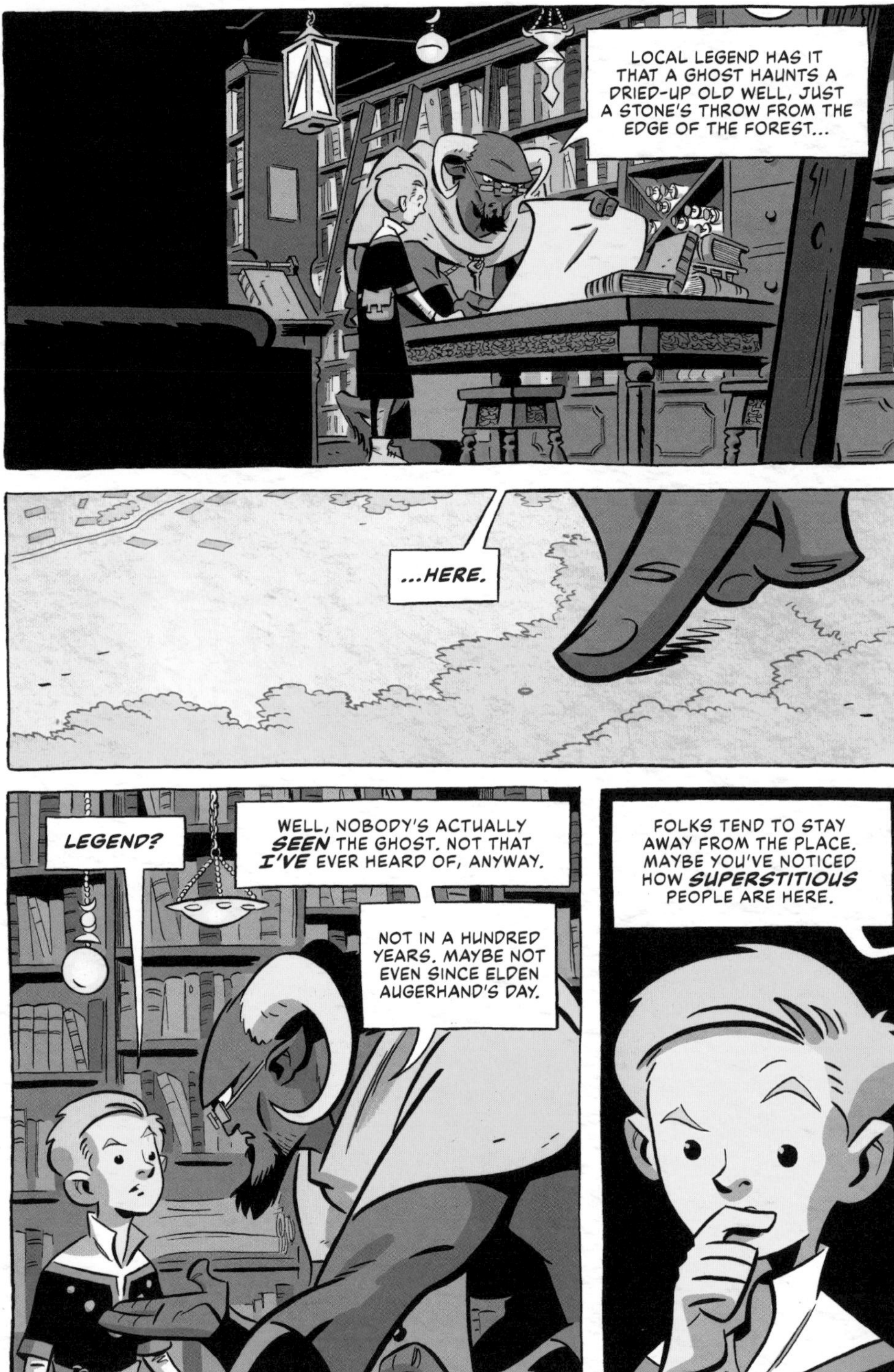

LOCAL LEGEND HAS IT THAT A GHOST HAUNTS A DRIED-UP OLD WELL, JUST A STONE'S THROW FROM THE EDGE OF THE FOREST...
...HERE.
LEGEND?
WELL, NOBODY'S ACTUALLY SEEN THE GHOST. NOT THAT I'VE EVER HEARD OF, ANYWAY.
NOT IN A HUNDRED YEARS. MAYBE NOT EVEN SINCE ELDEN AUGERHAND'S DAY.
FOLKS TEND TO STAY AWAY FROM THE PLACE. MAYBE YOU'VE NOTICED HOW SUPERSTITIOUS PEOPLE ARE HERE.

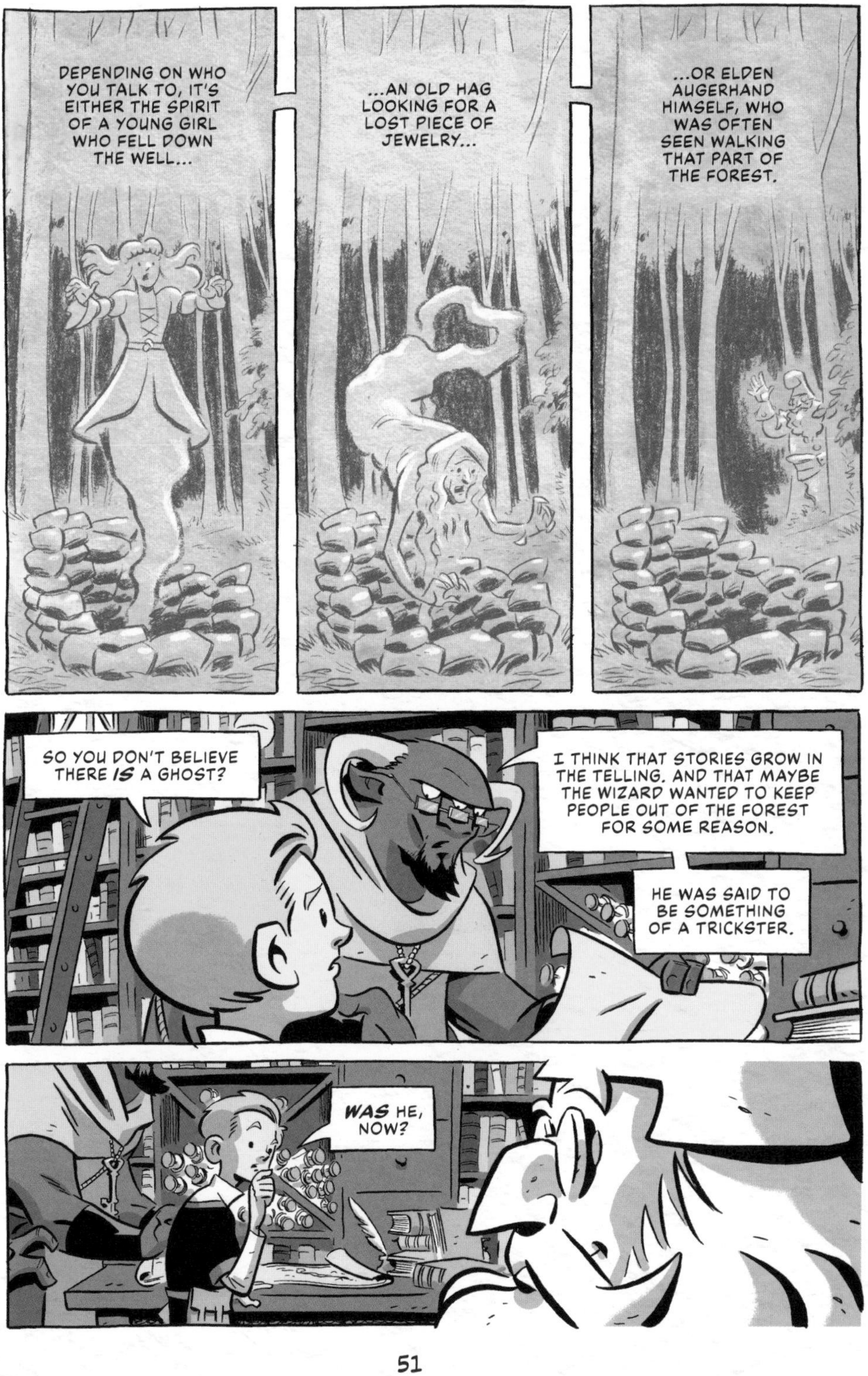
DEPENDING ON WHO YOU TALK TO, IT'S EITHER THE SPIRIT OF A YOUNG GIRL WHO FELL DOWN THE WELL...
...AN OLD HAG LOOKING FOR A LOST PIECE OF JEWELRY...
...OR ELDEN AUGERHAND HIMSELF, WHO WAS OFTEN SEEN WALKING THAT PART OF THE FOREST.
SO YOU DON'T BELIEVE THERE *IS* A GHOST?
I THINK THAT STORIES GROW IN THE TELLING. AND THAT MAYBE THE WIZARD WANTED TO KEEP PEOPLE OUT OF THE FOREST FOR SOME REASON.
HE WAS SAID TO BE SOMETHING OF A TRICKSTER.
*WAS* HE, NOW?

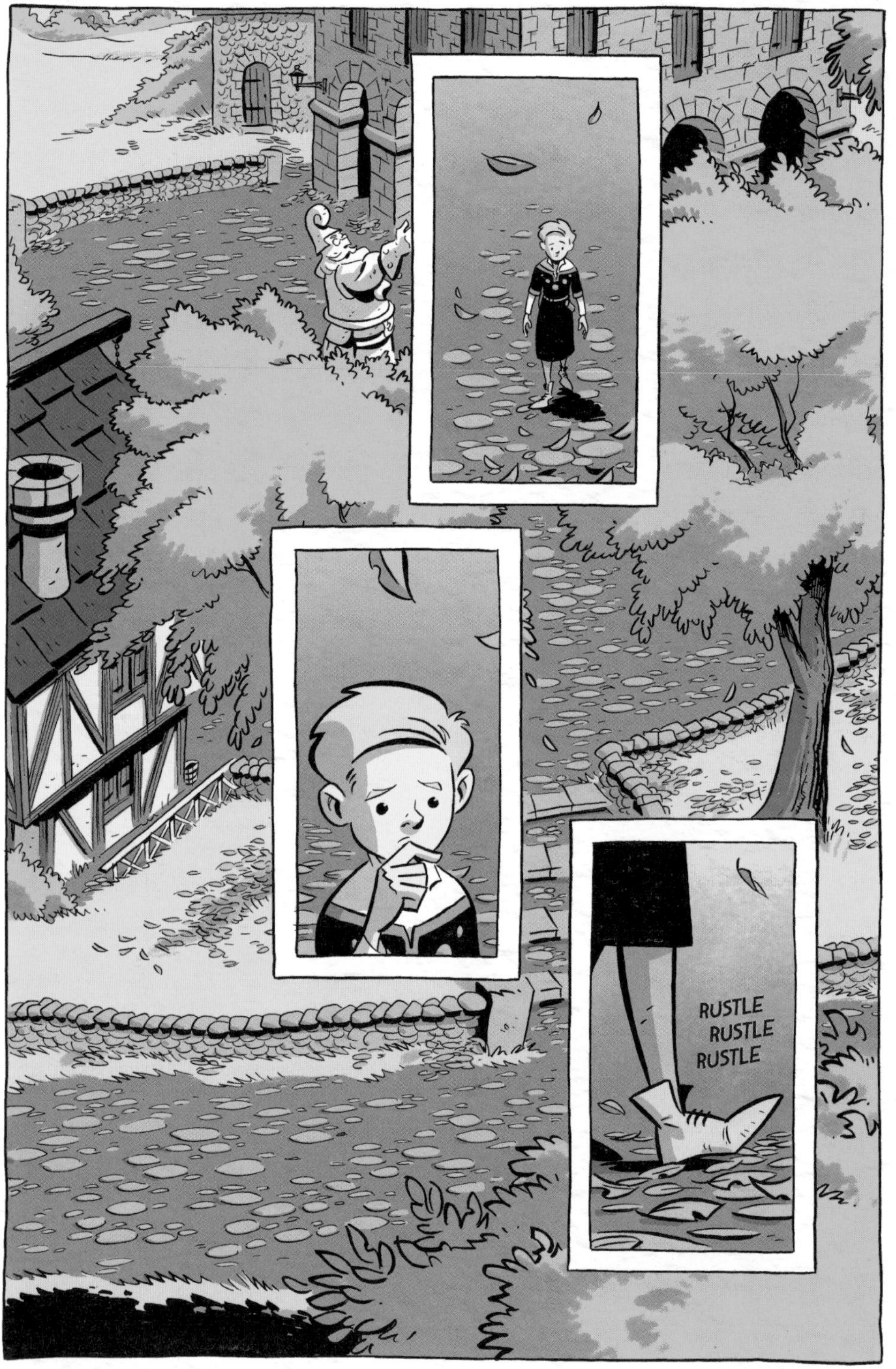
RUSTLE
RUSTLE
RUSTLE

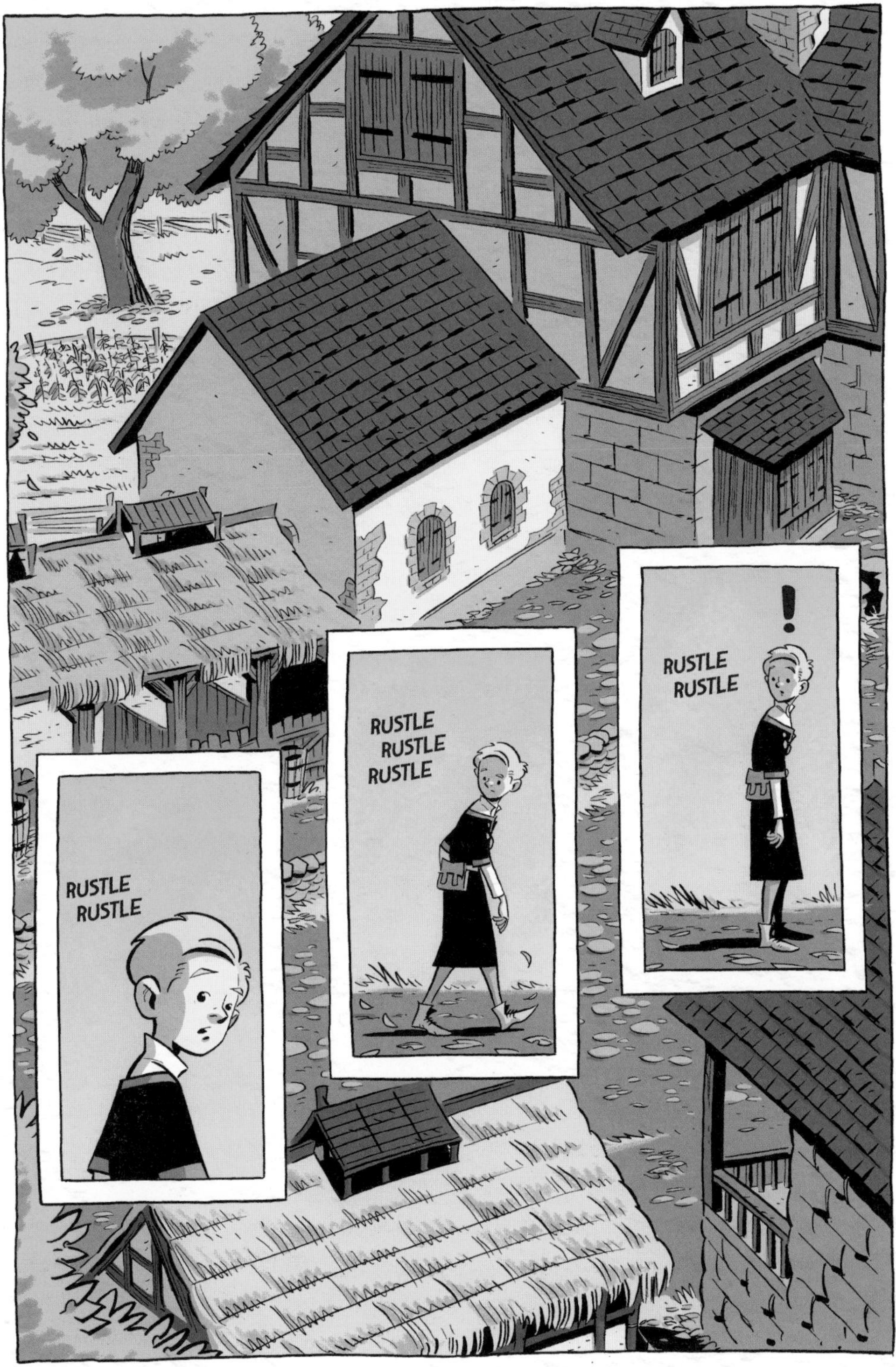
RUSTLE RUSTLE
RUSTLE RUSTLE RUSTLE
!
RUSTLE RUSTLE

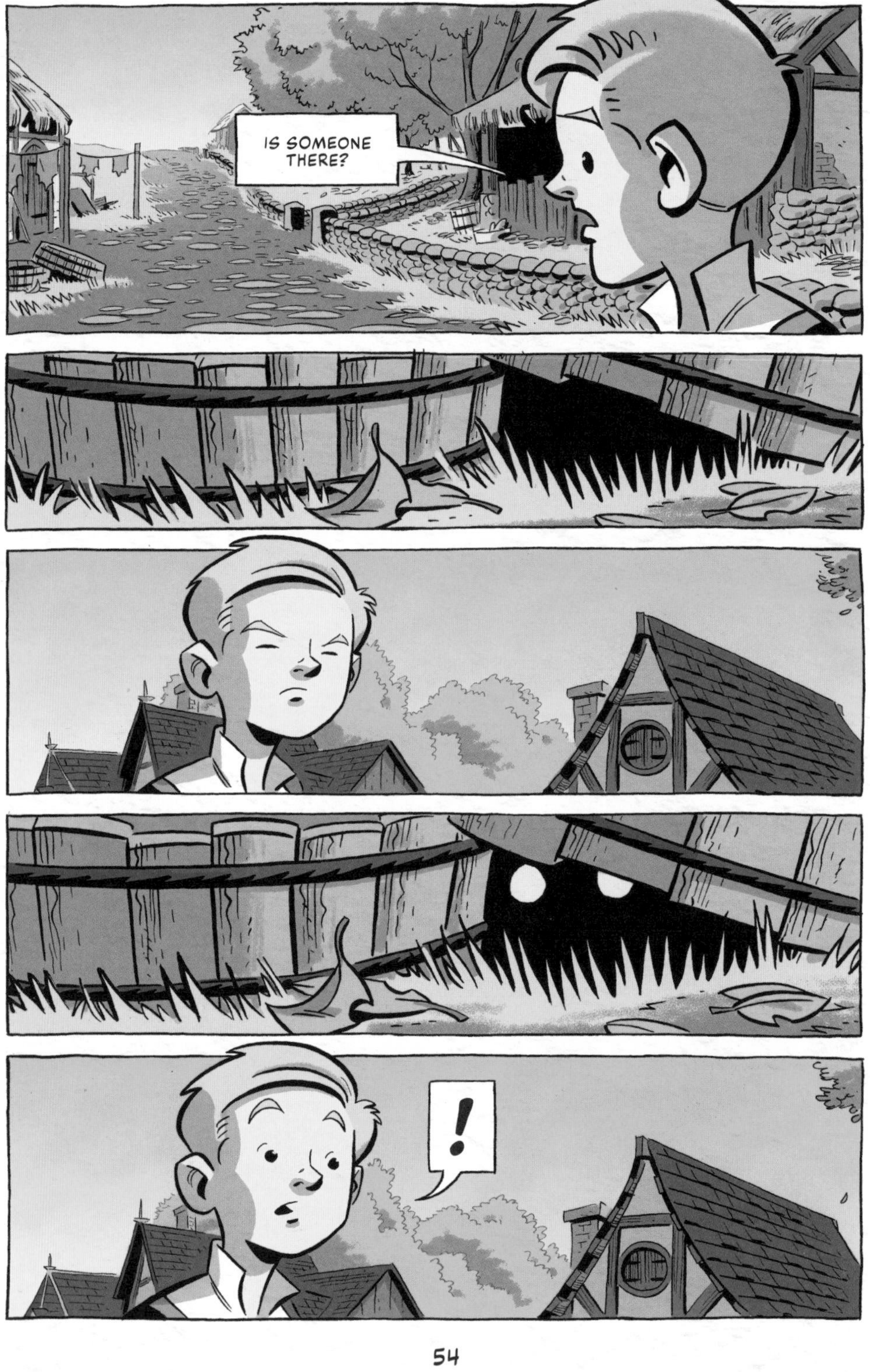
IS SOMEONE THERE?
!

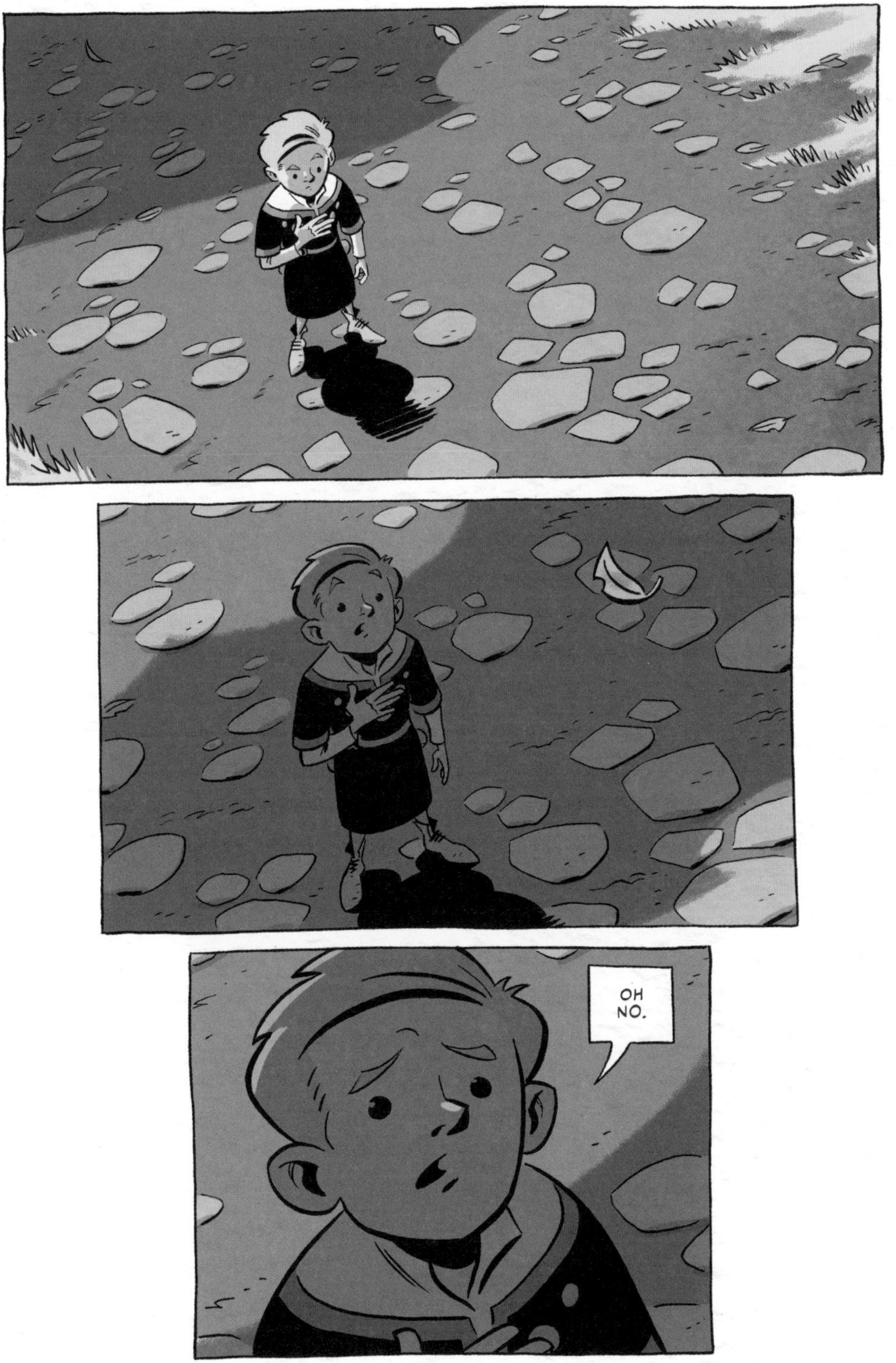
OH
NO.

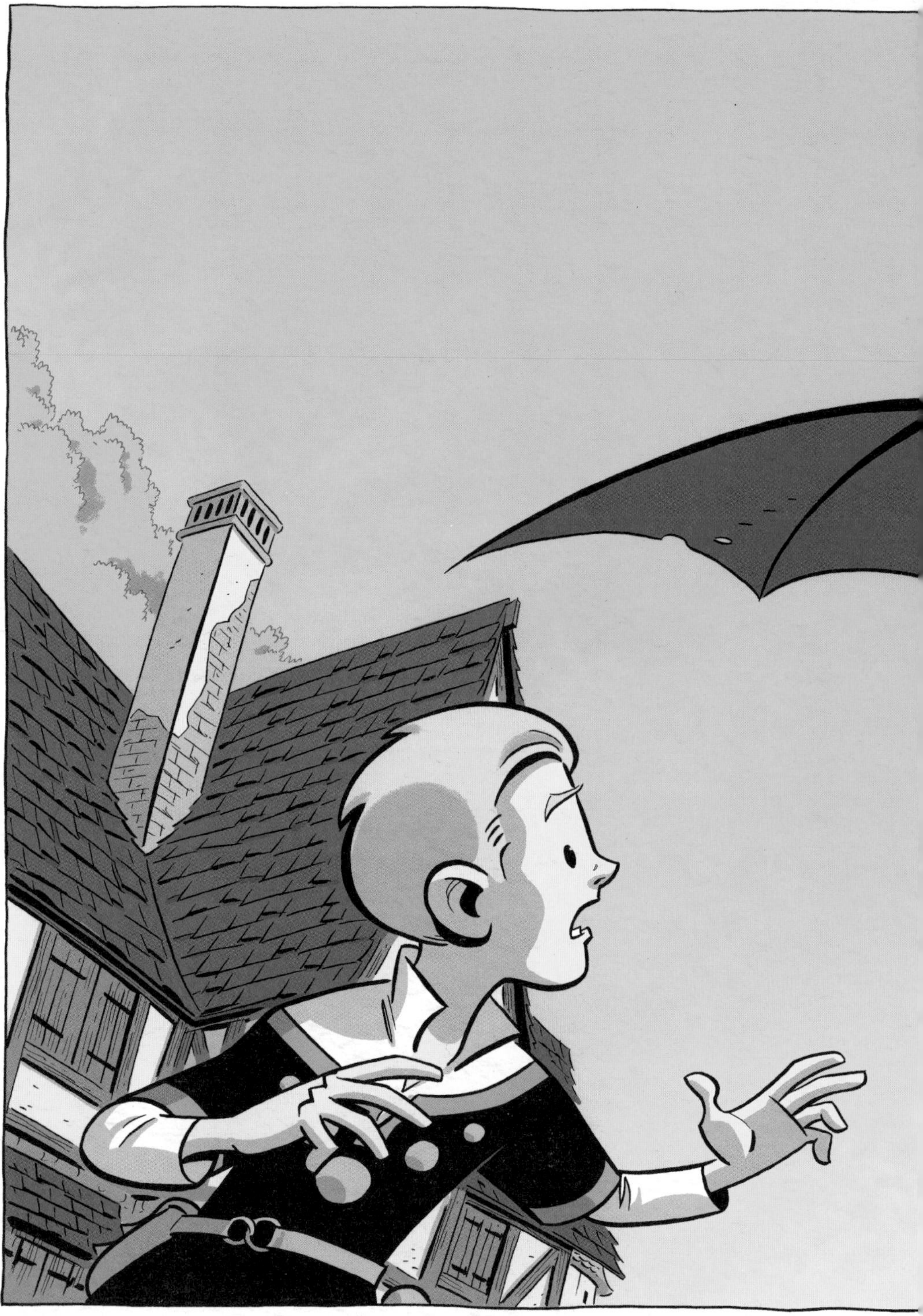

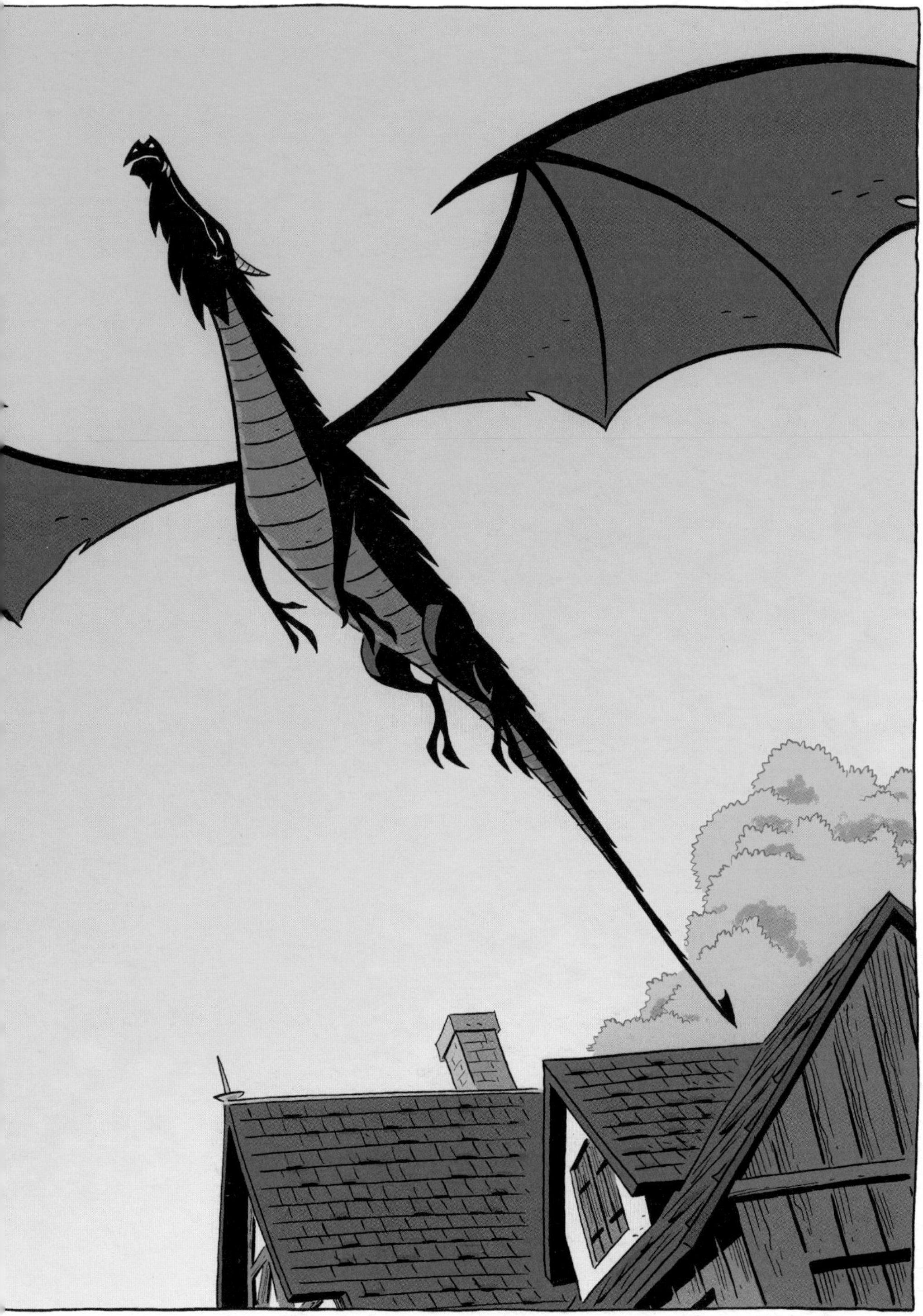

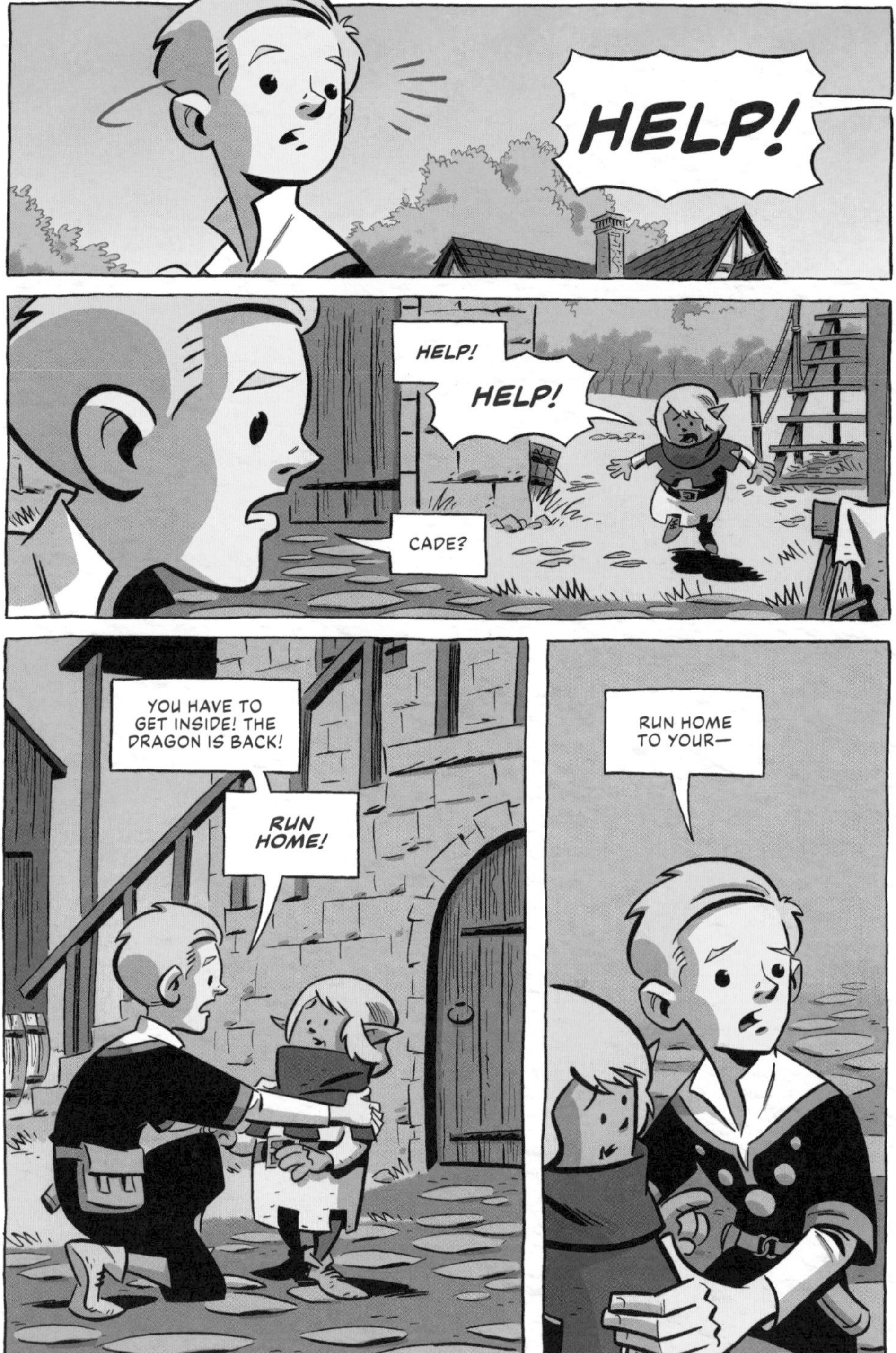
HELP!
HELP!
HELP!
CADE?
YOU HAVE TO GET INSIDE! THE DRAGON IS BACK!
RUN HOME!
RUN HOME TO YOUR—

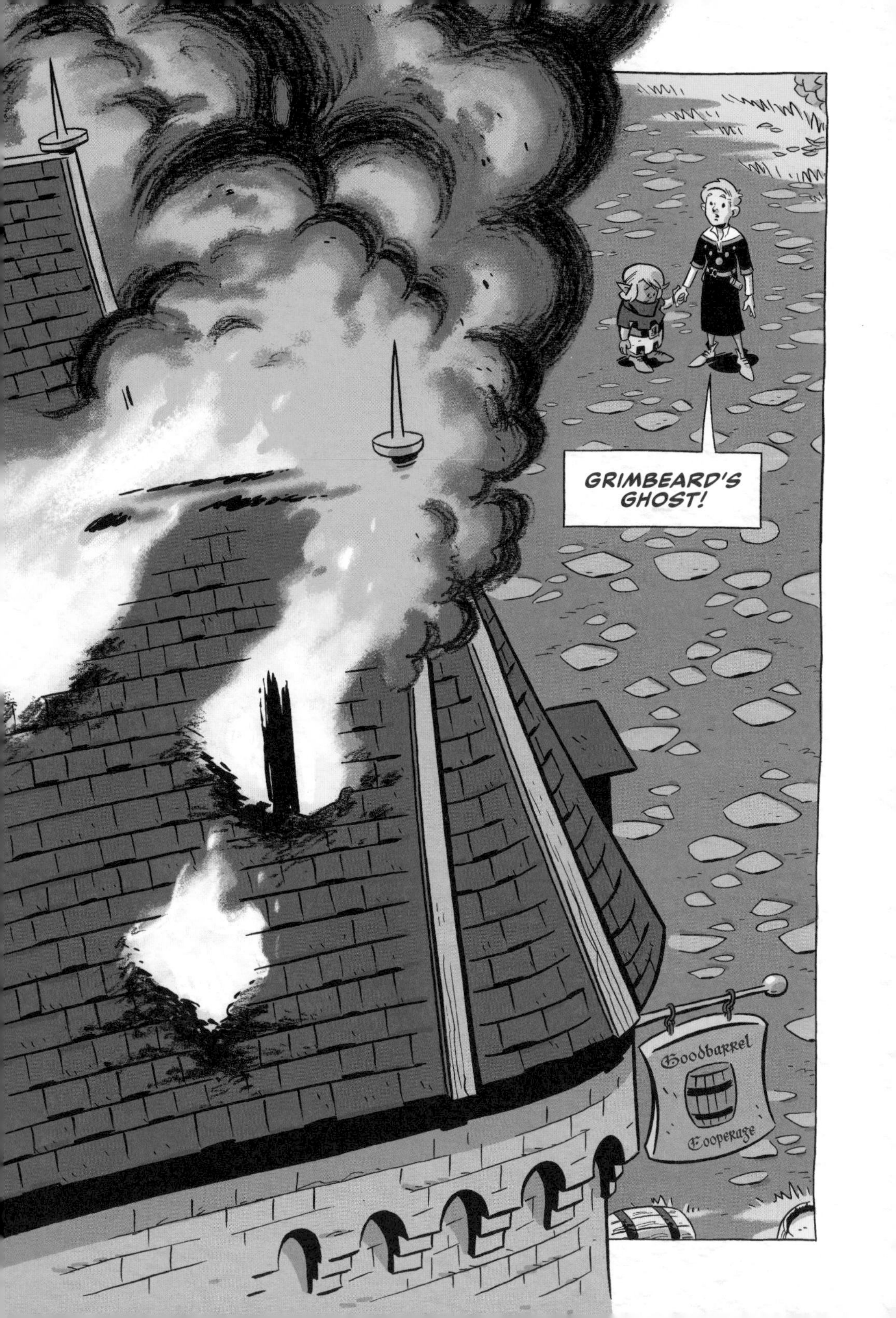
GRIMBEARD'S GHOST!
Goodbarrel
Cooperage

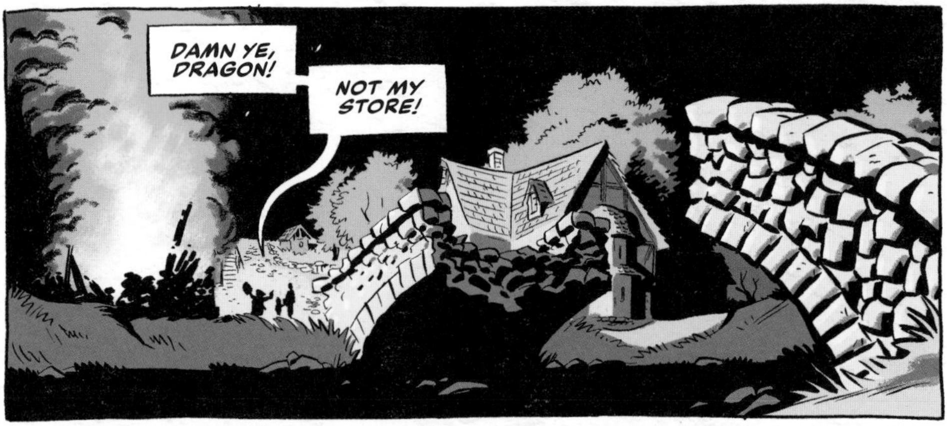
DAMN YE, DRAGON!
NOT MY STORE!

# CHAPTER FOUR

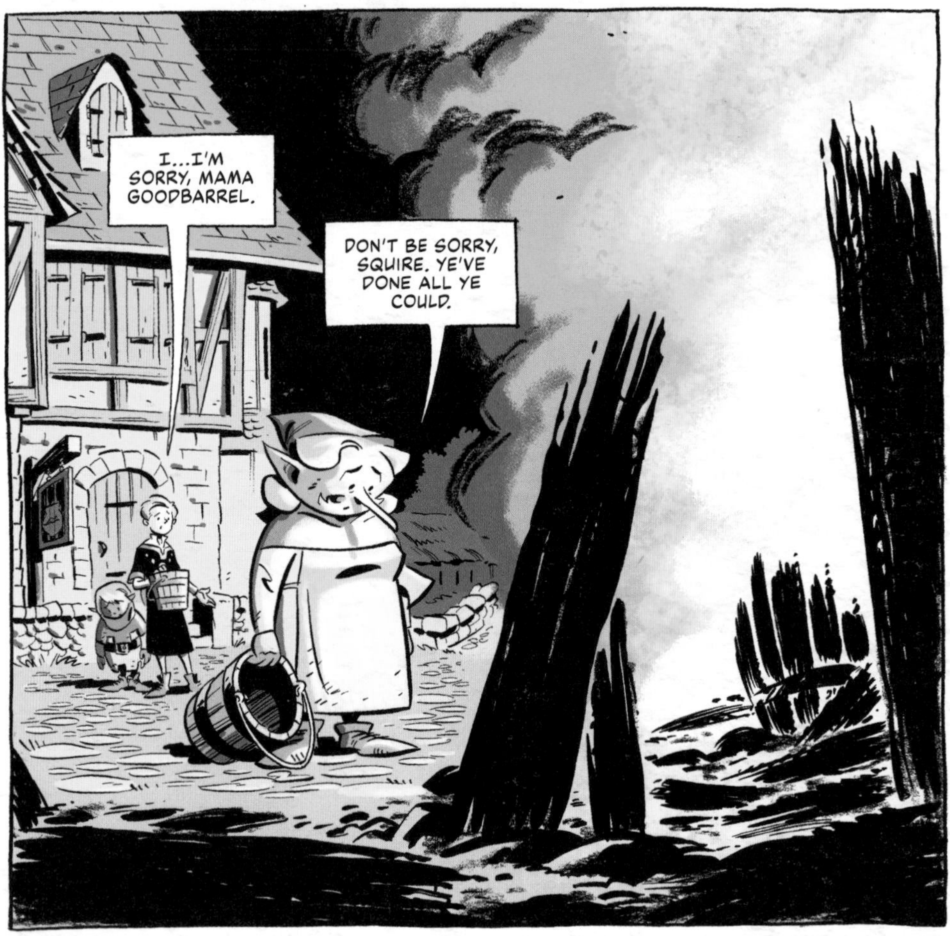
I...I'M SORRY, MAMA GOODBARREL.
DON'T BE SORRY, SQUIRE. YE'VE DONE ALL YE COULD.

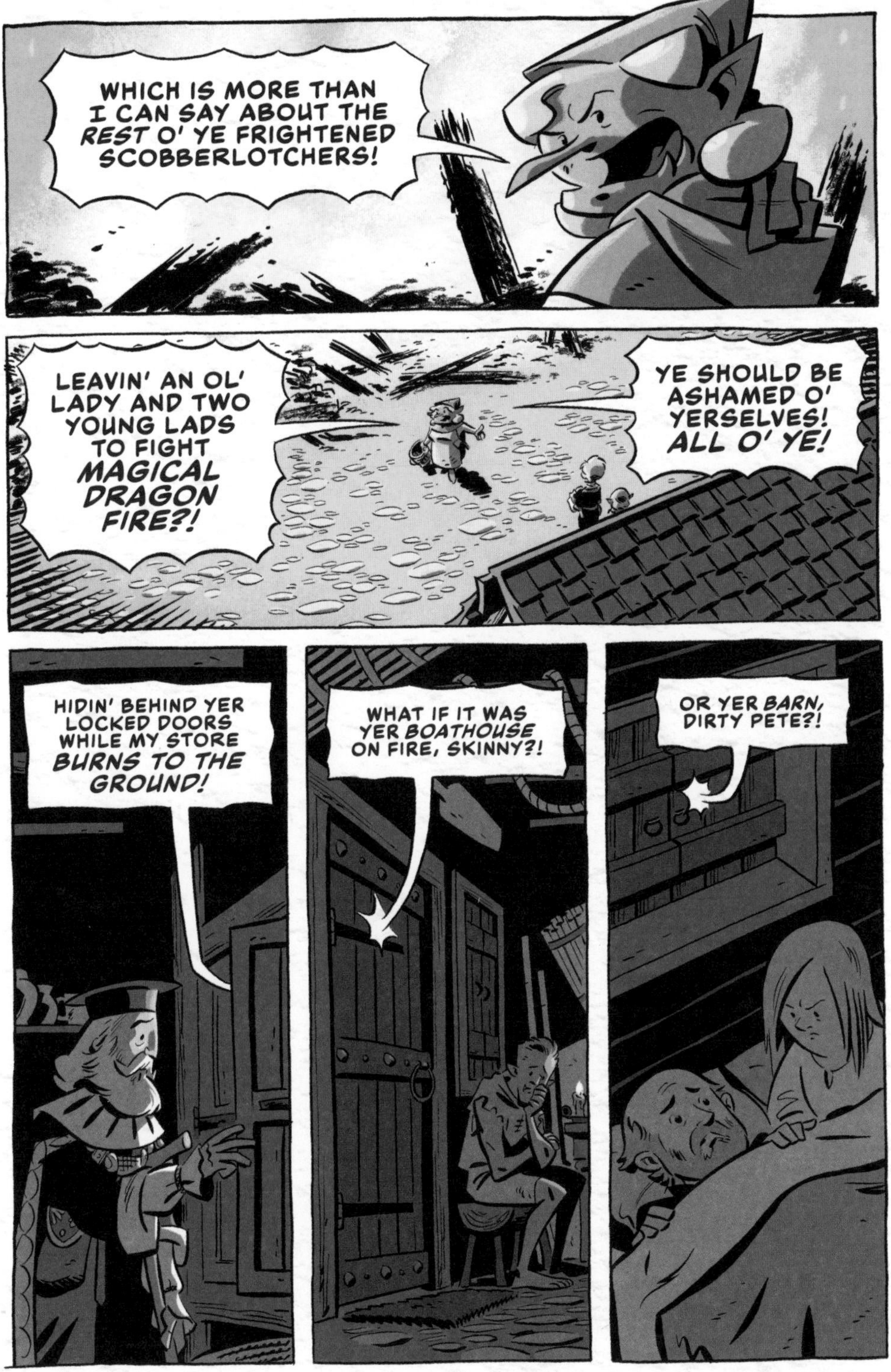

WHICH IS MORE THAN I CAN SAY ABOUT THE *REST* O' YE FRIGHTENED SCOBBERLOTCHERS!
LEAVIN' AN OL' LADY AND TWO YOUNG LADS TO FIGHT *MAGICAL DRAGON FIRE?!*
YE SHOULD BE ASHAMED O' YERSELVES! *ALL O' YE!*
HIDIN' BEHIND YER LOCKED DOORS WHILE MY STORE *BURNS TO THE GROUND!*
WHAT IF IT WAS YER *BOATHOUSE* ON FIRE, SKINNY?!
OR YER *BARN,* DIRTY PETE?!

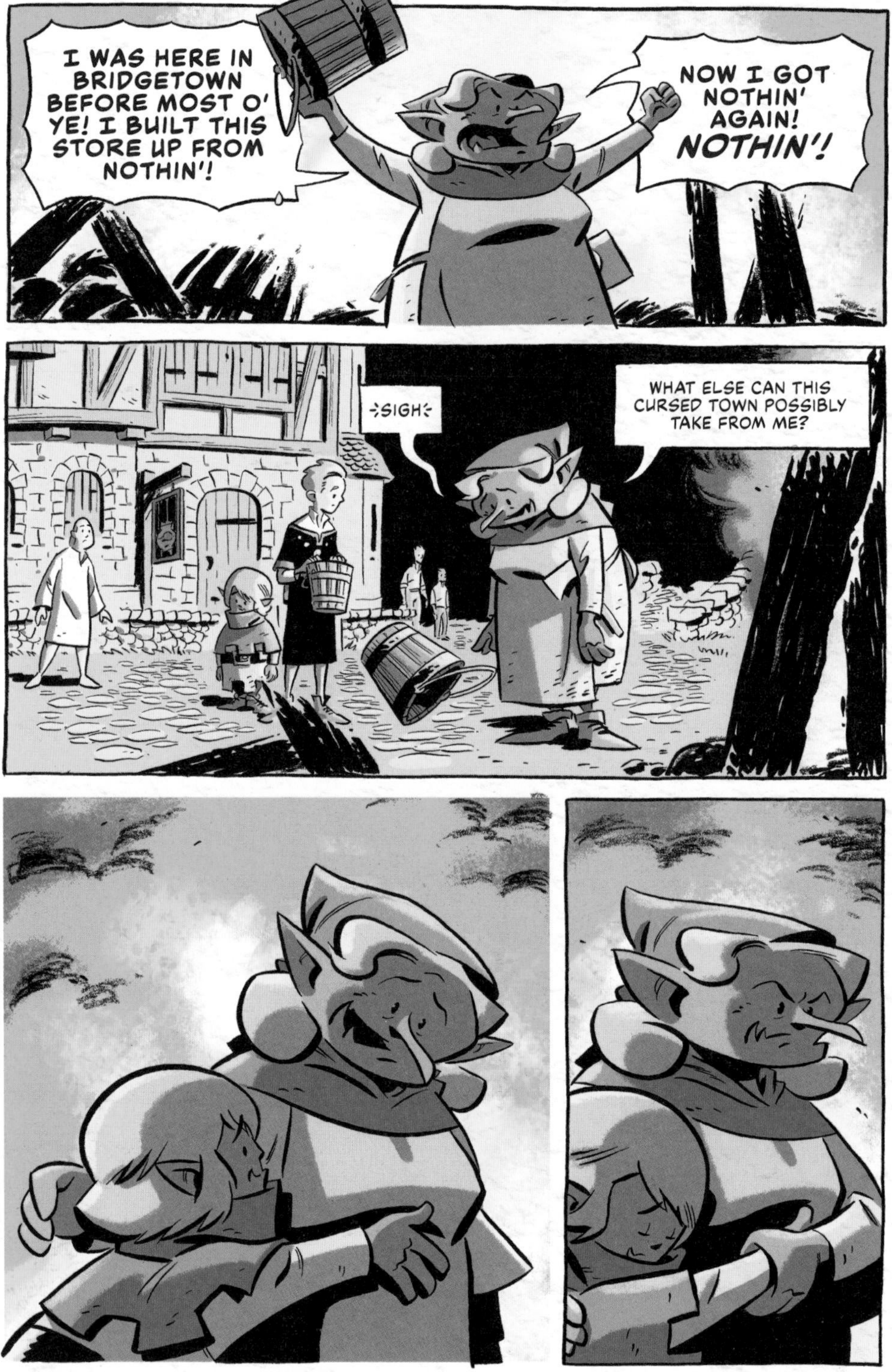
I WAS HERE IN BRIDGETOWN BEFORE MOST O' YE! I BUILT THIS STORE UP FROM NOTHIN'!
NOW I GOT NOTHIN' AGAIN! *NOTHIN'!*
SIGH
WHAT ELSE CAN THIS CURSED TOWN POSSIBLY TAKE FROM ME?

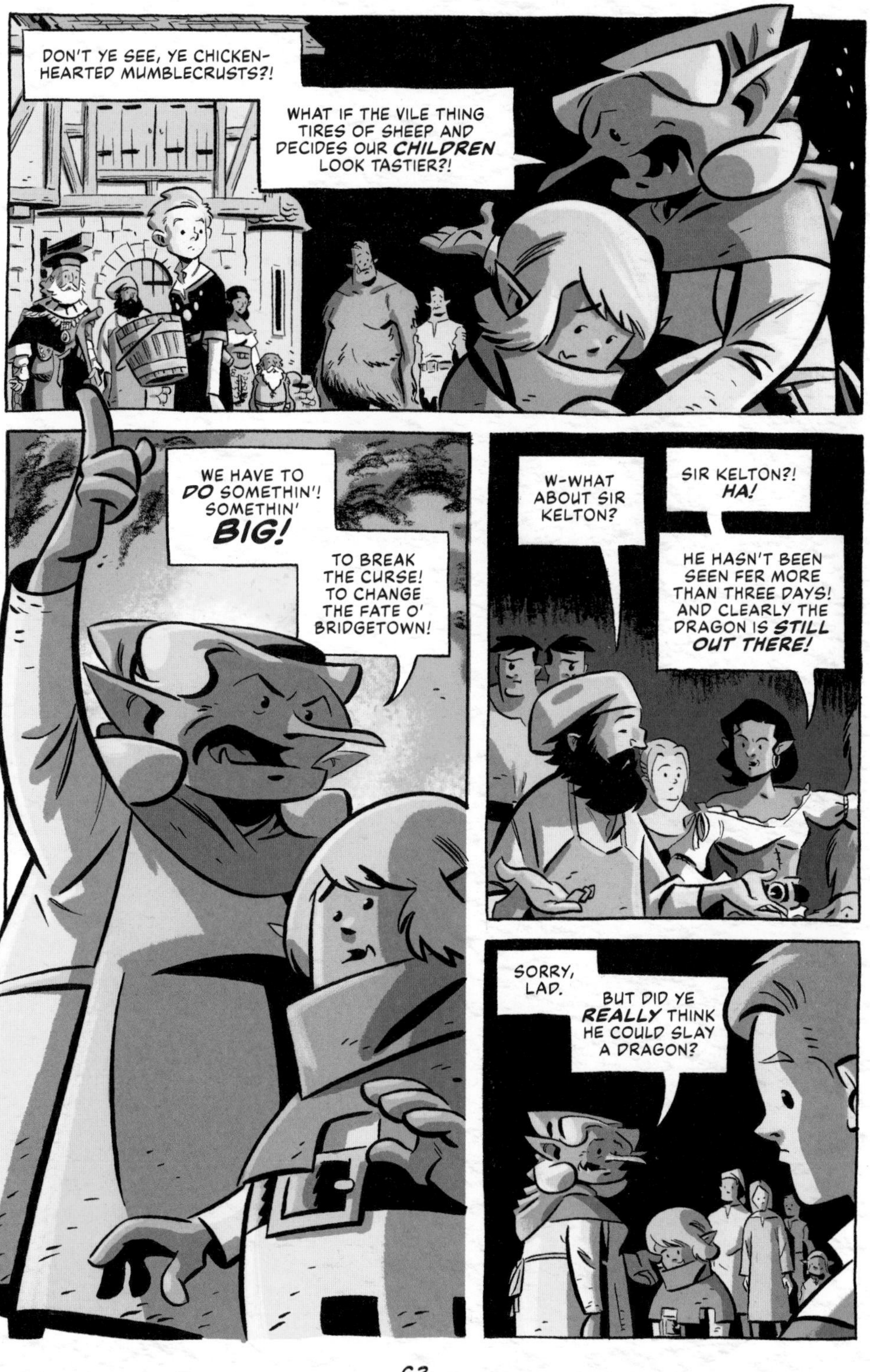
DON'T YE SEE, YE CHICKEN-HEARTED MUMBLECRUSTS?!
WHAT IF THE VILE THING TIRES OF SHEEP AND DECIDES OUR CHILDREN LOOK TASTIER?!
WE HAVE TO DO SOMETHIN'! SOMETHIN' BIG!
TO BREAK THE CURSE! TO CHANGE THE FATE O' BRIDGETOWN!
W-WHAT ABOUT SIR KELTON?
SIR KELTON?! HA!
HE HASN'T BEEN SEEN FER MORE THAN THREE DAYS! AND CLEARLY THE DRAGON IS STILL OUT THERE!
SORRY, LAD.
BUT DID YE REALLY THINK HE COULD SLAY A DRAGON?

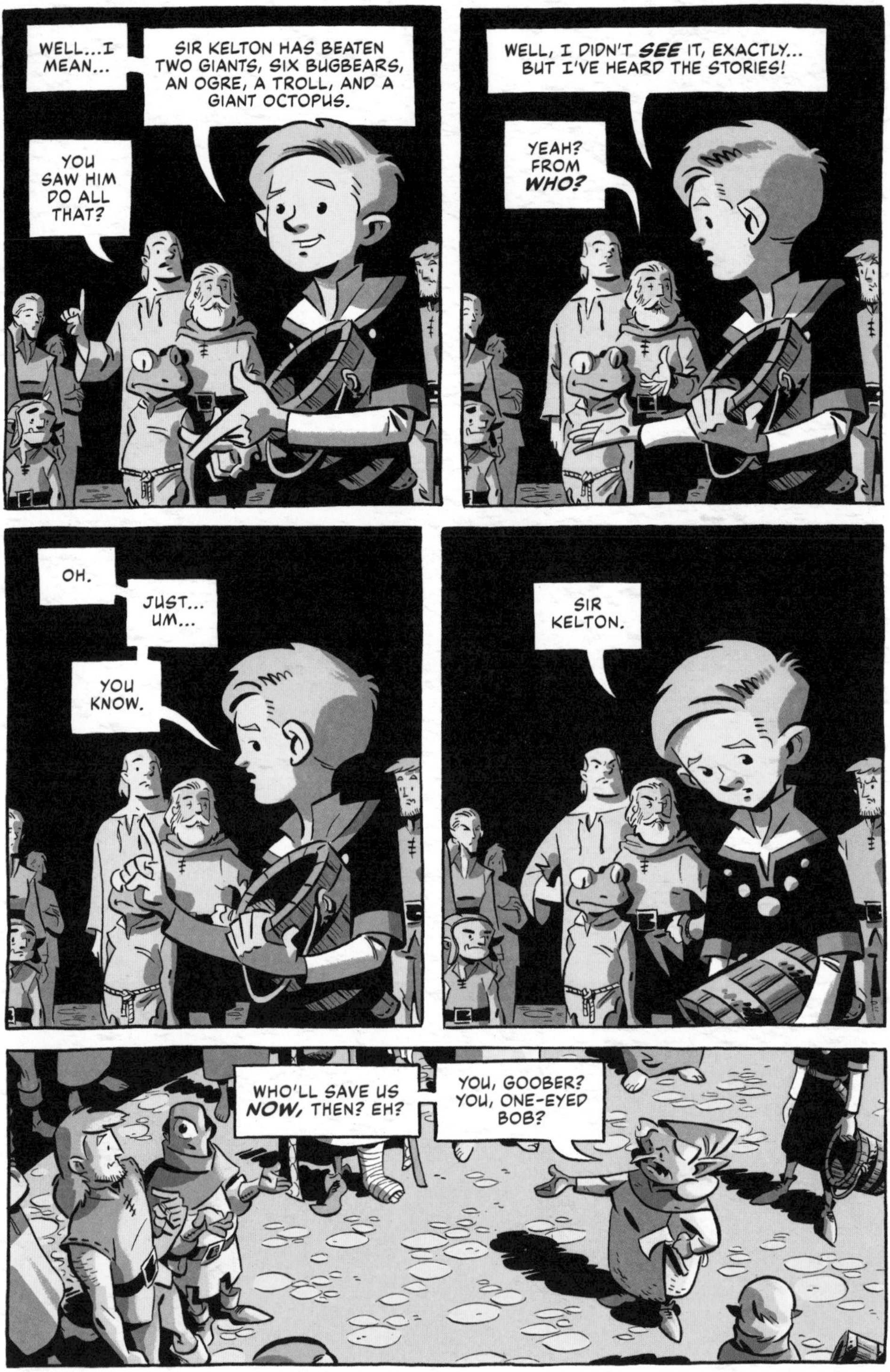
WELL...I MEAN...
SIR KELTON HAS BEATEN TWO GIANTS, SIX BUGBEARS, AN OGRE, A TROLL, AND A GIANT OCTOPUS.
YOU SAW HIM DO ALL THAT?
WELL, I DIDN'T SEE IT, EXACTLY... BUT I'VE HEARD THE STORIES!
YEAH? FROM WHO?
OH.
JUST... UM...
YOU KNOW.
SIR KELTON.
WHO'LL SAVE US NOW, THEN? EH?
YOU, GOOBER? YOU, ONE-EYED BOB?

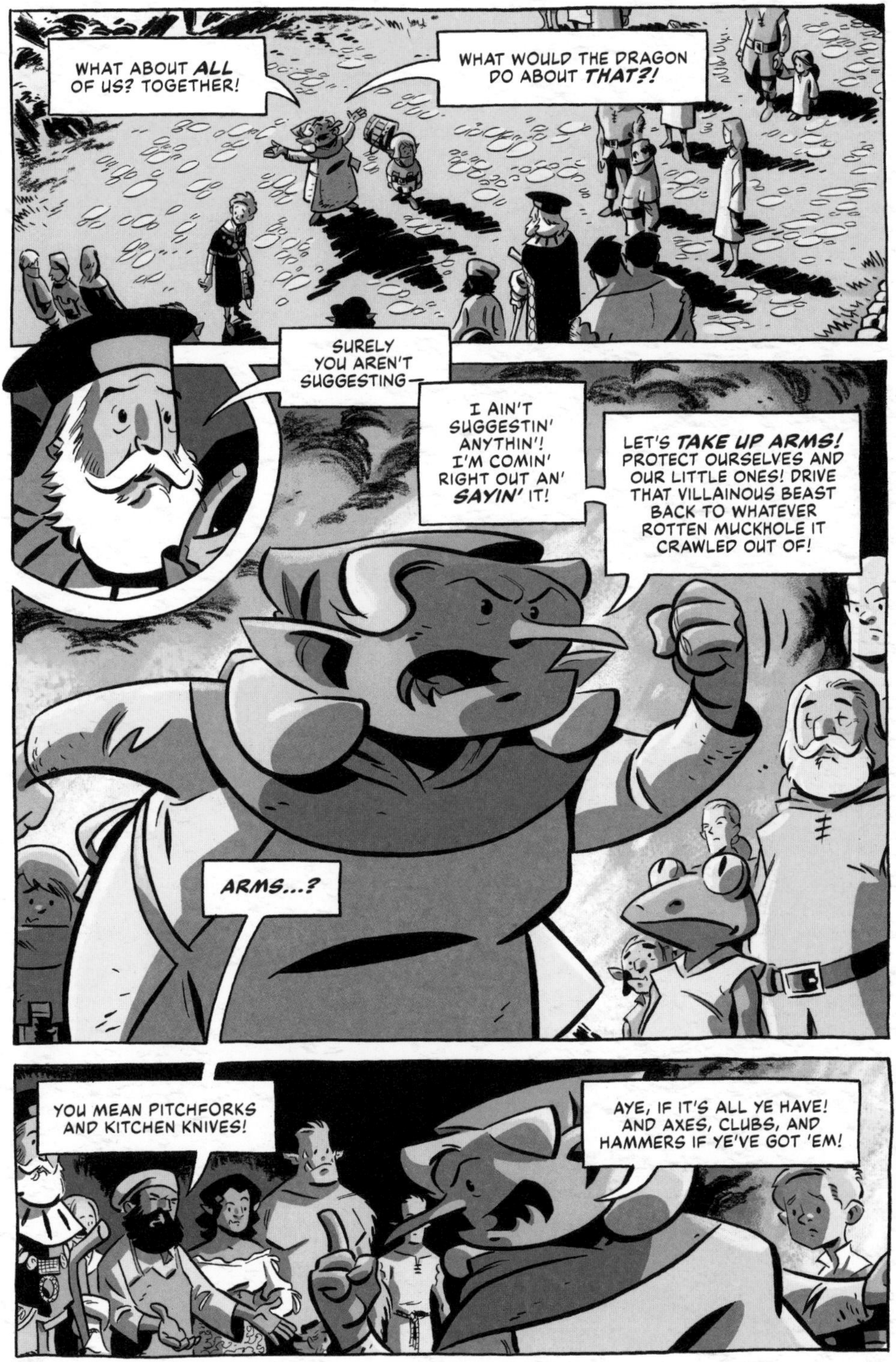
WHAT ABOUT ALL OF US? TOGETHER!
WHAT WOULD THE DRAGON DO ABOUT THAT?!
SURELY YOU AREN'T SUGGESTING—
I AIN'T SUGGESTIN' ANYTHIN'! I'M COMIN' RIGHT OUT AN' SAYIN' IT!
LET'S TAKE UP ARMS! PROTECT OURSELVES AND OUR LITTLE ONES! DRIVE THAT VILLAINOUS BEAST BACK TO WHATEVER ROTTEN MUCKHOLE IT CRAWLED OUT OF!
ARMS...?
YOU MEAN PITCHFORKS AND KITCHEN KNIVES!
AYE, IF IT'S ALL YE HAVE! AND AXES, CLUBS, AND HAMMERS IF YE'VE GOT 'EM!

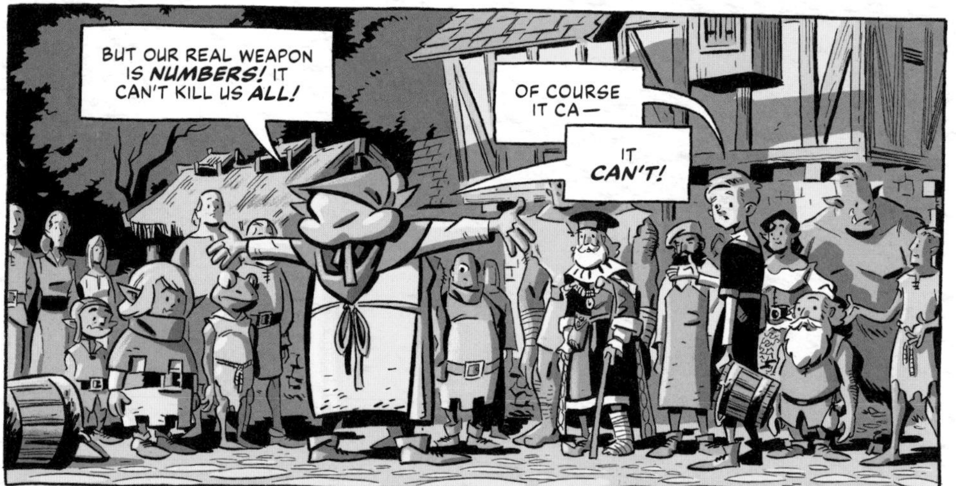
BUT OUR REAL WEAPON IS NUMBERS! IT CAN'T KILL US ALL!
OF COURSE IT CA—
IT CAN'T!

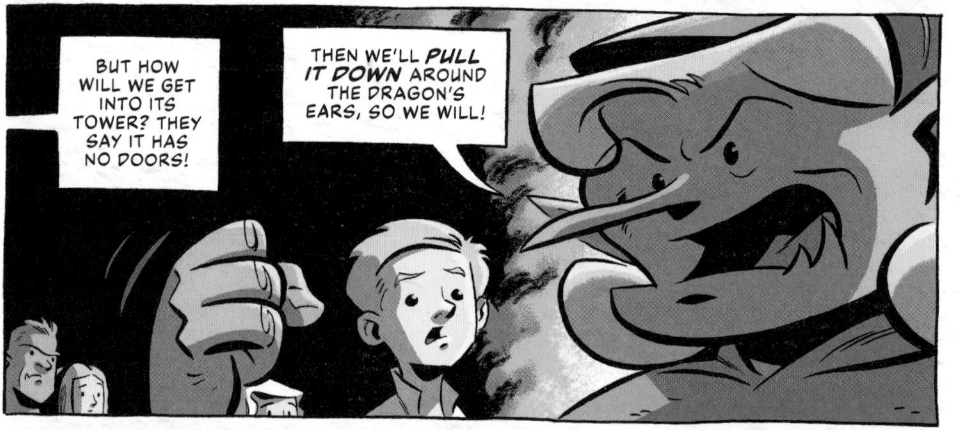
BUT HOW WILL WE GET INTO ITS TOWER? THEY SAY IT HAS NO DOORS!
THEN WE'LL PULL IT DOWN AROUND THE DRAGON'S EARS, SO WE WILL!

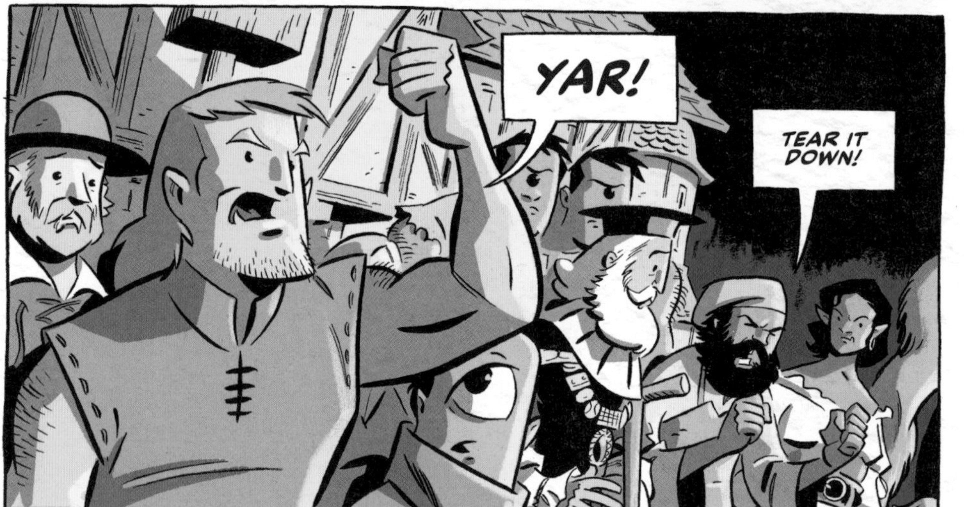
YAR!
TEAR IT DOWN!

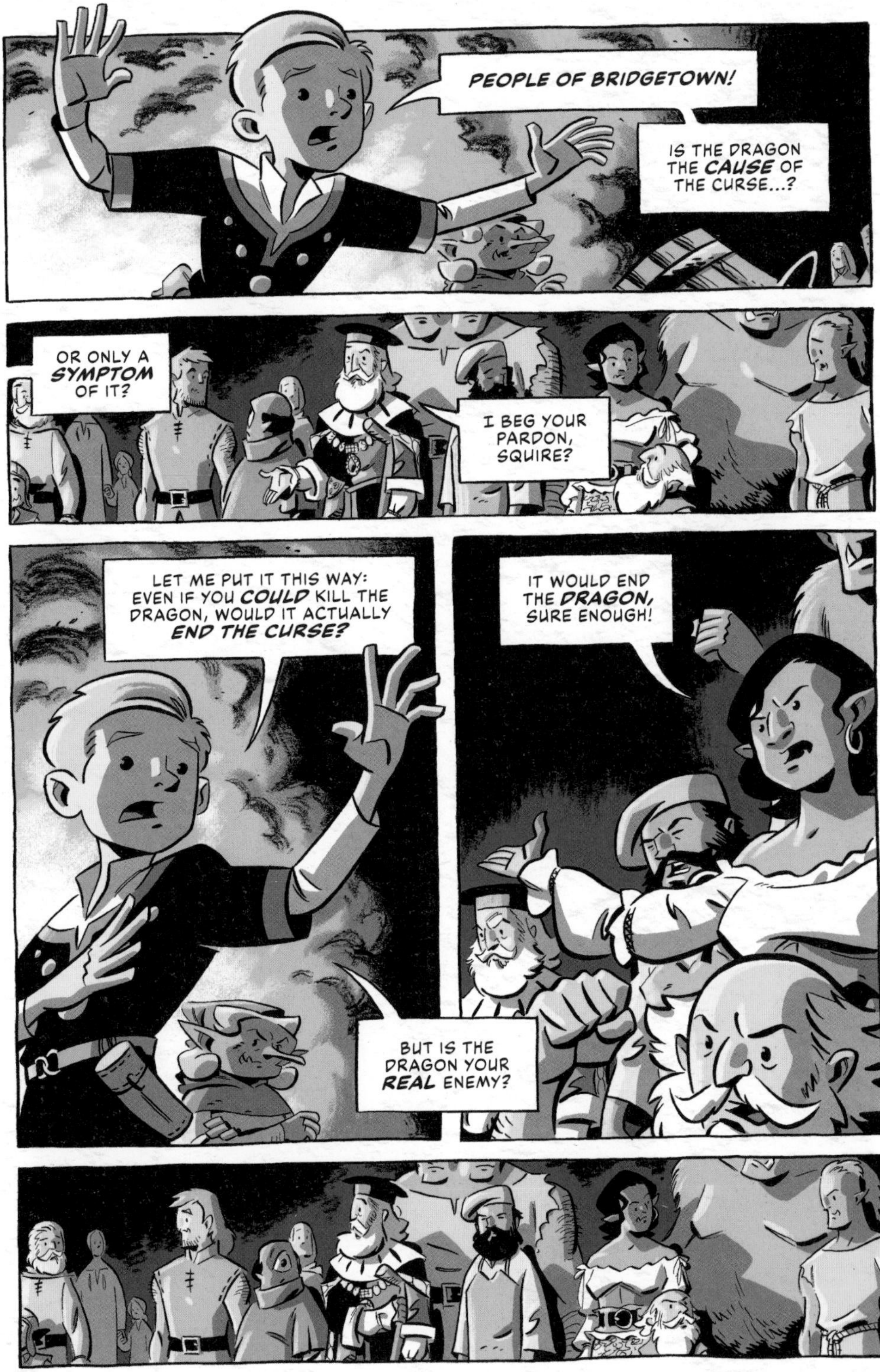

PEOPLE OF BRIDGETOWN!
IS THE DRAGON THE CAUSE OF THE CURSE...?
OR ONLY A SYMPTOM OF IT?
I BEG YOUR PARDON, SQUIRE?
LET ME PUT IT THIS WAY: EVEN IF YOU COULD KILL THE DRAGON, WOULD IT ACTUALLY END THE CURSE?
IT WOULD END THE DRAGON, SURE ENOUGH!
BUT IS THE DRAGON YOUR REAL ENEMY?

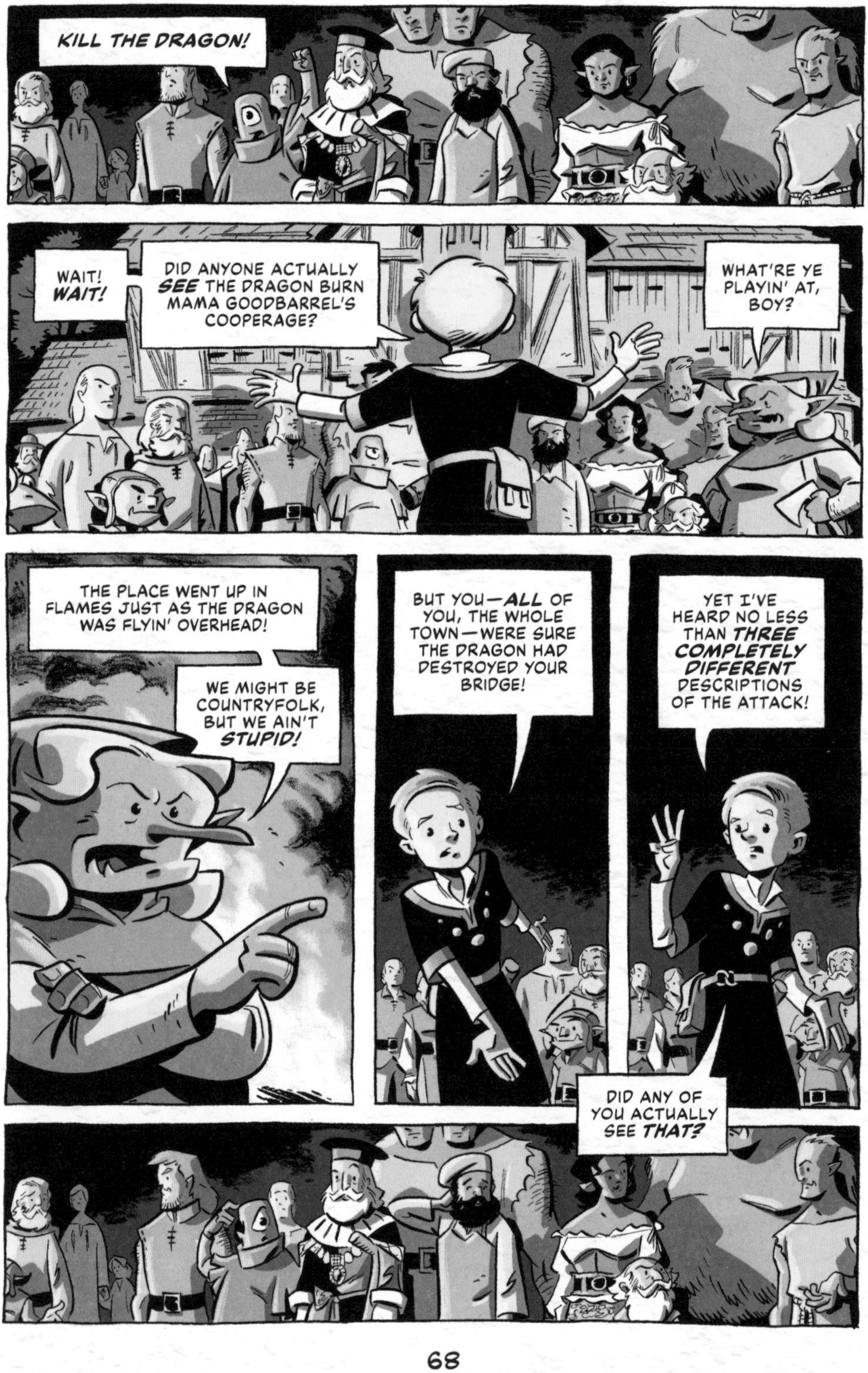
KILL THE DRAGON!
WAIT! WAIT!
DID ANYONE ACTUALLY SEE THE DRAGON BURN MAMA GOODBARREL'S COOPERAGE?
WHAT'RE YE PLAYIN' AT, BOY?
THE PLACE WENT UP IN FLAMES JUST AS THE DRAGON WAS FLYIN' OVERHEAD!
WE MIGHT BE COUNTRYFOLK, BUT WE AIN'T STUPID!
BUT YOU—ALL OF YOU, THE WHOLE TOWN—WERE SURE THE DRAGON HAD DESTROYED YOUR BRIDGE!
YET I'VE HEARD NO LESS THAN THREE COMPLETELY DIFFERENT DESCRIPTIONS OF THE ATTACK!
DID ANY OF YOU ACTUALLY SEE THAT?

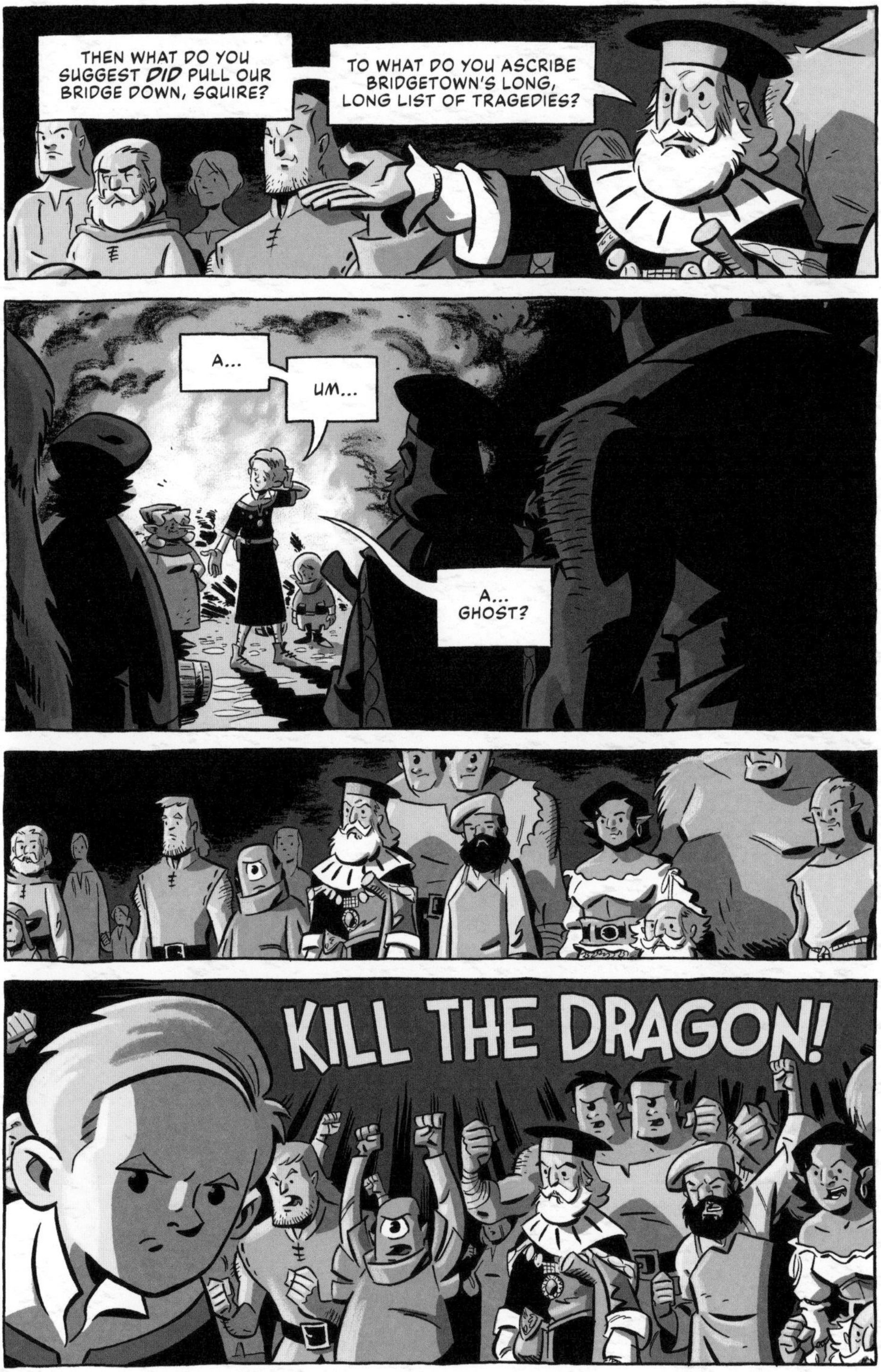

THEN WHAT DO YOU SUGGEST DID PULL OUR BRIDGE DOWN, SQUIRE?
TO WHAT DO YOU ASCRIBE BRIDGETOWN'S LONG, LONG LIST OF TRAGEDIES?
A...
UM...
A... GHOST?
KILL THE DRAGON!

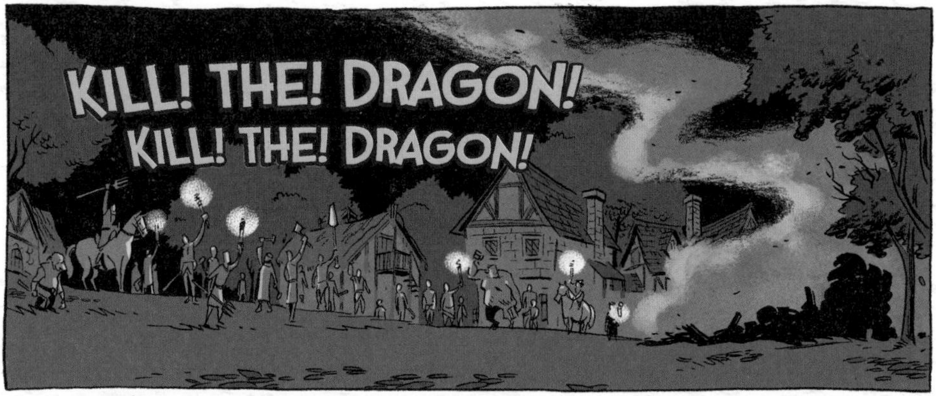
KILL! THE! DRAGON!
KILL! THE! DRAGON!

# CHAPTER FIVE

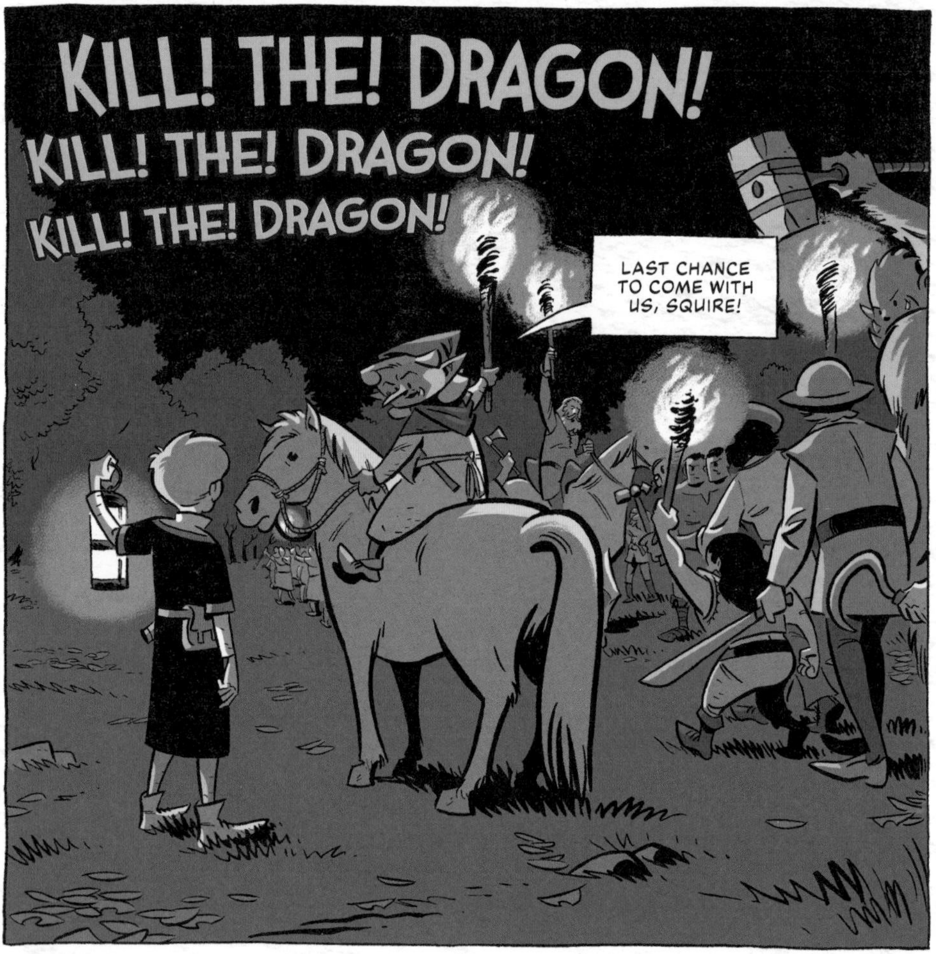
KILL! THE! DRAGON!
KILL! THE! DRAGON!
KILL! THE! DRAGON!
LAST CHANCE TO COME WITH US, SQUIRE!

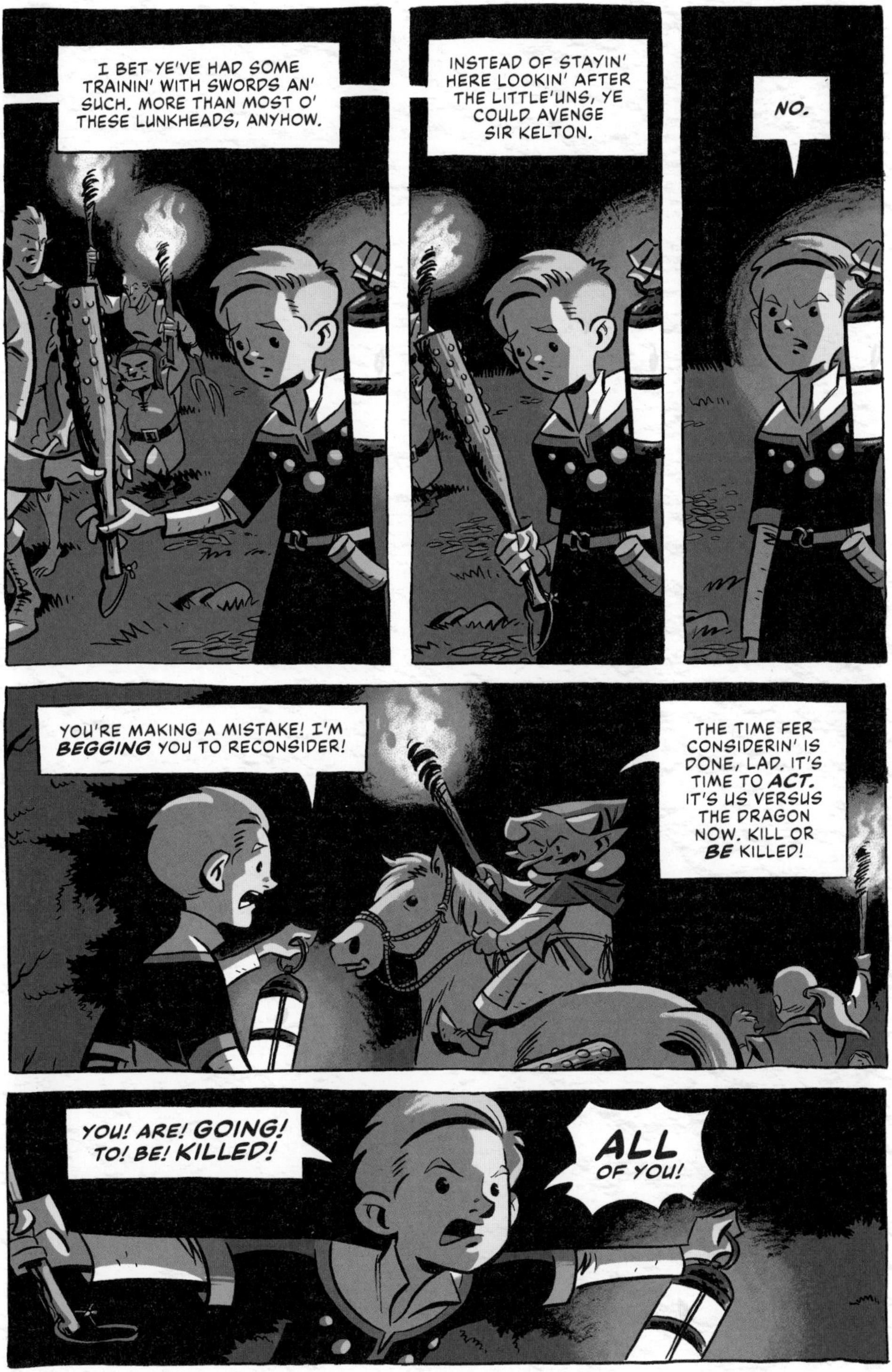
I BET YE'VE HAD SOME TRAININ' WITH SWORDS AN' SUCH. MORE THAN MOST O' THESE LUNKHEADS, ANYHOW.
INSTEAD OF STAYIN' HERE LOOKIN' AFTER THE LITTLE'UNS, YE COULD AVENGE SIR KELTON.
NO.
YOU'RE MAKING A MISTAKE! I'M BEGGING YOU TO RECONSIDER!
THE TIME FER CONSIDERIN' IS DONE, LAD. IT'S TIME TO ACT. IT'S US VERSUS THE DRAGON NOW. KILL OR BE KILLED!
YOU! ARE! GOING! TO! BE! KILLED!
ALL OF YOU!

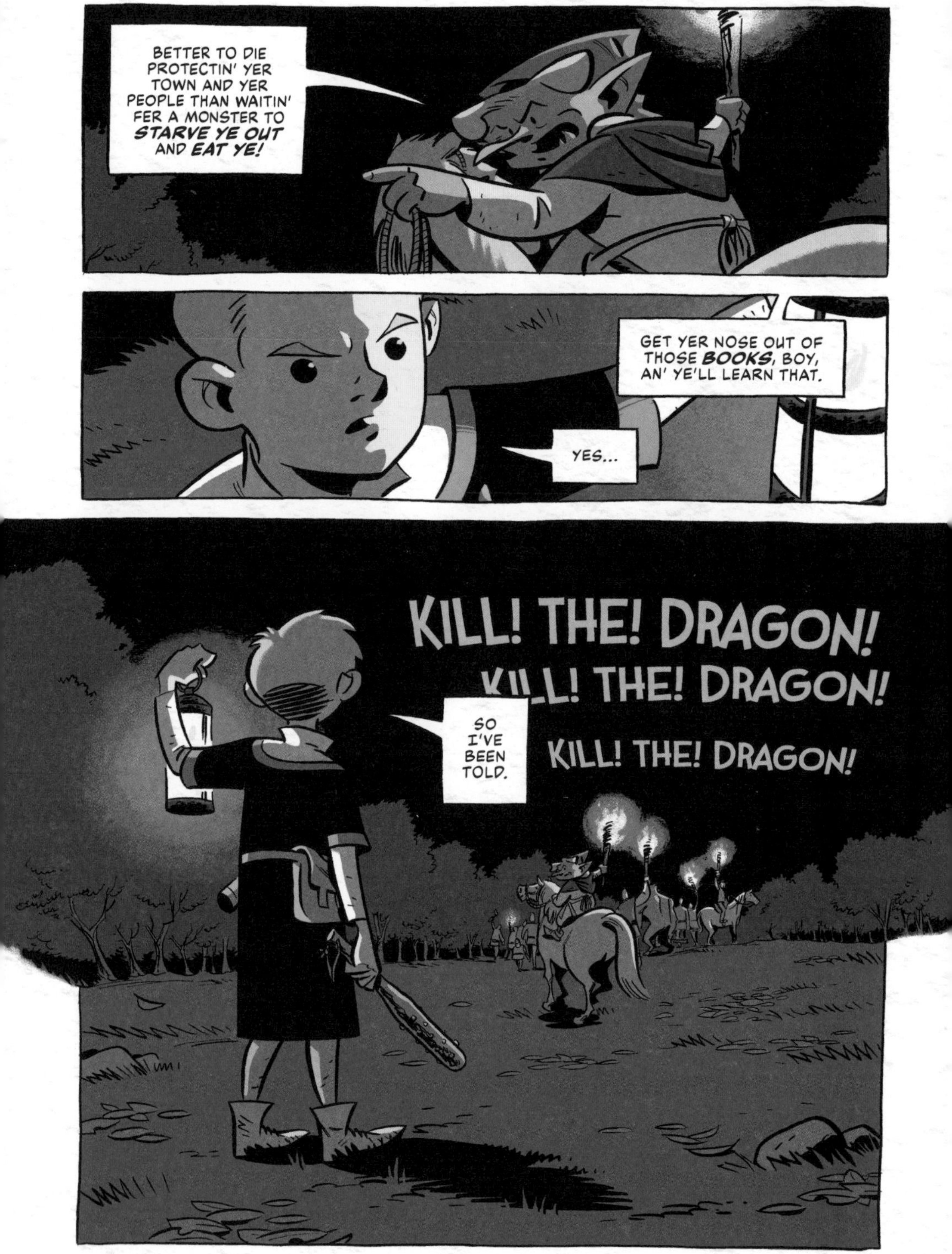

BETTER TO DIE PROTECTIN' YER TOWN AND YER PEOPLE THAN WAITIN' FER A MONSTER TO ***STARVE YE OUT*** AND ***EAT YE!***
GET YER NOSE OUT OF THOSE ***BOOKS***, BOY, AN' YE'LL LEARN THAT.
YES...
KILL! THE! DRAGON!
KILL! THE! DRAGON!
KILL! THE! DRAGON!
SO I'VE BEEN TOLD.

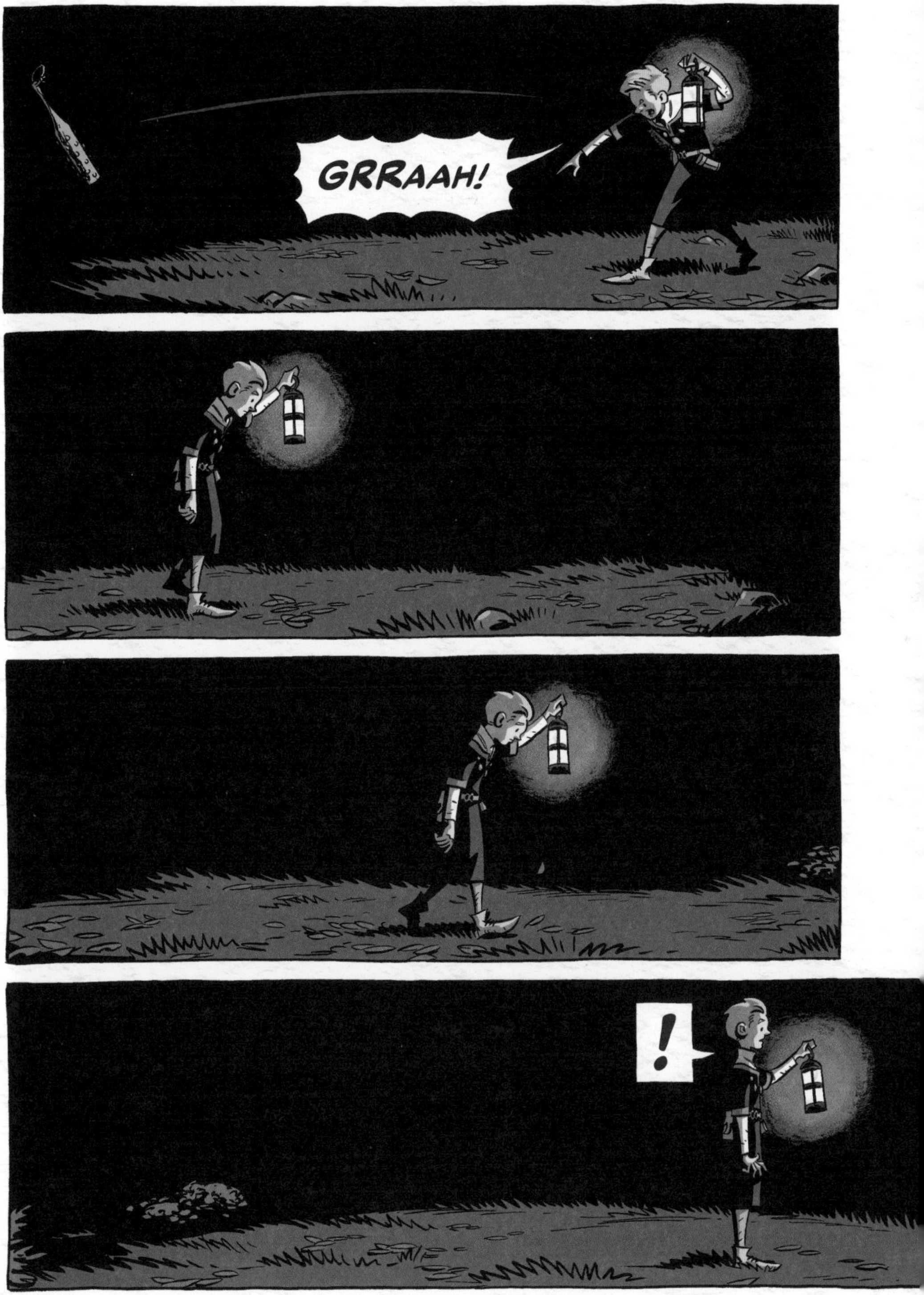
GRRAAH!
!

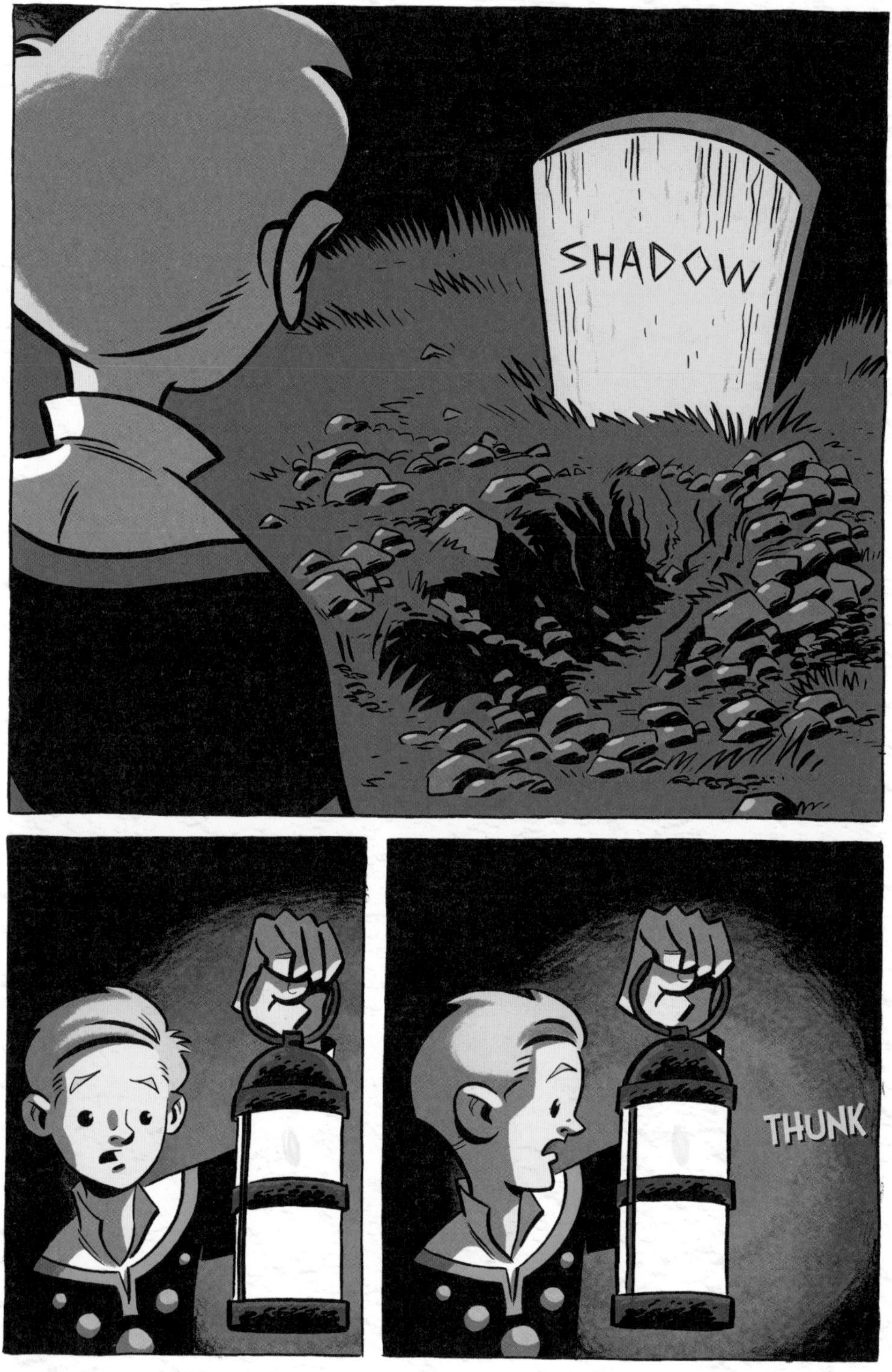
SHADOW
THUNK

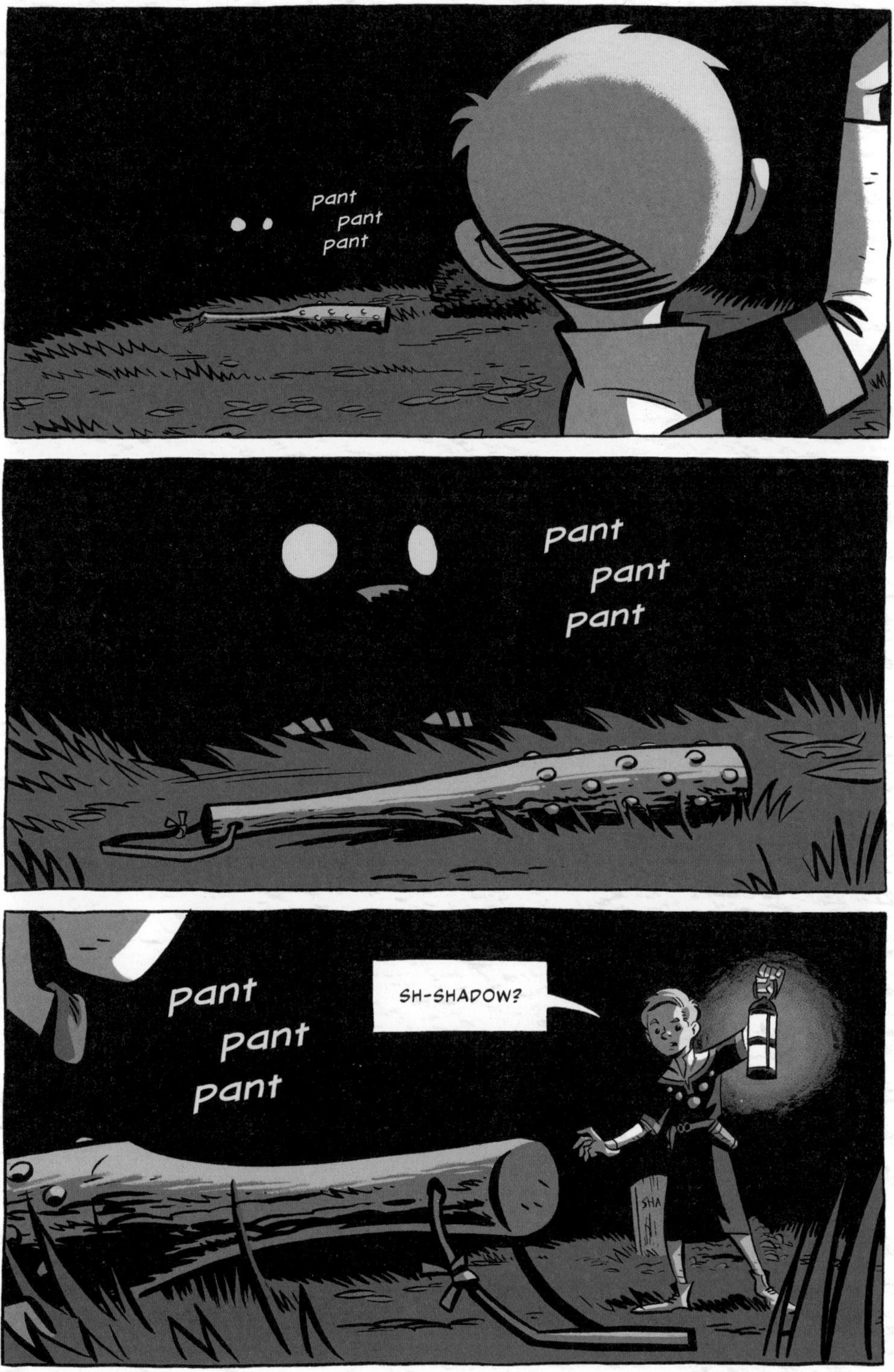
pant
pant
pant
pant
pant
pant
pant
pant
pant
SH-SHADOW?
SHA

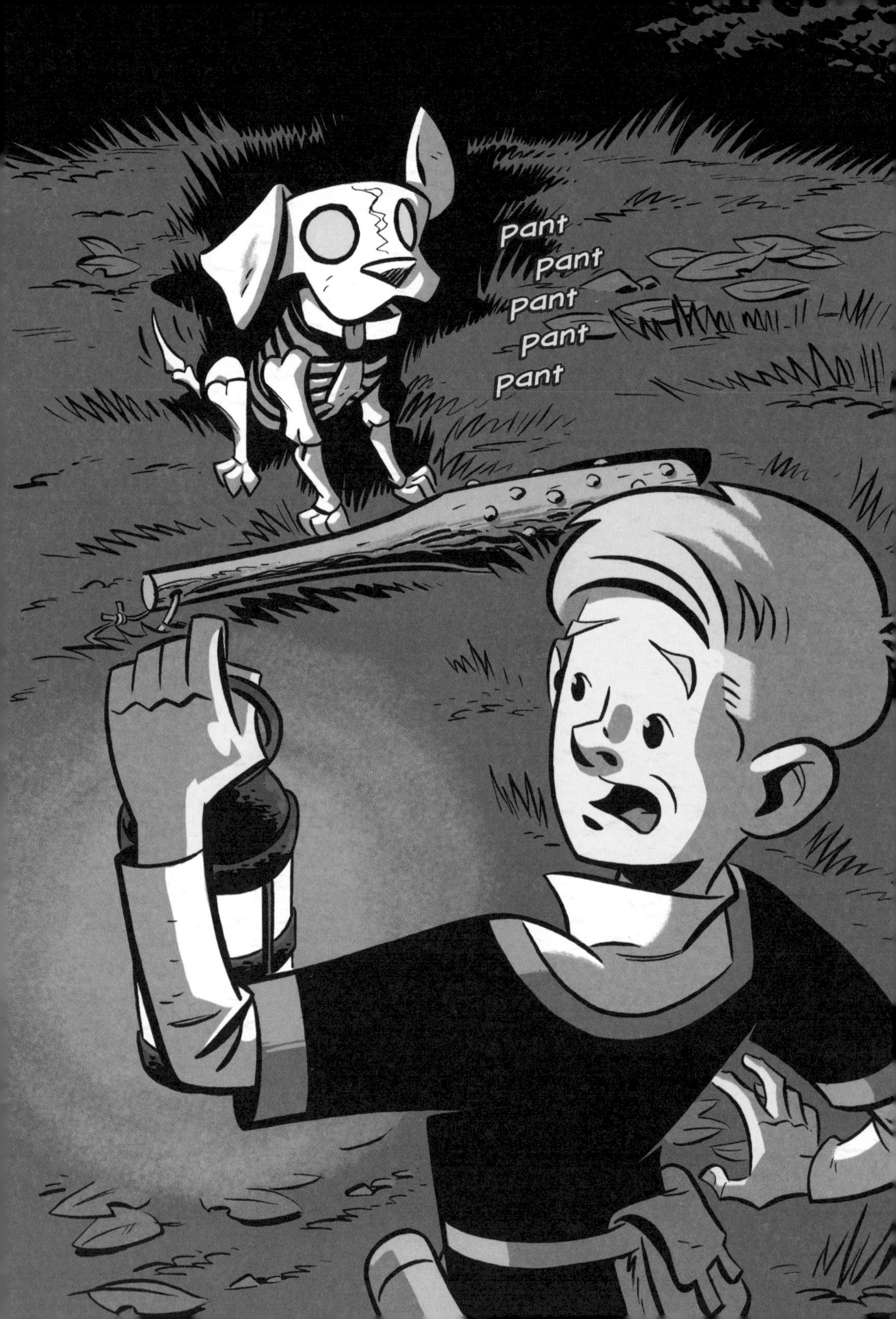
pant
pant
pant
pant
pant

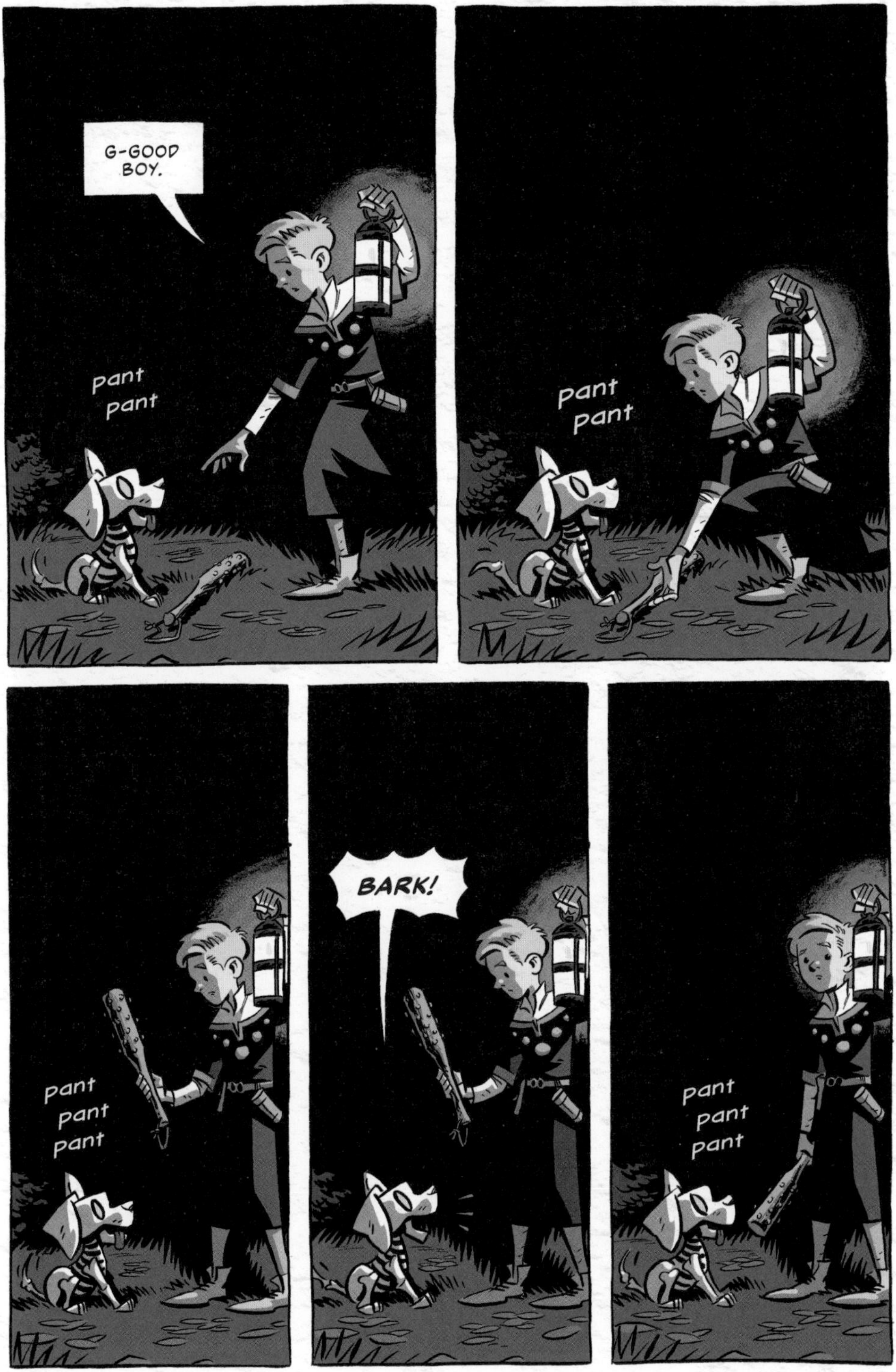
G-GOOD BOY.
pant pant
pant pant
pant pant pant
BARK!
pant pant pant

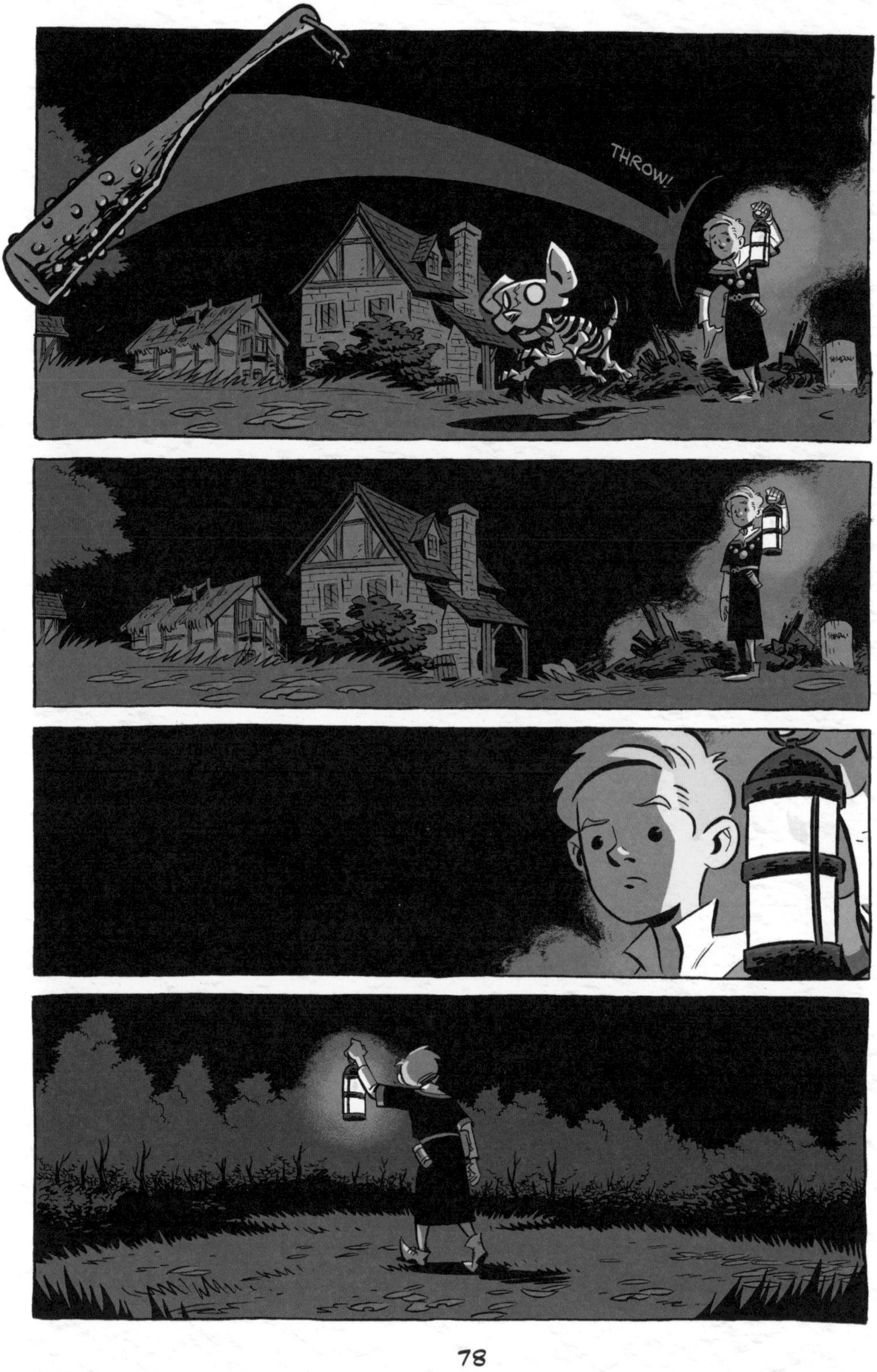
THROW!

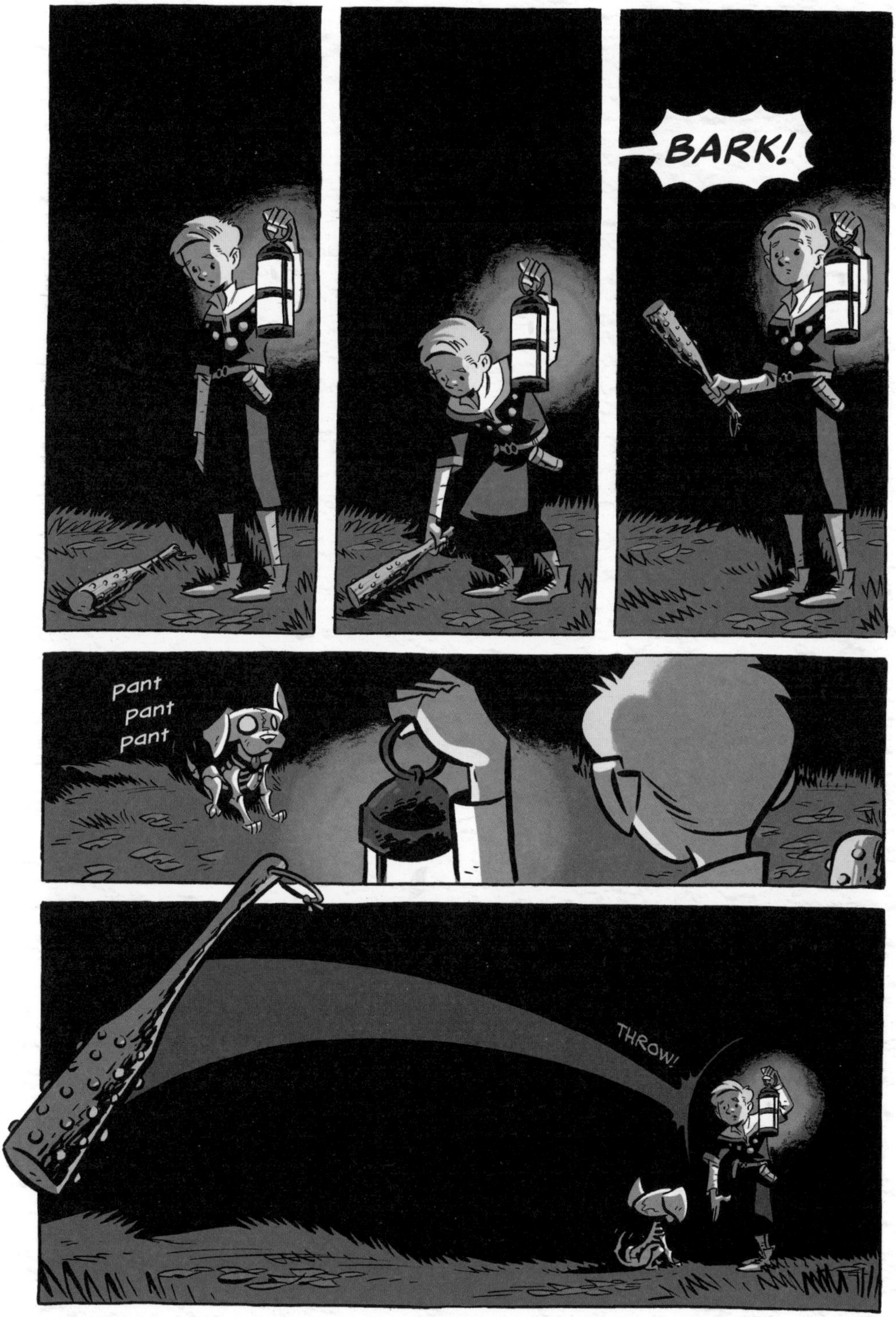
BARK!
pant
pant
pant
THROW!

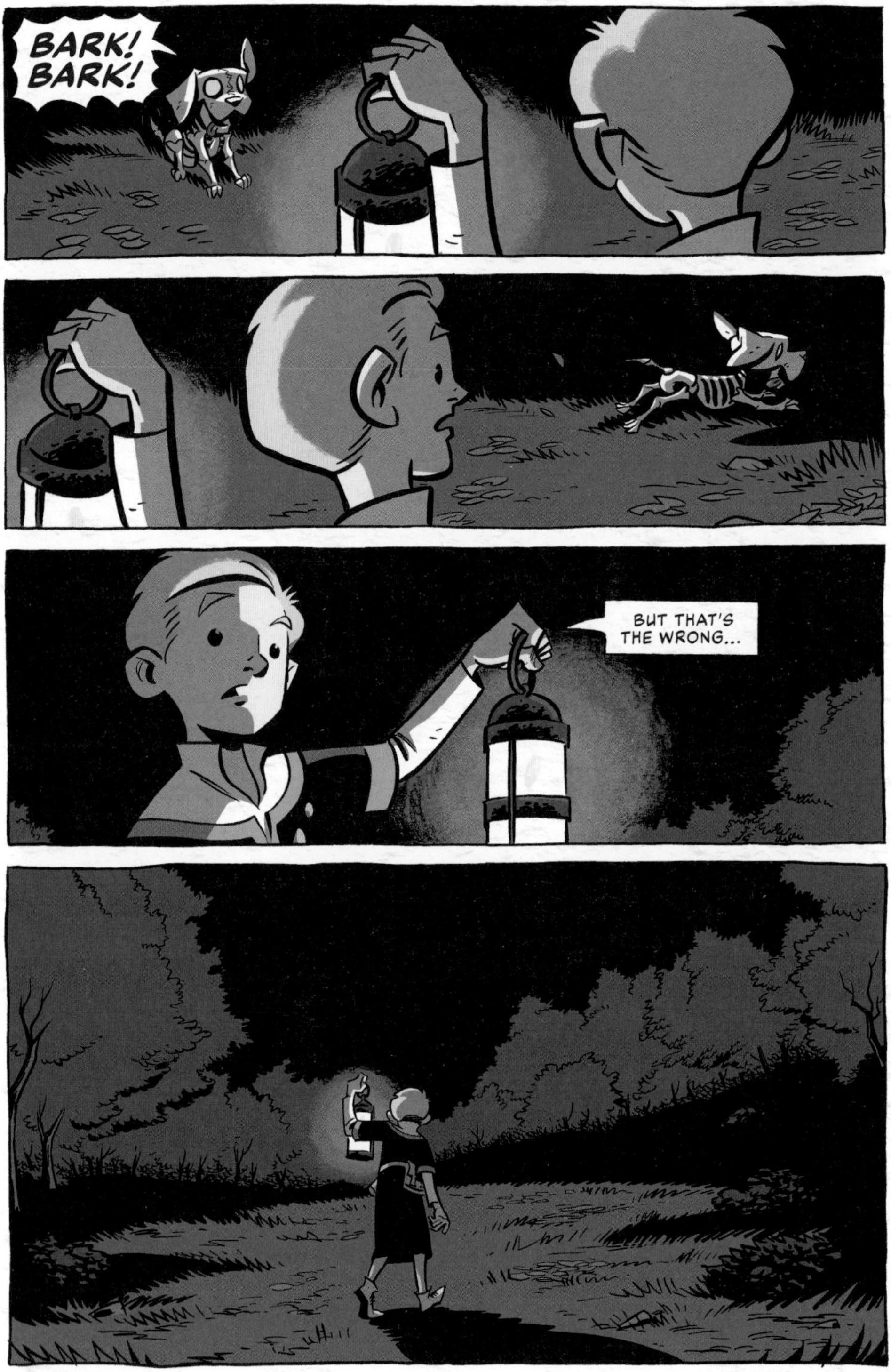
BARK! BARK!
BUT THAT'S THE WRONG...

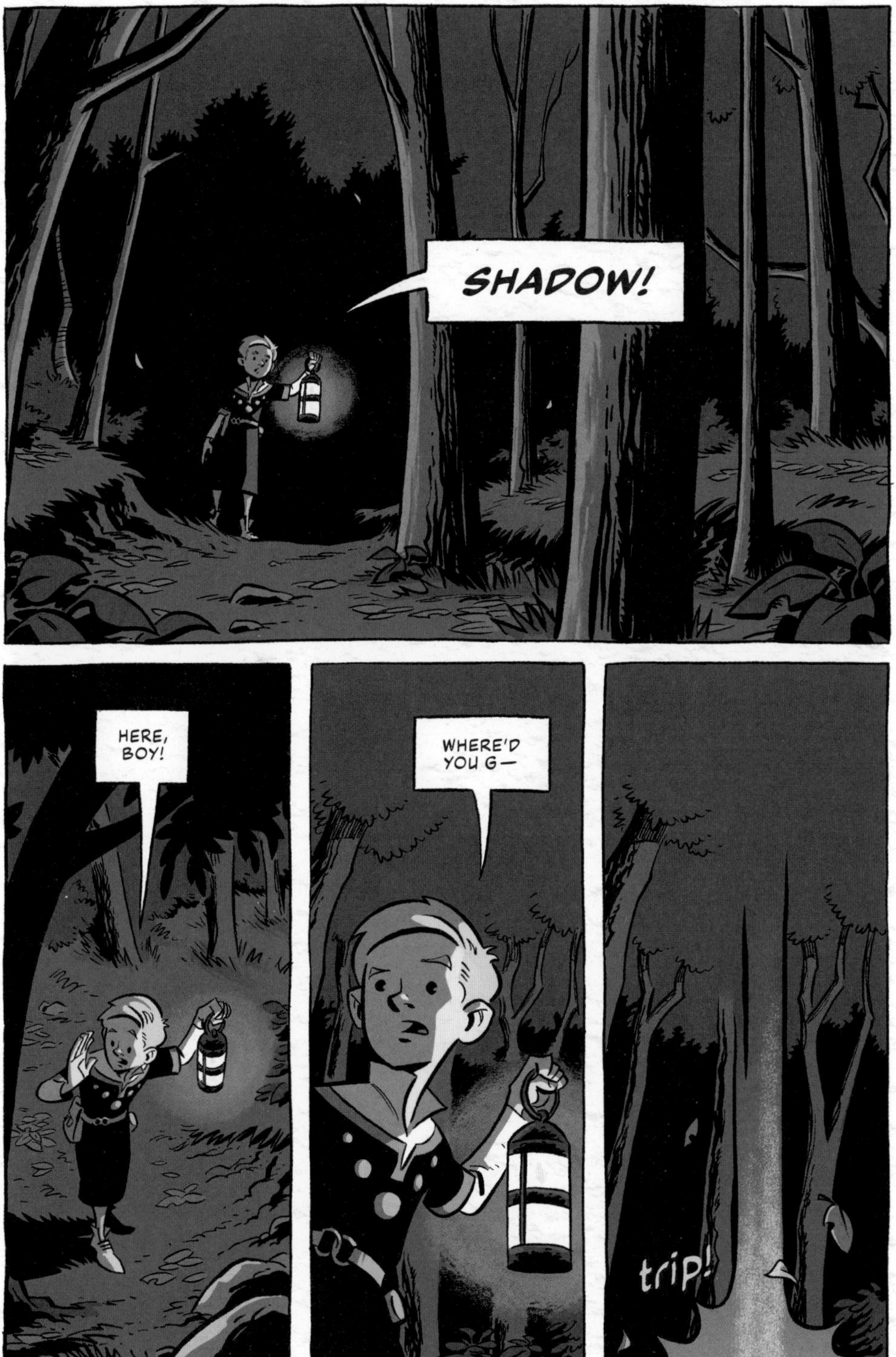
SHADOW!
HERE, BOY!
WHERE'D YOU G—
trip!

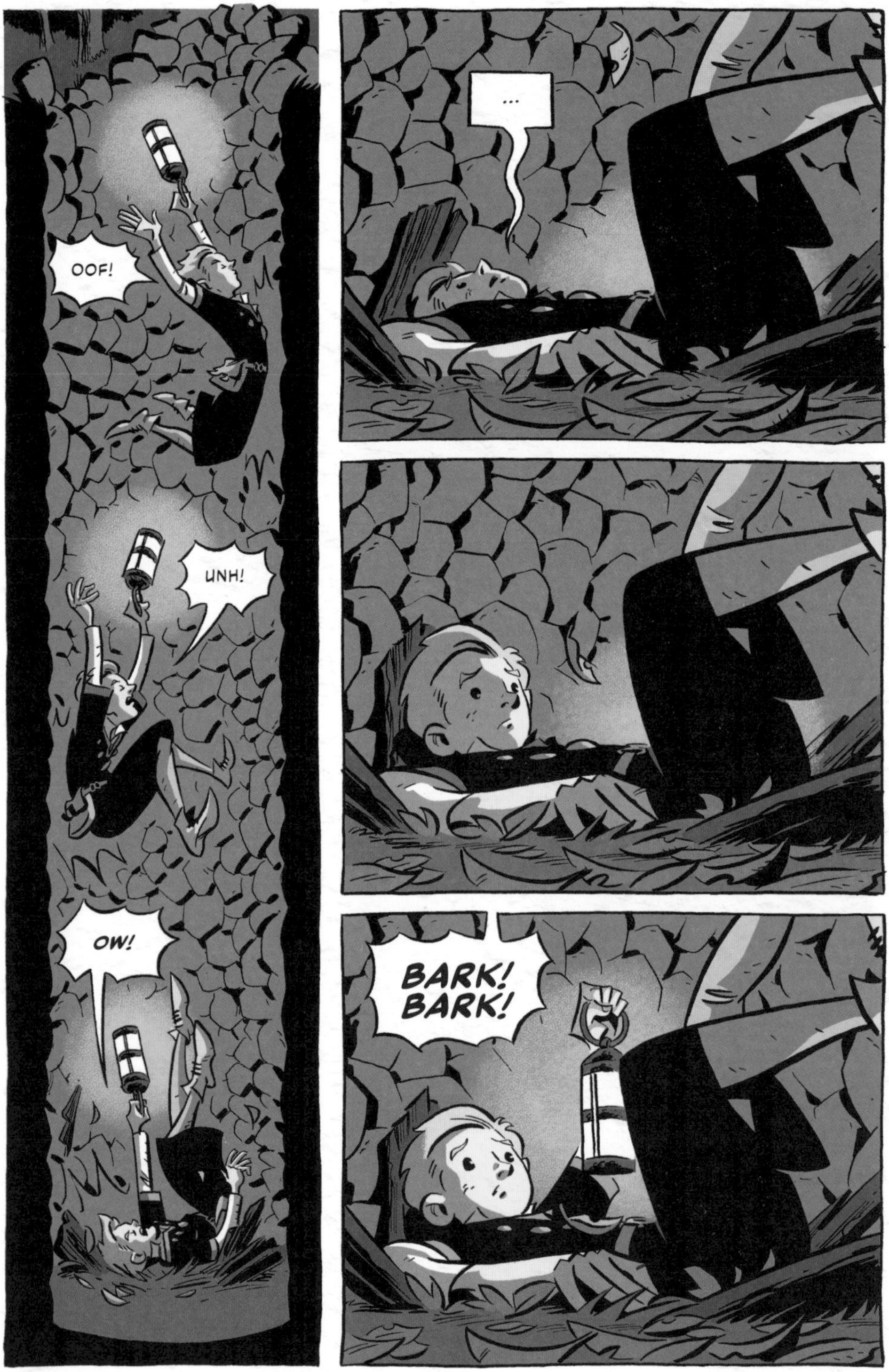
OOF!
UNH!
OW!
...
BARK! BARK!

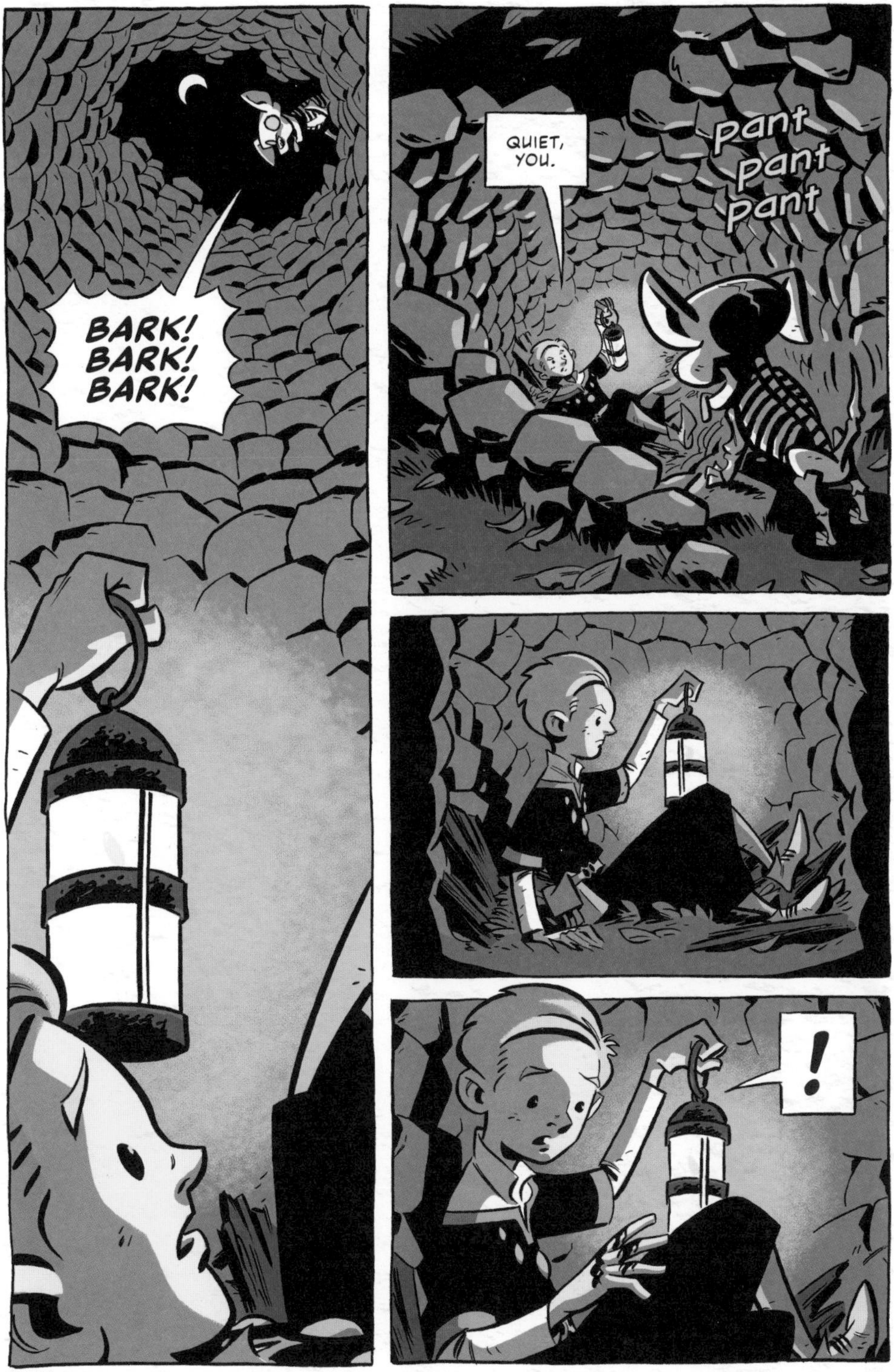
BARK! BARK! BARK!
QUIET, YOU.
pant pant pant
!

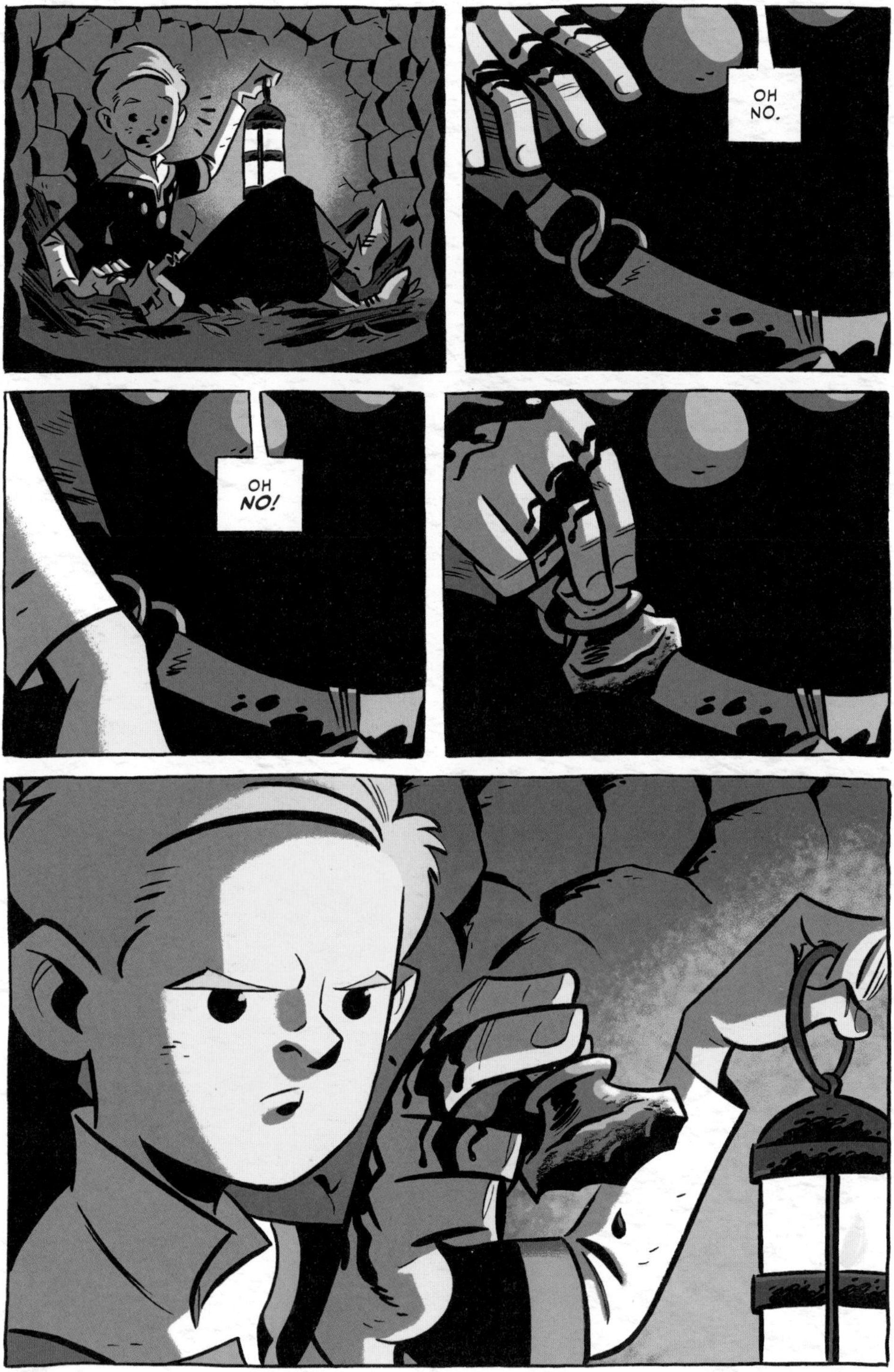
OH
NO.
OH
NO!

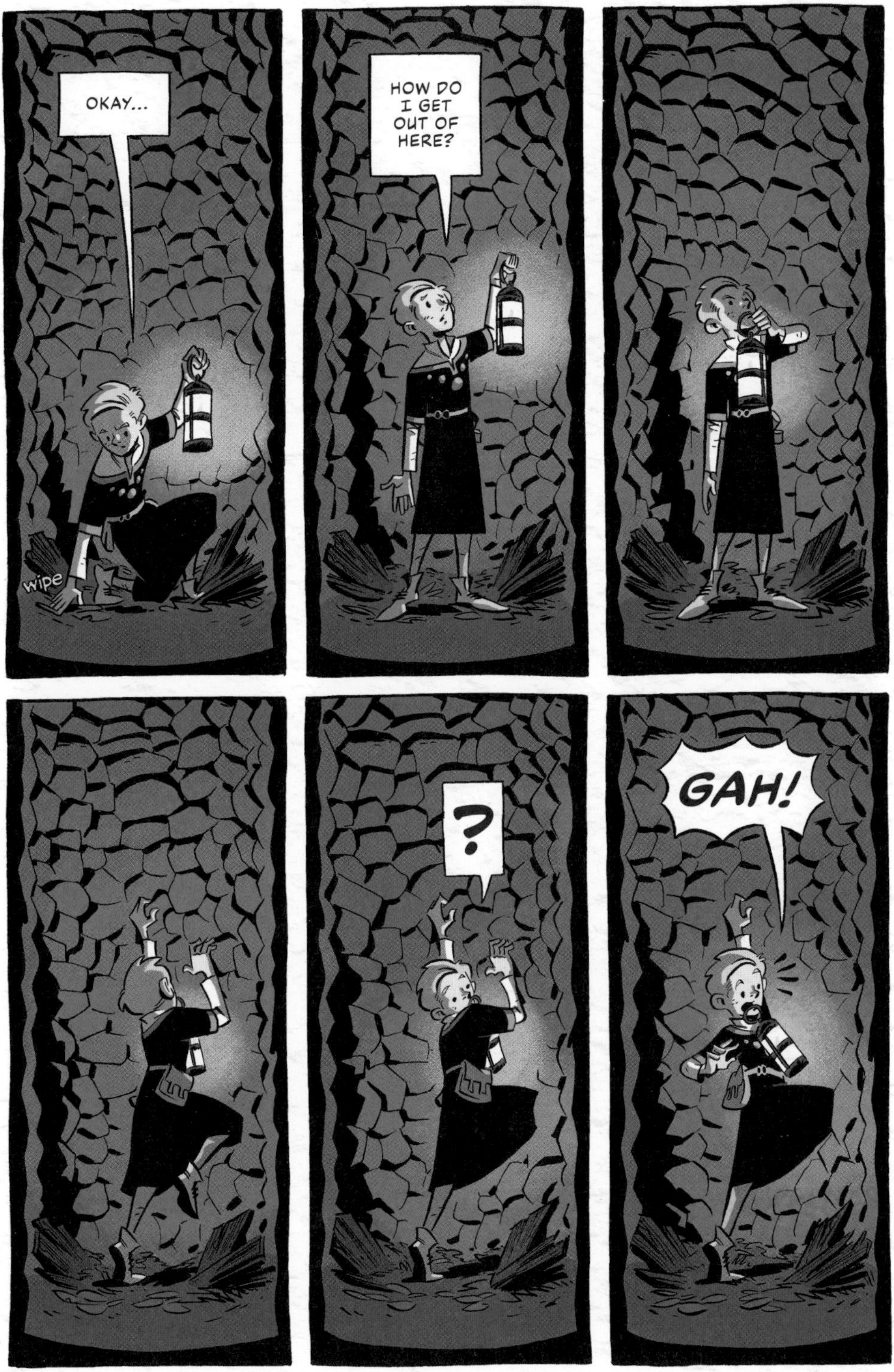
OKAY...
wipe
HOW DO I GET OUT OF HERE?
?
GAH!

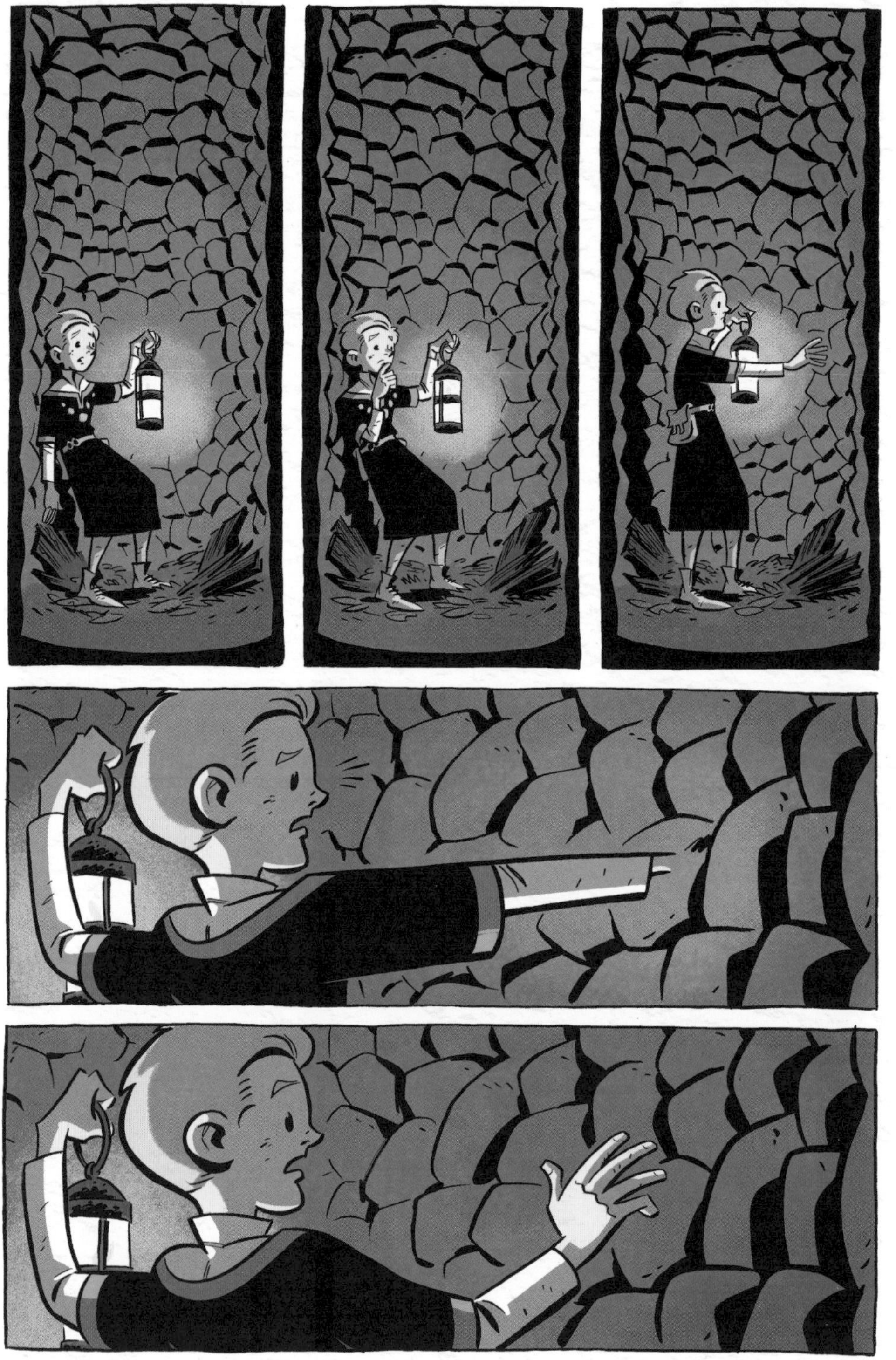

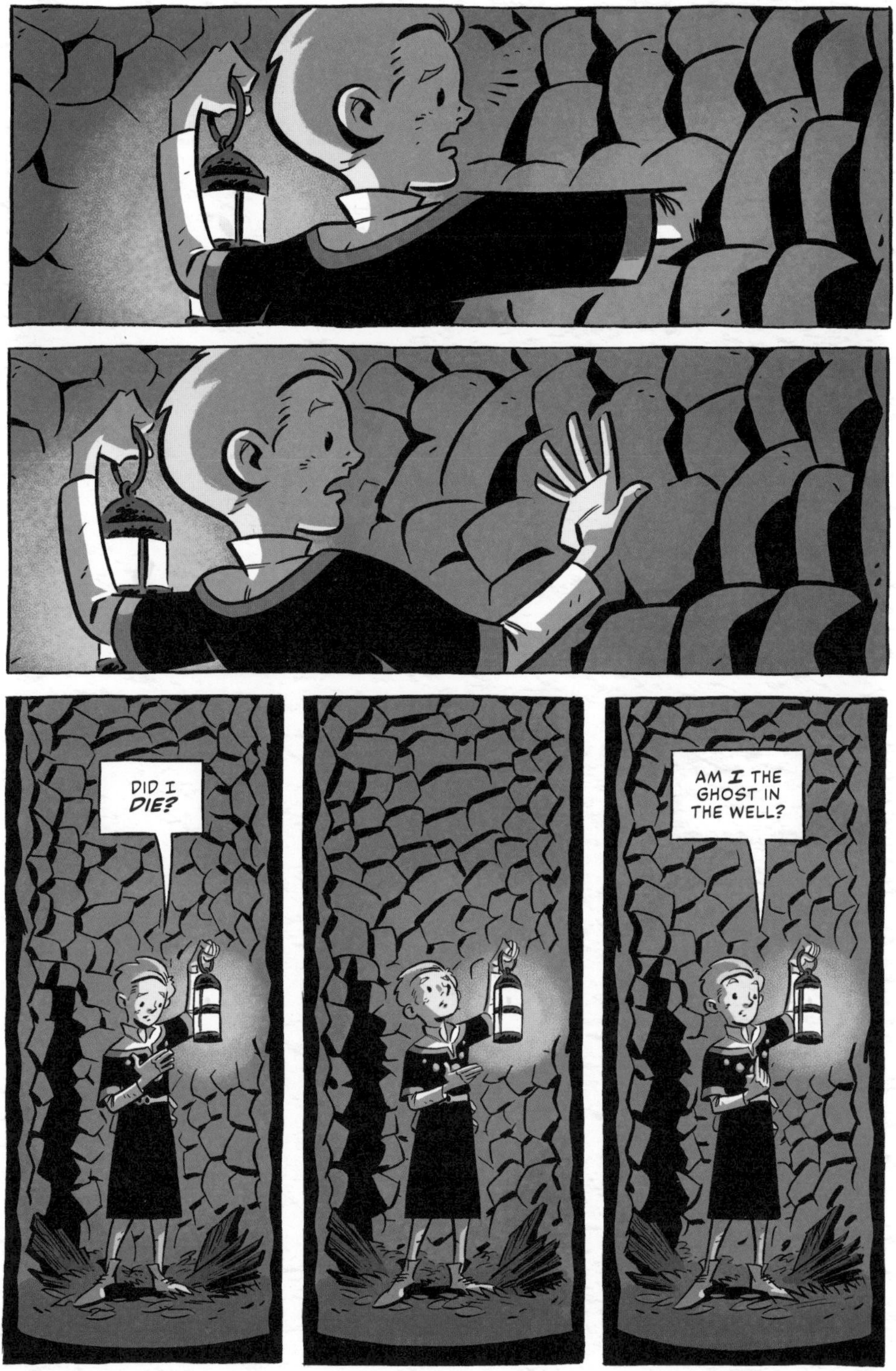
DID I DIE?
AM I THE GHOST IN THE WELL?

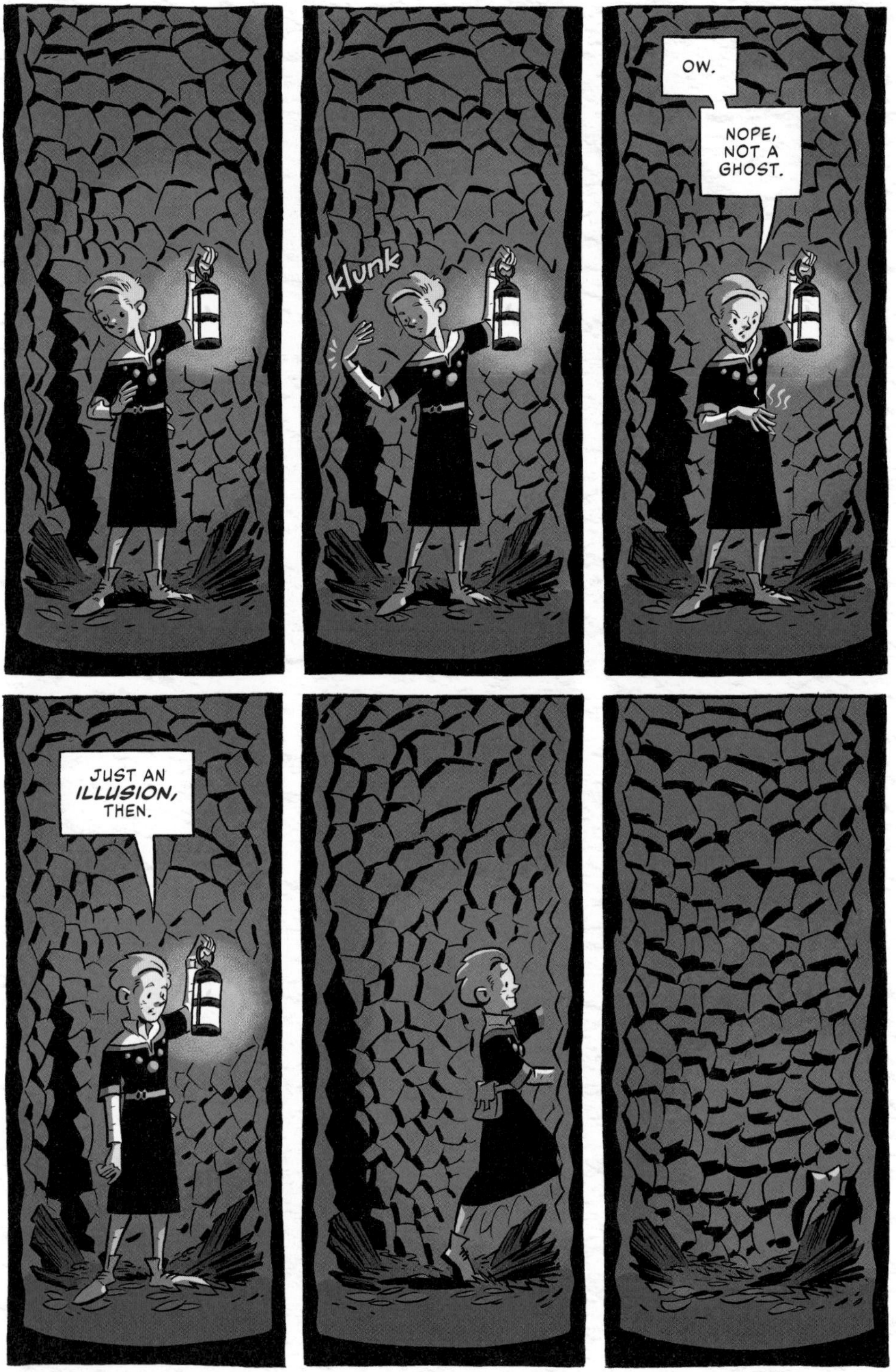
klunk
OW.
NOPE, NOT A GHOST.
JUST AN ***ILLUSION,*** THEN.

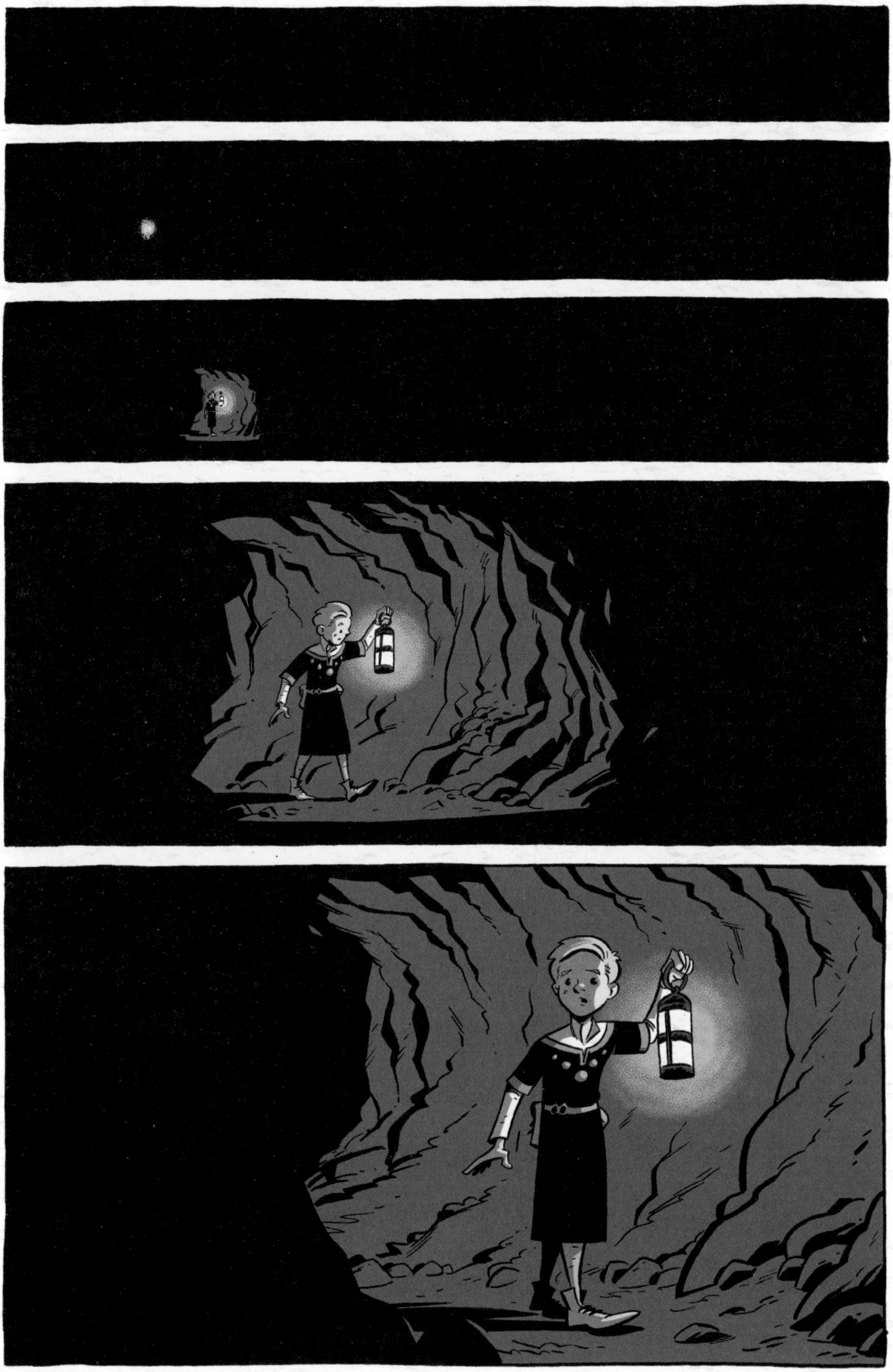

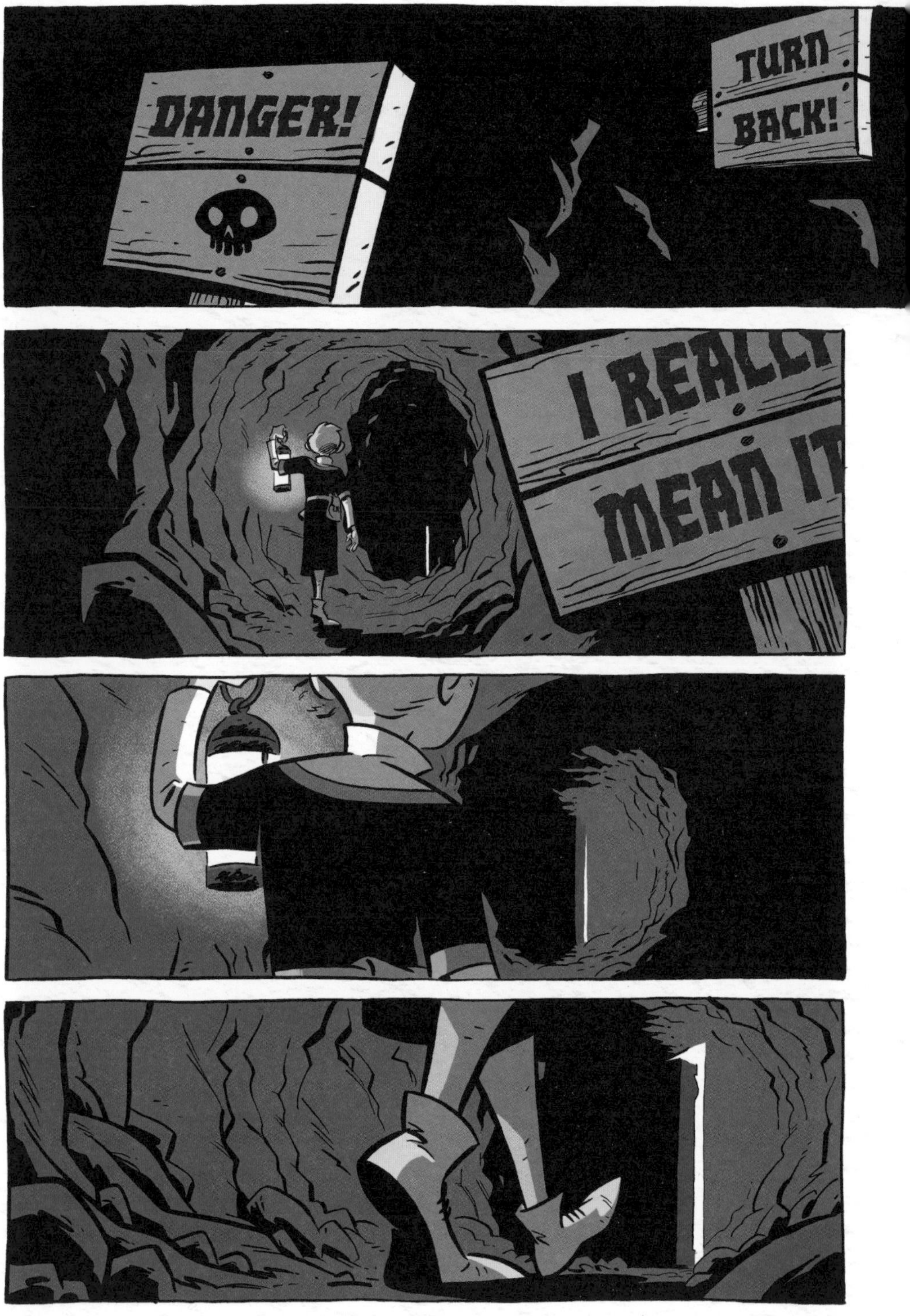
DANGER!
TURN BACK!
I REALLY MEAN IT

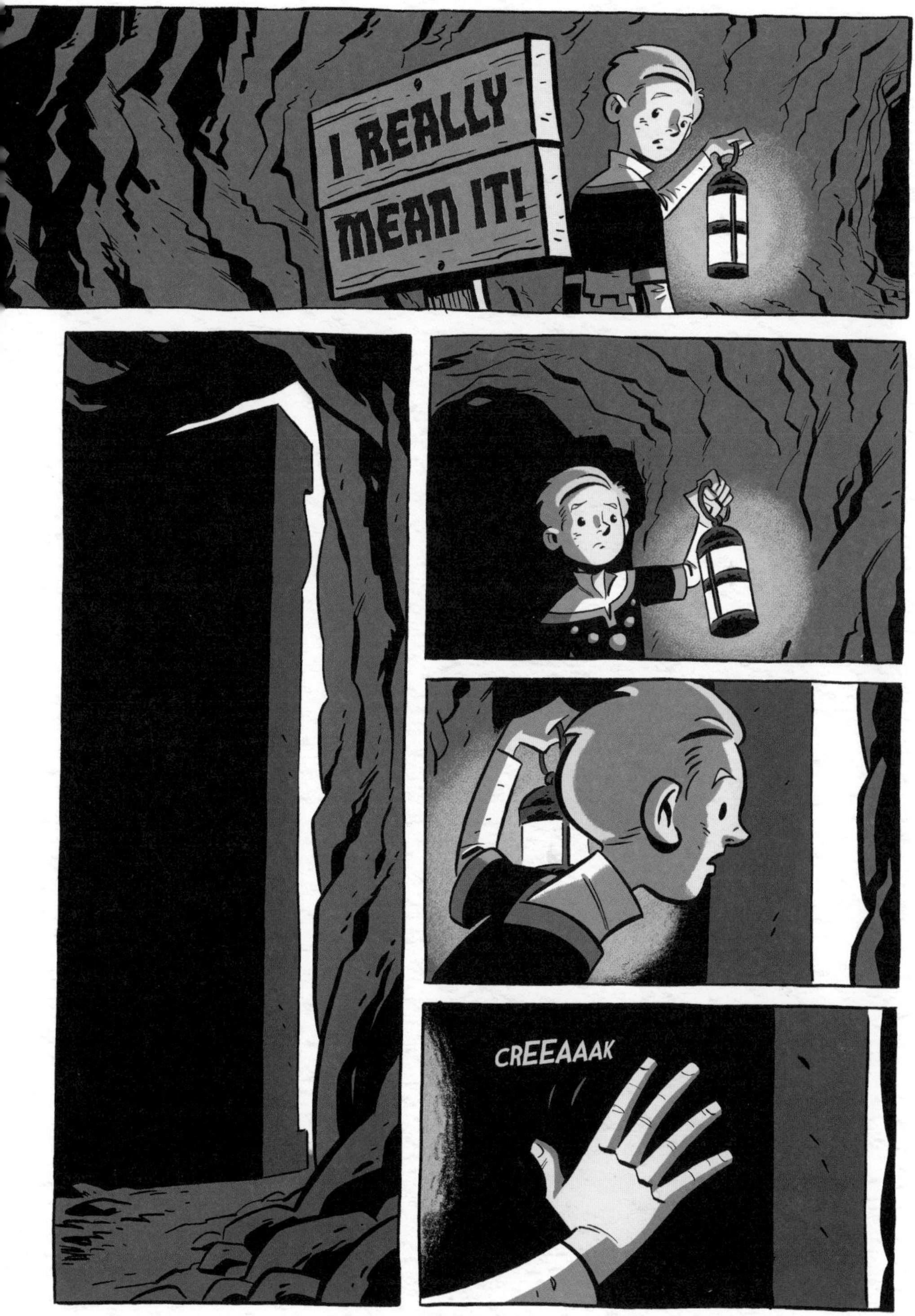
I REALLY
MEAN IT!
CREEAAAK

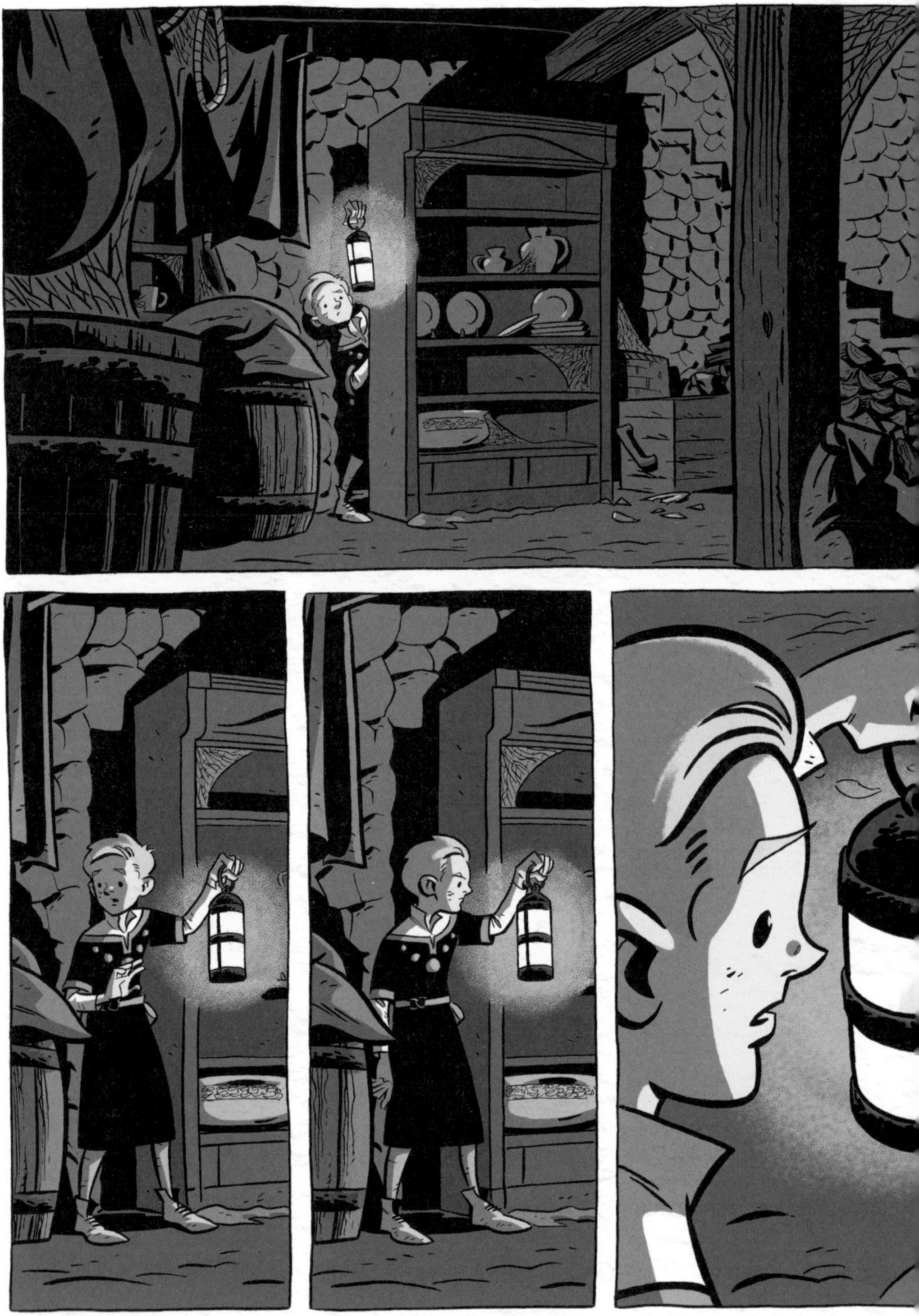

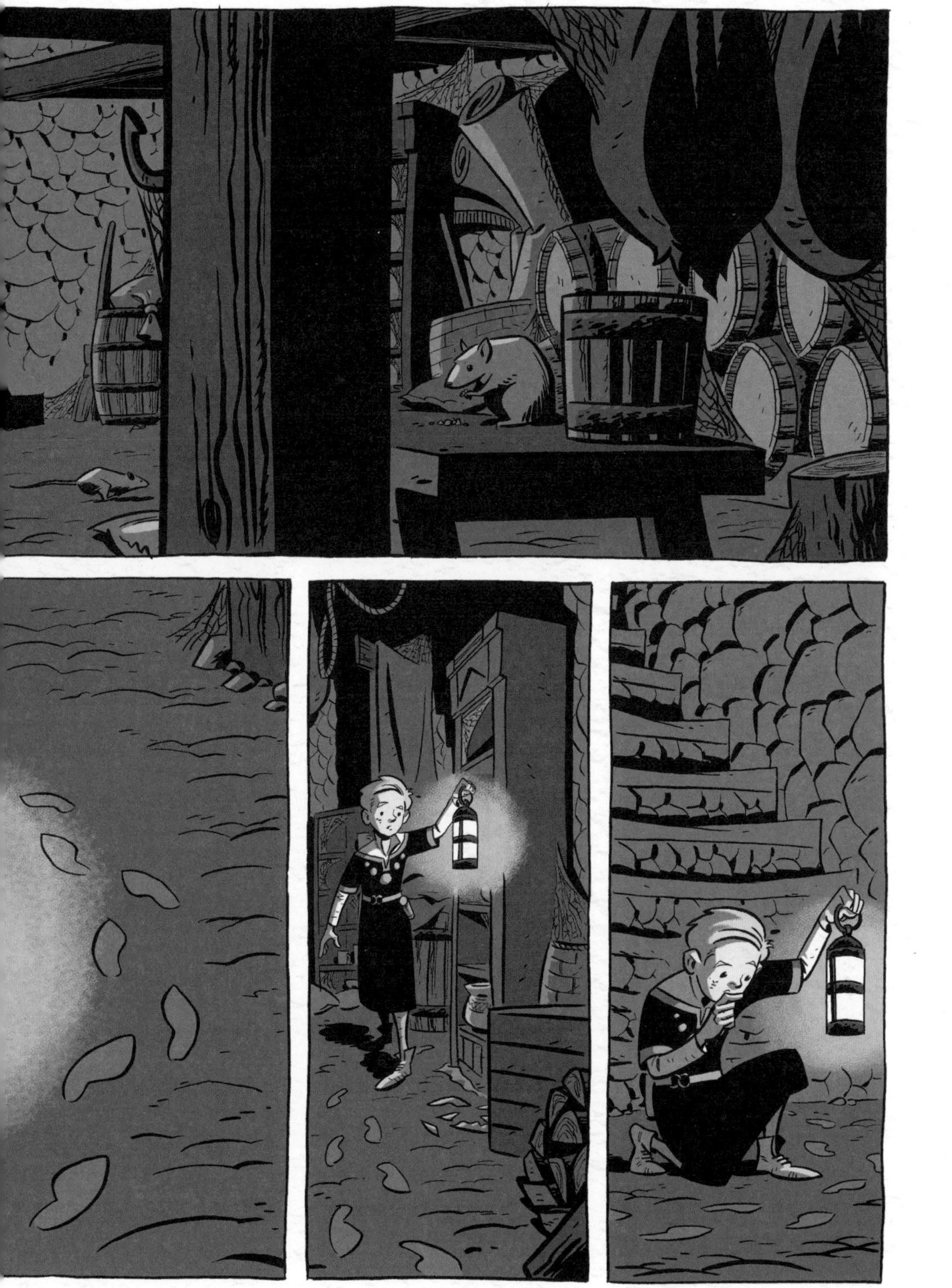

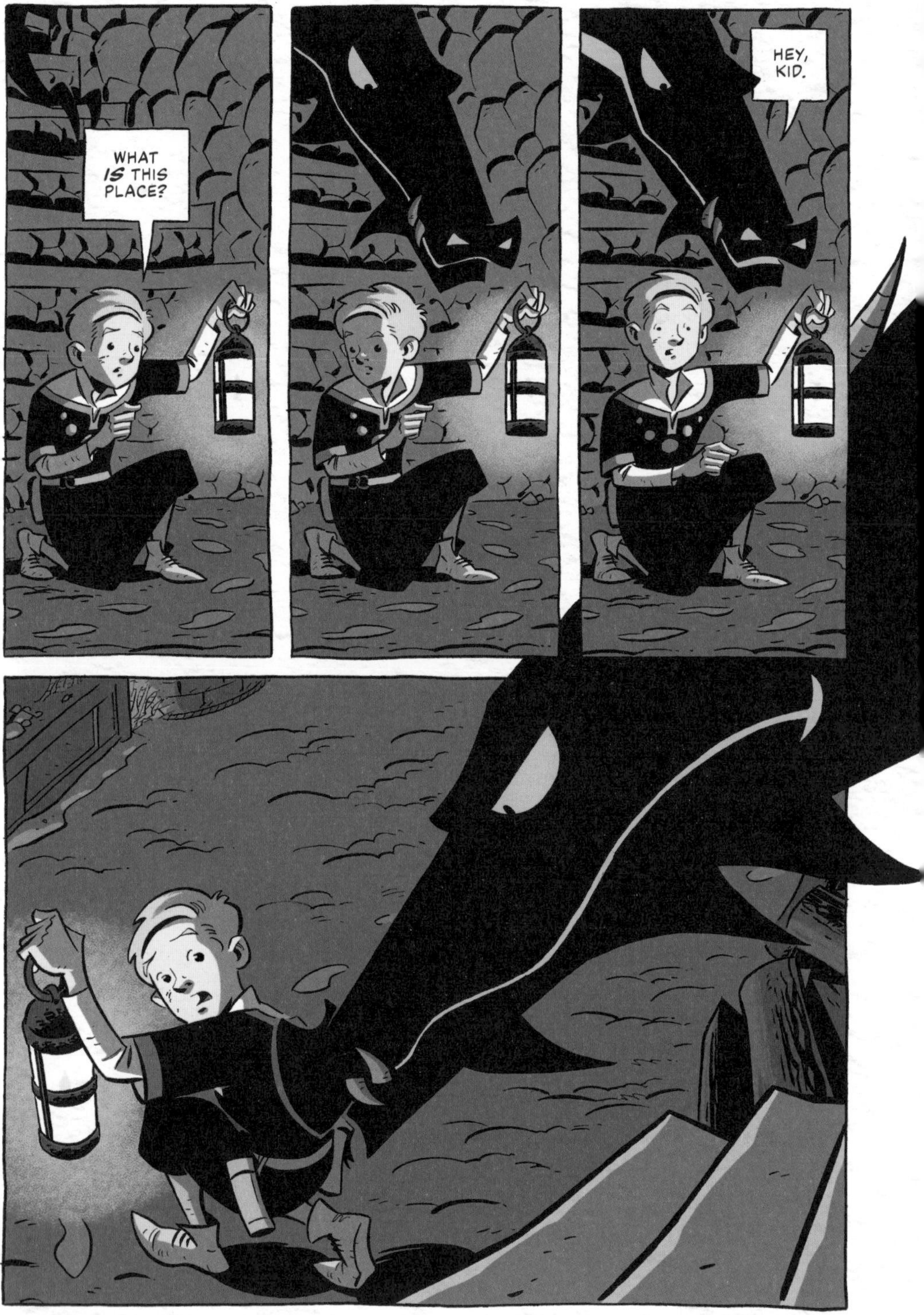
WHAT *IS* THIS PLACE?
HEY, KID.

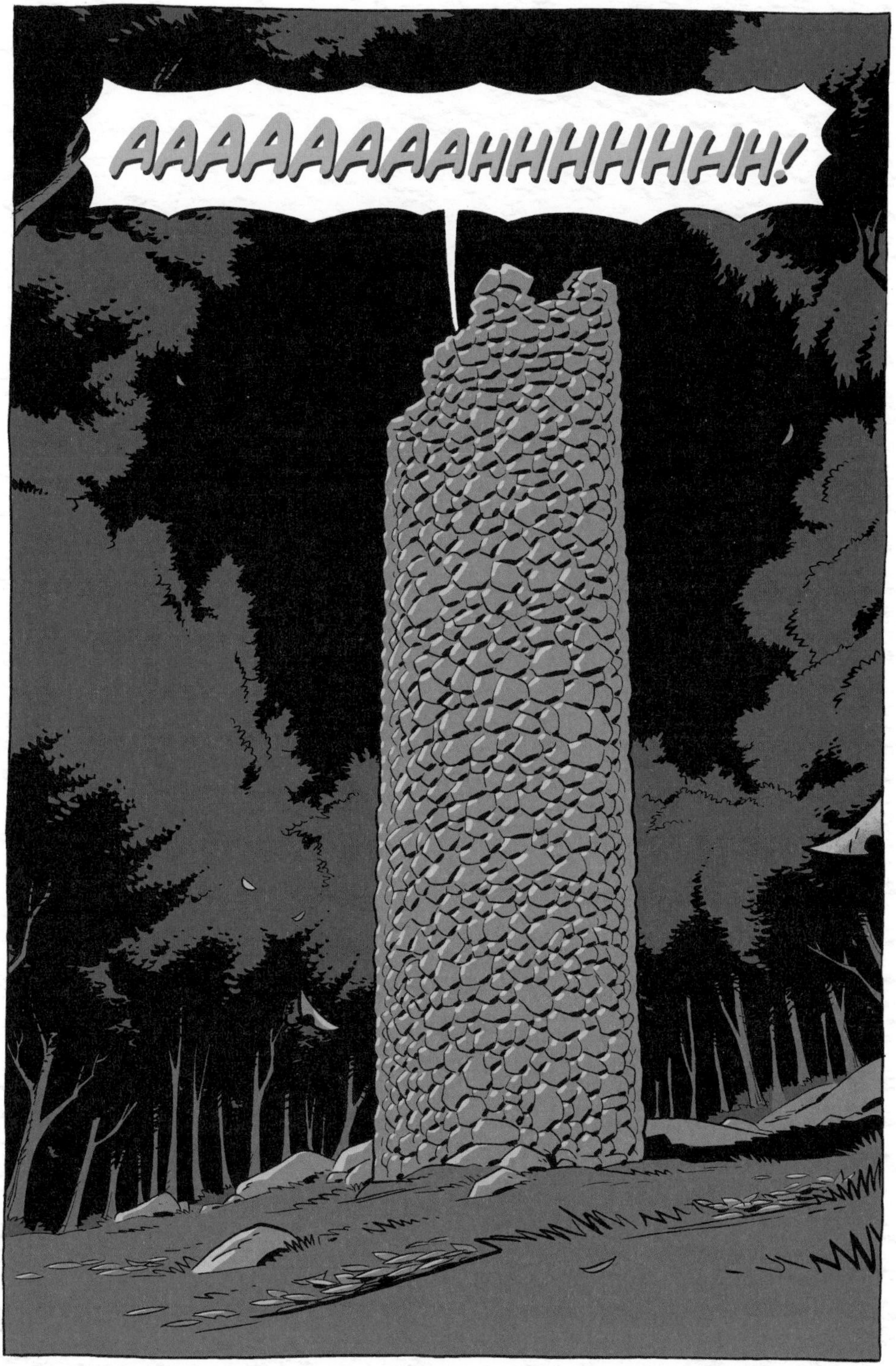
AAAAAAAAHHHHHHH!

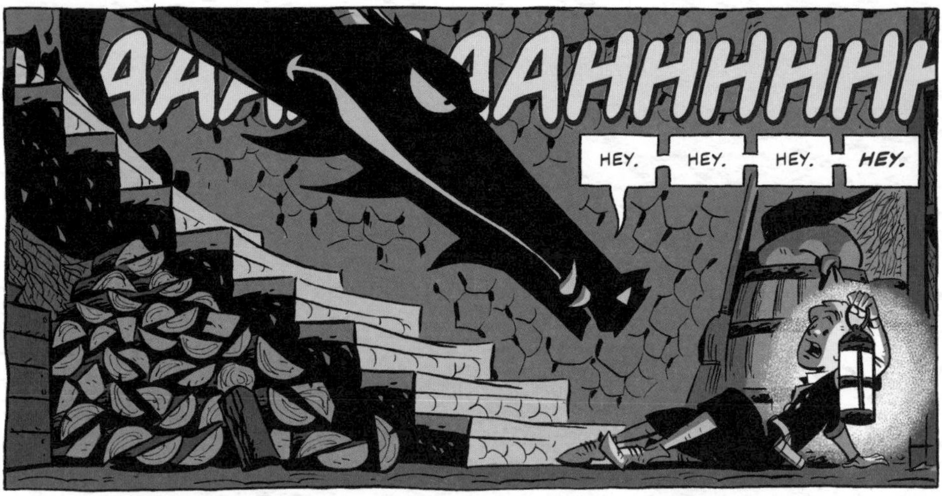
HEY.
HEY.
HEY.
*HEY.*

# CHAPTER SIX

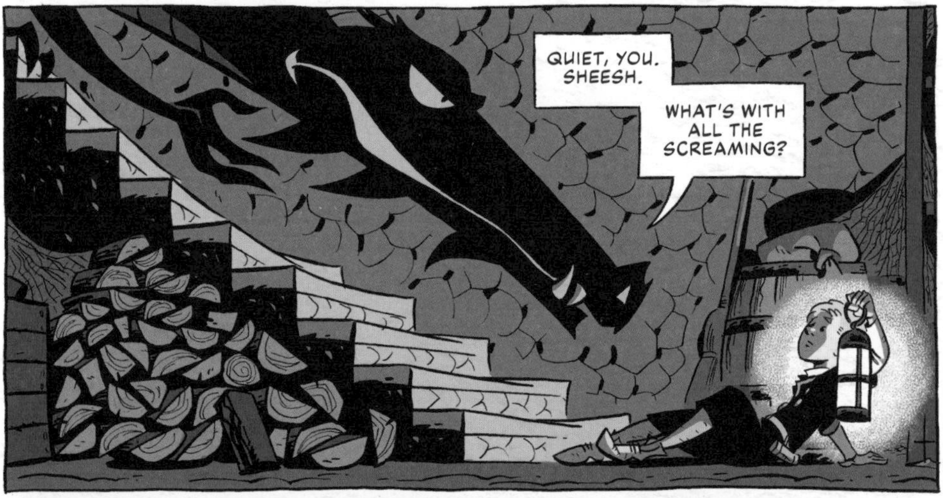
QUIET, YOU. SHEESH.
WHAT'S WITH ALL THE SCREAMING?

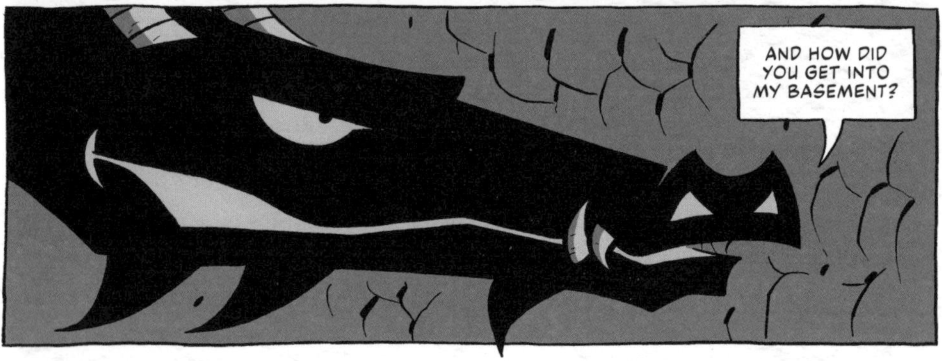
AND HOW DID YOU GET INTO MY BASEMENT?

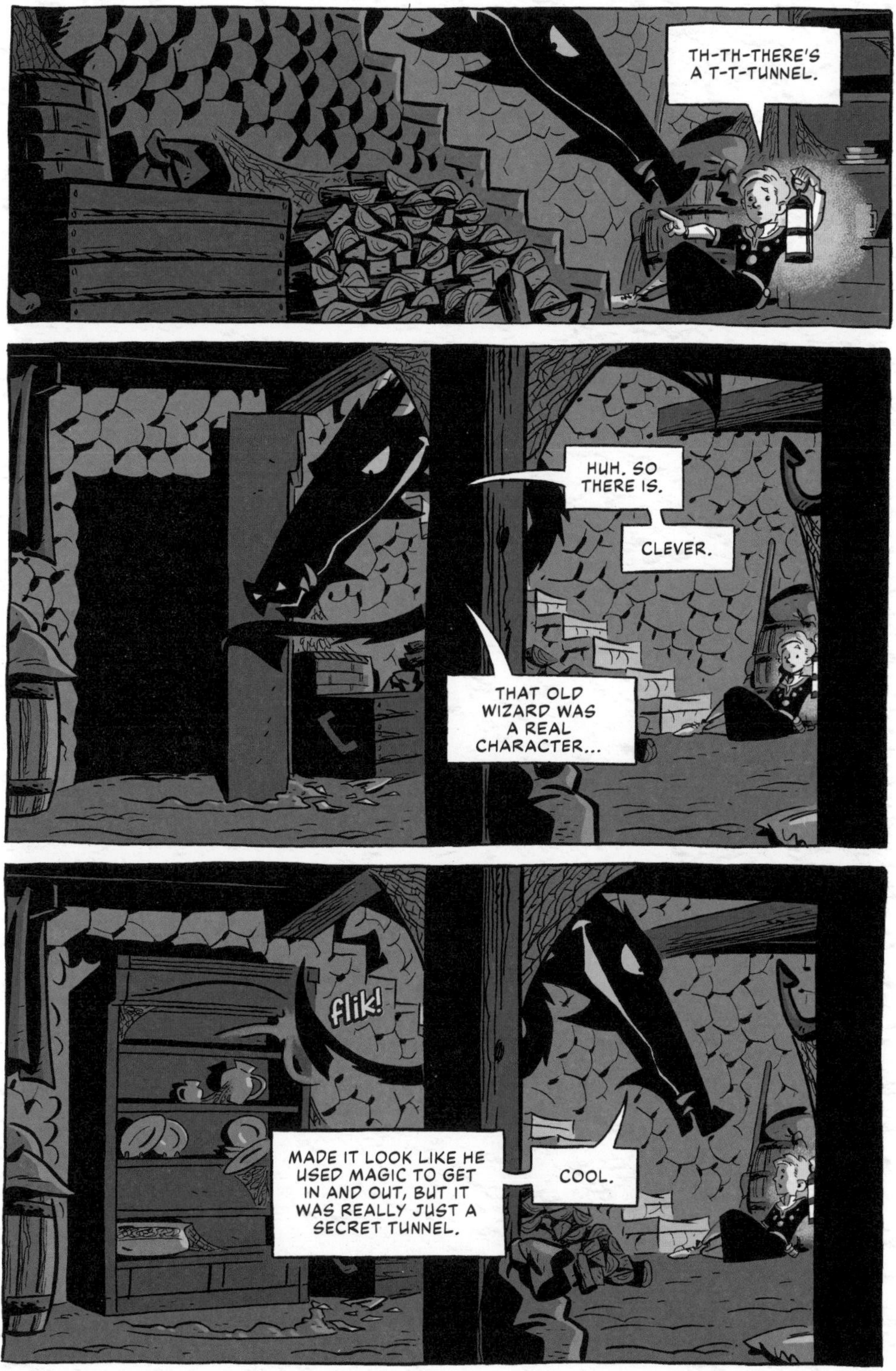
TH-TH-THERE'S A T-T-TUNNEL.
HUH. SO THERE IS.
CLEVER.
THAT OLD WIZARD WAS A REAL CHARACTER...
flik!
MADE IT LOOK LIKE HE USED MAGIC TO GET IN AND OUT, BUT IT WAS REALLY JUST A SECRET TUNNEL.
COOL.

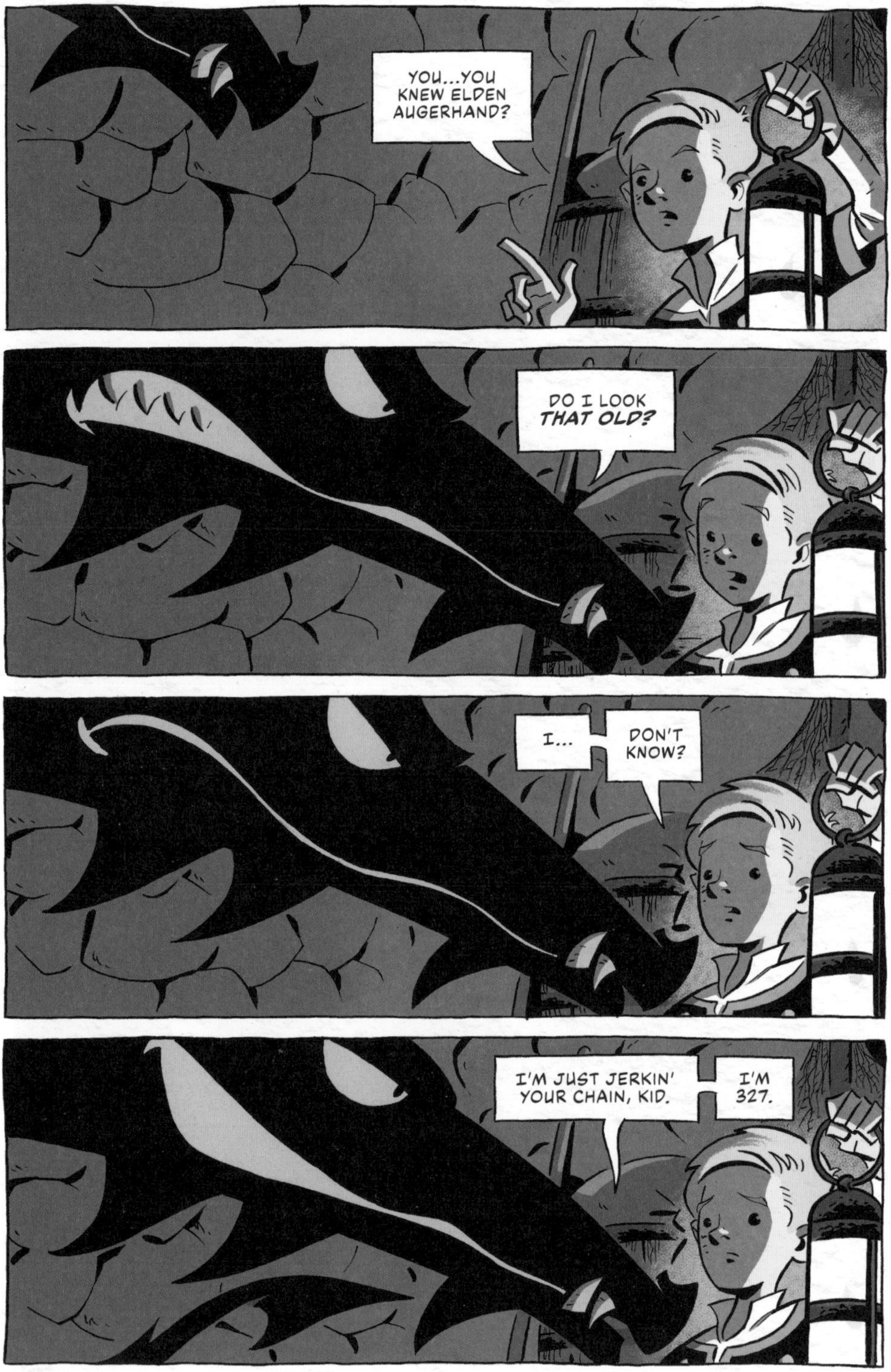
YOU...YOU KNEW ELDEN AUGERHAND?
DO I LOOK *THAT OLD?*
I...
DON'T KNOW?
I'M JUST JERKIN' YOUR CHAIN, KID.
I'M 327.

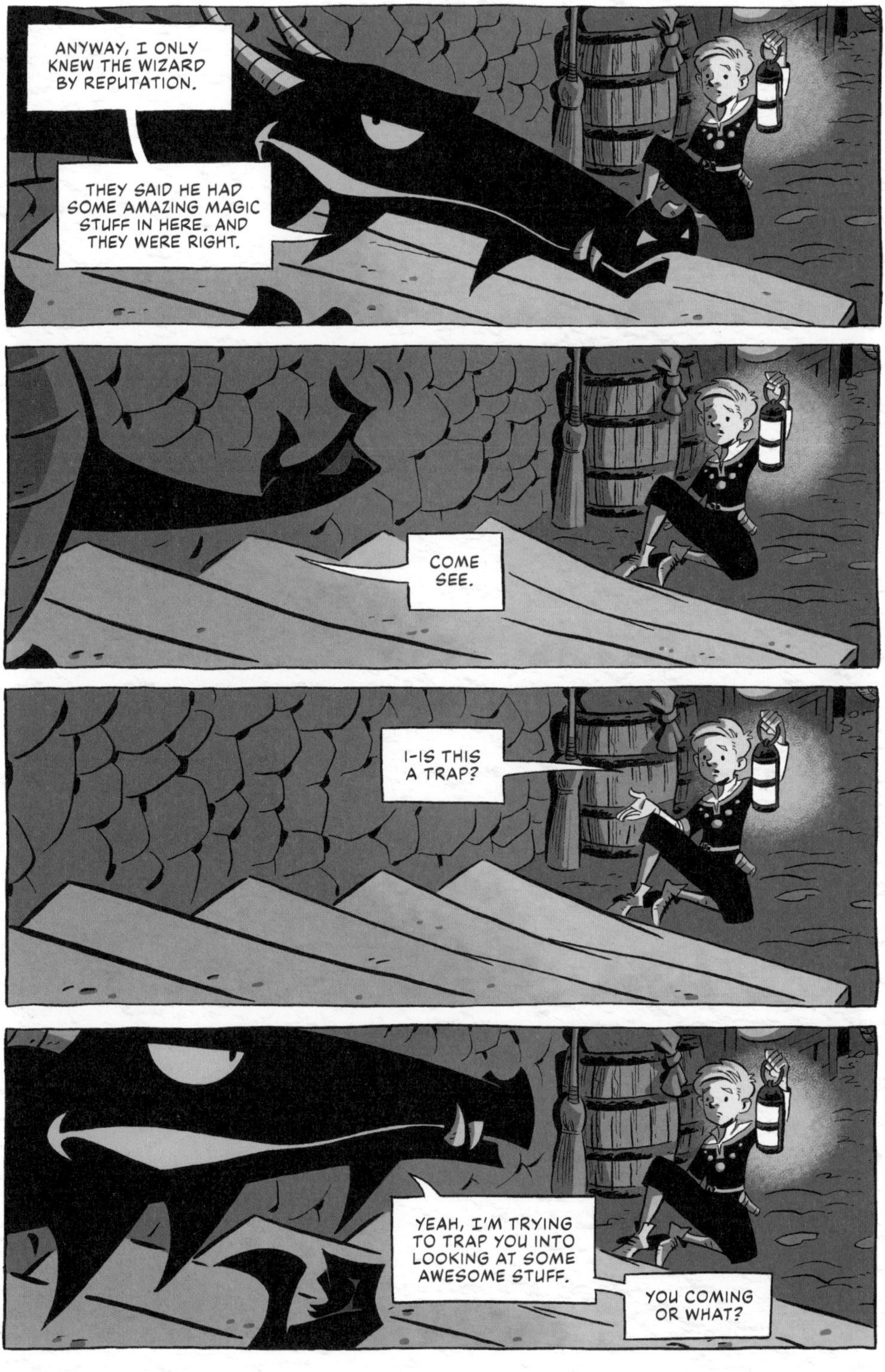
ANYWAY, I ONLY KNEW THE WIZARD BY REPUTATION.
THEY SAID HE HAD SOME AMAZING MAGIC STUFF IN HERE. AND THEY WERE RIGHT.
COME SEE.
I-IS THIS A TRAP?
YEAH, I'M TRYING TO TRAP YOU INTO LOOKING AT SOME AWESOME STUFF.
YOU COMING OR WHAT?

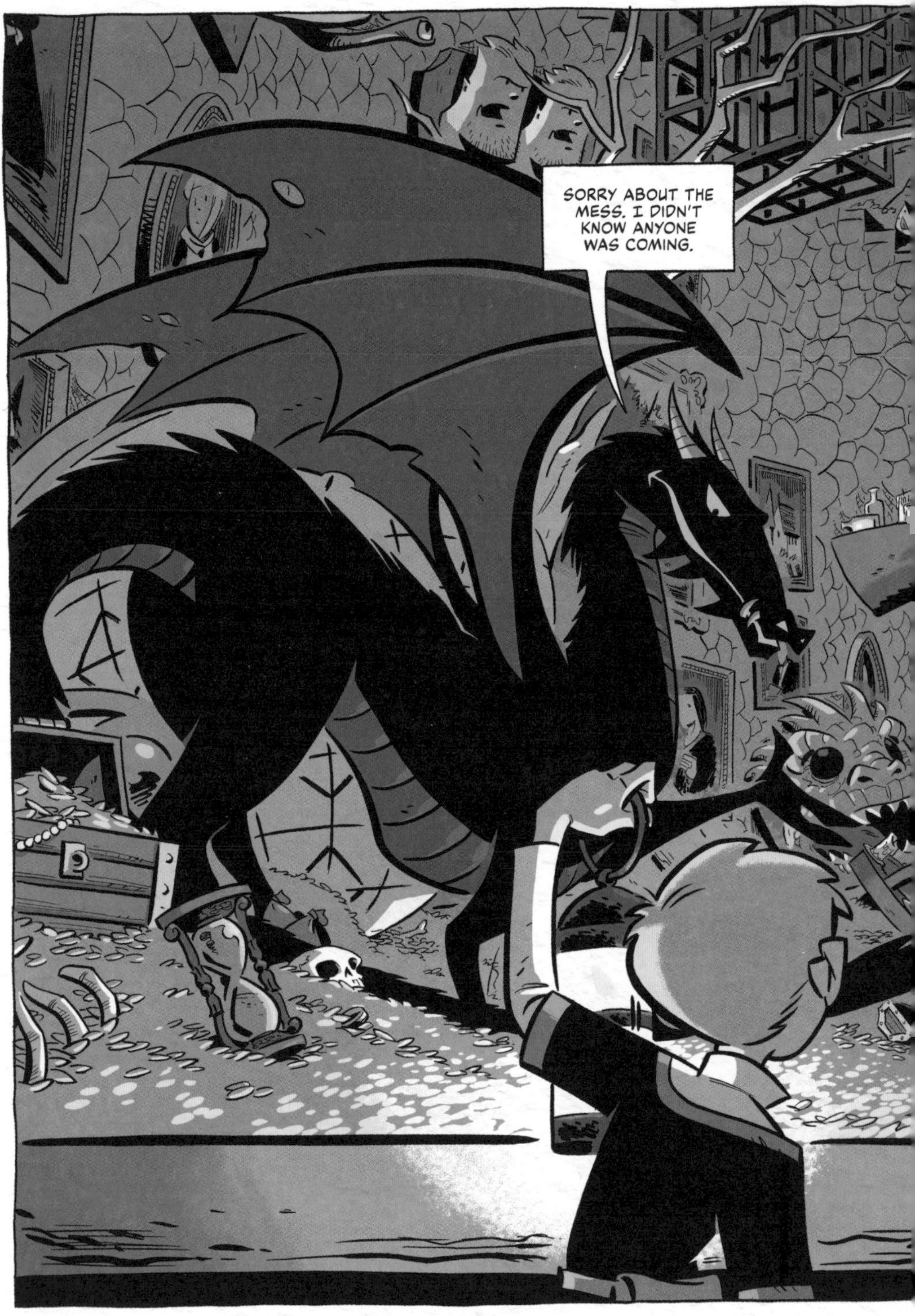
SORRY ABOUT THE MESS. I DIDN'T KNOW ANYONE WAS COMING.

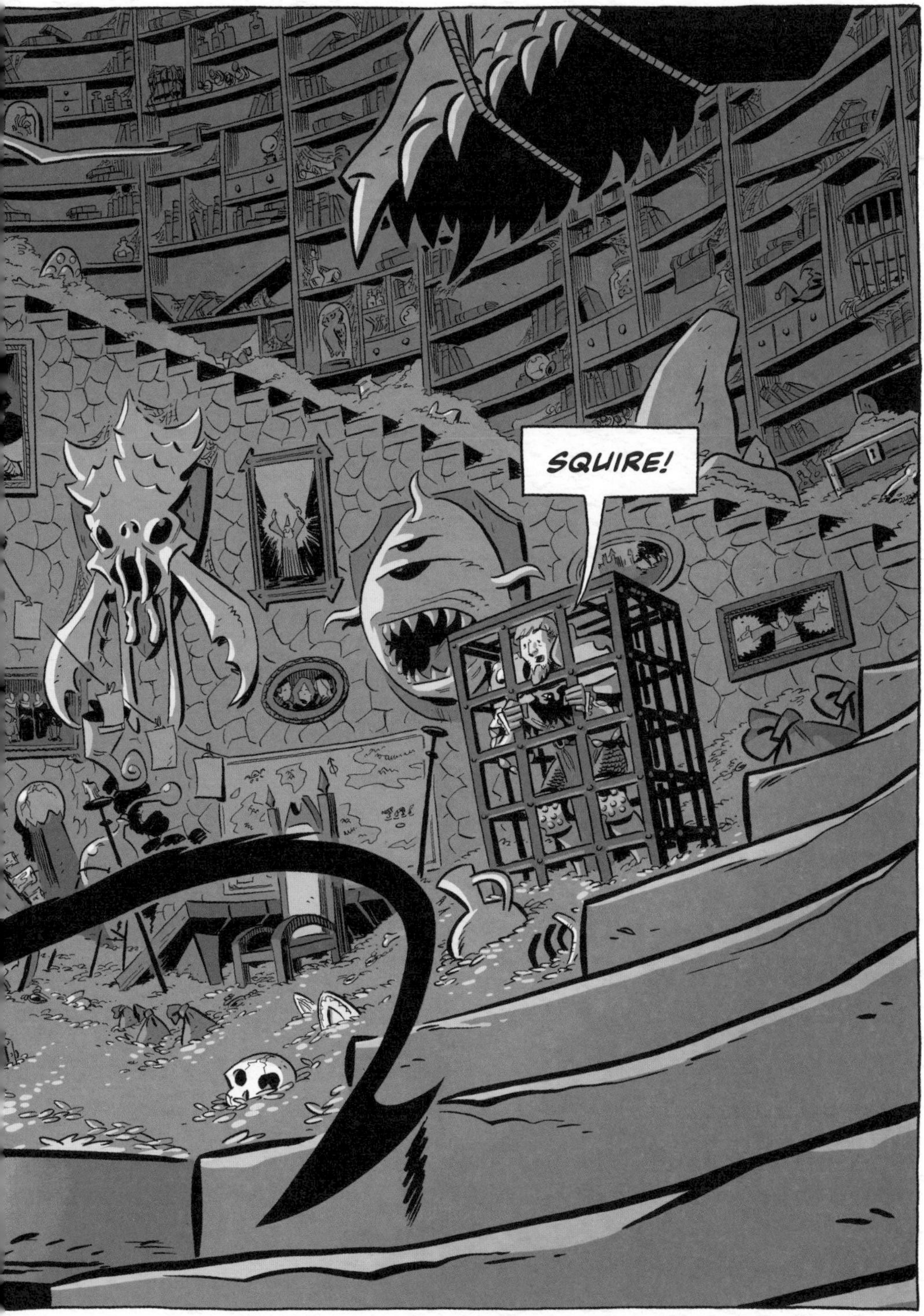
SQUIRE!

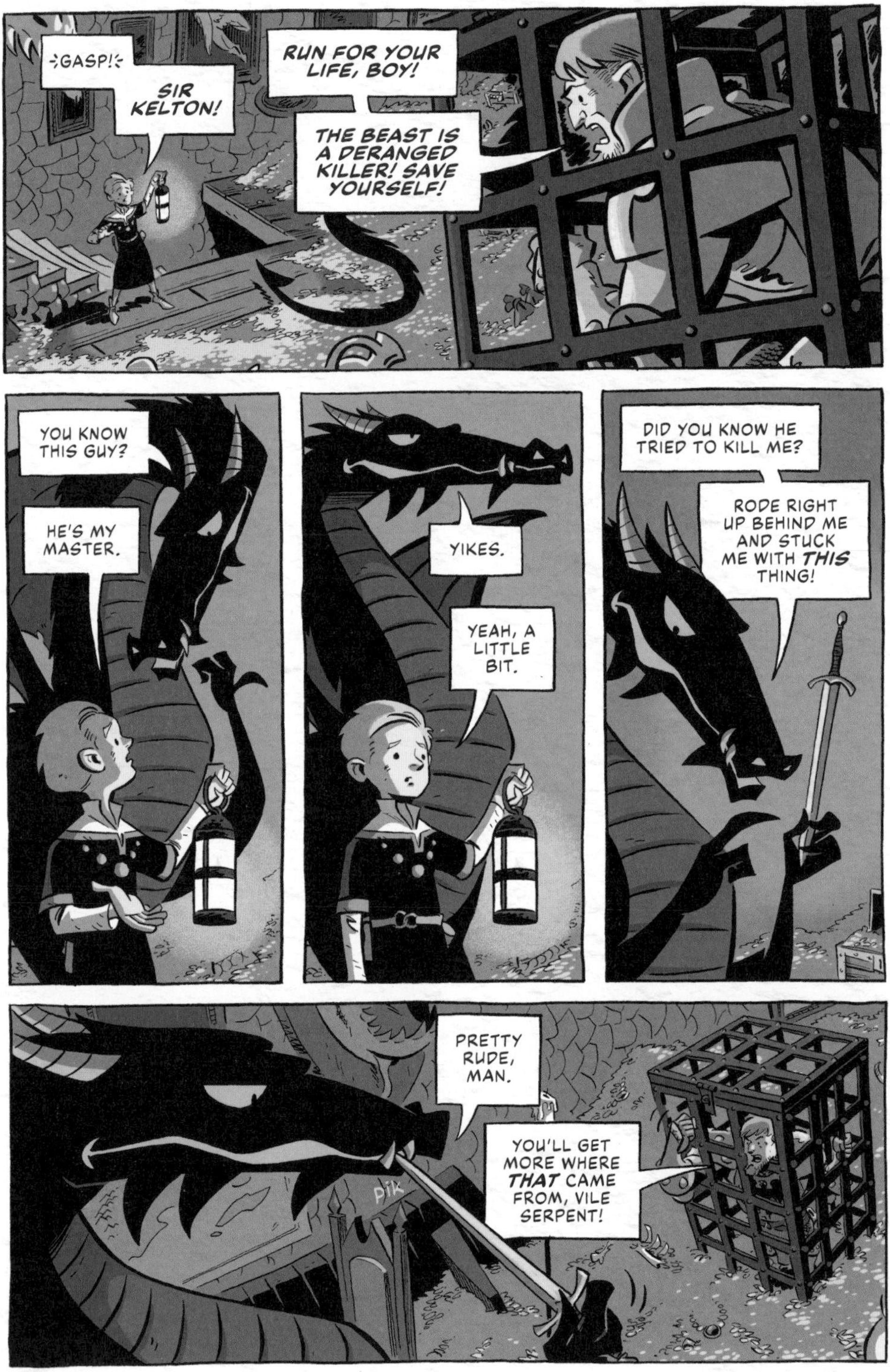

GASP!
SIR KELTON!
RUN FOR YOUR LIFE, BOY!
THE BEAST IS A DERANGED KILLER! SAVE YOURSELF!
YOU KNOW THIS GUY?
HE'S MY MASTER.
YIKES.
YEAH, A LITTLE BIT.
DID YOU KNOW HE TRIED TO KILL ME?
RODE RIGHT UP BEHIND ME AND STUCK ME WITH THIS THING!
PRETTY RUDE, MAN.
PIK
YOU'LL GET MORE WHERE THAT CAME FROM, VILE SERPENT!

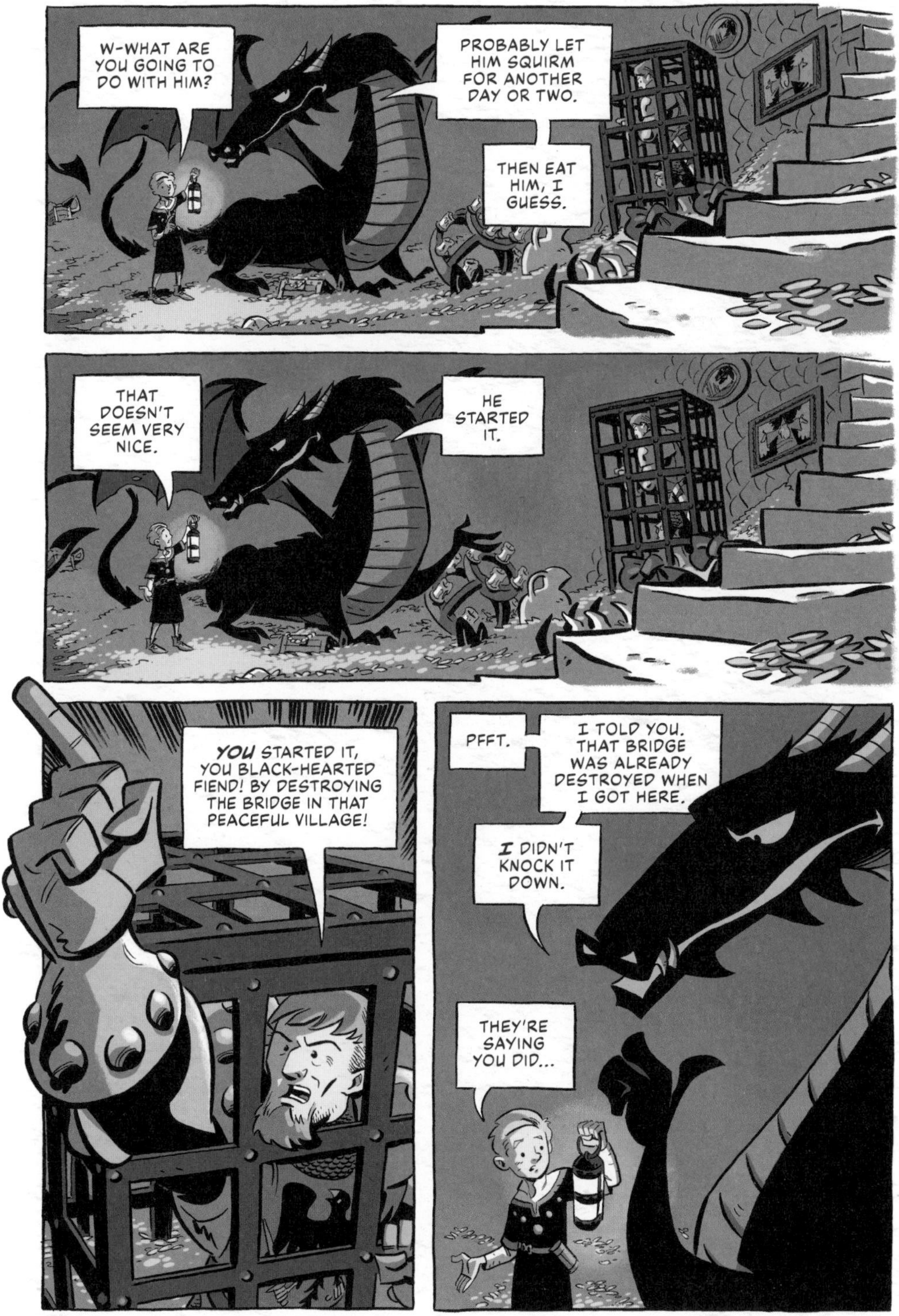

W-WHAT ARE YOU GOING TO DO WITH HIM?
PROBABLY LET HIM SQUIRM FOR ANOTHER DAY OR TWO.
THEN EAT HIM, I GUESS.
THAT DOESN'T SEEM VERY NICE.
HE STARTED IT.
YOU STARTED IT, YOU BLACK-HEARTED FIEND! BY DESTROYING THE BRIDGE IN THAT PEACEFUL VILLAGE!
PFFT.
I TOLD YOU. THAT BRIDGE WAS ALREADY DESTROYED WHEN I GOT HERE.
I DIDN'T KNOCK IT DOWN.
THEY'RE SAYING YOU DID...

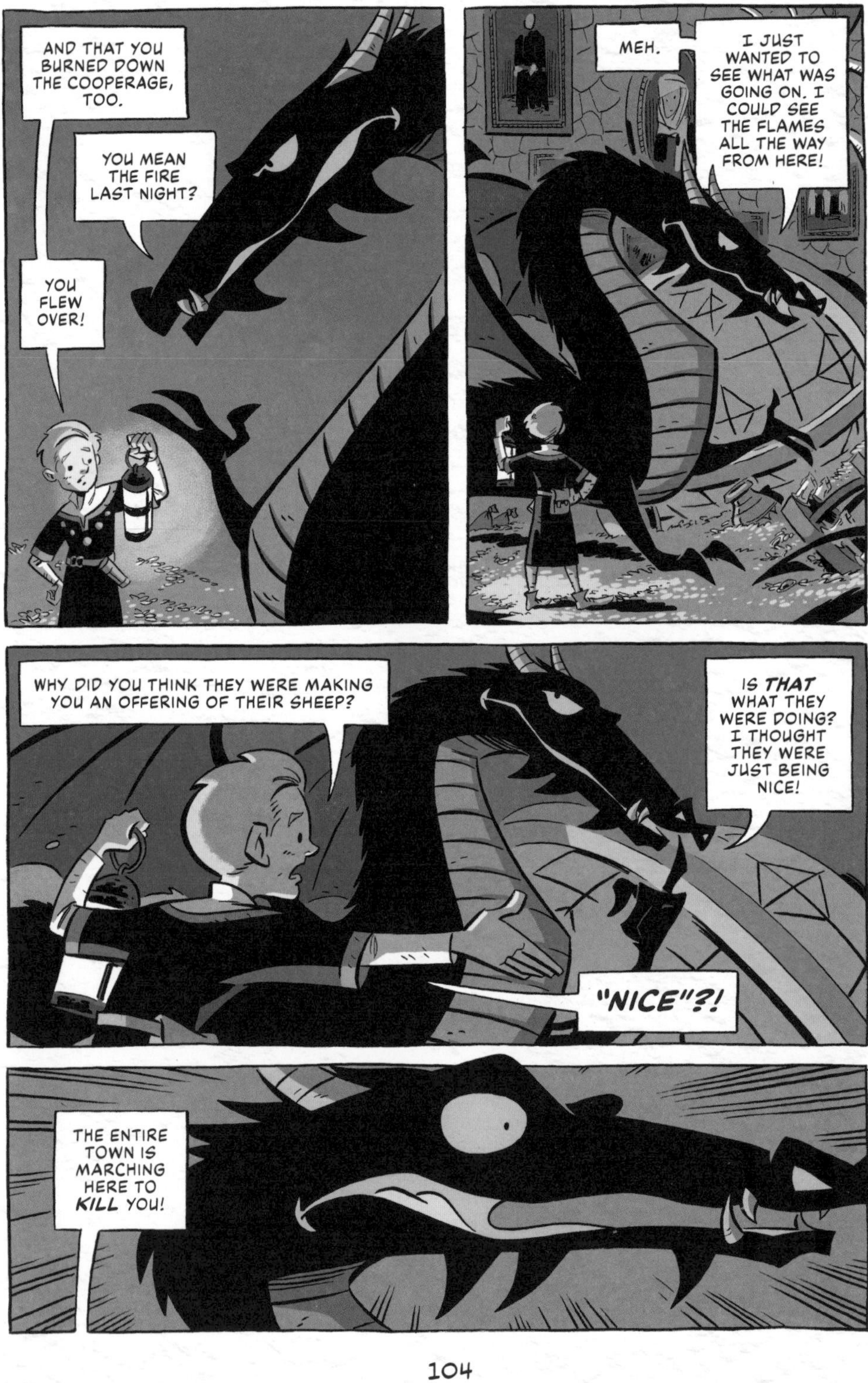
AND THAT YOU BURNED DOWN THE COOPERAGE, TOO.
YOU MEAN THE FIRE LAST NIGHT?
YOU FLEW OVER!
MEH.
I JUST WANTED TO SEE WHAT WAS GOING ON. I COULD SEE THE FLAMES ALL THE WAY FROM HERE!
WHY DID YOU THINK THEY WERE MAKING YOU AN OFFERING OF THEIR SHEEP?
IS **THAT** WHAT THEY WERE DOING? I THOUGHT THEY WERE JUST BEING NICE!
**"NICE"?!**
THE ENTIRE TOWN IS MARCHING HERE TO **KILL** YOU!

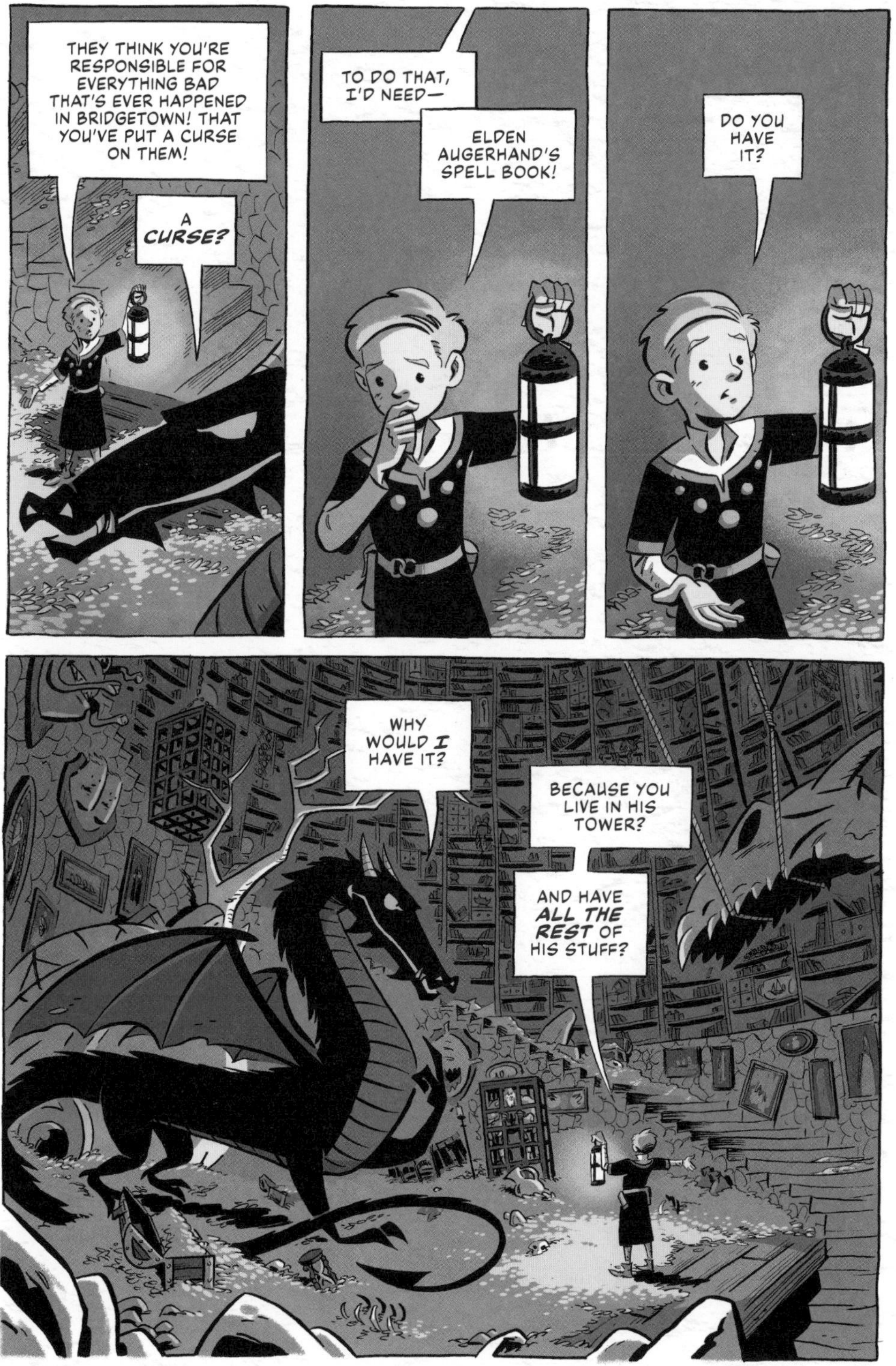
THEY THINK YOU'RE RESPONSIBLE FOR EVERYTHING BAD THAT'S EVER HAPPENED IN BRIDGETOWN! THAT YOU'VE PUT A CURSE ON THEM!
A *CURSE?*
TO DO THAT, I'D NEED—
ELDEN AUGERHAND'S SPELL BOOK!
DO YOU HAVE IT?
WHY WOULD *I* HAVE IT?
BECAUSE YOU LIVE IN HIS TOWER?
AND HAVE *ALL THE REST* OF HIS STUFF?

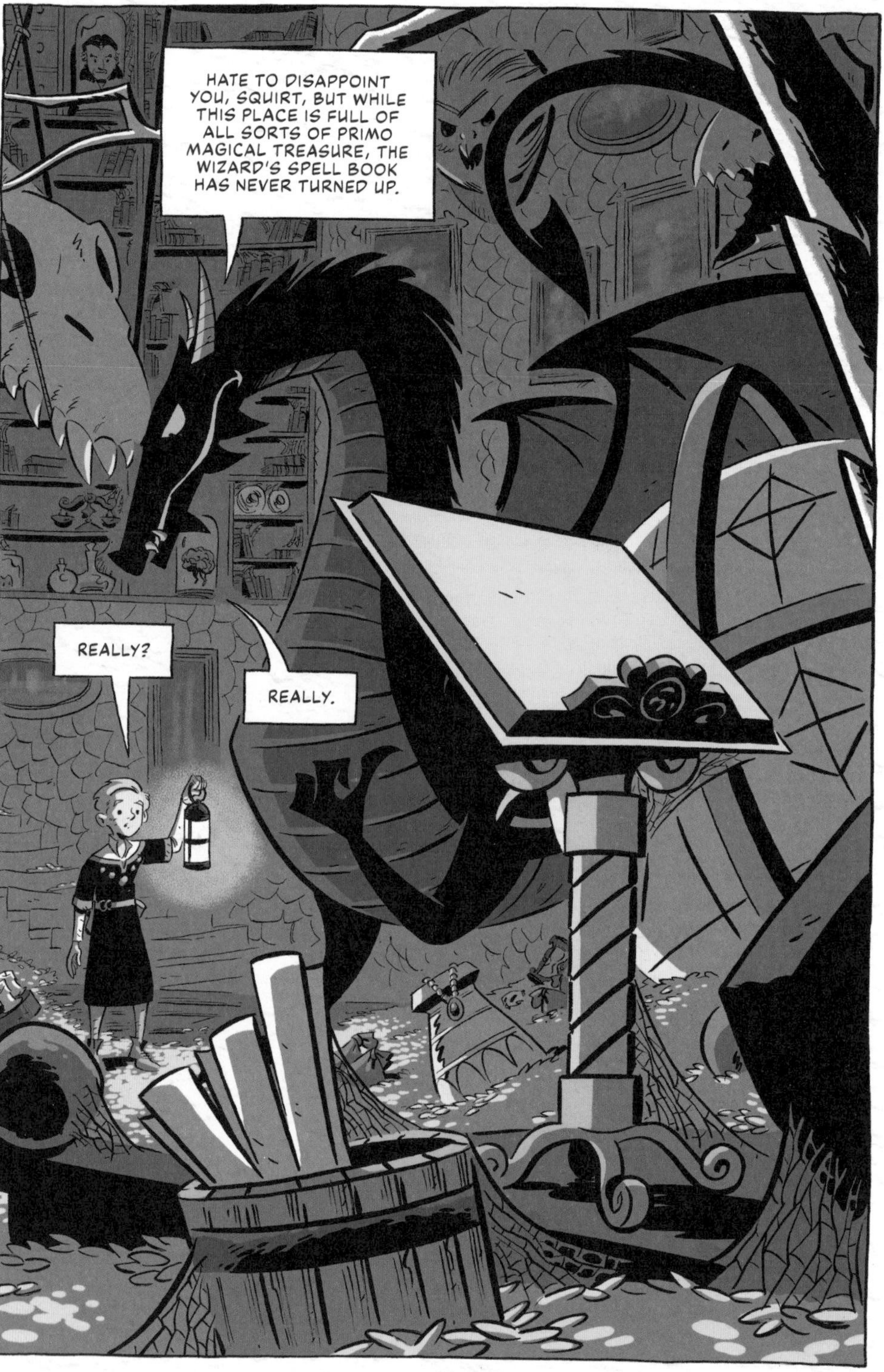
HATE TO DISAPPOINT YOU, SQUIRT, BUT WHILE THIS PLACE IS FULL OF ALL SORTS OF PRIMO MAGICAL TREASURE, THE WIZARD'S SPELL BOOK HAS NEVER TURNED UP.
REALLY?
REALLY.

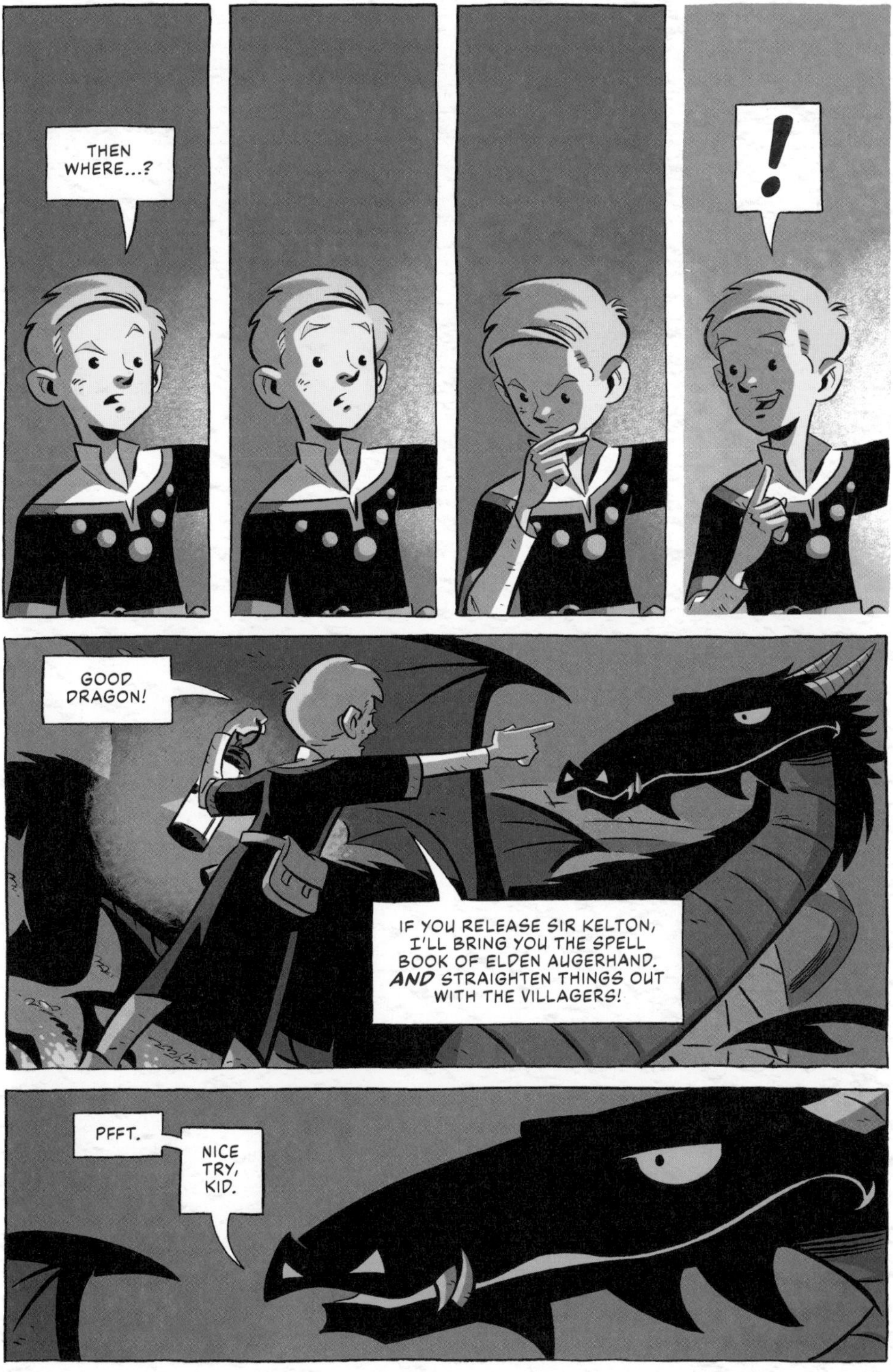
THEN WHERE...?
!
GOOD DRAGON!
IF YOU RELEASE SIR KELTON, I'LL BRING YOU THE SPELL BOOK OF ELDEN AUGERHAND. **AND** STRAIGHTEN THINGS OUT WITH THE VILLAGERS!
PFFT.
NICE TRY, KID.

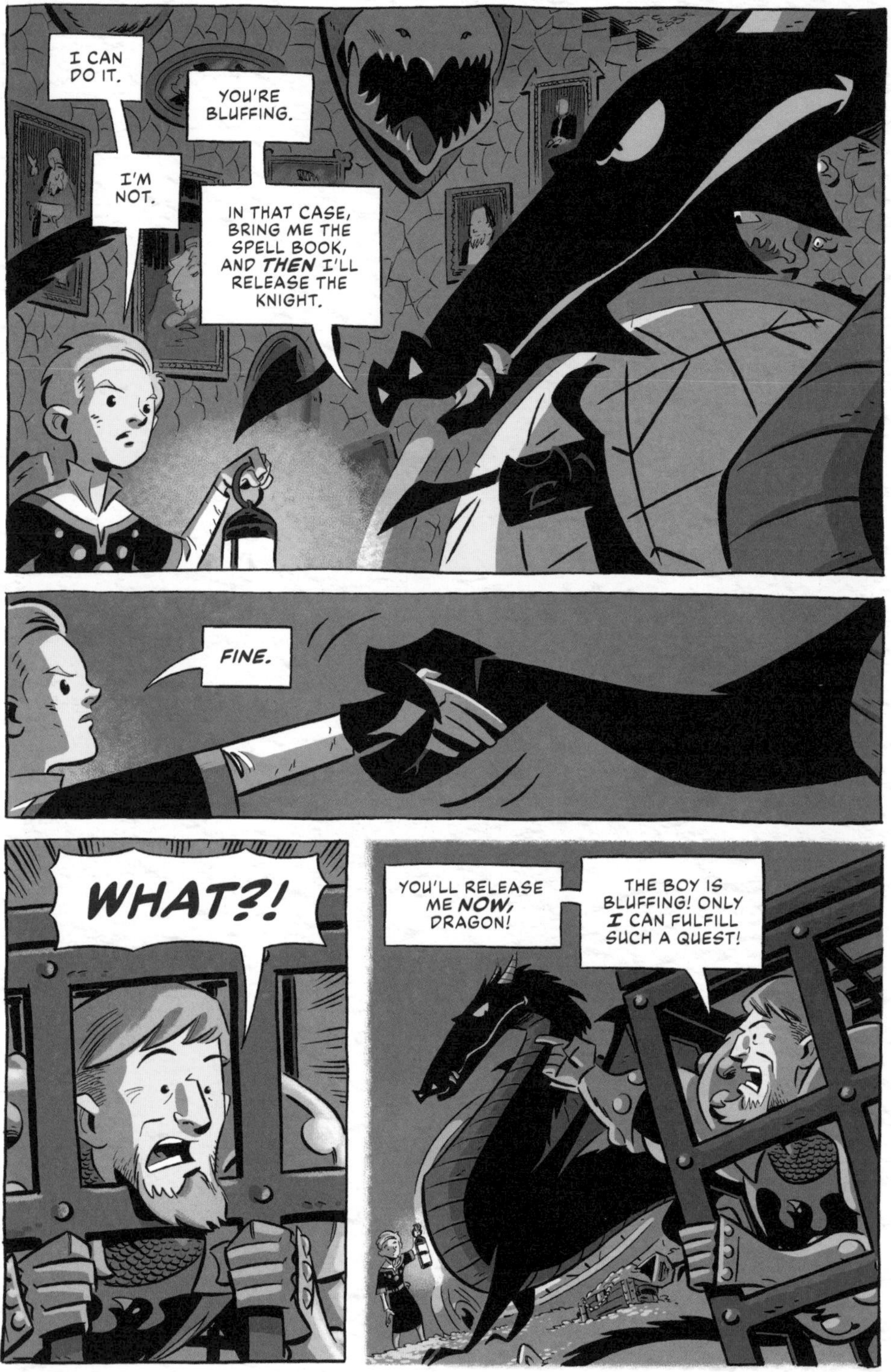
I CAN DO IT.
YOU'RE BLUFFING.
I'M NOT.
IN THAT CASE, BRING ME THE SPELL BOOK, AND *THEN* I'LL RELEASE THE KNIGHT.
*FINE.*
*WHAT?!*
YOU'LL RELEASE ME *NOW*, DRAGON!
THE BOY IS BLUFFING! ONLY *I* CAN FULFILL SUCH A QUEST!

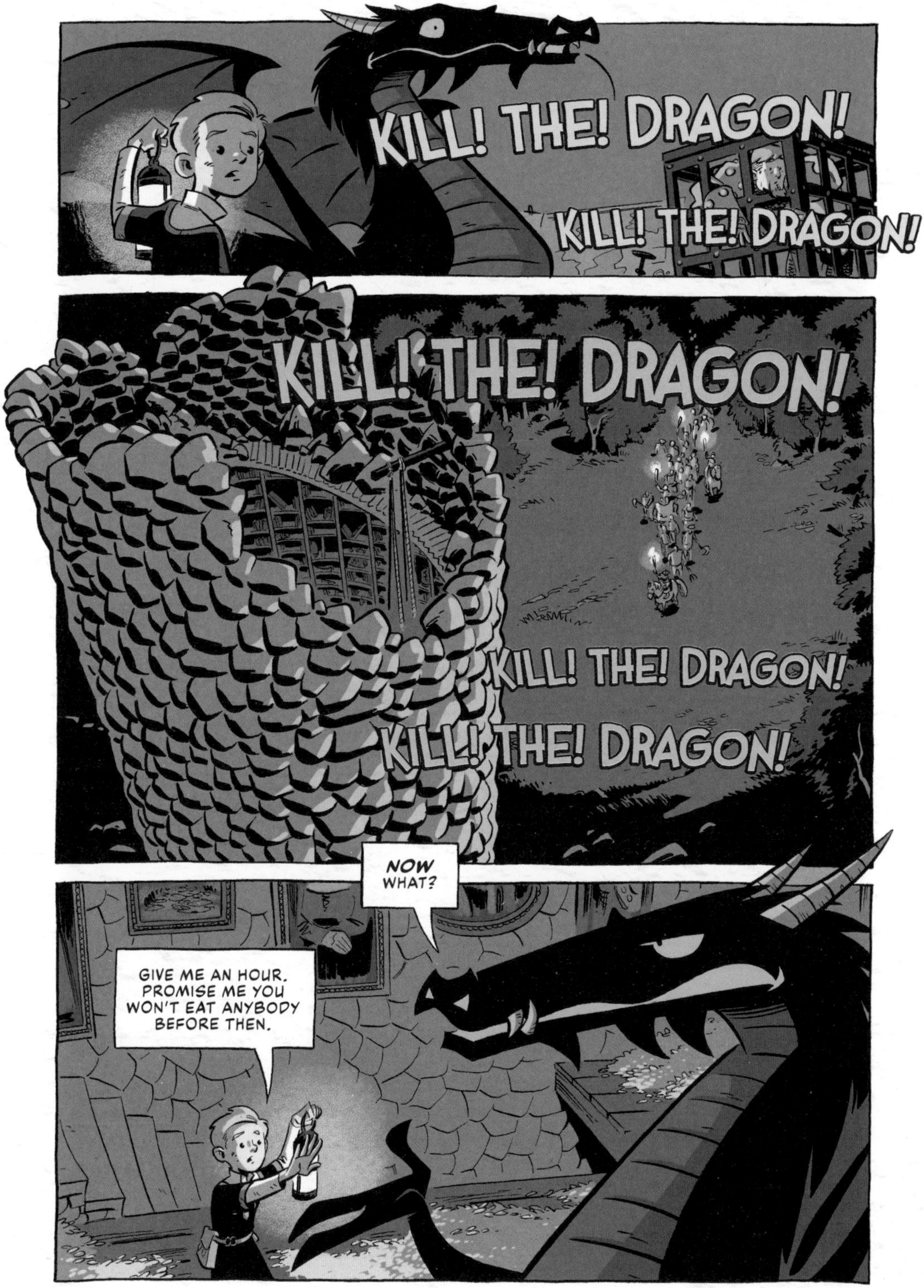
KILL! THE! DRAGON!
KILL! THE! DRAGON!
KILL! THE! DRAGON!
KILL! THE! DRAGON!
KILL! THE! DRAGON!
NOW WHAT?
GIVE ME AN HOUR. PROMISE ME YOU WON'T EAT ANYBODY BEFORE THEN.

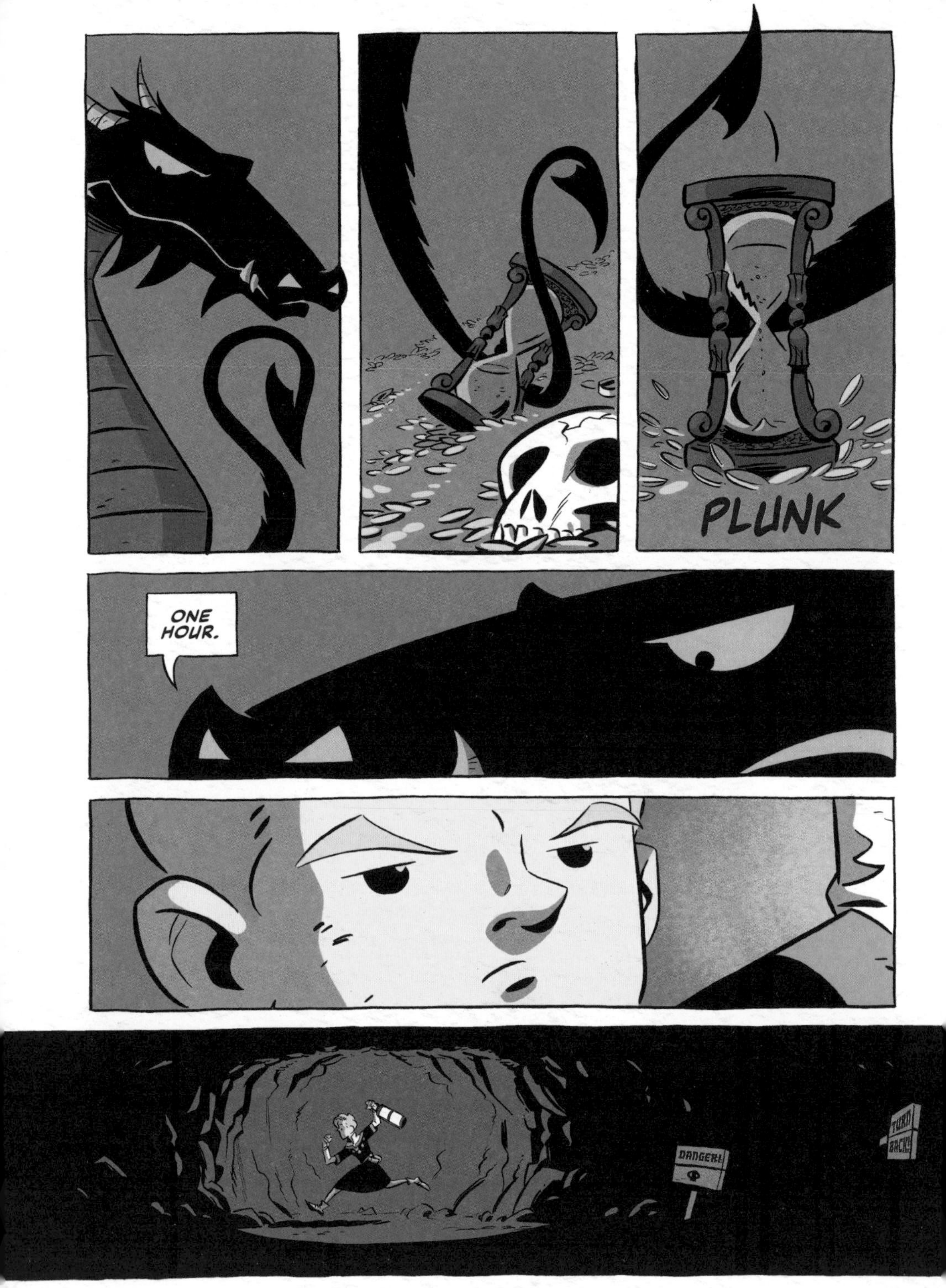
PLUNK
ONE HOUR.
DANGER!
TURN BACK!

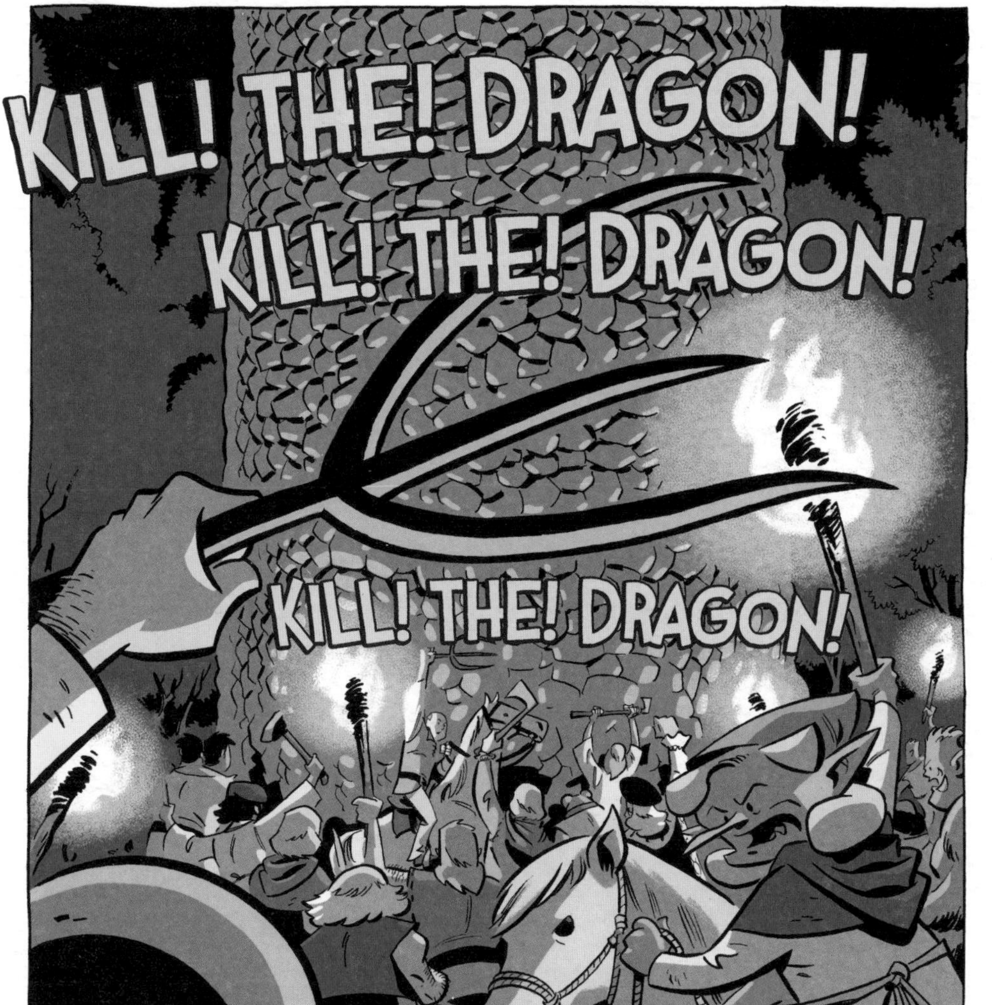
KILL! THE! DRAGON!
KILL! THE! DRAGON!
KILL! THE! DRAGON!

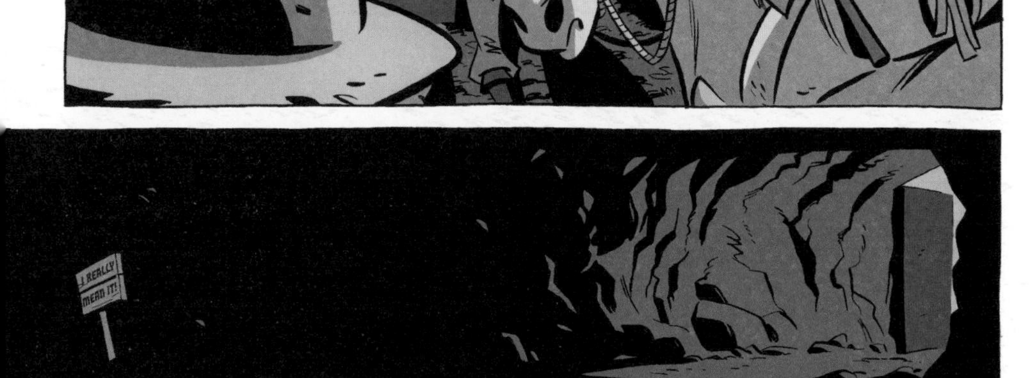
I REALLY MEAN IT!

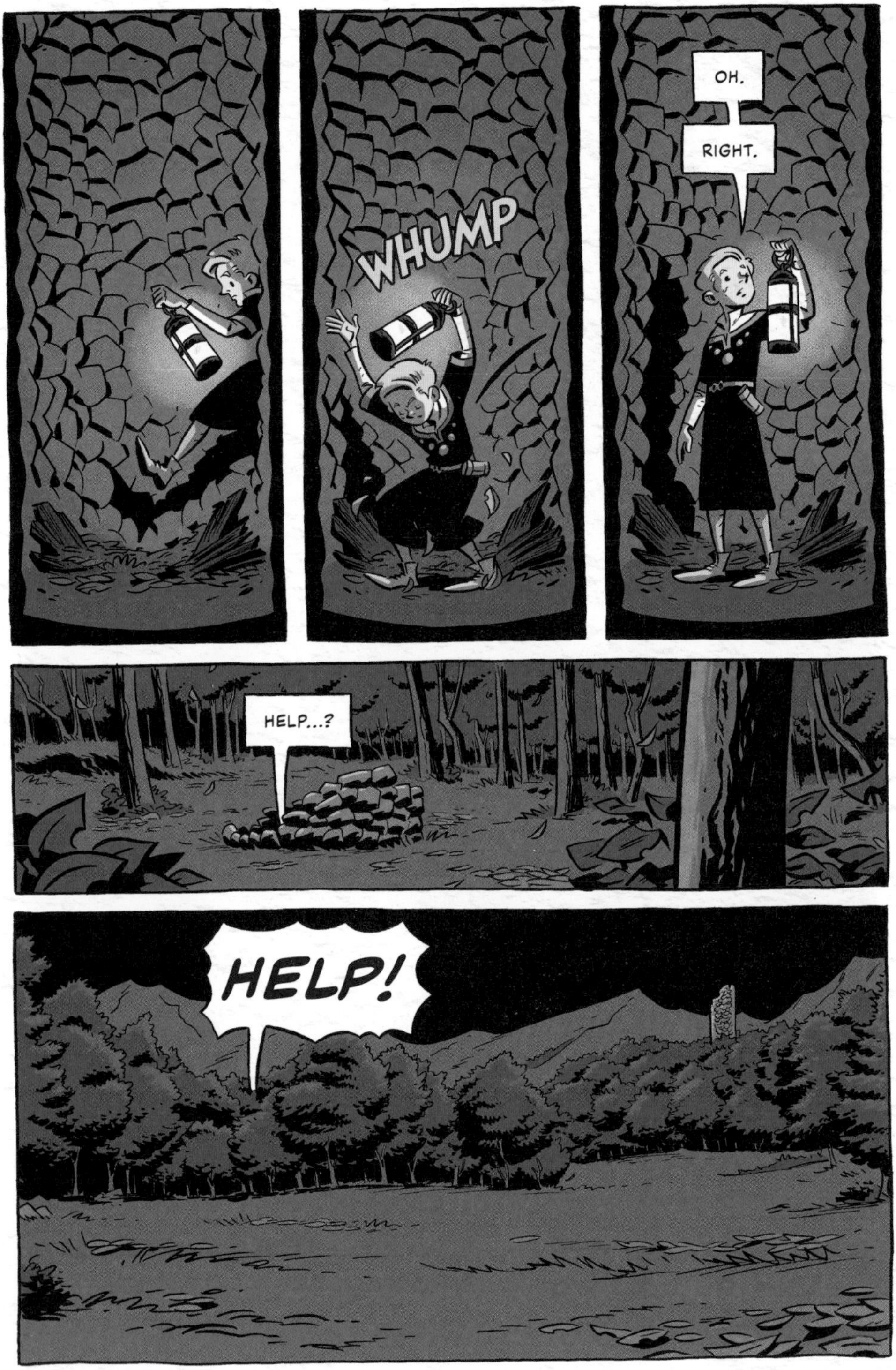
WHUMP
OH.
RIGHT.
HELP...?
HELP!

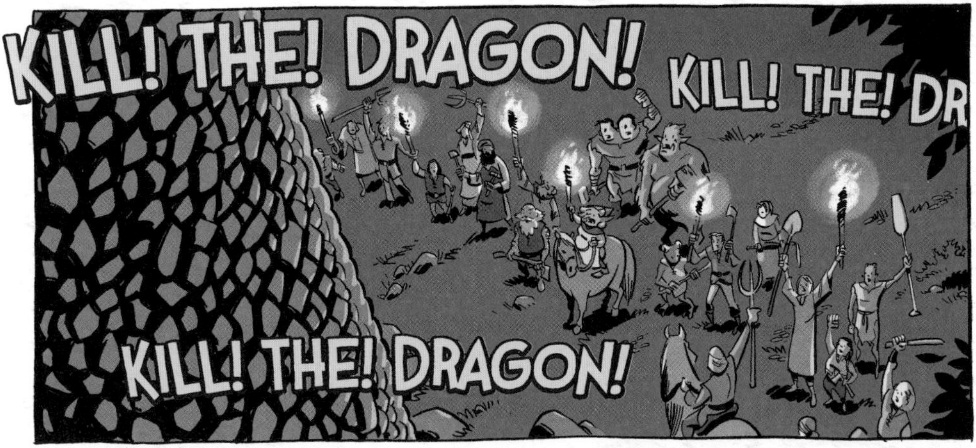
KILL! THE! DRAGON!
KILL! THE! DR
KILL! THE! DRAGON!

# Chapter Seven

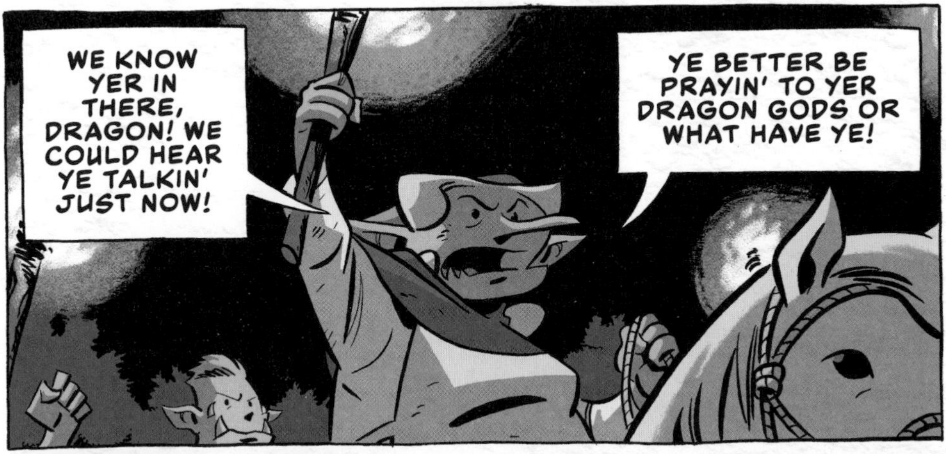
WE KNOW YER IN THERE, DRAGON! WE COULD HEAR YE TALKIN' JUST NOW!
YE BETTER BE PRAYIN' TO YER DRAGON GODS OR WHAT HAVE YE!

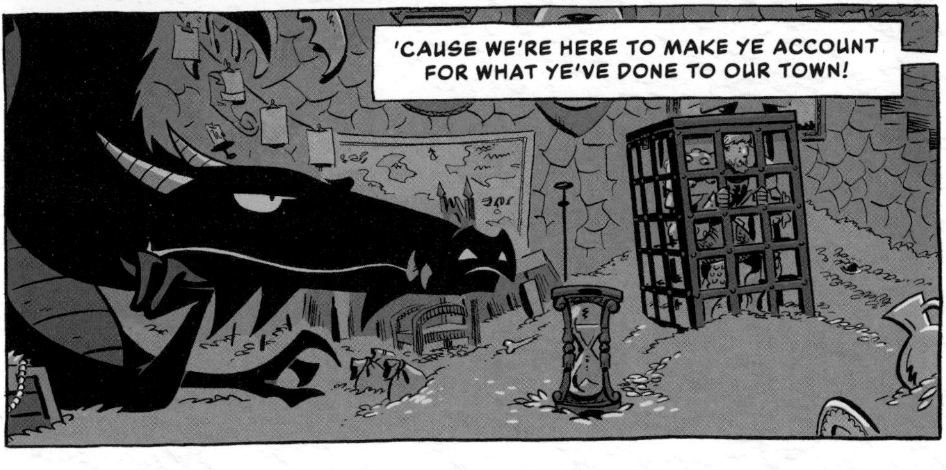
'CAUSE WE'RE HERE TO MAKE YE ACCOUNT FOR WHAT YE'VE DONE TO OUR TOWN!

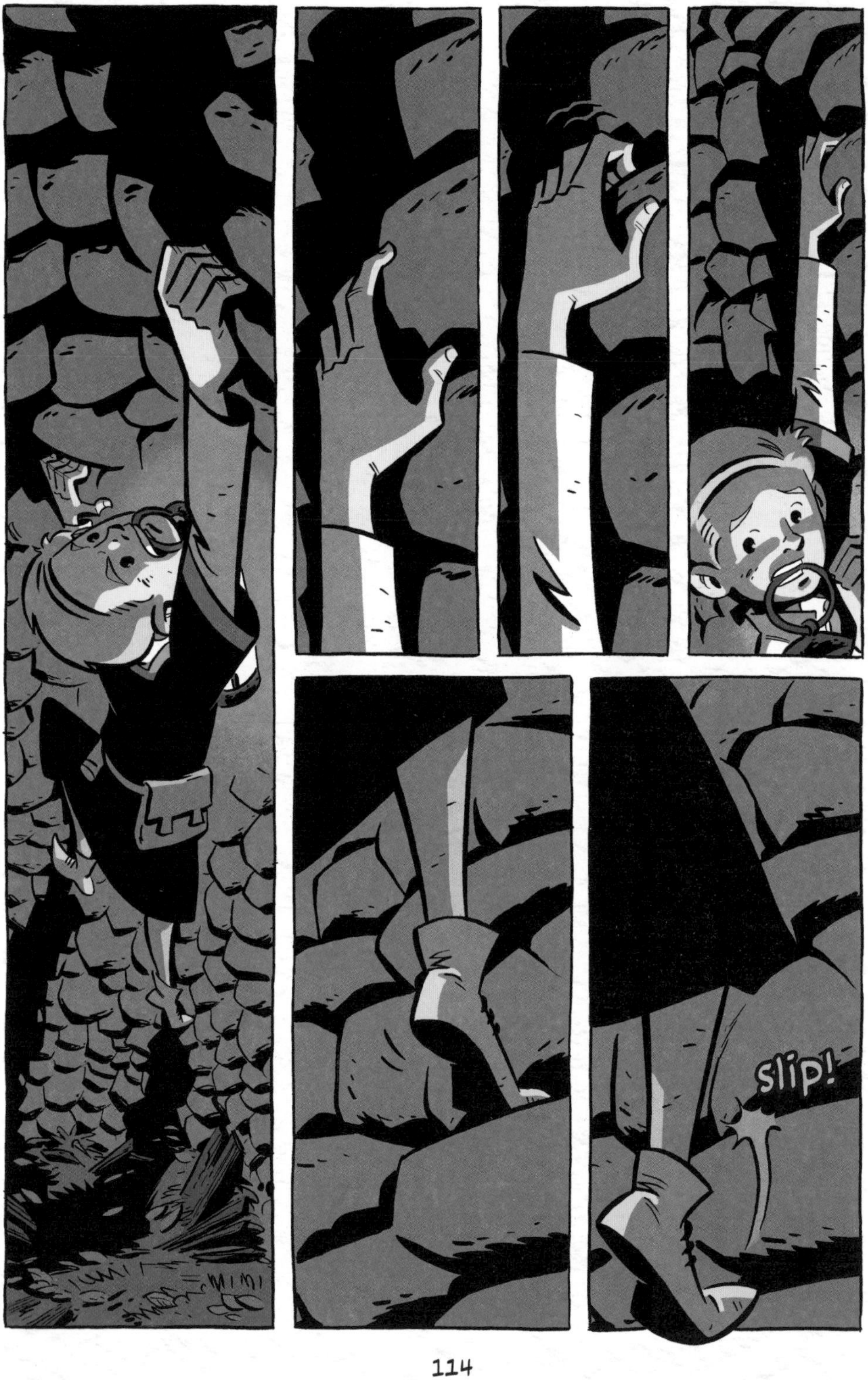
slip!

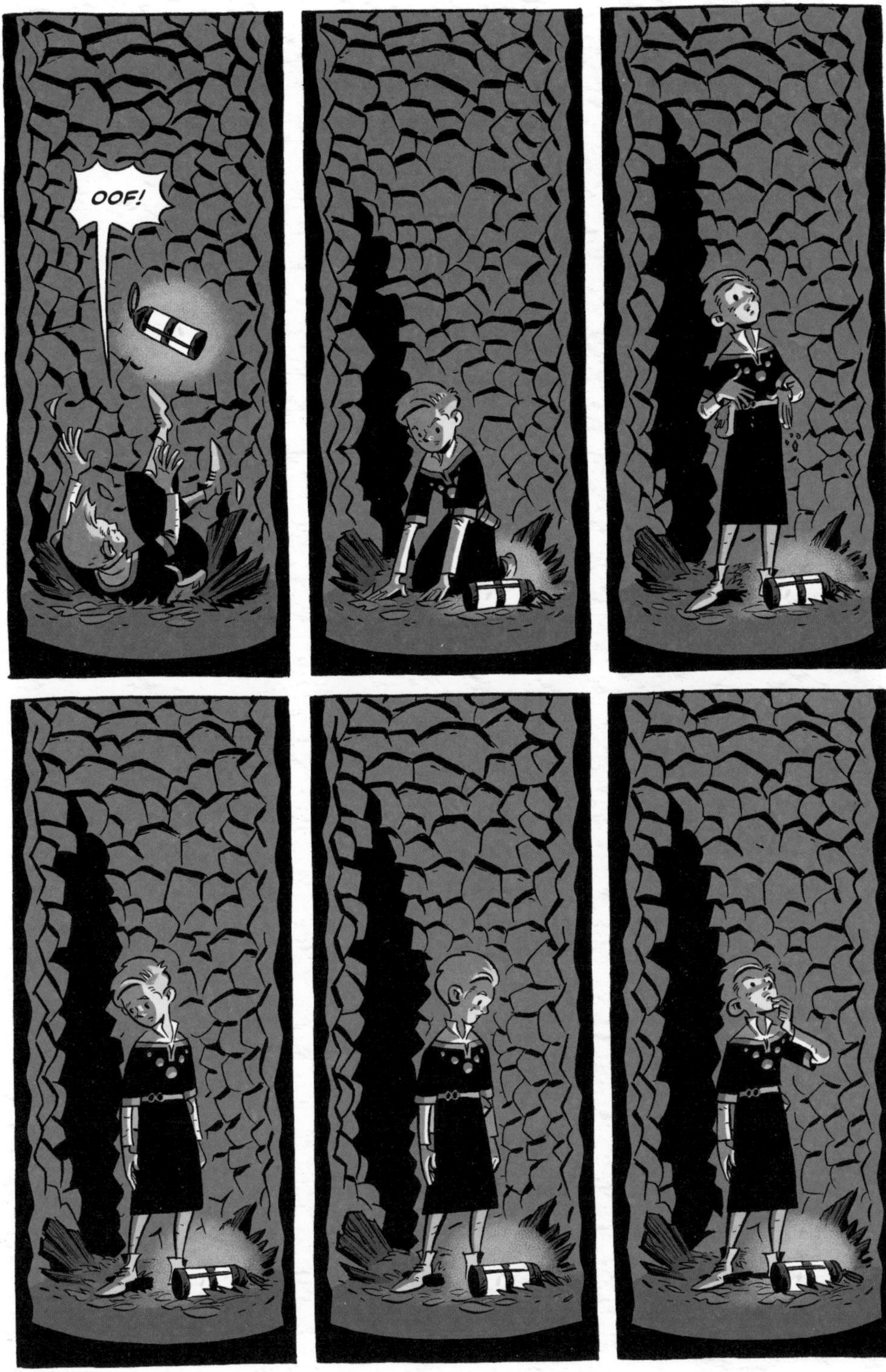
OOF!

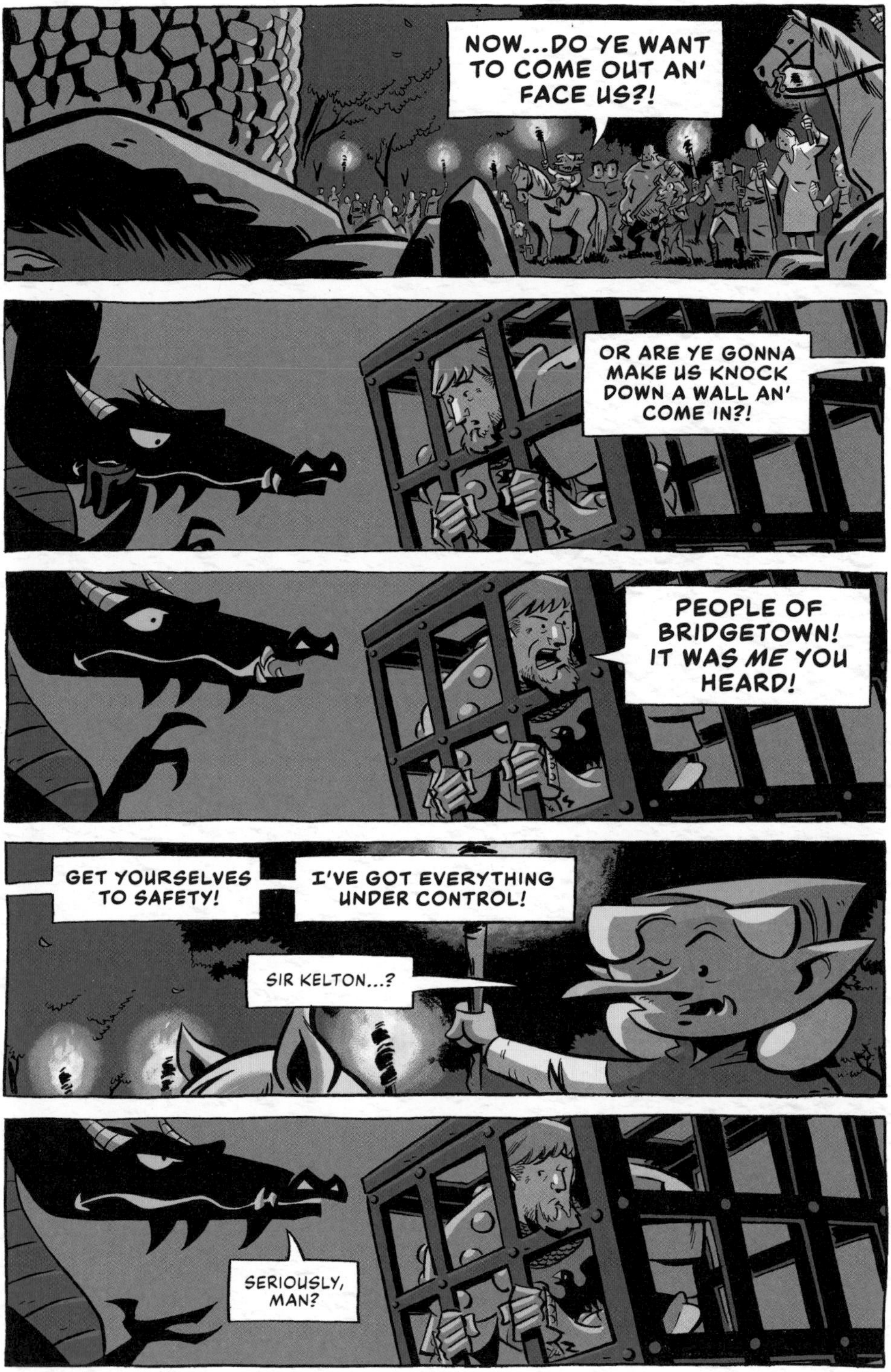
NOW...DO YE WANT TO COME OUT AN' FACE US?!
OR ARE YE GONNA MAKE US KNOCK DOWN A WALL AN' COME IN?!
PEOPLE OF BRIDGETOWN! IT WAS *ME* YOU HEARD!
GET YOURSELVES TO SAFETY!
I'VE GOT EVERYTHING UNDER CONTROL!
SIR KELTON...?
SERIOUSLY, MAN?

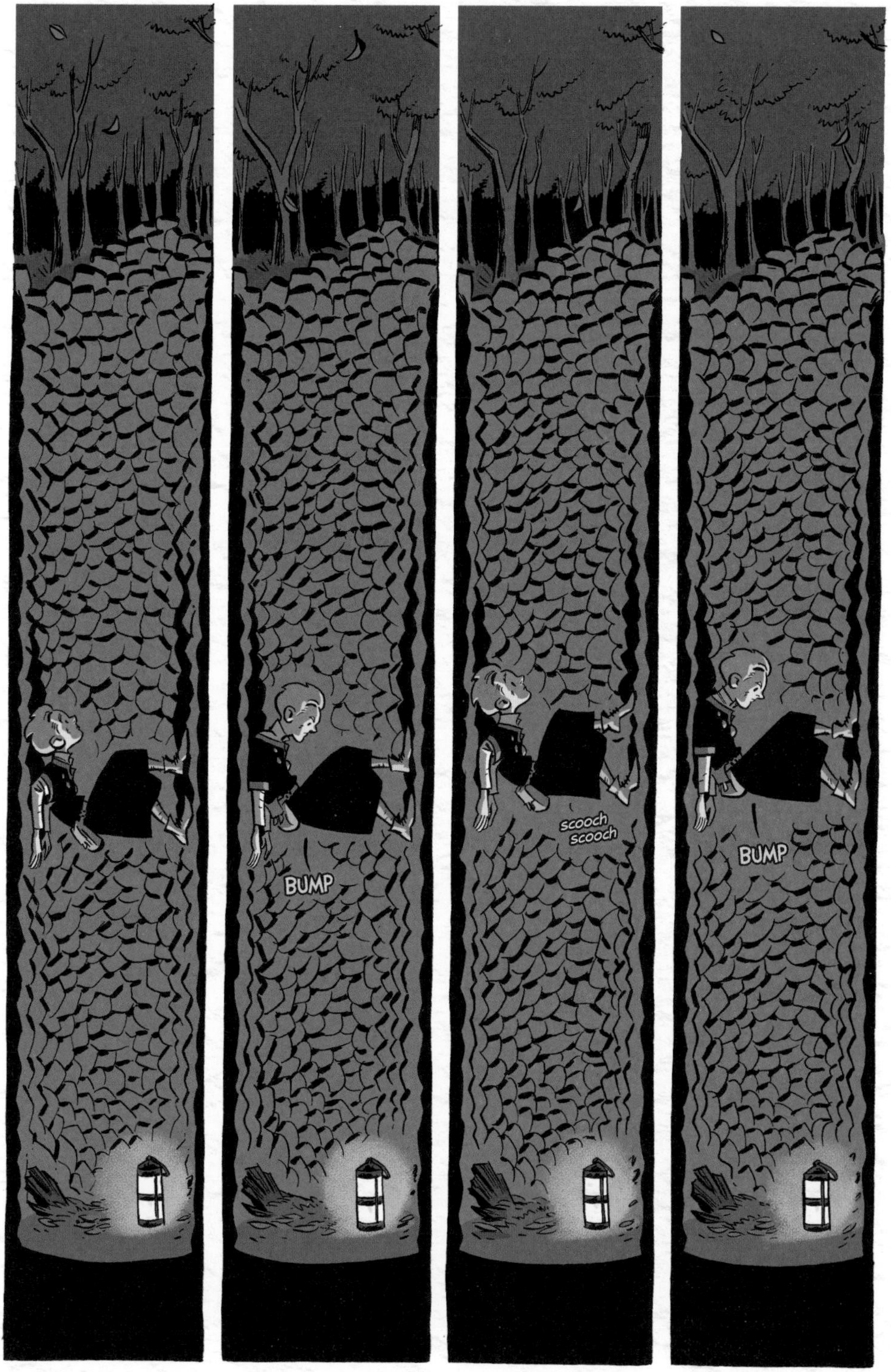
BUMP
scooch
scooch
BUMP

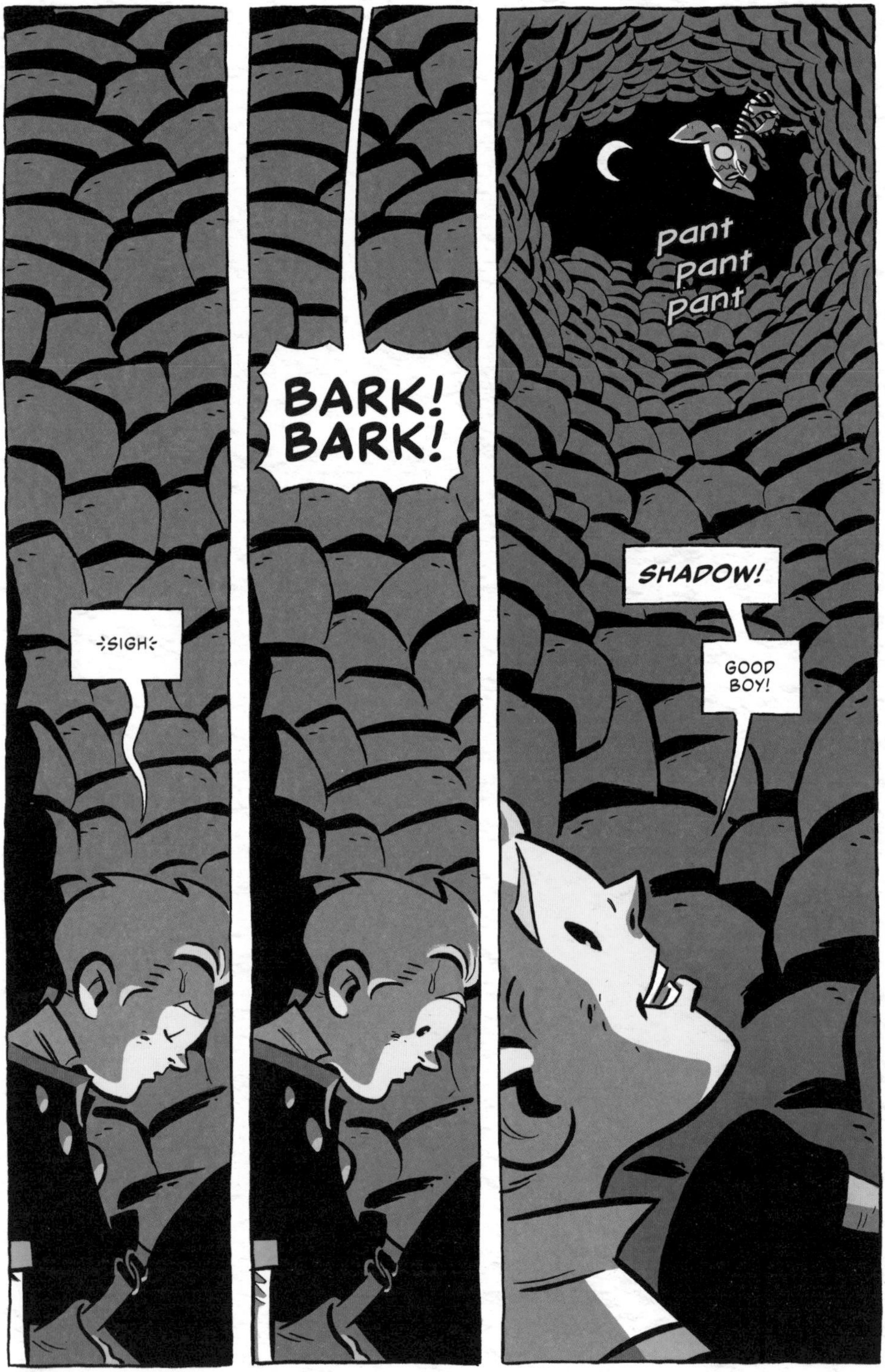
-SIGH-
BARK! BARK!
pant
pant
pant
SHADOW!
GOOD BOY!

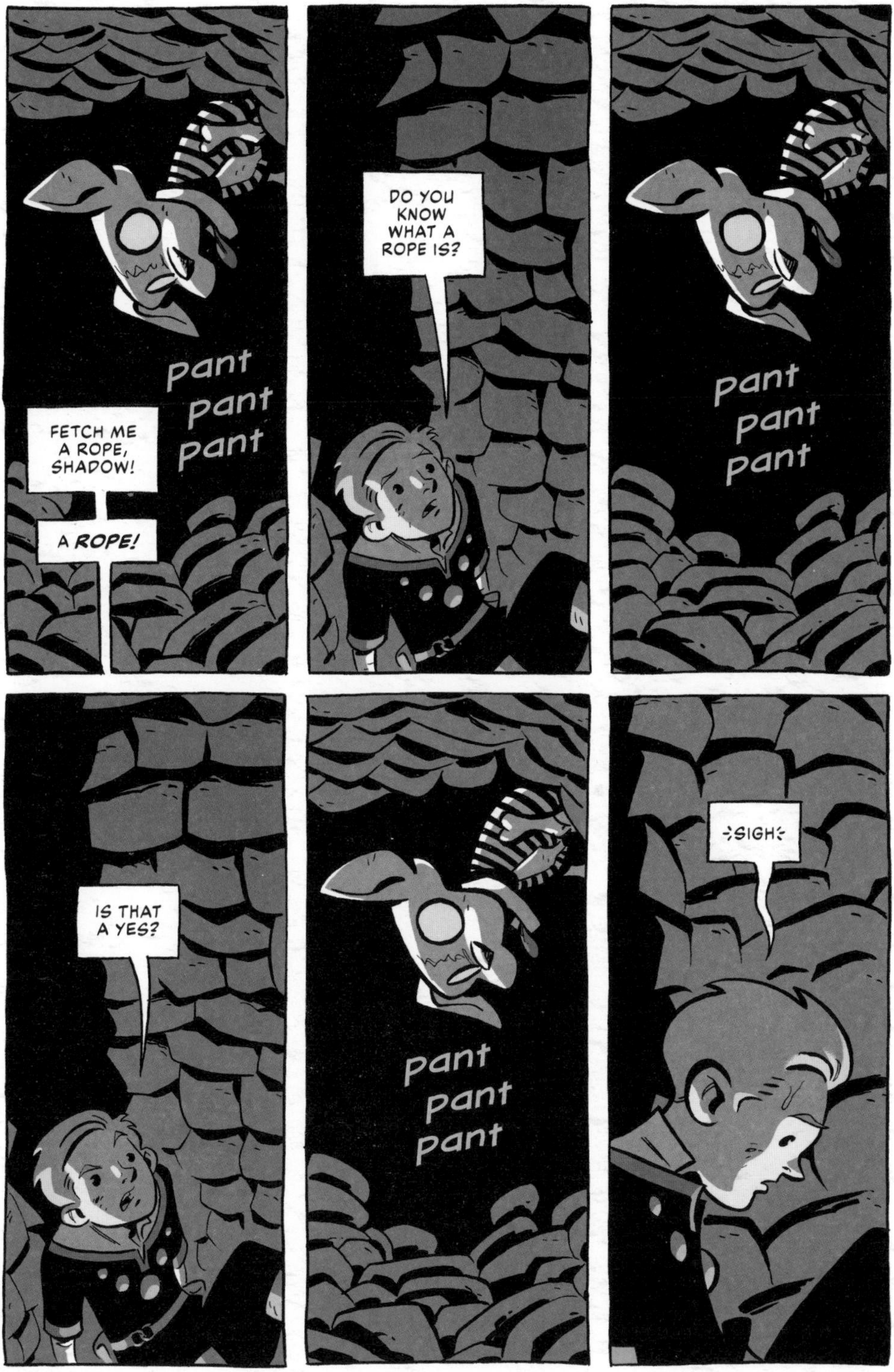
pant
pant
pant
FETCH ME A ROPE, SHADOW!
A ROPE!
DO YOU KNOW WHAT A ROPE IS?
pant
pant
pant
IS THAT A YES?
pant
pant
pant
-SIGH-

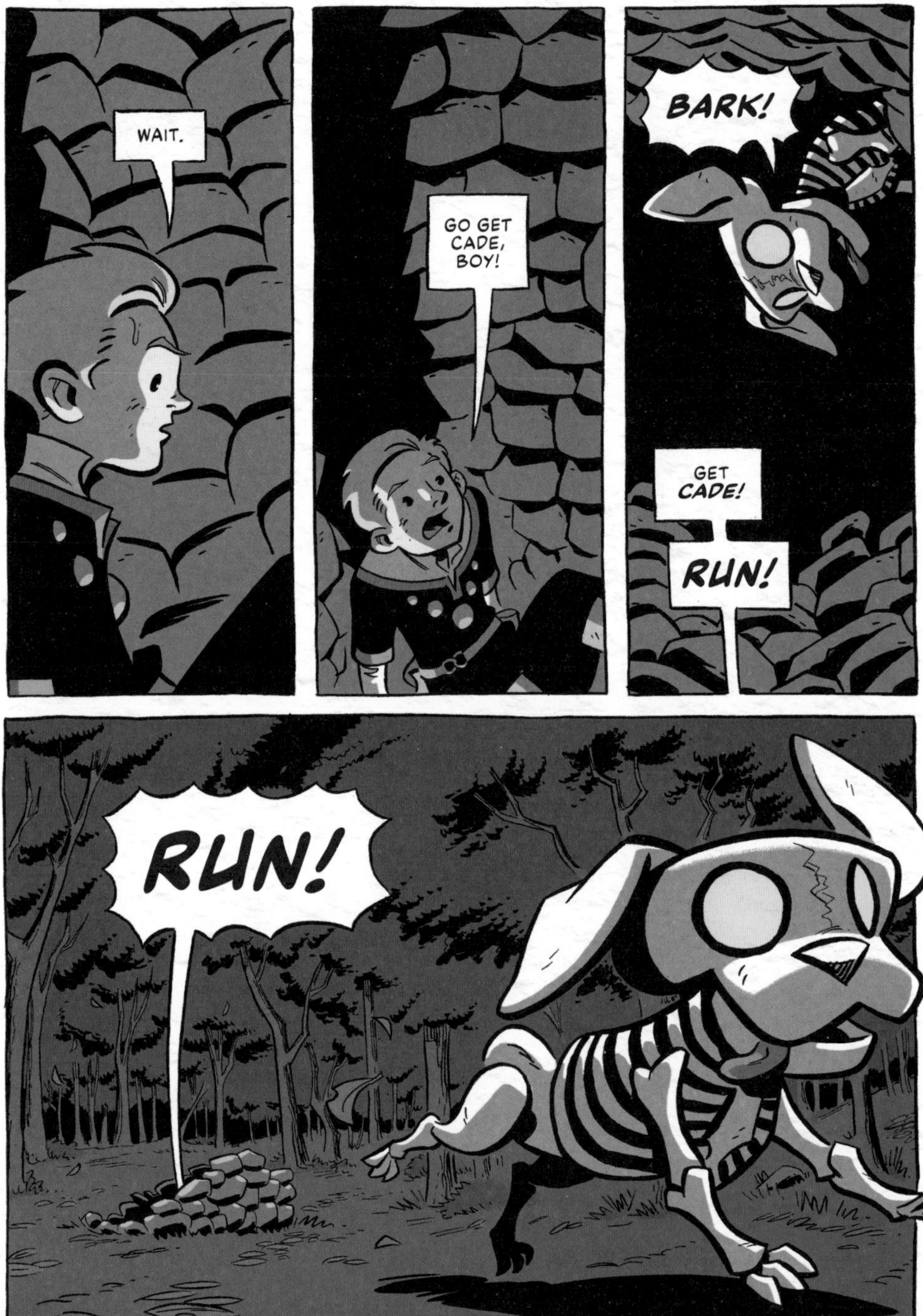
WAIT.
GO GET CADE, BOY!
BARK!
GET CADE!
RUN!
RUN!

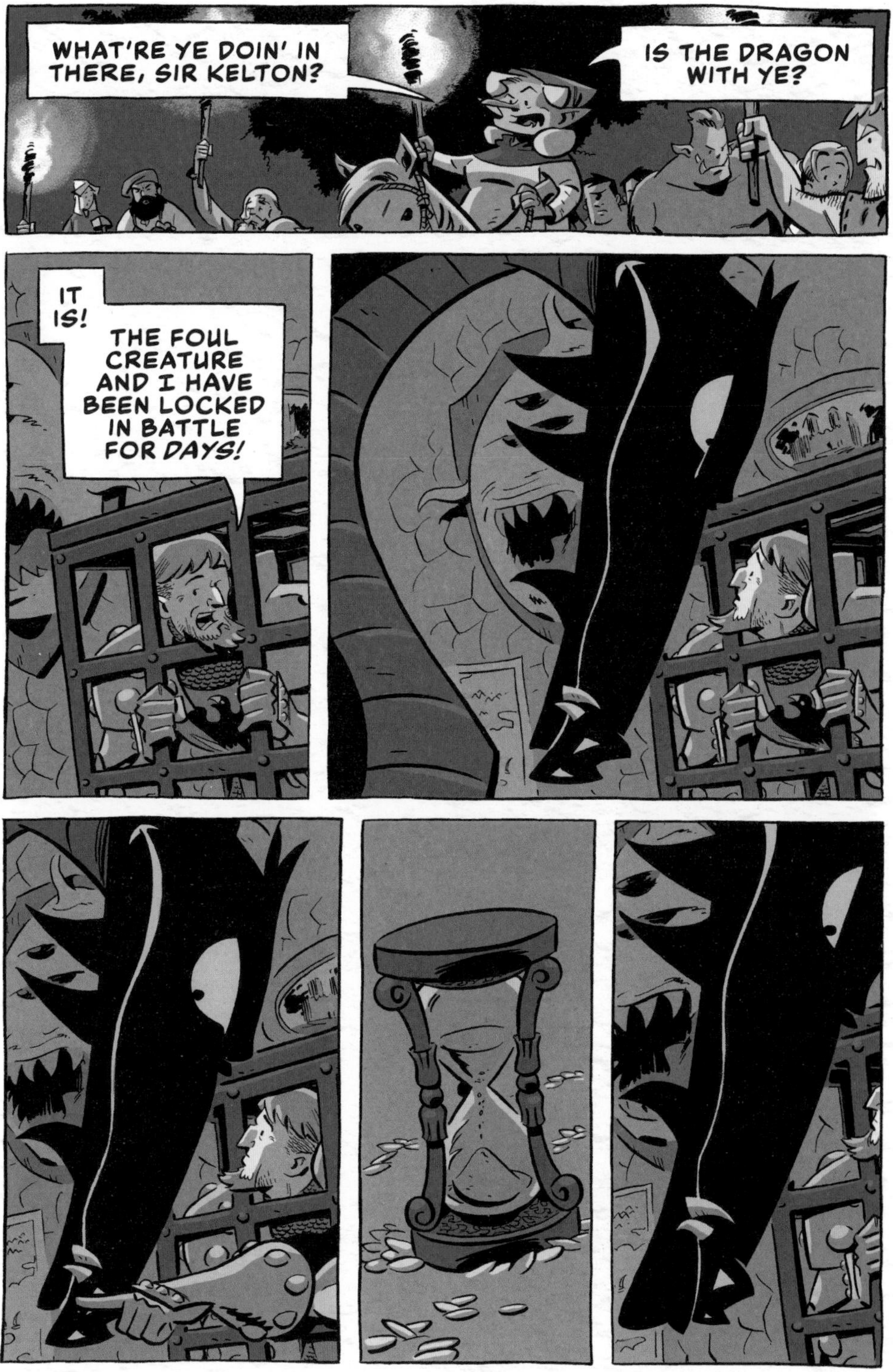
WHAT'RE YE DOIN' IN THERE, SIR KELTON?
IS THE DRAGON WITH YE?
IT IS!
THE FOUL CREATURE AND I HAVE BEEN LOCKED IN BATTLE FOR *DAYS!*

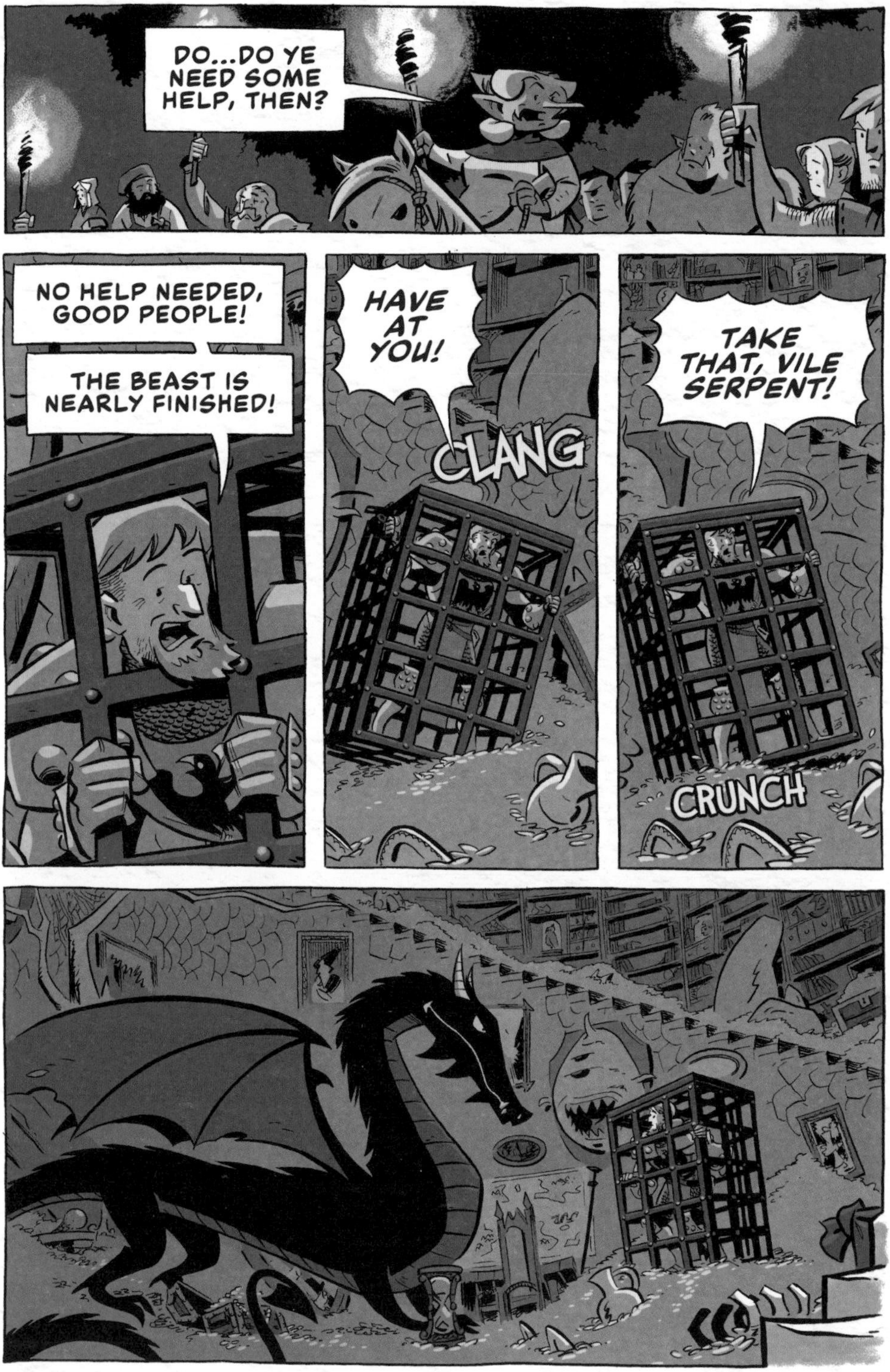
DO...DO YE NEED SOME HELP, THEN?
NO HELP NEEDED, GOOD PEOPLE!
THE BEAST IS NEARLY FINISHED!
HAVE AT YOU!
CLANG
TAKE THAT, VILE SERPENT!
CRUNCH

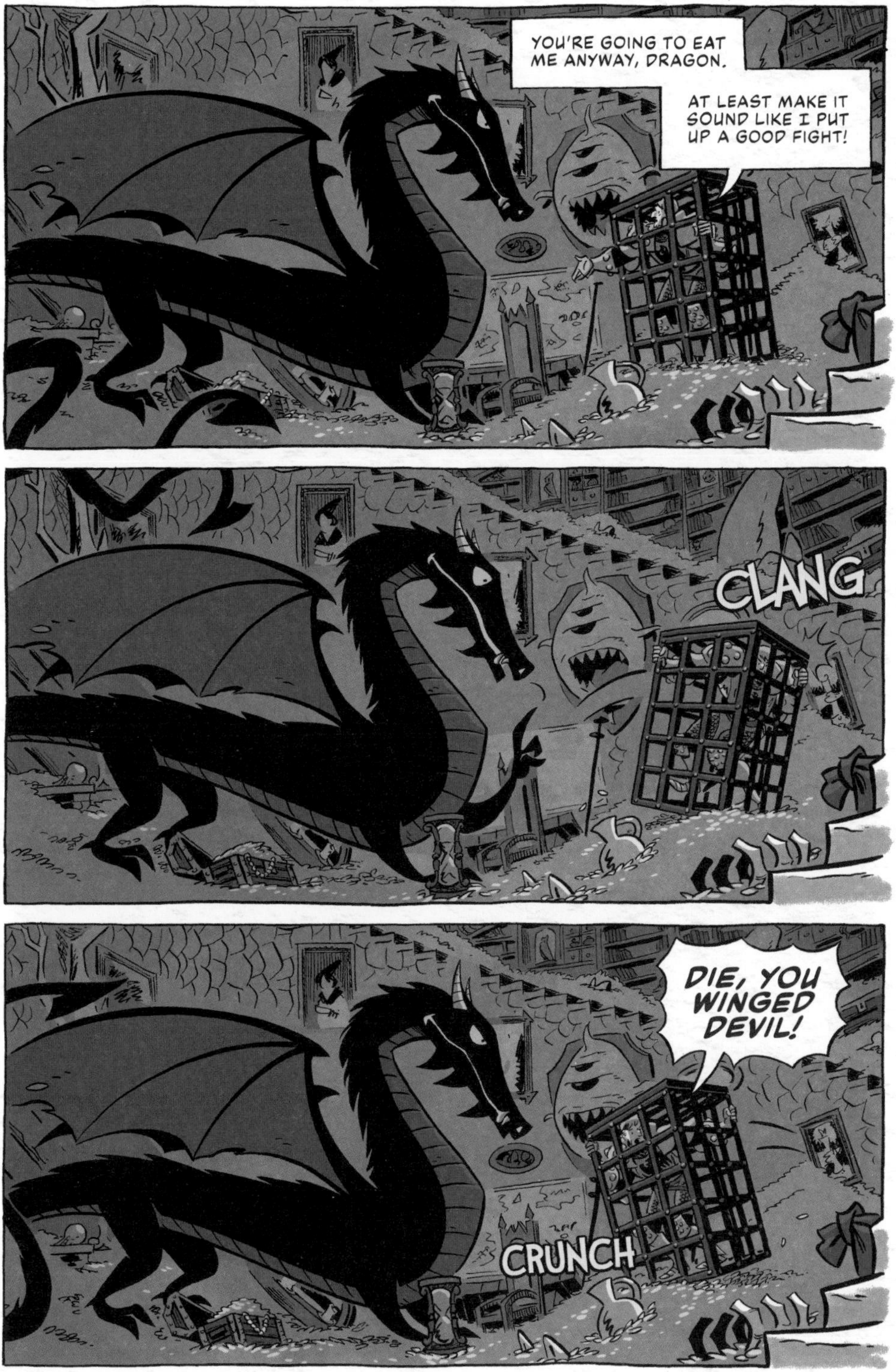
YOU'RE GOING TO EAT ME ANYWAY, DRAGON.
AT LEAST MAKE IT SOUND LIKE I PUT UP A GOOD FIGHT!
CLANG
DIE, YOU WINGED DEVIL!
CRUNCH

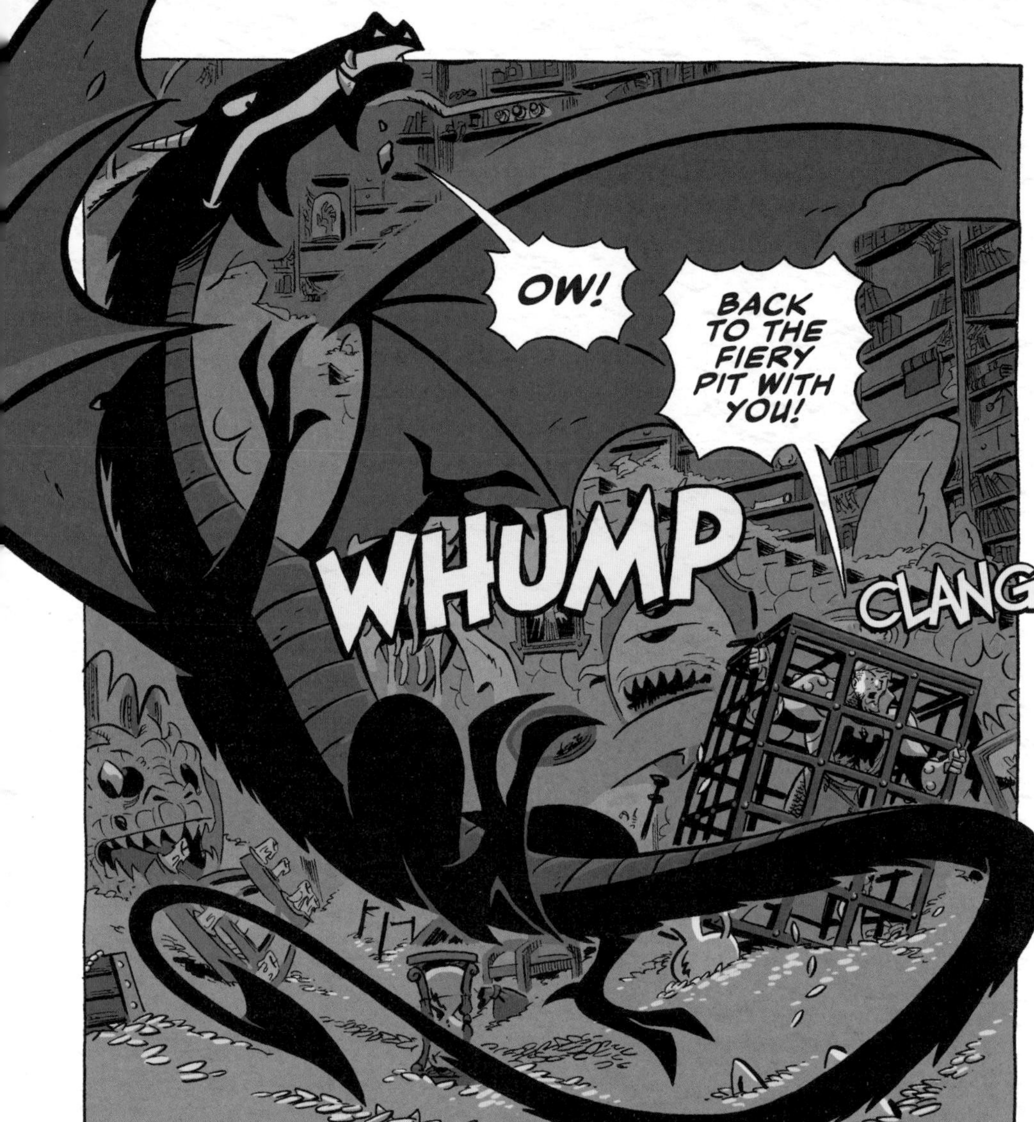
OW!
BACK TO THE FIERY PIT WITH YOU!
WHUMP
CLANG

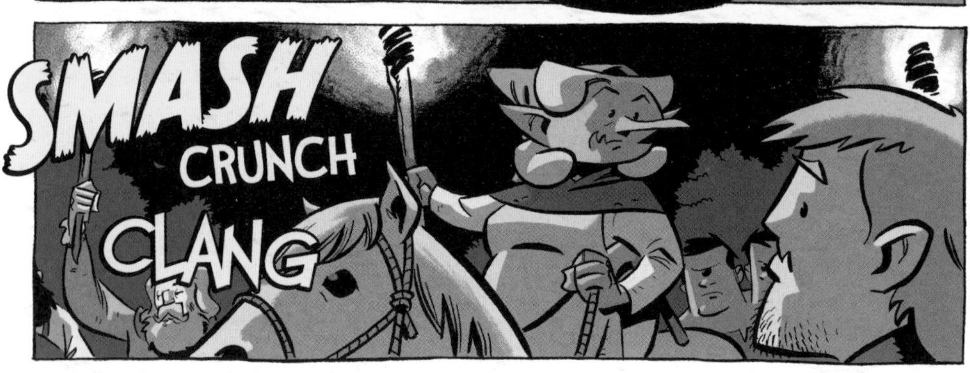
SMASH
CRUNCH
CLANG

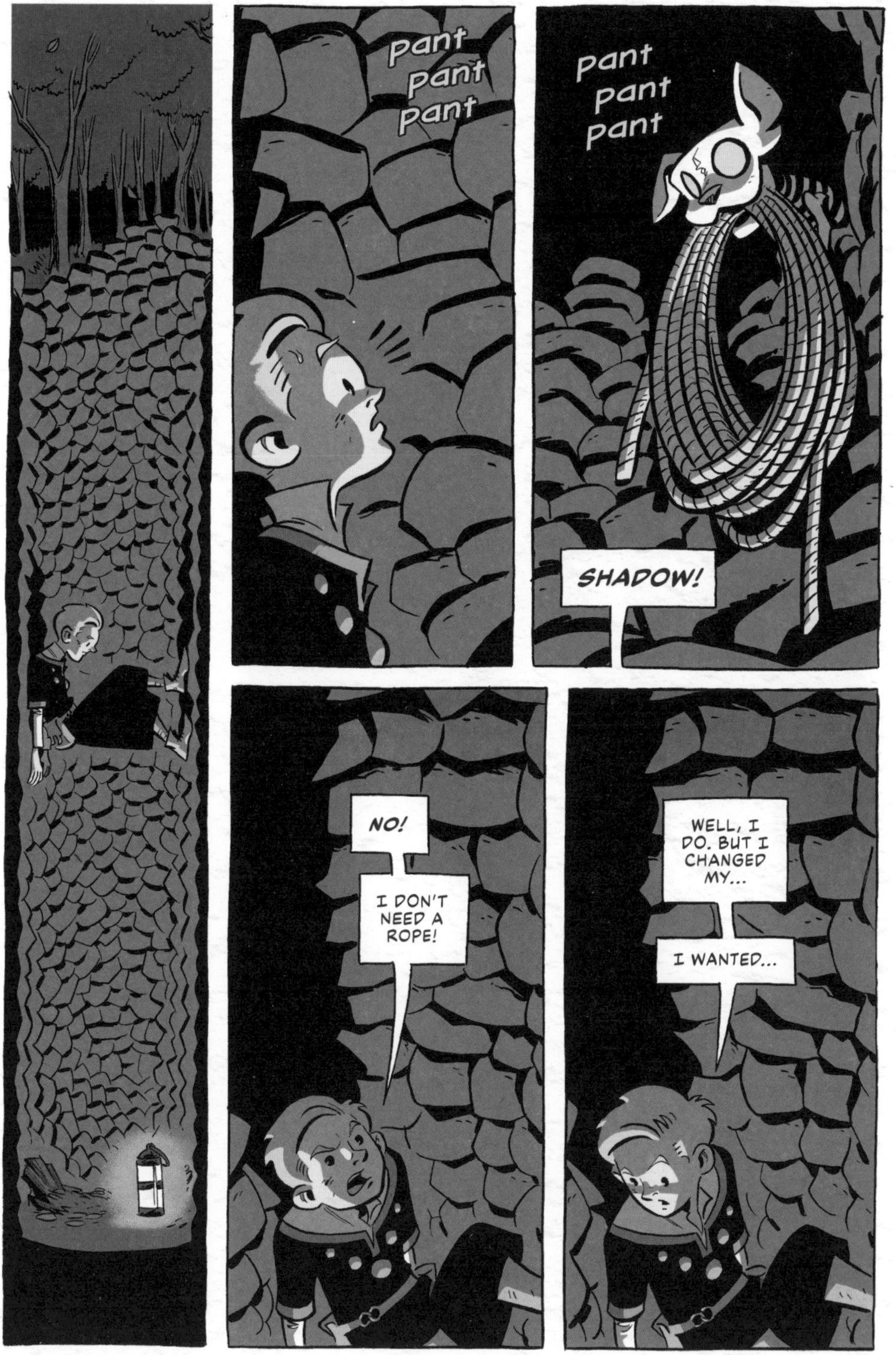
pant
pant
pant
pant
pant
pant
SHADOW!
NO!
I DON'T NEED A ROPE!
WELL, I DO. BUT I CHANGED MY...
I WANTED...

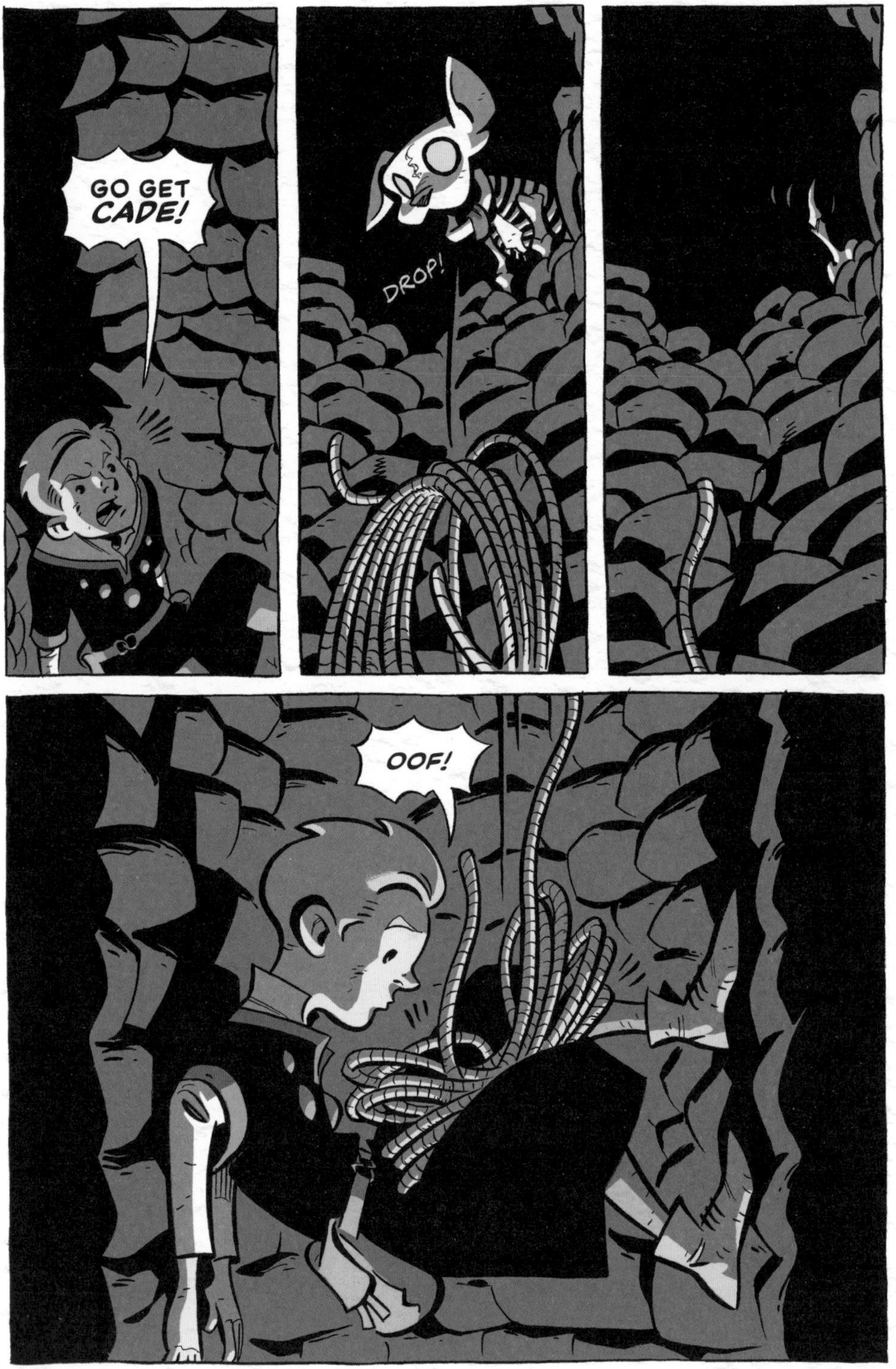
GO GET CADE!
DROP!
OOF!

CRASH

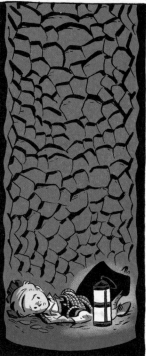

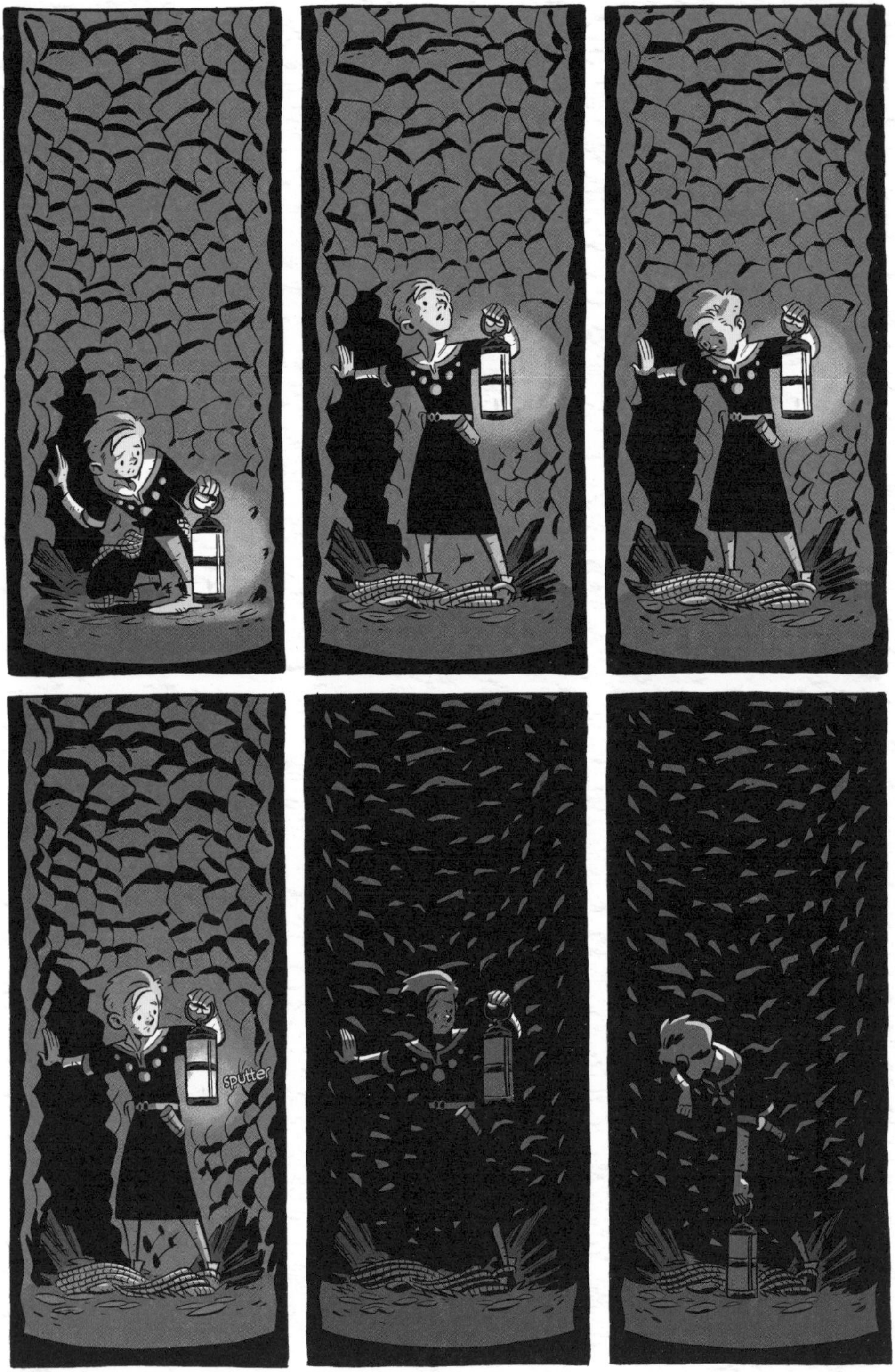
sputter

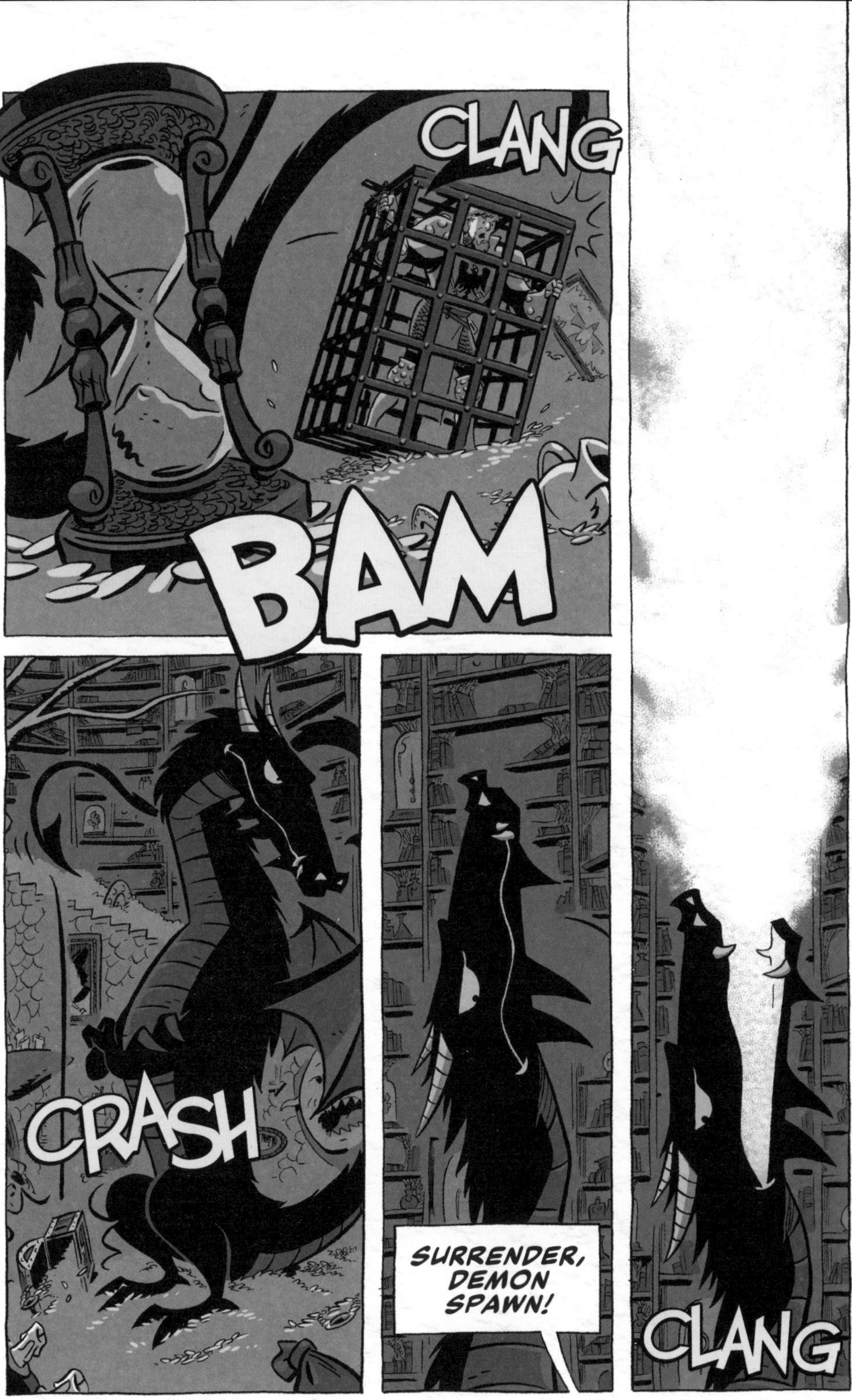
CLANG
BAM
CRASH
SURRENDER, DEMON SPAWN!
CLANG

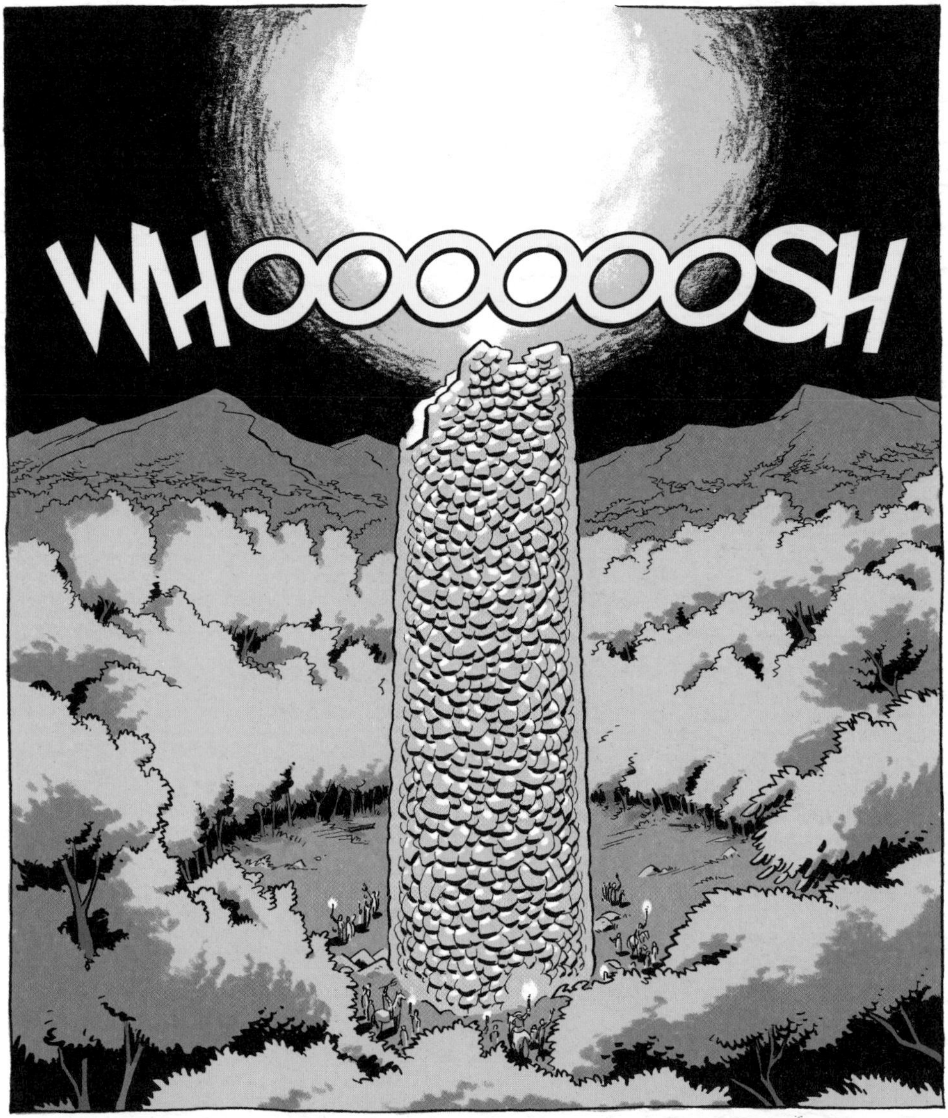
WHOOOOOOSH

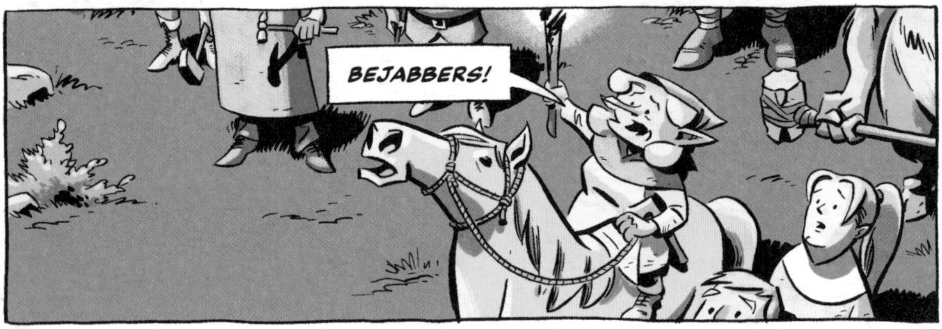
BEJABBERS!

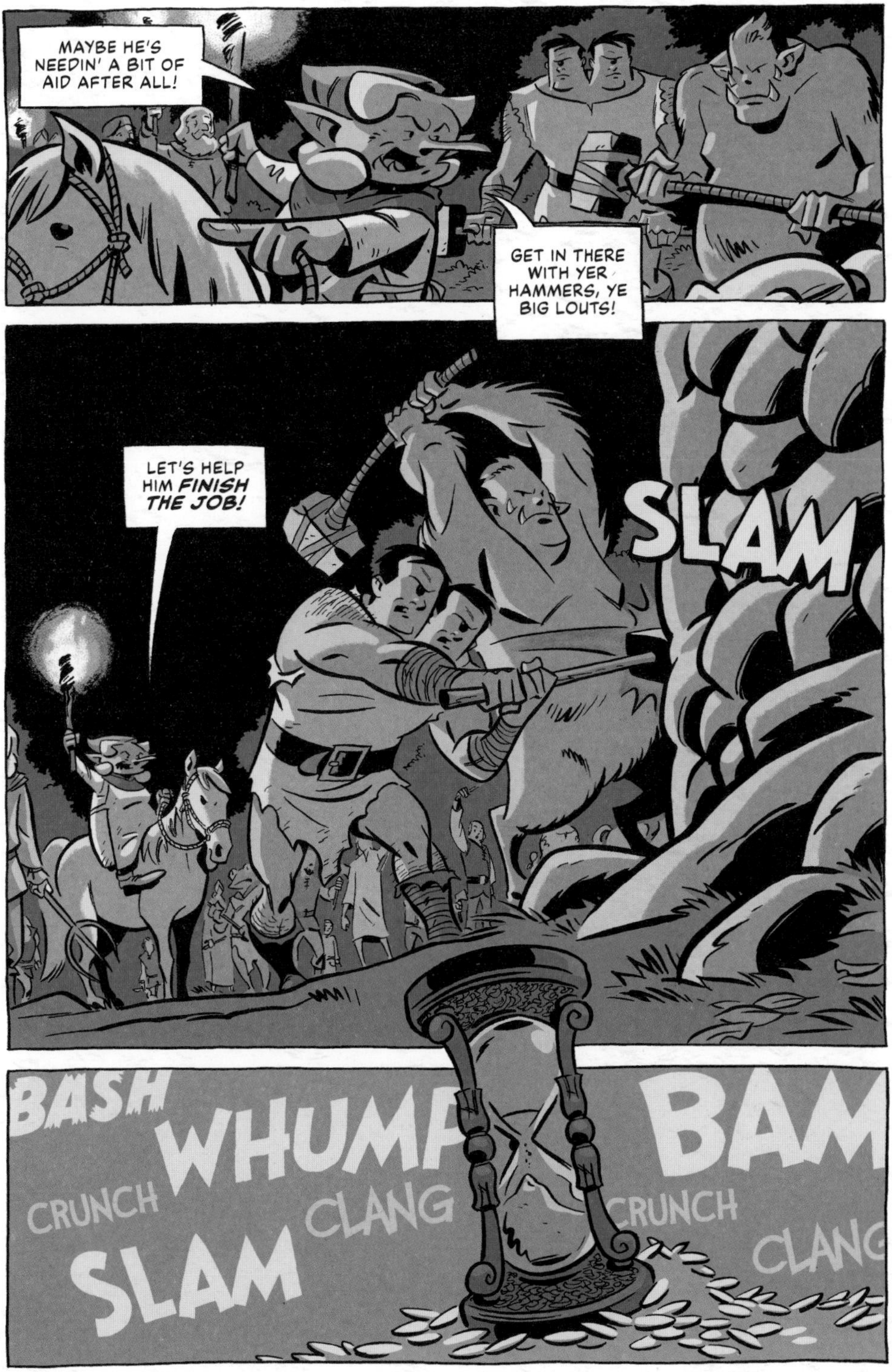
MAYBE HE'S NEEDIN' A BIT OF AID AFTER ALL!
GET IN THERE WITH YER HAMMERS, YE BIG LOUTS!
LET'S HELP HIM *FINISH THE JOB!*
SLAM
BASH
WHUMP
BAM
CRUNCH
CLANG
CRUNCH
SLAM
CLANG

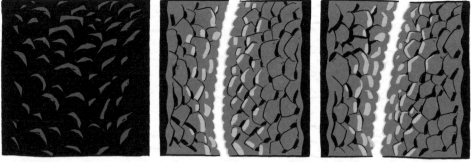

# CHAPTER EIGHT

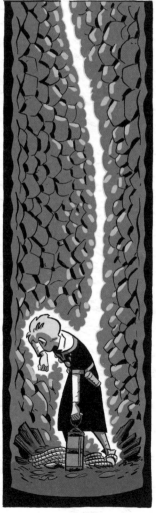

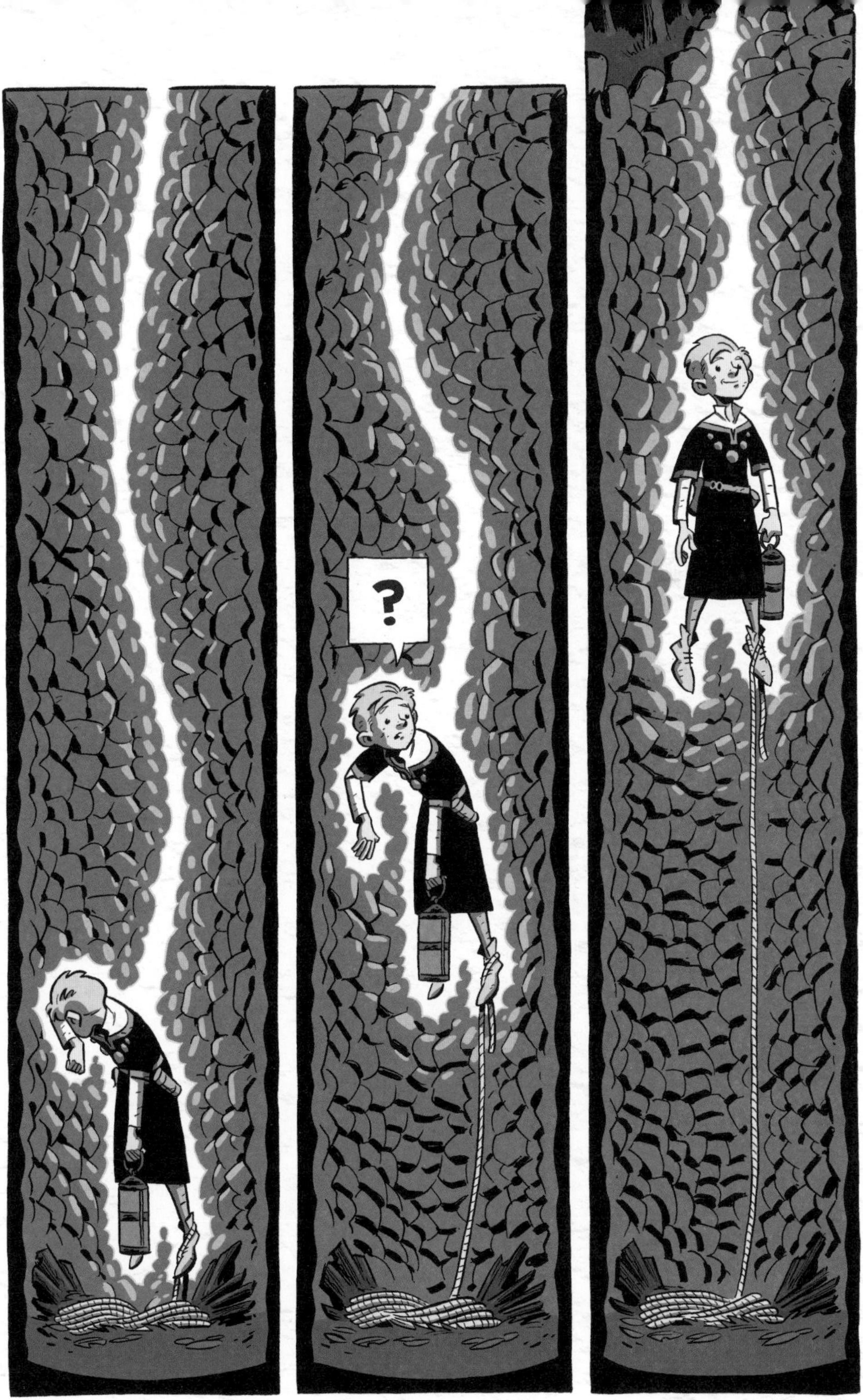
?

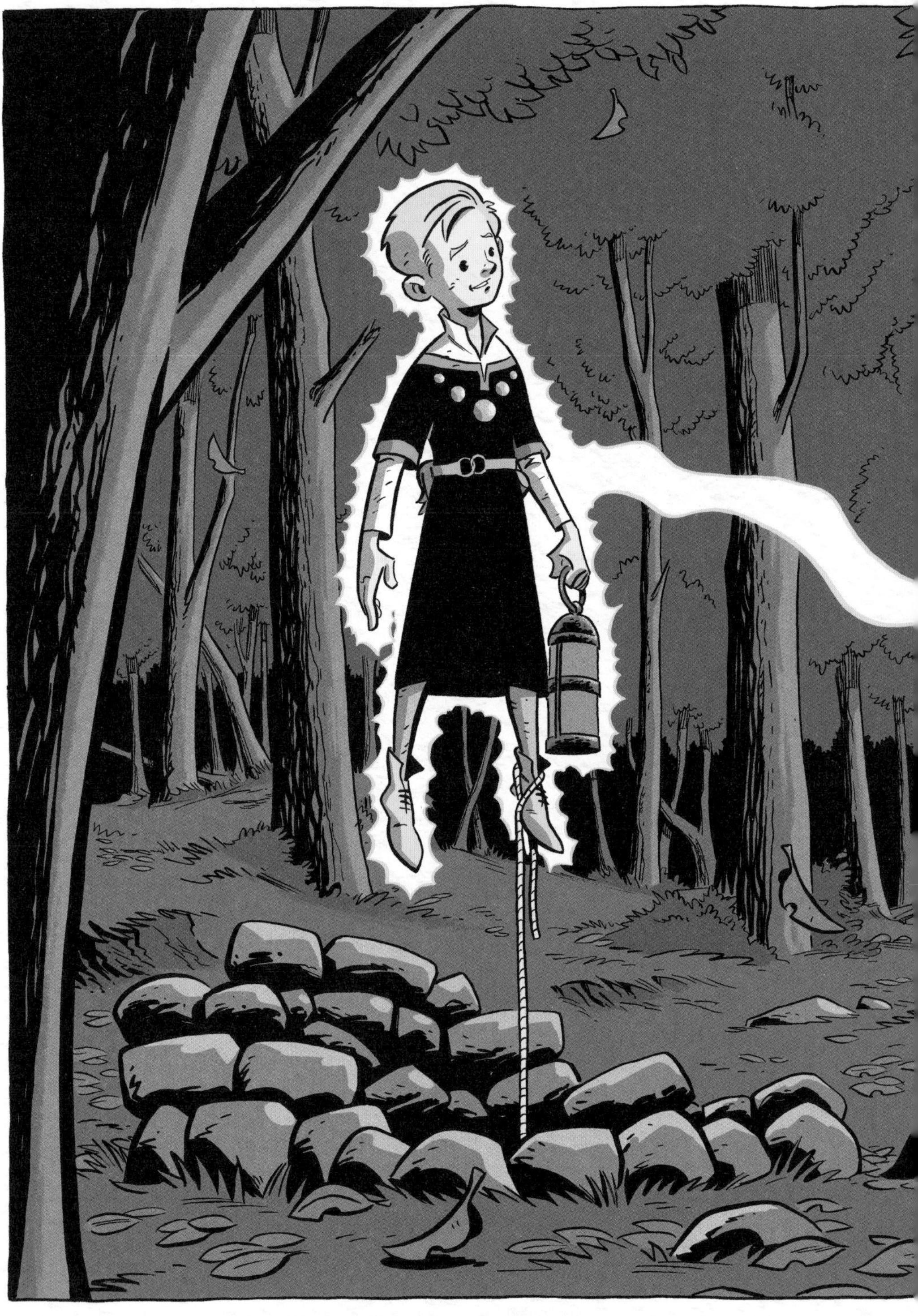

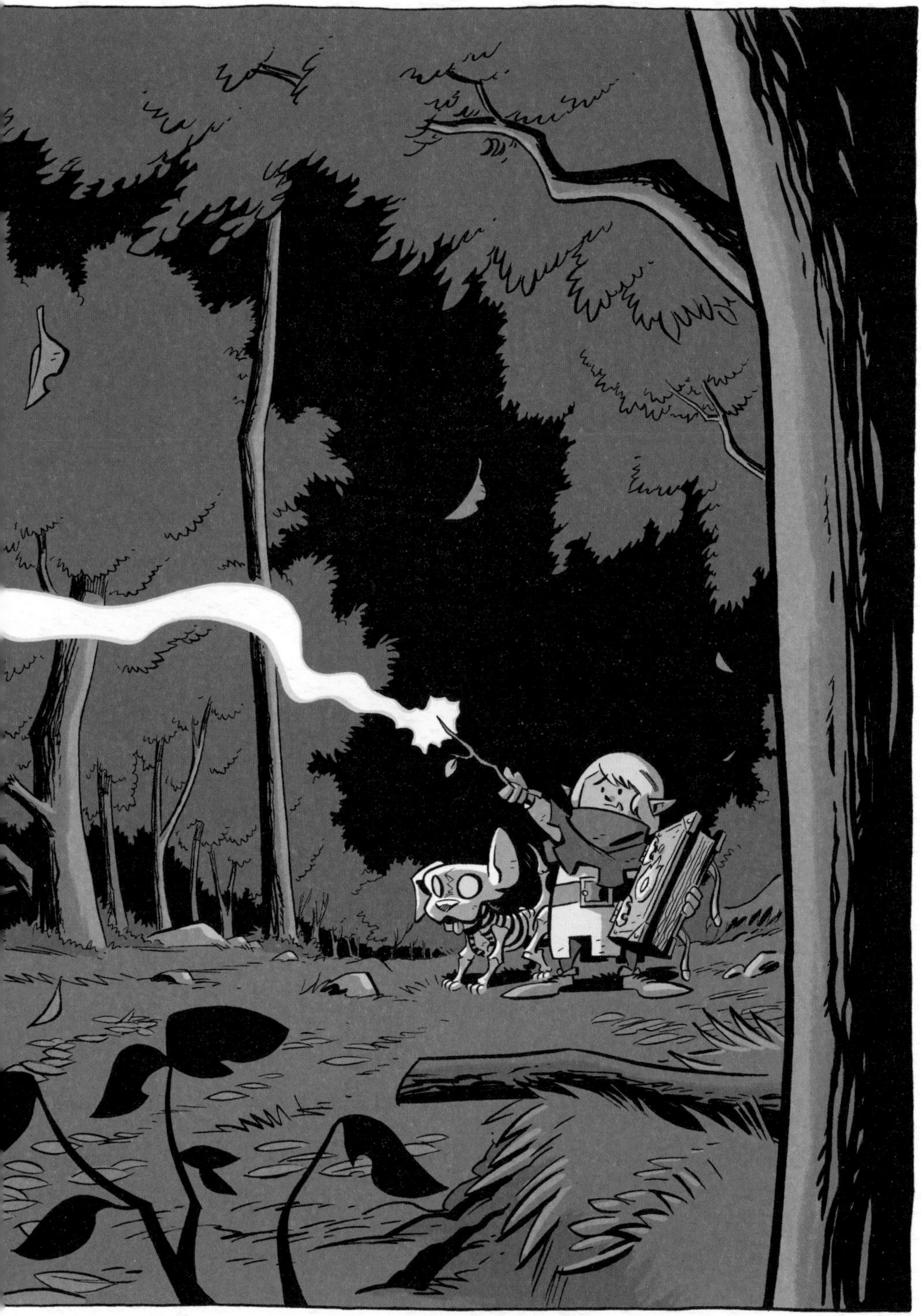

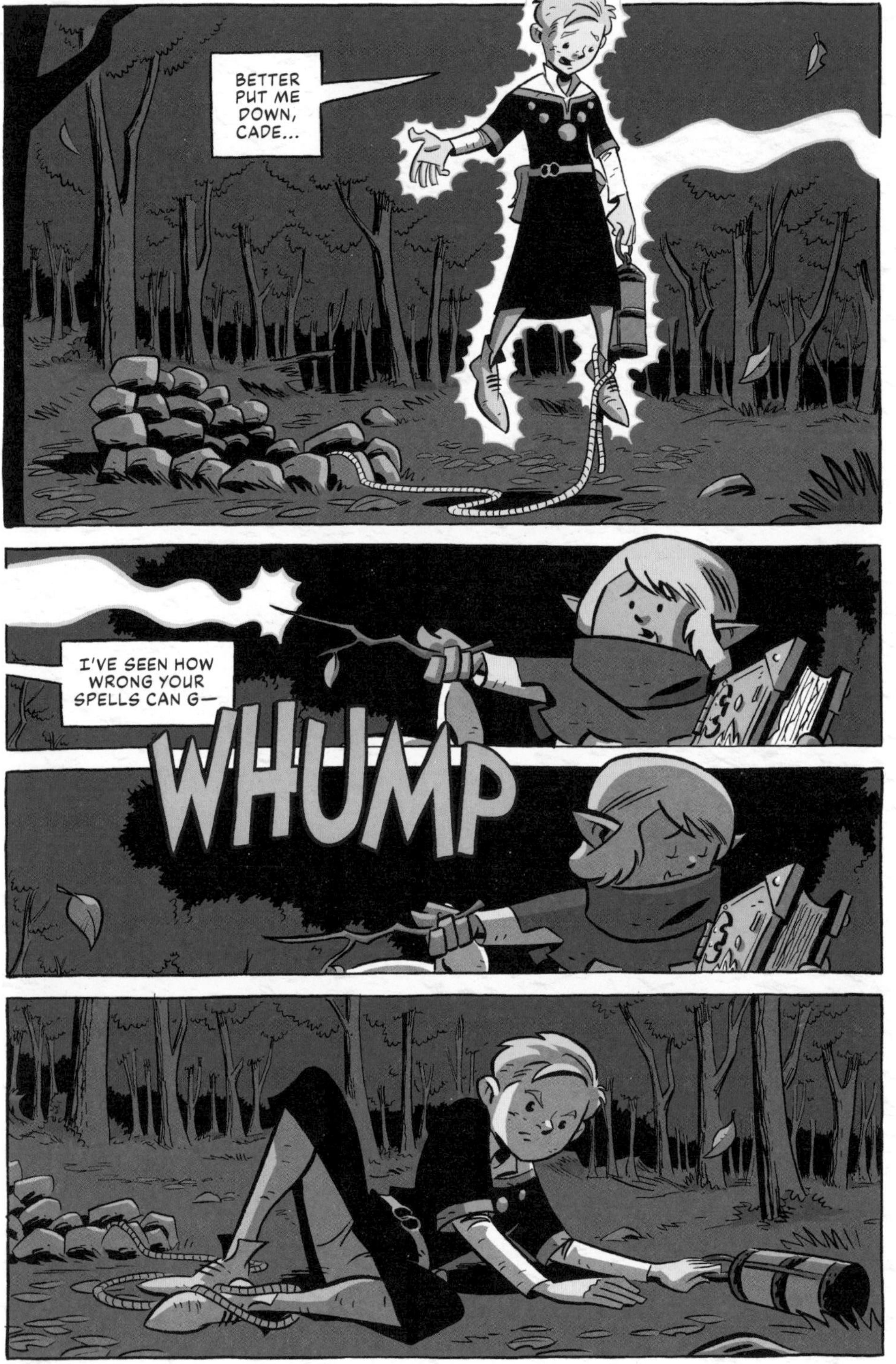
BETTER PUT ME DOWN, CADE...
I'VE SEEN HOW WRONG YOUR SPELLS CAN G—
WHUMP

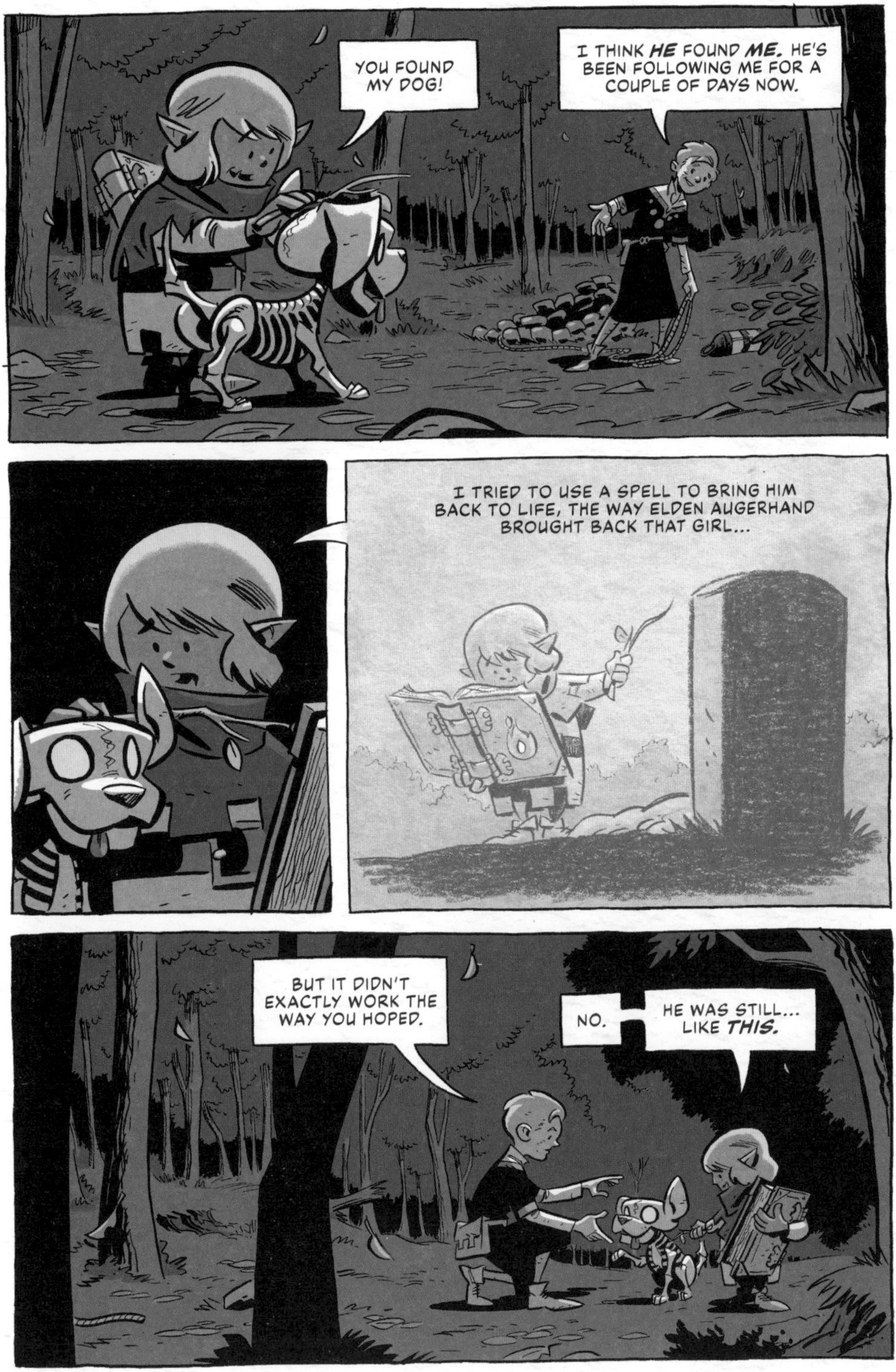
YOU FOUND MY DOG!
I THINK HE FOUND ME. HE'S BEEN FOLLOWING ME FOR A COUPLE OF DAYS NOW.
I TRIED TO USE A SPELL TO BRING HIM BACK TO LIFE, THE WAY ELDEN AUGERHAND BROUGHT BACK THAT GIRL...
BUT IT DIDN'T EXACTLY WORK THE WAY YOU HOPED.
NO.
HE WAS STILL... LIKE THIS.

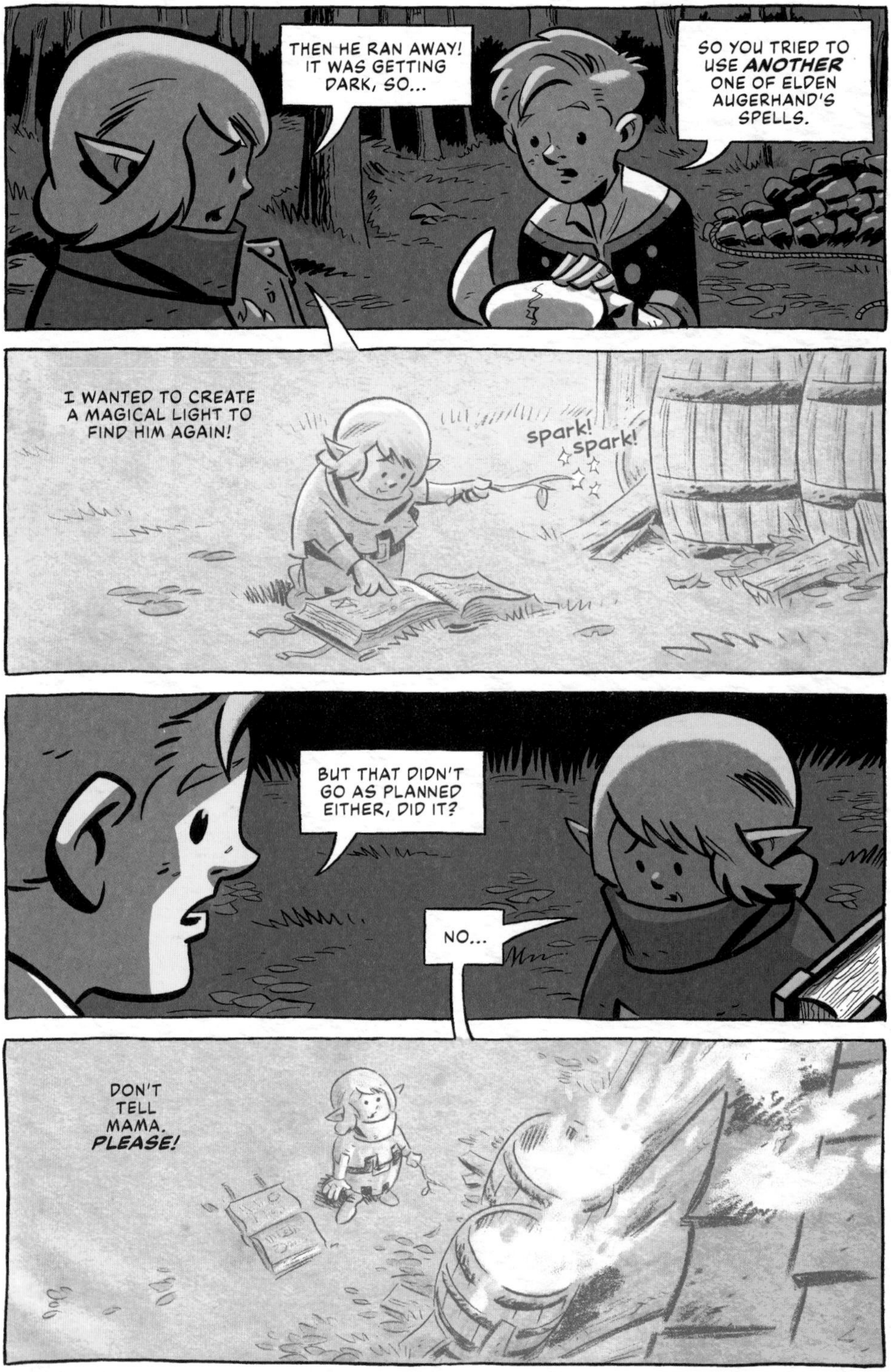
THEN HE RAN AWAY! IT WAS GETTING DARK, SO...
SO YOU TRIED TO USE ANOTHER ONE OF ELDEN AUGERHAND'S SPELLS.
I WANTED TO CREATE A MAGICAL LIGHT TO FIND HIM AGAIN!
spark! spark!
BUT THAT DIDN'T GO AS PLANNED EITHER, DID IT?
NO...
DON'T TELL MAMA. PLEASE!

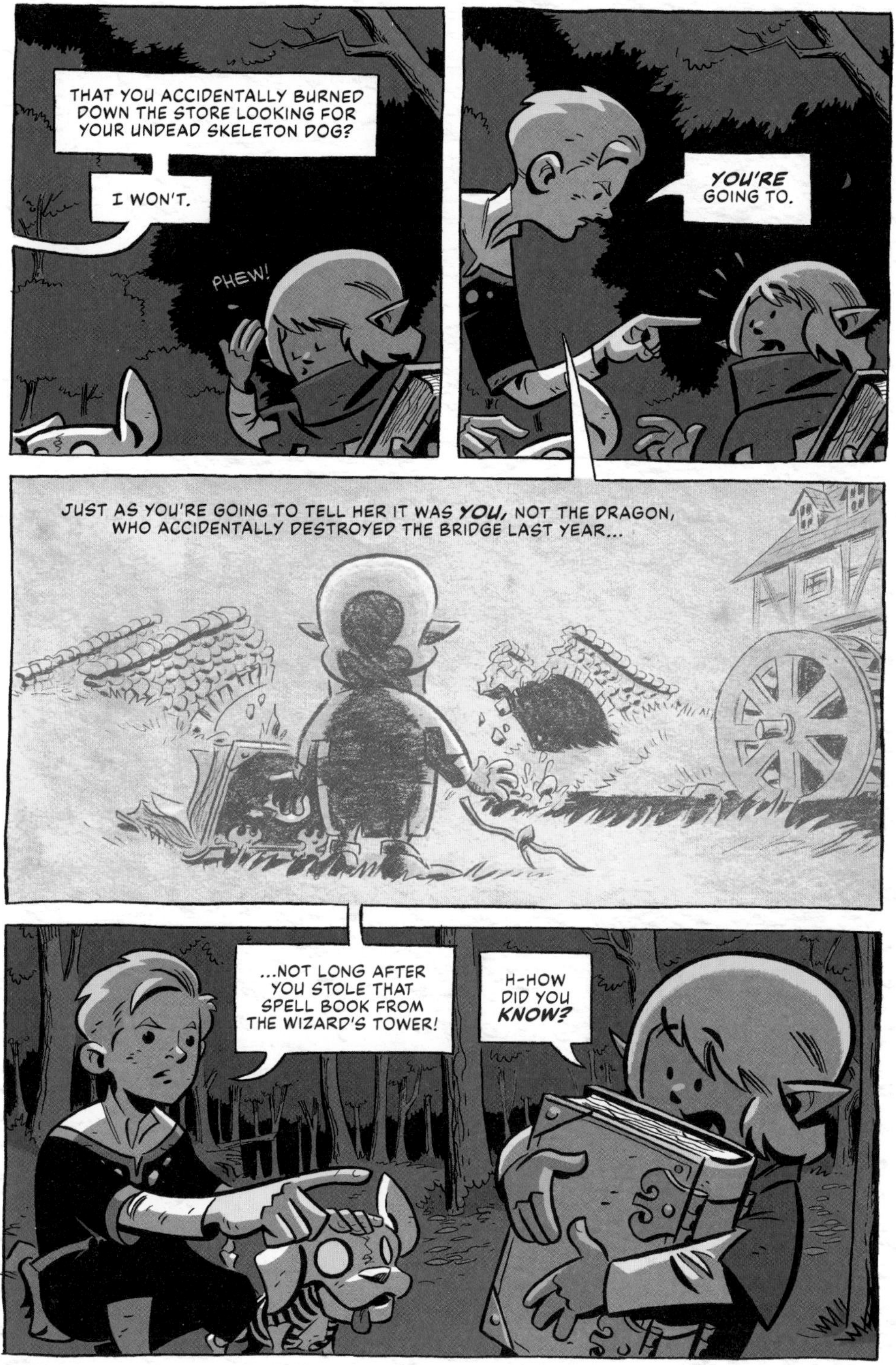
THAT YOU ACCIDENTALLY BURNED DOWN THE STORE LOOKING FOR YOUR UNDEAD SKELETON DOG?
I WON'T.
PHEW!
YOU'RE GOING TO.
JUST AS YOU'RE GOING TO TELL HER IT WAS YOU, NOT THE DRAGON, WHO ACCIDENTALLY DESTROYED THE BRIDGE LAST YEAR...
...NOT LONG AFTER YOU STOLE THAT SPELL BOOK FROM THE WIZARD'S TOWER!
H-HOW DID YOU KNOW?

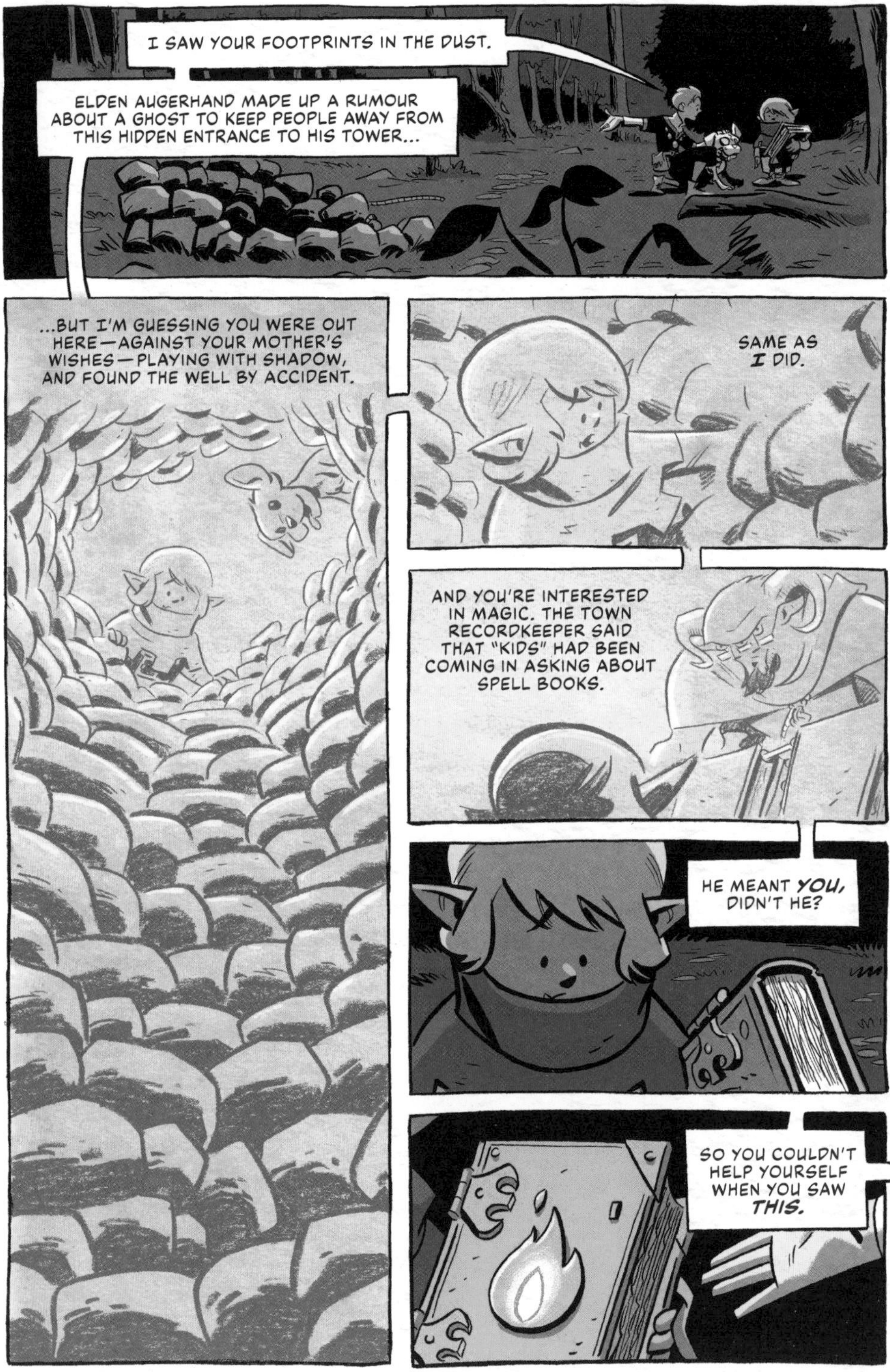

I SAW YOUR FOOTPRINTS IN THE DUST.
ELDEN AUGERHAND MADE UP A RUMOUR ABOUT A GHOST TO KEEP PEOPLE AWAY FROM THIS HIDDEN ENTRANCE TO HIS TOWER...
...BUT I'M GUESSING YOU WERE OUT HERE—AGAINST YOUR MOTHER'S WISHES—PLAYING WITH SHADOW, AND FOUND THE WELL BY ACCIDENT.
SAME AS *I* DID.
AND YOU'RE INTERESTED IN MAGIC. THE TOWN RECORDKEEPER SAID THAT "KIDS" HAD BEEN COMING IN ASKING ABOUT SPELL BOOKS.
HE MEANT *YOU,* DIDN'T HE?
SO YOU COULDN'T HELP YOURSELF WHEN YOU SAW *THIS.*

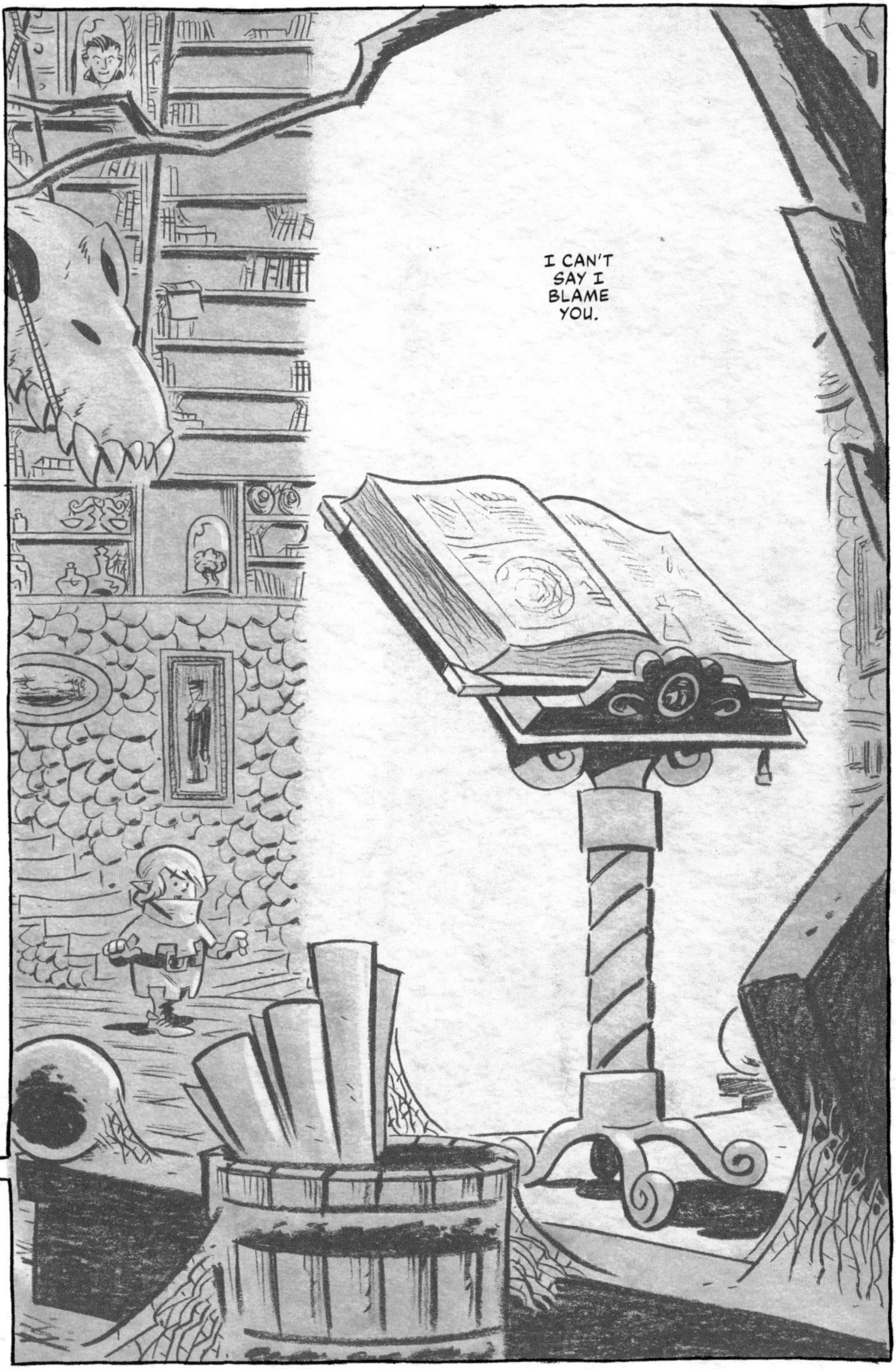
I CAN'T SAY I BLAME YOU.

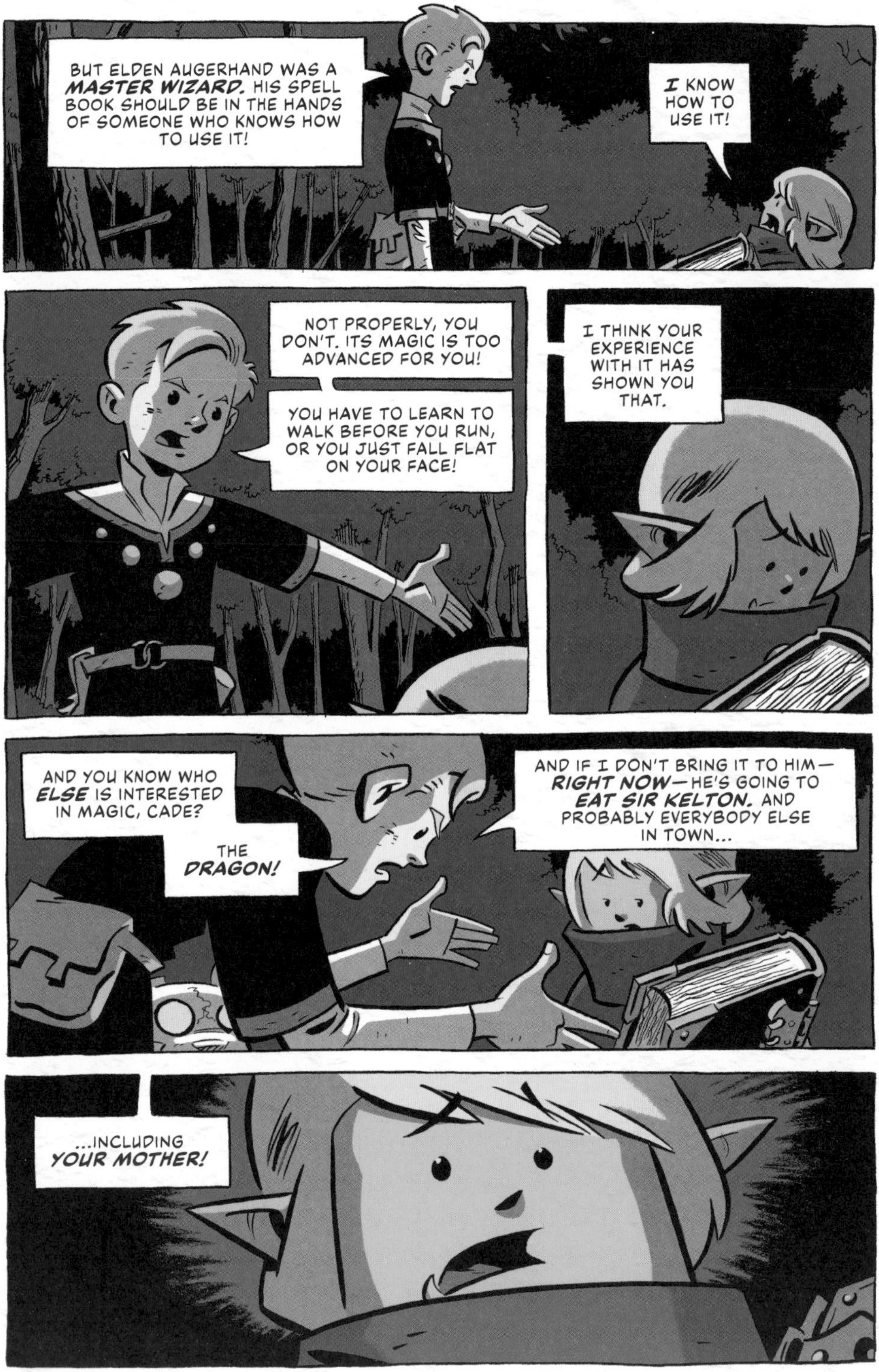
BUT ELDEN AUGERHAND WAS A MASTER WIZARD. HIS SPELL BOOK SHOULD BE IN THE HANDS OF SOMEONE WHO KNOWS HOW TO USE IT!
I KNOW HOW TO USE IT!
NOT PROPERLY, YOU DON'T. ITS MAGIC IS TOO ADVANCED FOR YOU!
YOU HAVE TO LEARN TO WALK BEFORE YOU RUN, OR YOU JUST FALL FLAT ON YOUR FACE!
I THINK YOUR EXPERIENCE WITH IT HAS SHOWN YOU THAT.
AND YOU KNOW WHO ELSE IS INTERESTED IN MAGIC, CADE?
THE DRAGON!
AND IF I DON'T BRING IT TO HIM— RIGHT NOW—HE'S GOING TO EAT SIR KELTON. AND PROBABLY EVERYBODY ELSE IN TOWN...
...INCLUDING YOUR MOTHER!

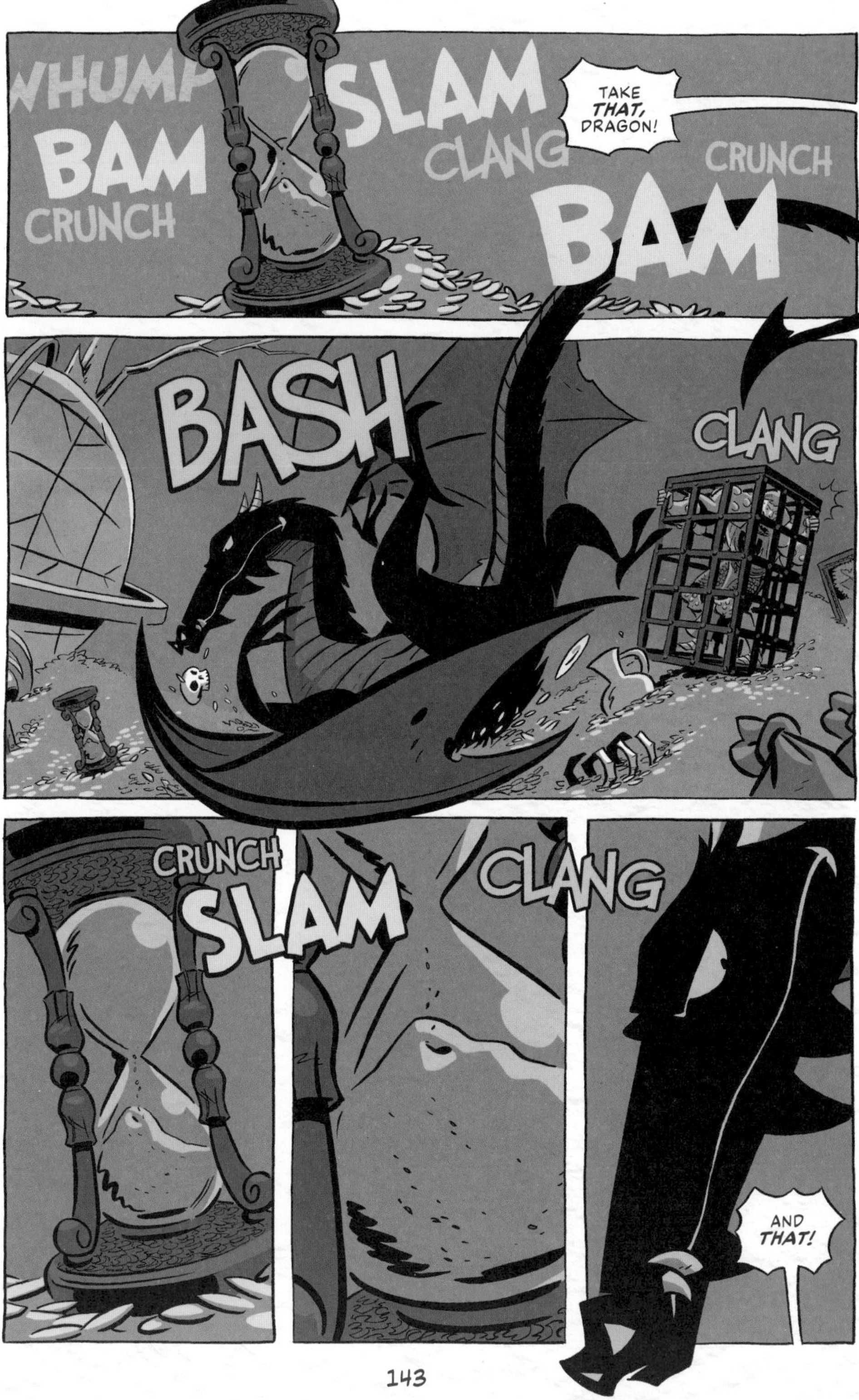

WHUMP
BAM
CRUNCH
SLAM
CLANG
TAKE *THAT,* DRAGON!
CRUNCH
BAM
BASH
CLANG
CRUNCH
SLAM
CLANG
AND *THAT!*

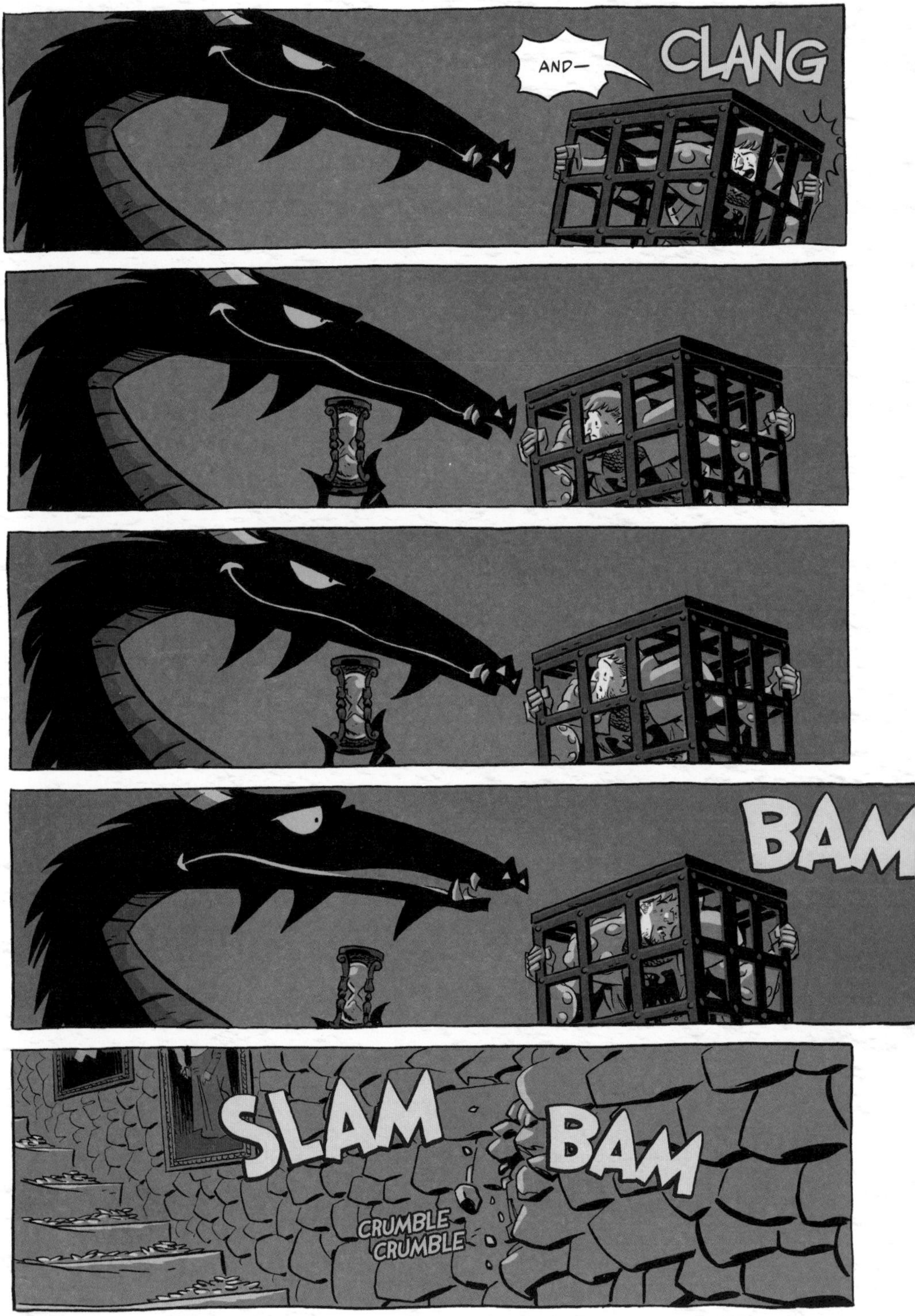
AND—
CLANG
BAM
SLAM
BAM
CRUMBLE
CRUMBLE

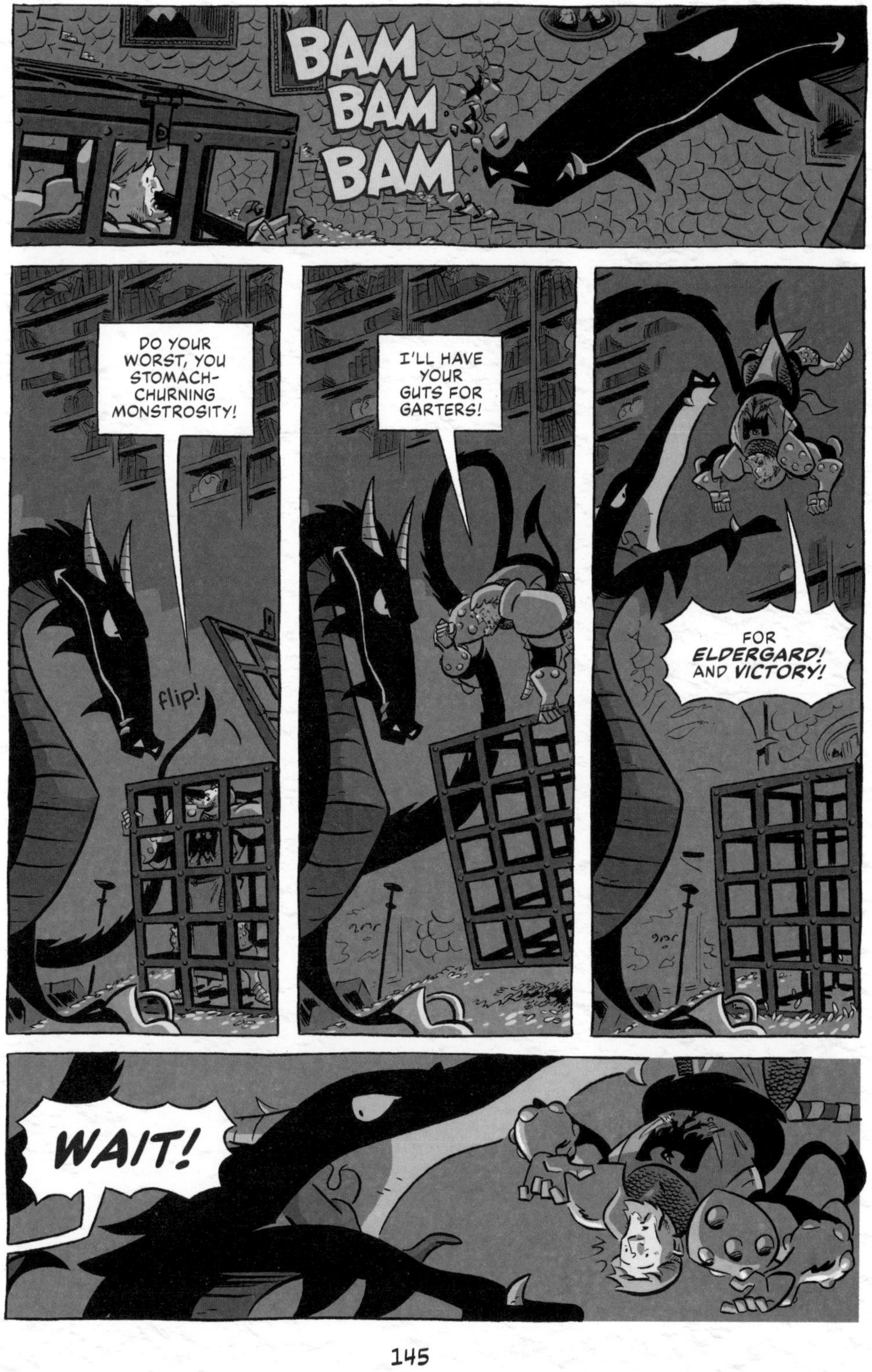
BAM
BAM
BAM
DO YOUR WORST, YOU STOMACH-CHURNING MONSTROSITY!
flip!
I'LL HAVE YOUR GUTS FOR GARTERS!
FOR ELDERGARD! AND VICTORY!
WAIT!

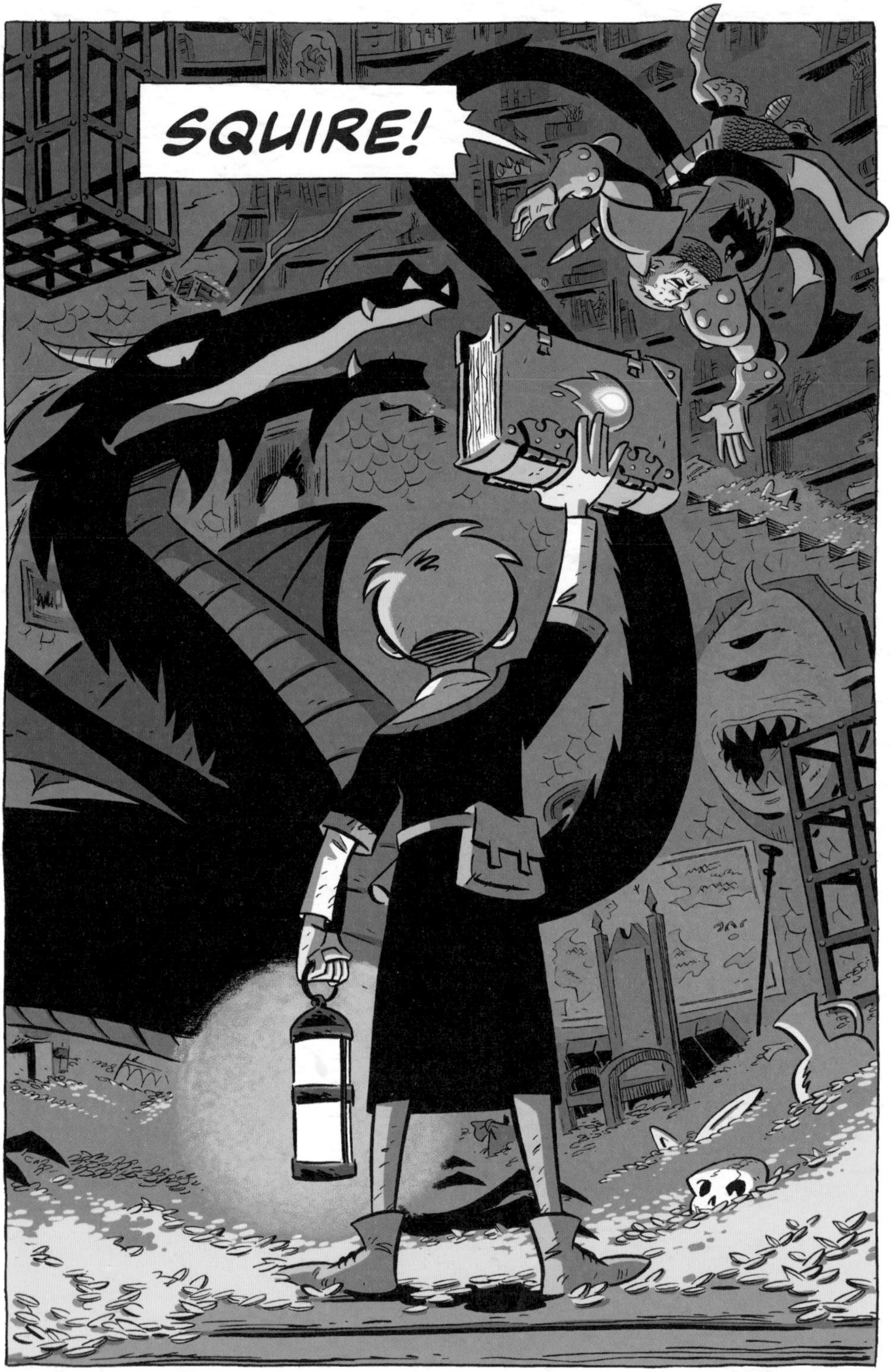
SQUIRE!

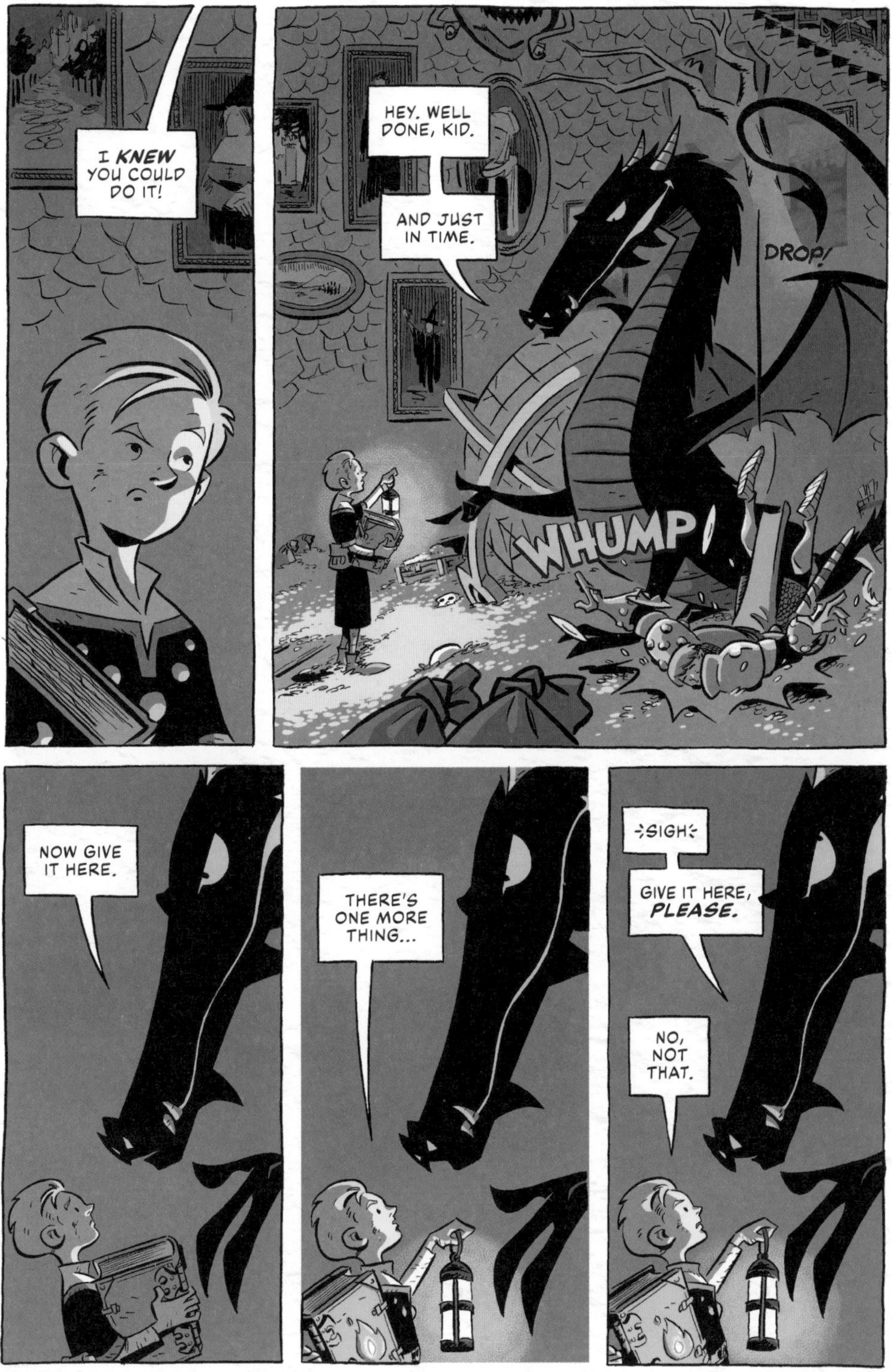
I *KNEW* YOU COULD DO IT!
HEY. WELL DONE, KID.
AND JUST IN TIME.
DROP!
WHUMP
NOW GIVE IT HERE.
THERE'S ONE MORE THING...
SIGH
GIVE IT HERE, *PLEASE.*
NO, NOT THAT.

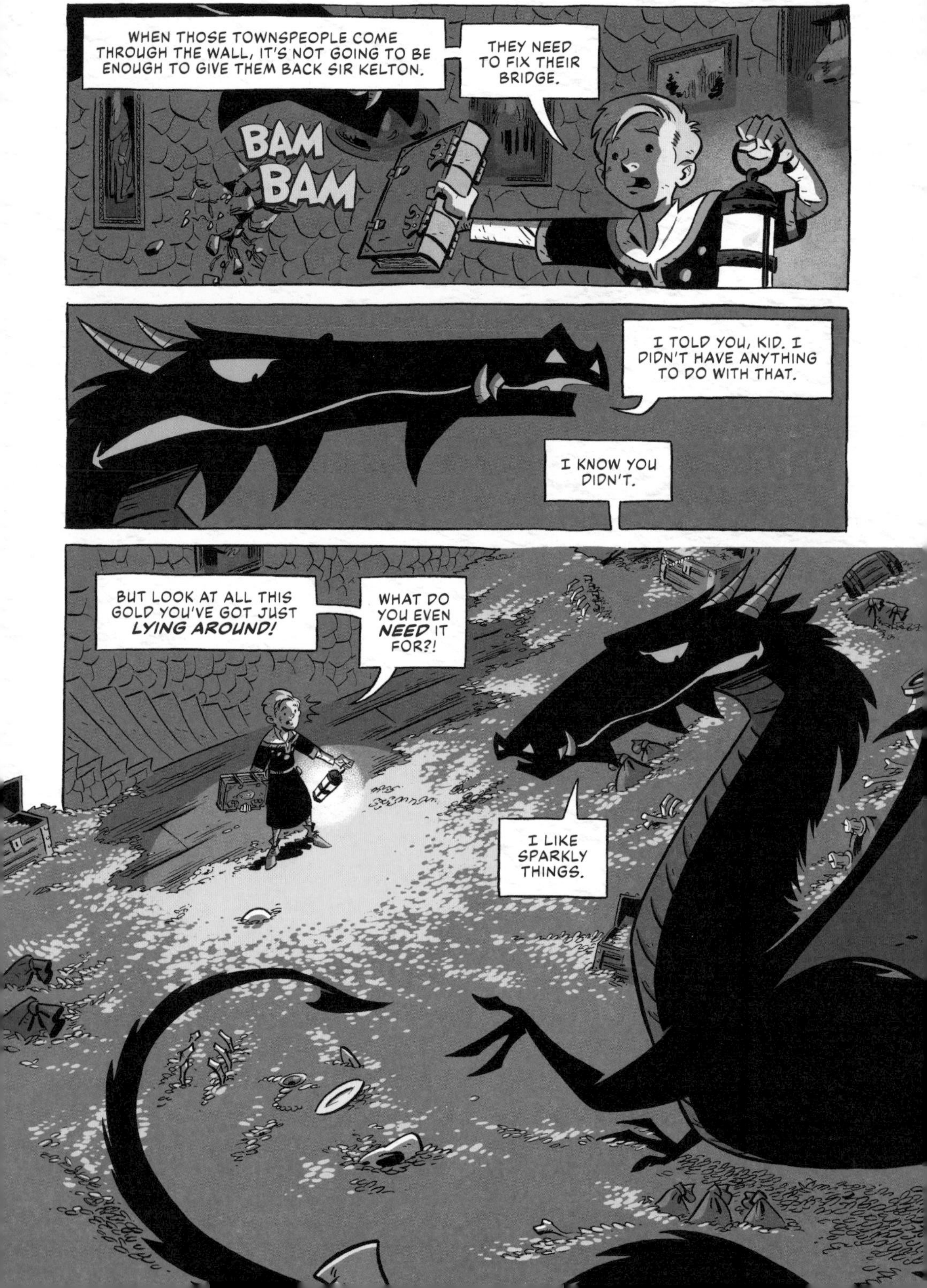
WHEN THOSE TOWNSPEOPLE COME THROUGH THE WALL, IT'S NOT GOING TO BE ENOUGH TO GIVE THEM BACK SIR KELTON.
THEY NEED TO FIX THEIR BRIDGE.
BAM BAM
I TOLD YOU, KID. I DIDN'T HAVE ANYTHING TO DO WITH THAT.
I KNOW YOU DIDN'T.
BUT LOOK AT ALL THIS GOLD YOU'VE GOT JUST ***LYING AROUND!***
WHAT DO YOU EVEN ***NEED*** IT FOR?!
I LIKE SPARKLY THINGS.

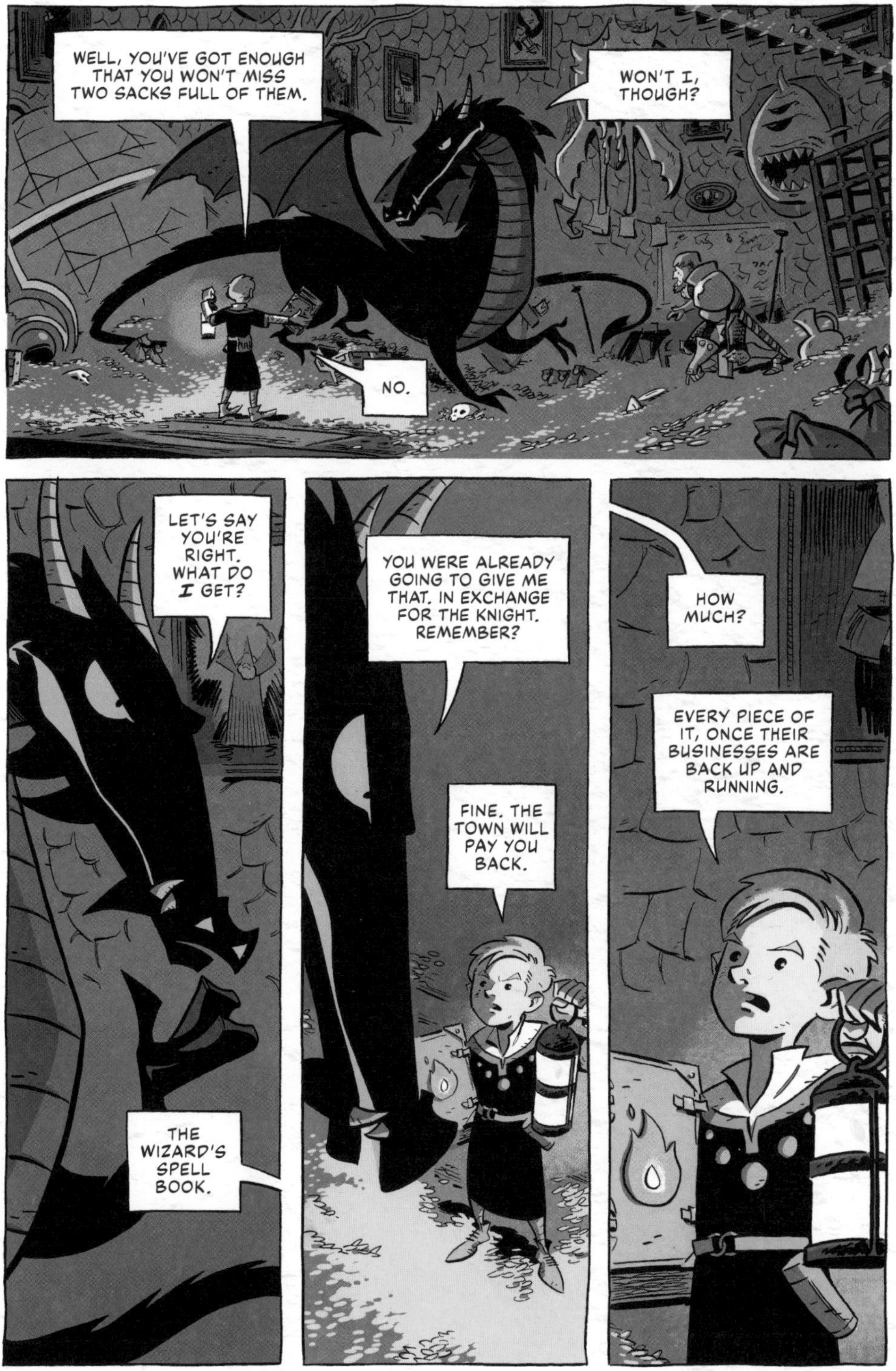
WELL, YOU'VE GOT ENOUGH THAT YOU WON'T MISS TWO SACKS FULL OF THEM.
WON'T I, THOUGH?
NO.
LET'S SAY YOU'RE RIGHT. WHAT DO *I* GET?
THE WIZARD'S SPELL BOOK.
YOU WERE ALREADY GOING TO GIVE ME THAT. IN EXCHANGE FOR THE KNIGHT. REMEMBER?
FINE. THE TOWN WILL PAY YOU BACK.
HOW MUCH?
EVERY PIECE OF IT, ONCE THEIR BUSINESSES ARE BACK UP AND RUNNING.

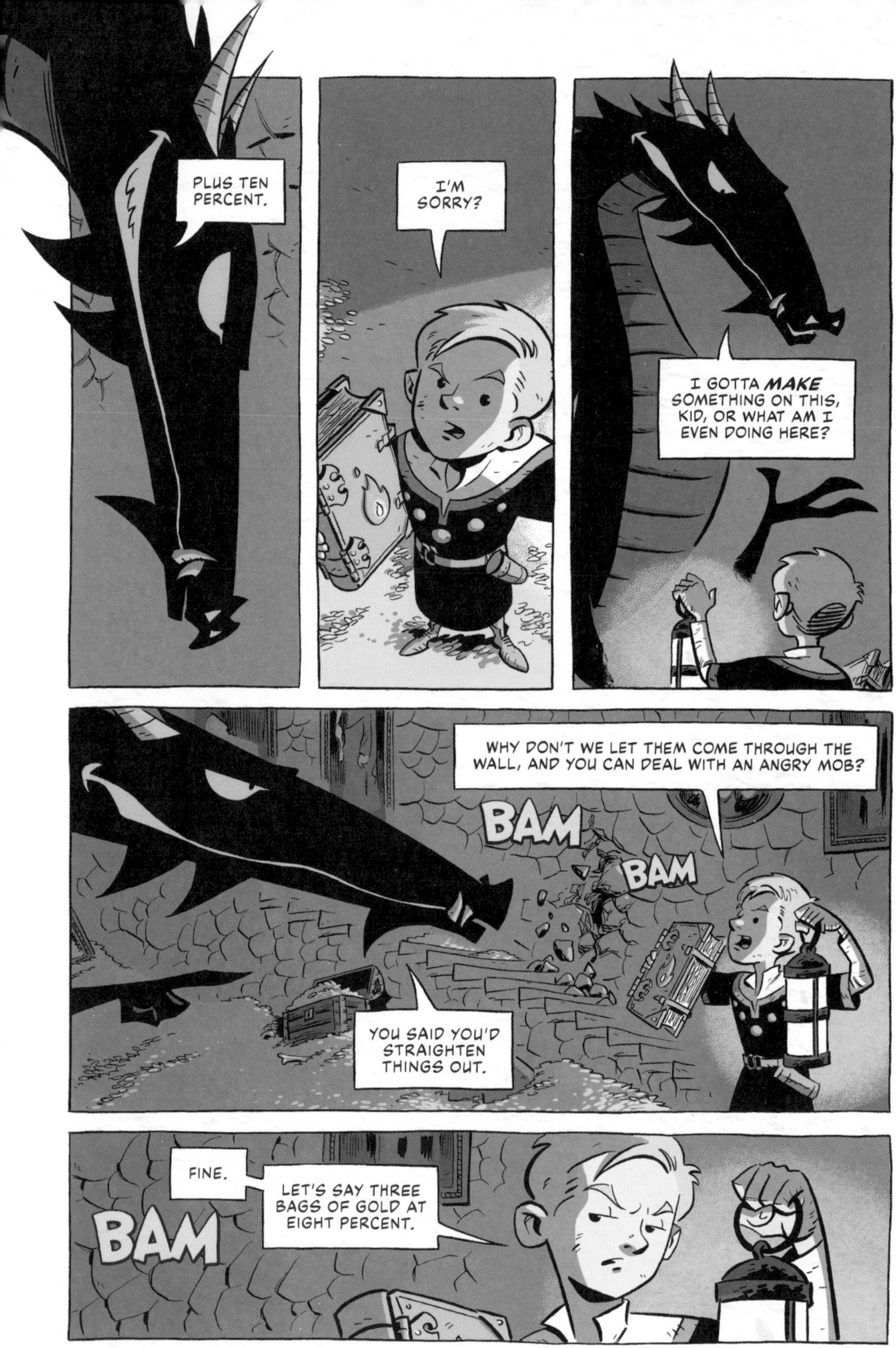
PLUS TEN PERCENT.
I'M SORRY?
I GOTTA MAKE SOMETHING ON THIS, KID, OR WHAT AM I EVEN DOING HERE?
WHY DON'T WE LET THEM COME THROUGH THE WALL, AND YOU CAN DEAL WITH AN ANGRY MOB?
BAM
BAM
YOU SAID YOU'D STRAIGHTEN THINGS OUT.
FINE.
LET'S SAY THREE BAGS OF GOLD AT EIGHT PERCENT.
BAM

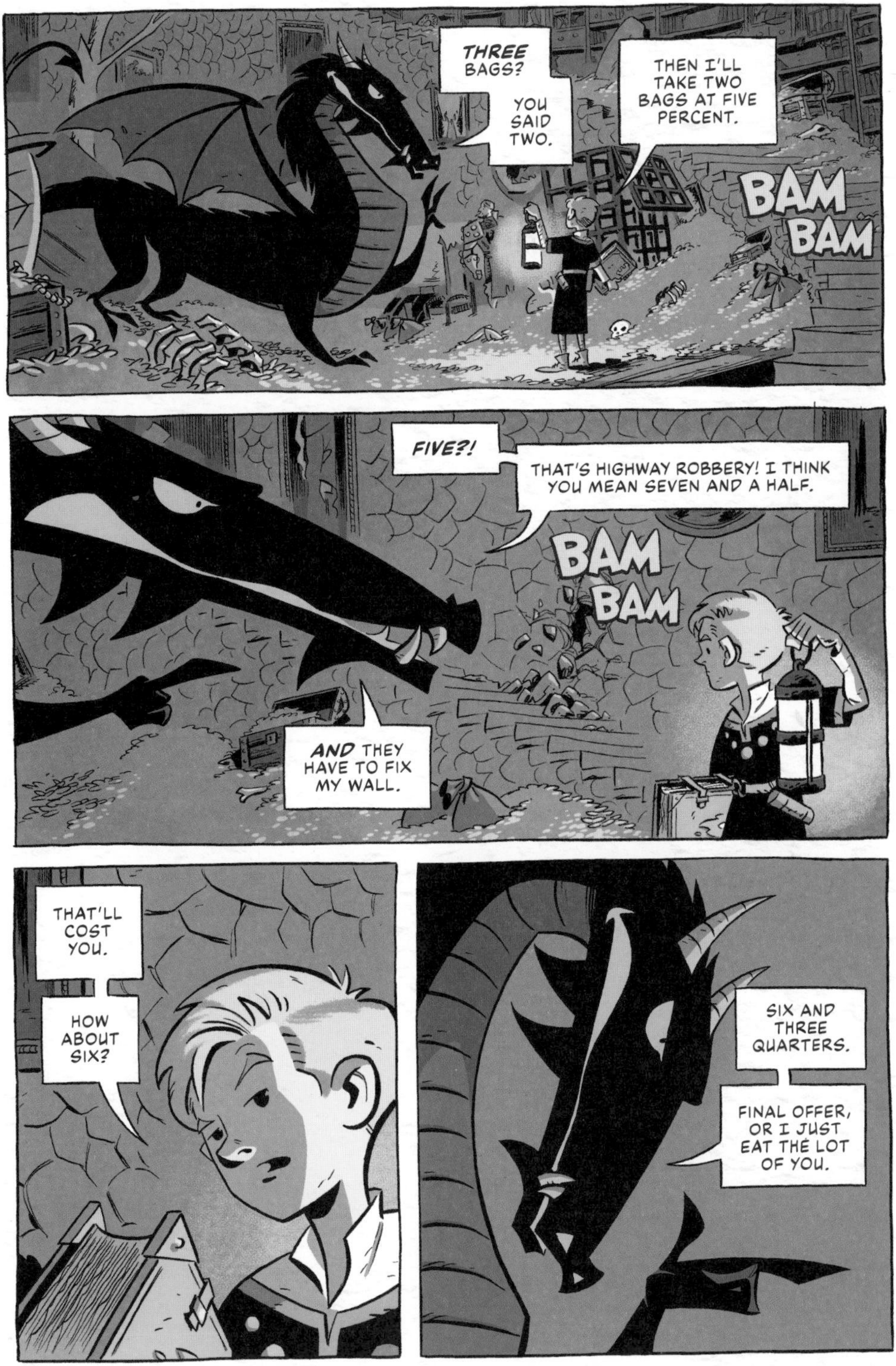
THREE BAGS?
YOU SAID TWO.
THEN I'LL TAKE TWO BAGS AT FIVE PERCENT.
BAM BAM
FIVE?!
THAT'S HIGHWAY ROBBERY! I THINK YOU MEAN SEVEN AND A HALF.
BAM BAM
AND THEY HAVE TO FIX MY WALL.
THAT'LL COST YOU.
HOW ABOUT SIX?
SIX AND THREE QUARTERS.
FINAL OFFER, OR I JUST EAT THE LOT OF YOU.

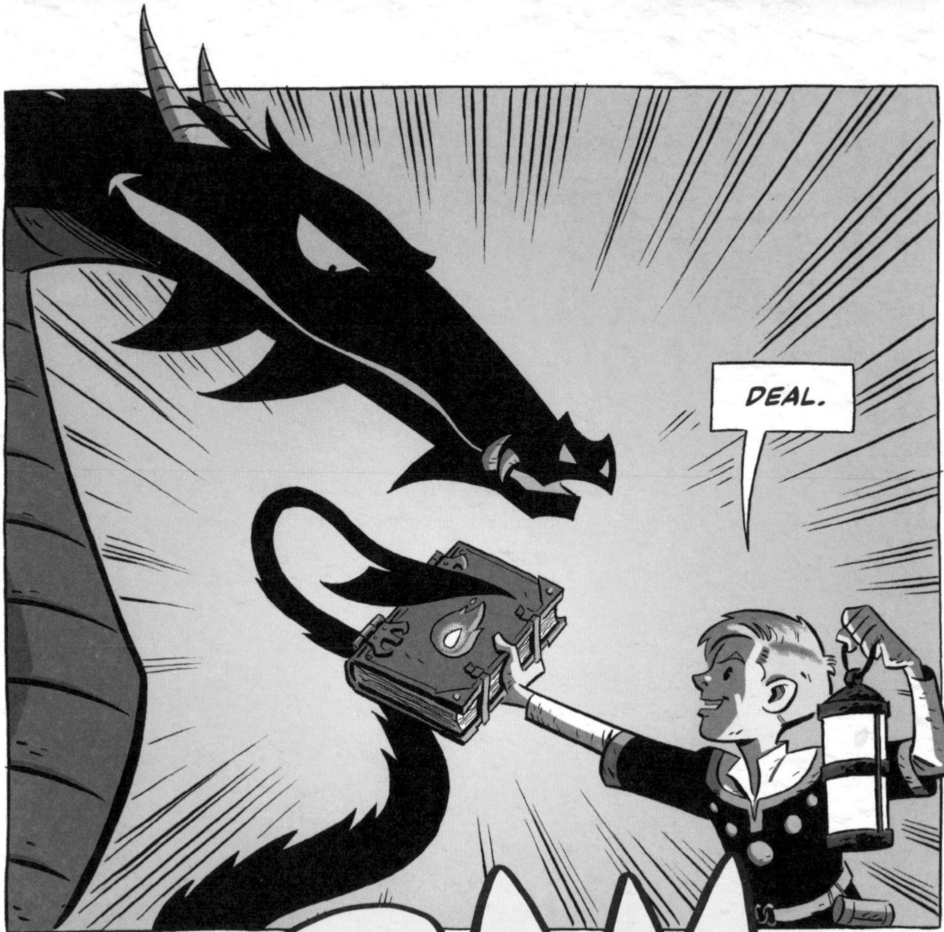
DEAL.

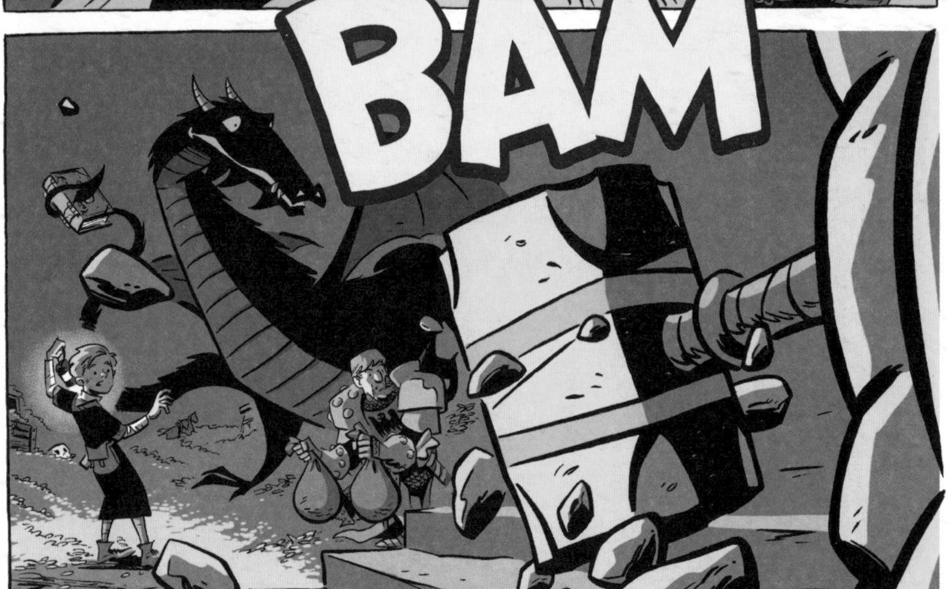
BAM

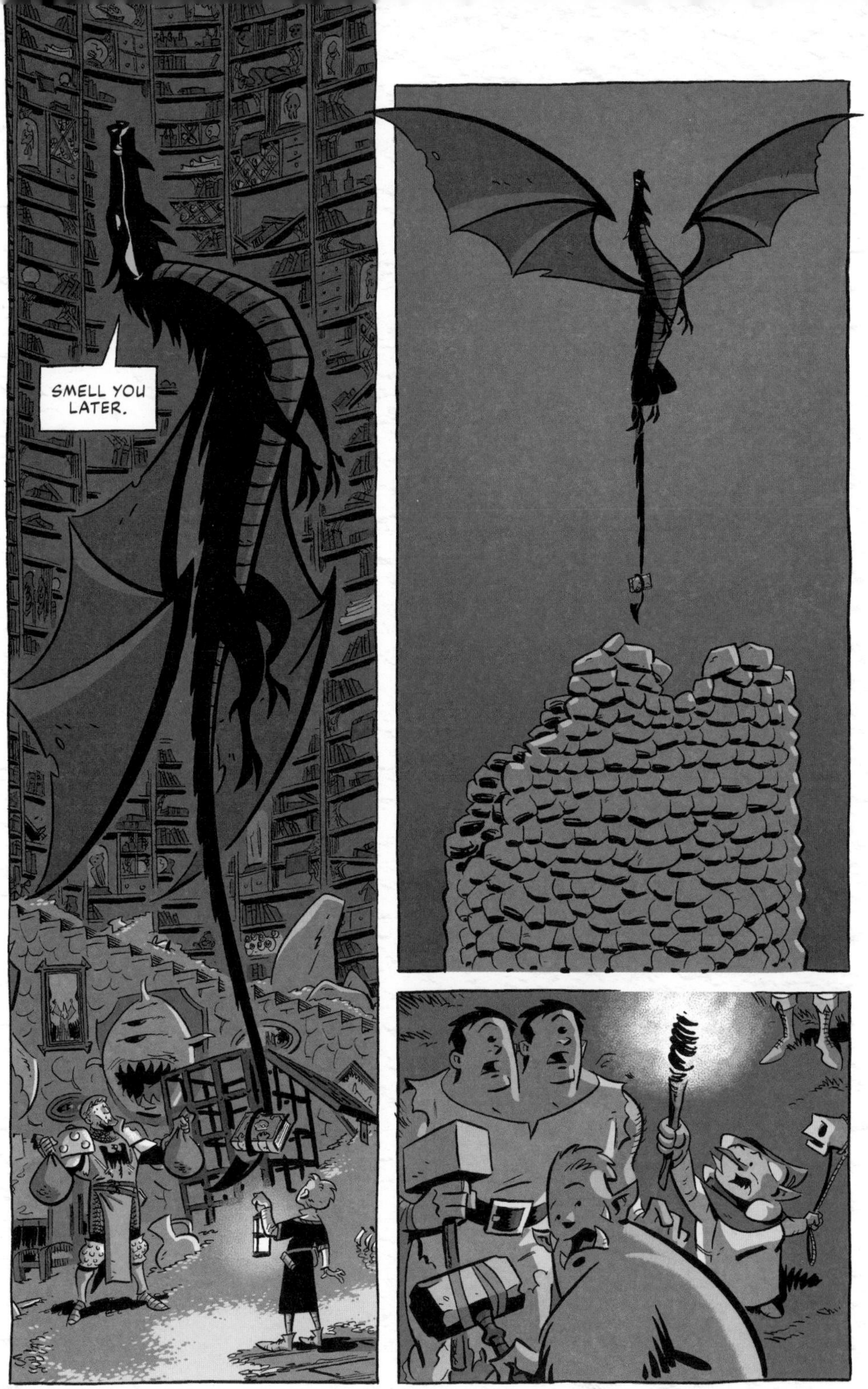
SMELL YOU LATER.

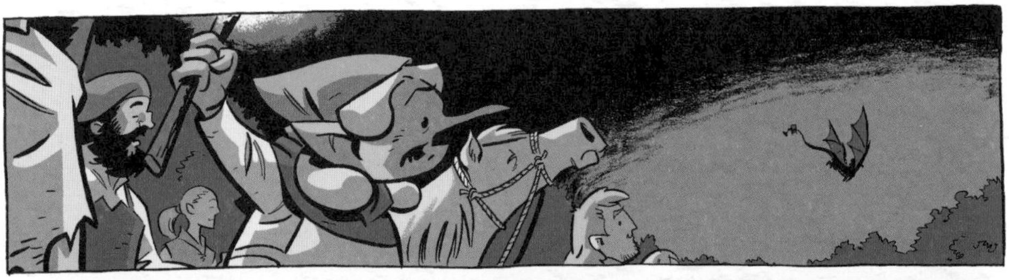

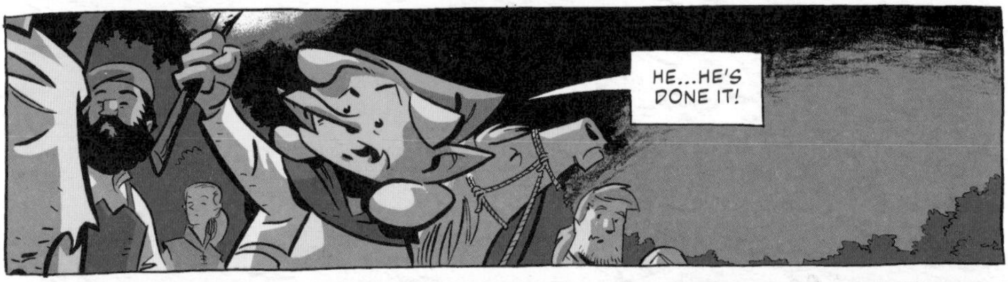
HE...HE'S DONE IT!

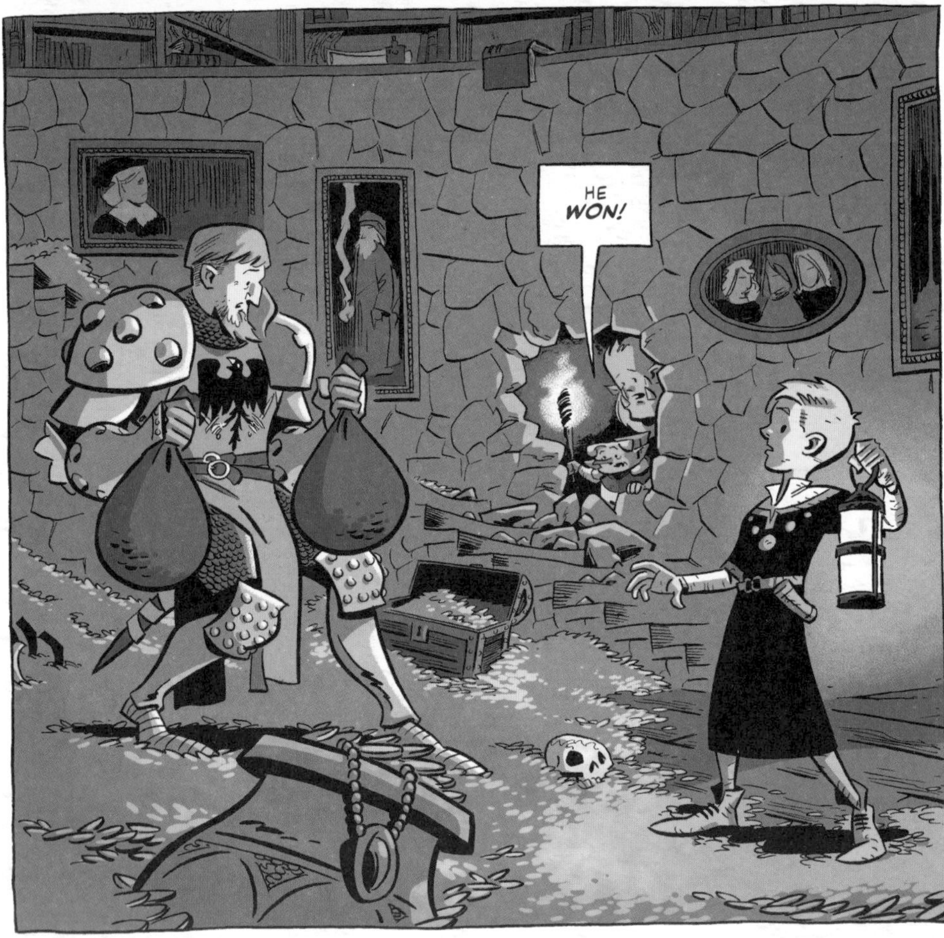
HE *WON!*

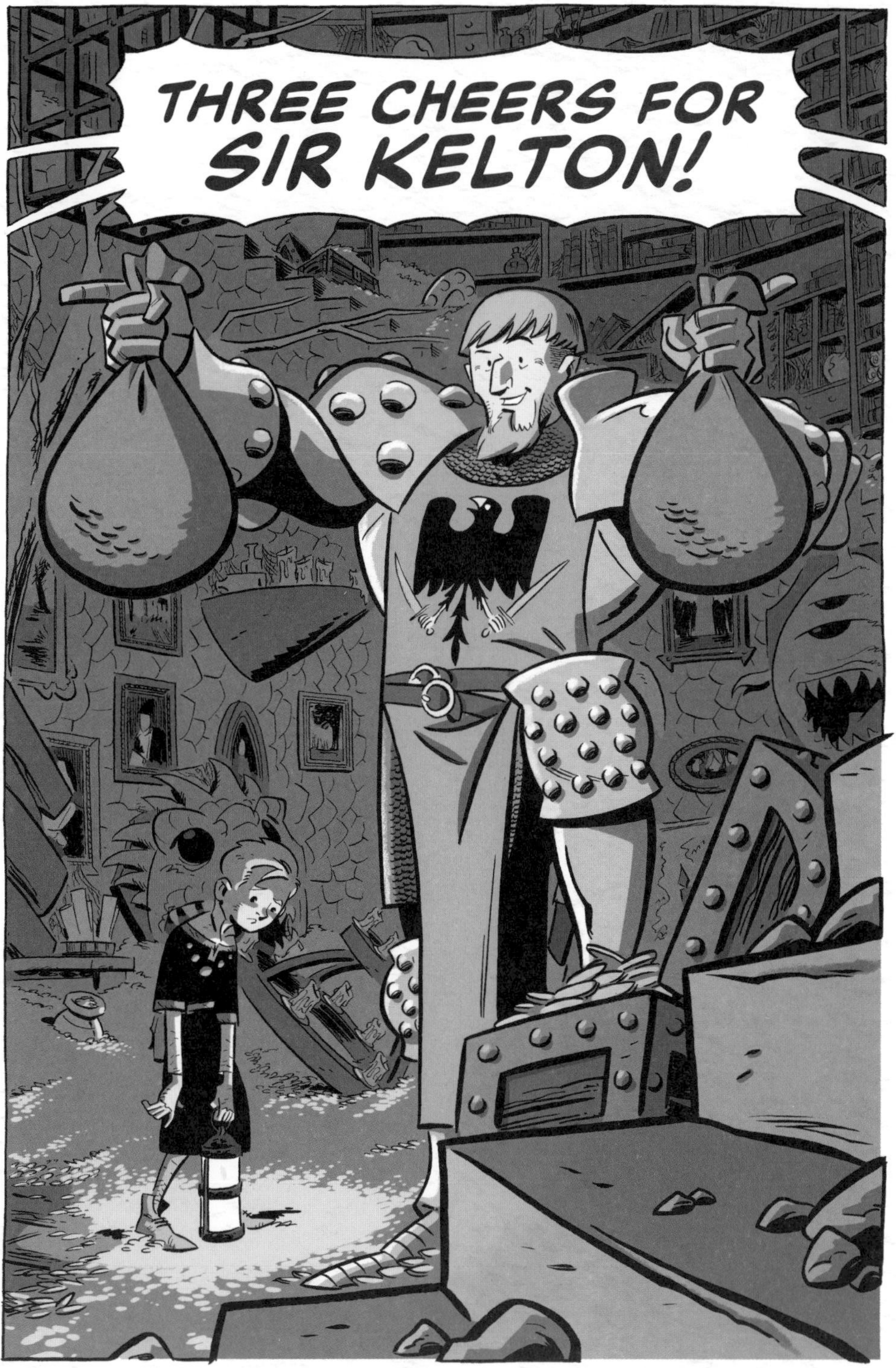
THREE CHEERS FOR SIR KELTON!

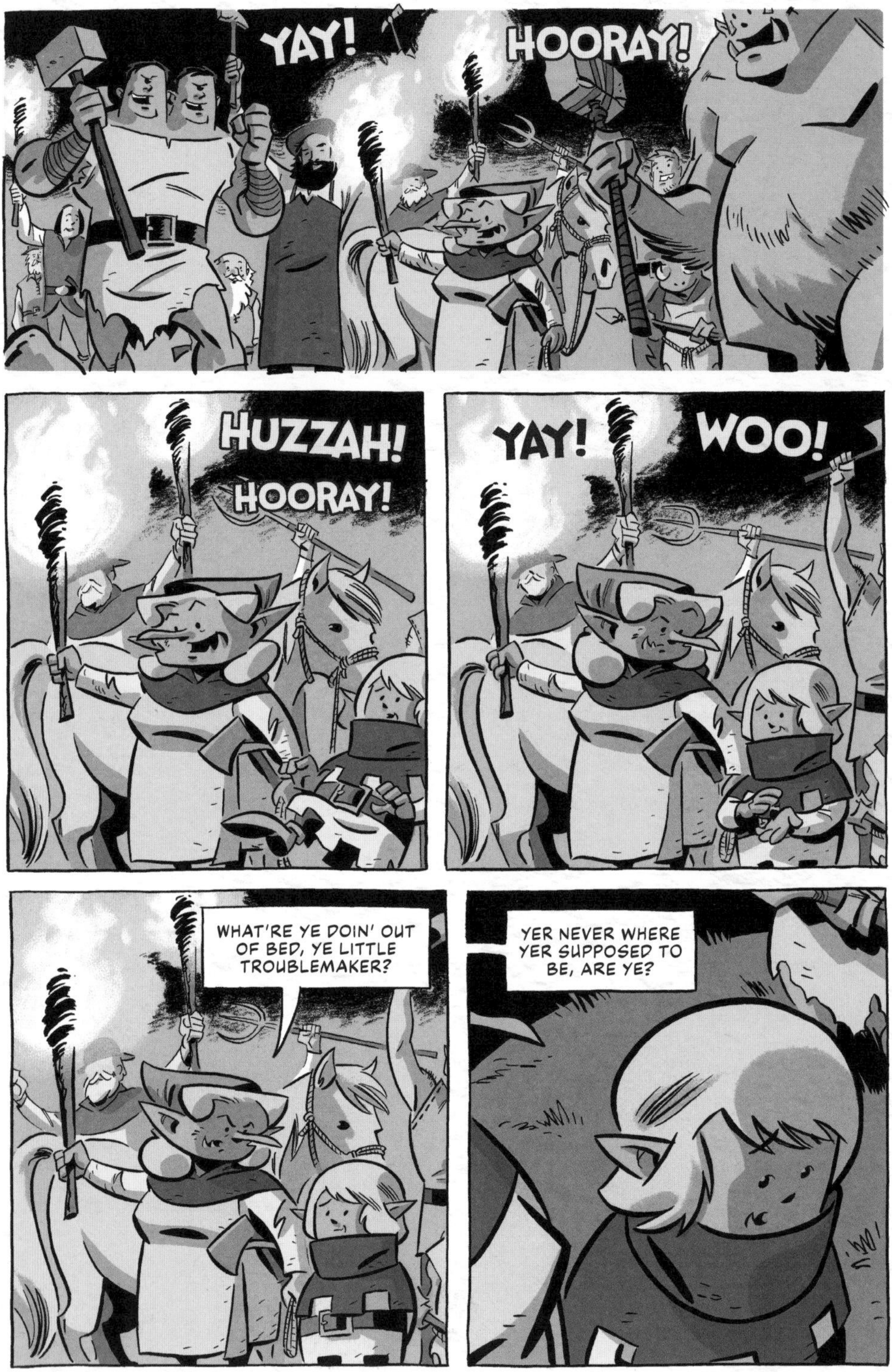
YAY!
HOORAY!
HUZZAH!
HOORAY!
YAY!
WOO!
WHAT'RE YE DOIN' OUT OF BED, YE LITTLE TROUBLEMAKER?
YER NEVER WHERE YER SUPPOSED TO BE, ARE YE?

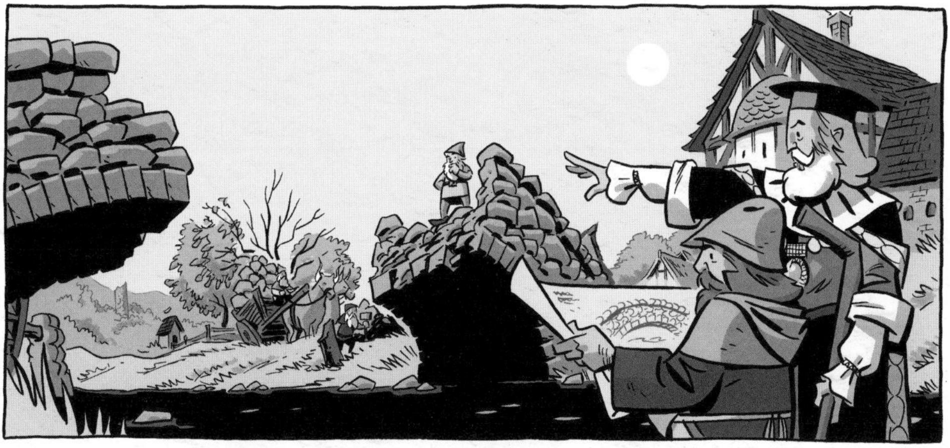

# EPILOGUE

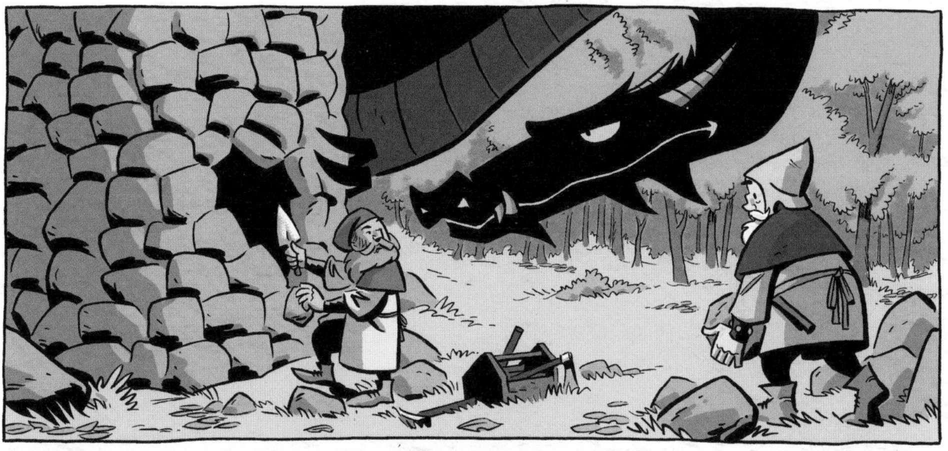

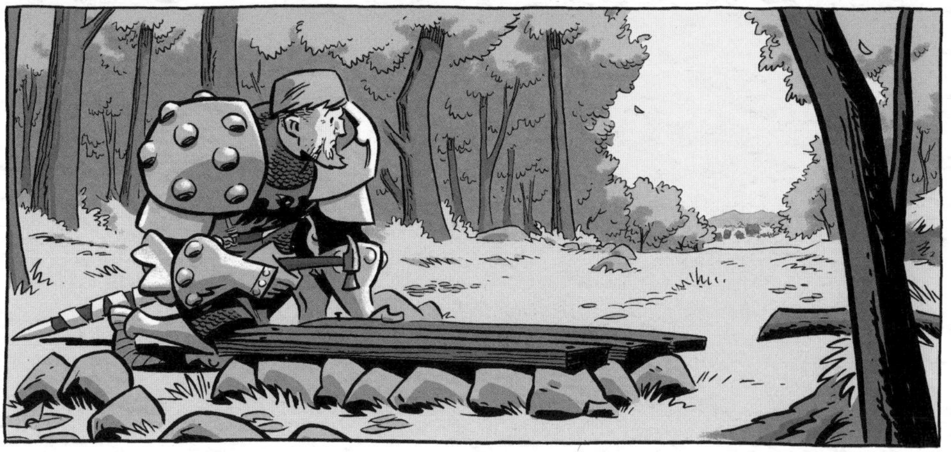

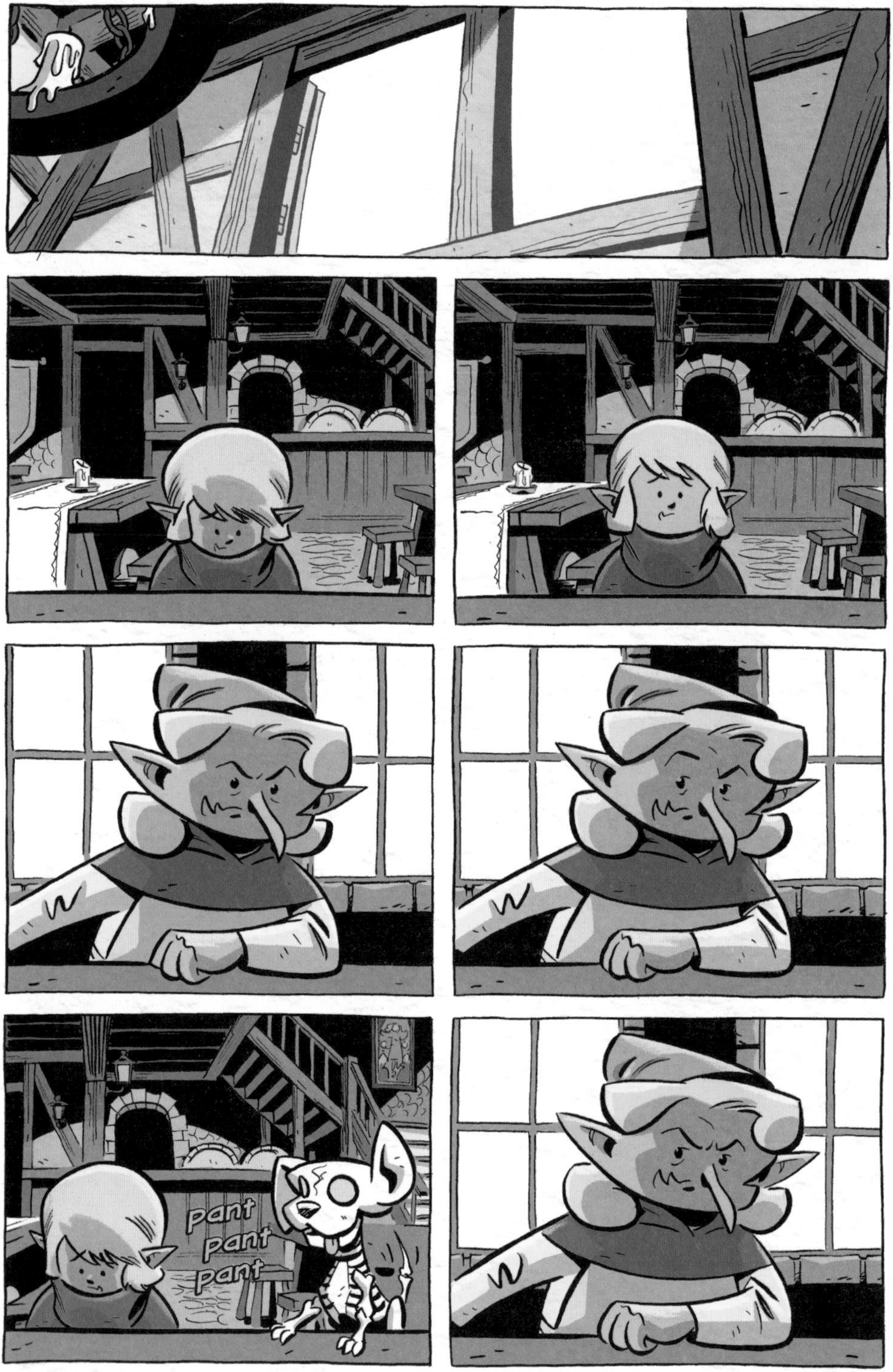
pant
pant
pant

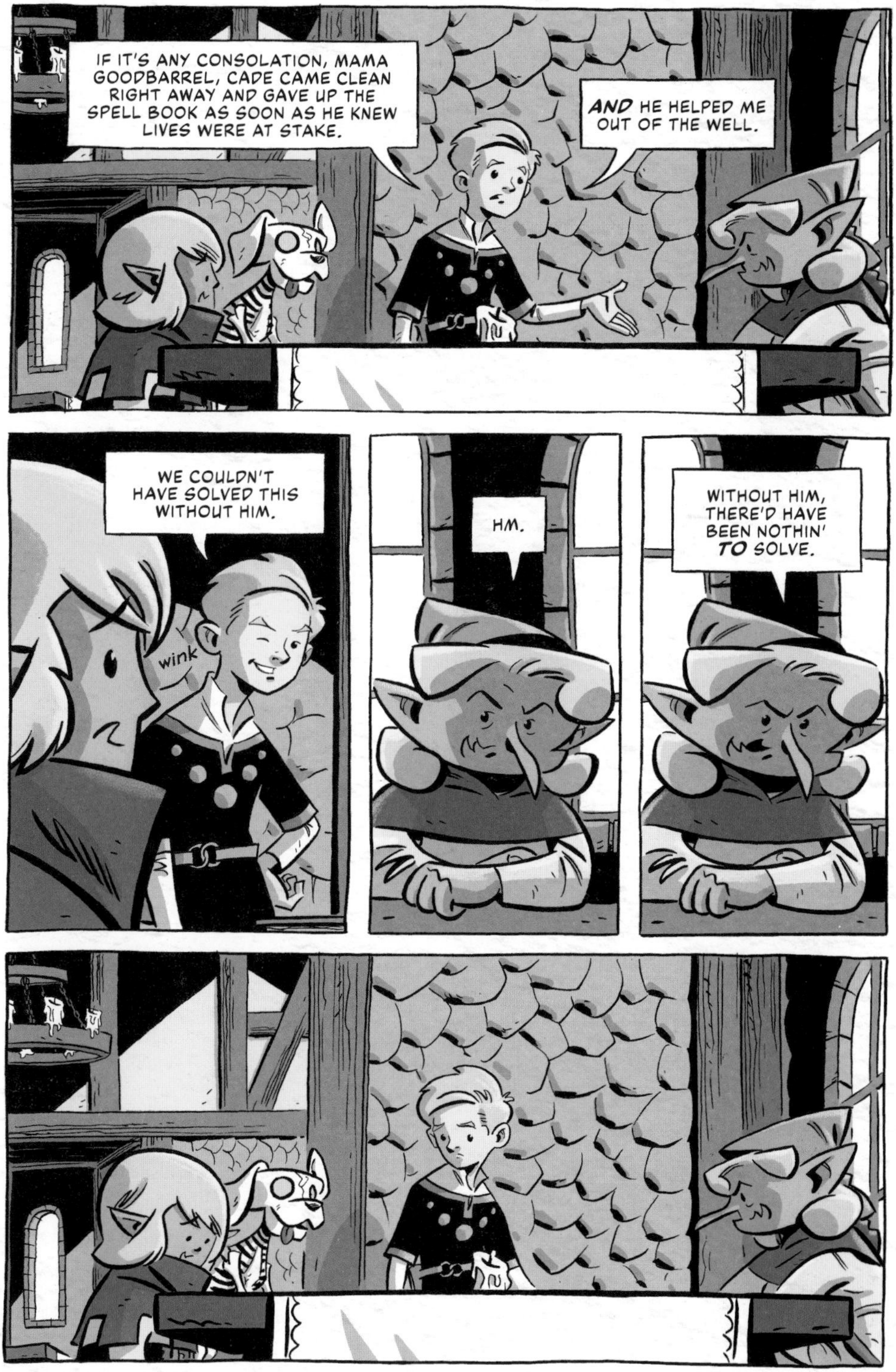
IF IT'S ANY CONSOLATION, MAMA GOODBARREL, CADE CAME CLEAN RIGHT AWAY AND GAVE UP THE SPELL BOOK AS SOON AS HE KNEW LIVES WERE AT STAKE.
AND HE HELPED ME OUT OF THE WELL.
WE COULDN'T HAVE SOLVED THIS WITHOUT HIM.
wink
HM.
WITHOUT HIM, THERE'D HAVE BEEN NOTHIN' TO SOLVE.

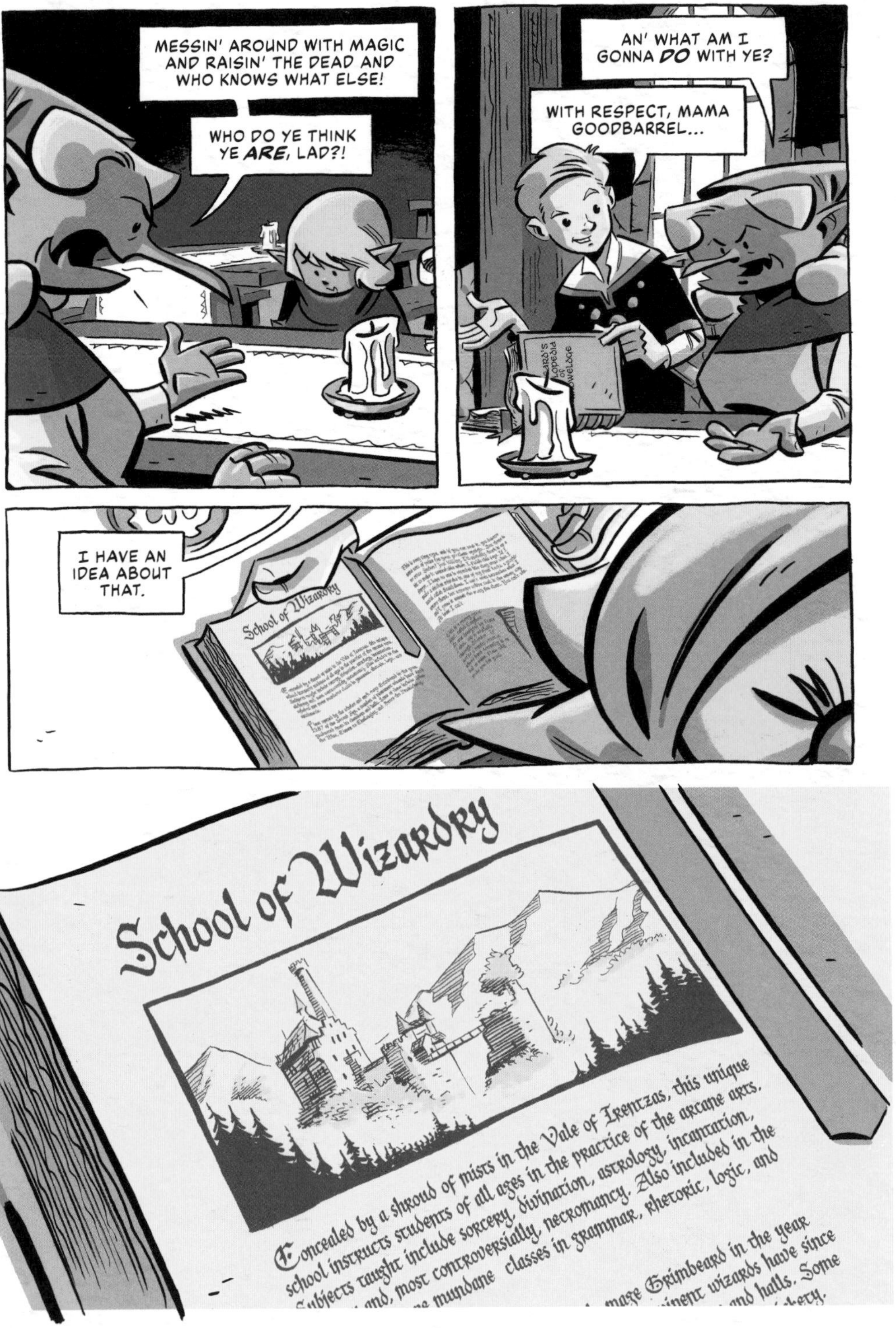

MESSIN' AROUND WITH MAGIC AND RAISIN' THE DEAD AND WHO KNOWS WHAT ELSE!
WHO DO YE THINK YE *ARE*, LAD?!
AN' WHAT AM I GONNA *DO* WITH YE?
WITH RESPECT, MAMA GOODBARREL...
I HAVE AN IDEA ABOUT THAT.
School of Wizardry
Concealed by a shroud of mists in the Vale of Irentzas, this unique
school instructs students of all ages in the practice of the arcane arts.
Subjects taught include sorcery, divination, astrology, incantation,
and, most controversially, necromancy. Also included in the
mundane classes in grammar, rhetoric, logic, and
Grimbeard in the year
wizards have since
and halls. Some

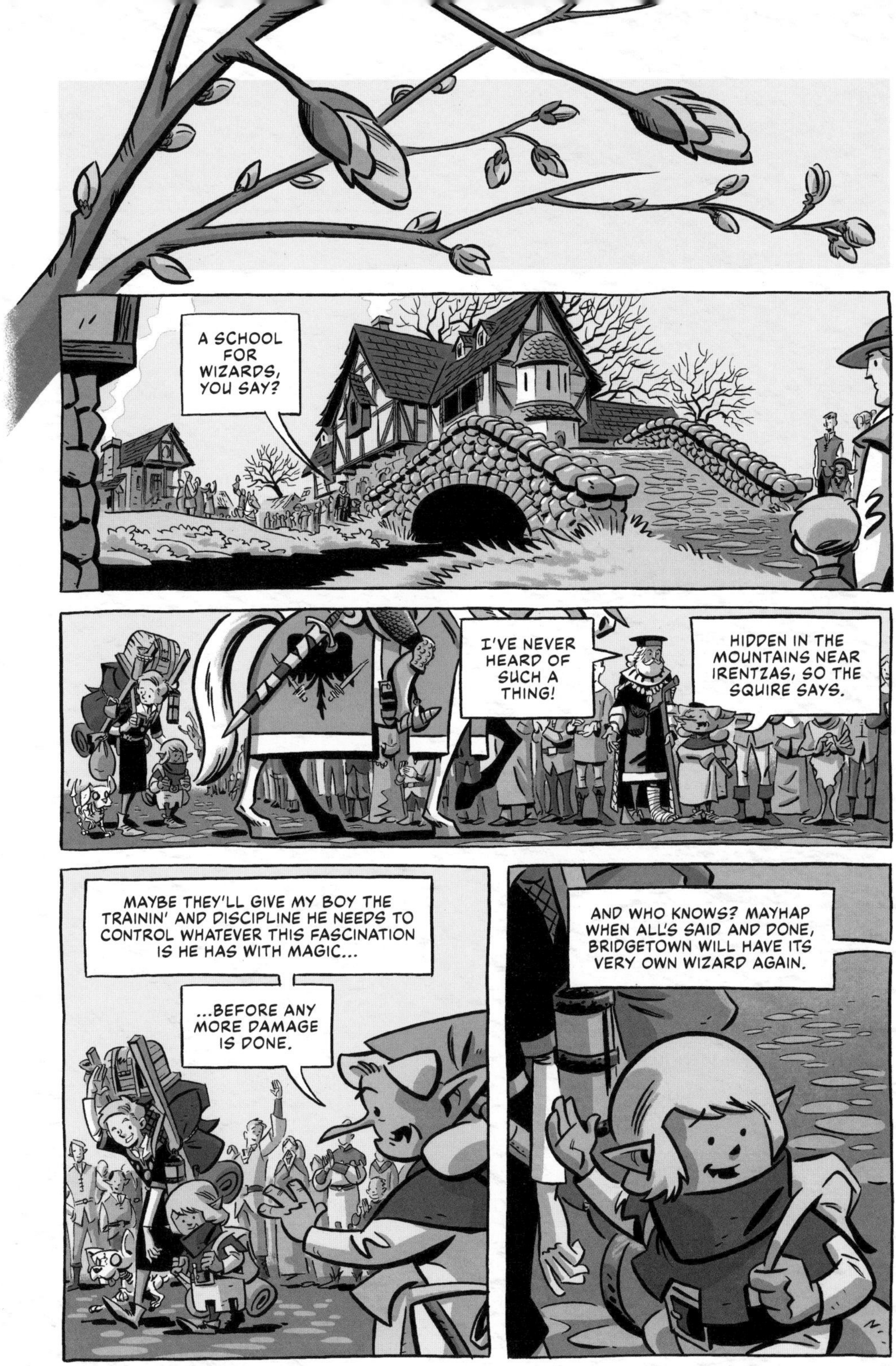
A SCHOOL FOR WIZARDS, YOU SAY?
I'VE NEVER HEARD OF SUCH A THING!
HIDDEN IN THE MOUNTAINS NEAR IRENTZAS, SO THE SQUIRE SAYS.
MAYBE THEY'LL GIVE MY BOY THE TRAININ' AND DISCIPLINE HE NEEDS TO CONTROL WHATEVER THIS FASCINATION IS HE HAS WITH MAGIC...
...BEFORE ANY MORE DAMAGE IS DONE.
AND WHO KNOWS? MAYHAP WHEN ALL'S SAID AND DONE, BRIDGETOWN WILL HAVE ITS VERY OWN WIZARD AGAIN.

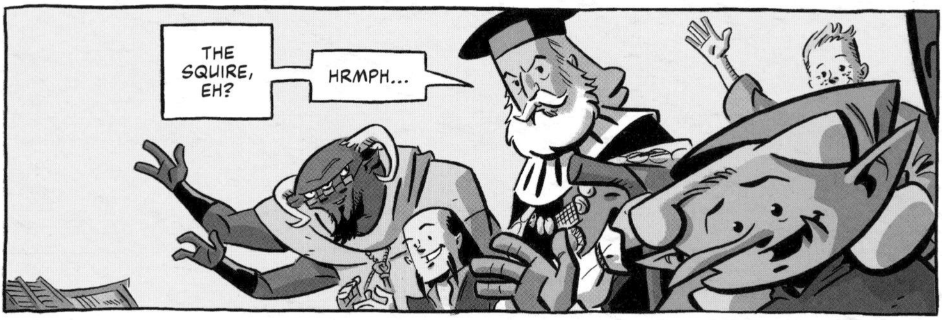
THE SQUIRE, EH?
HRMPH...

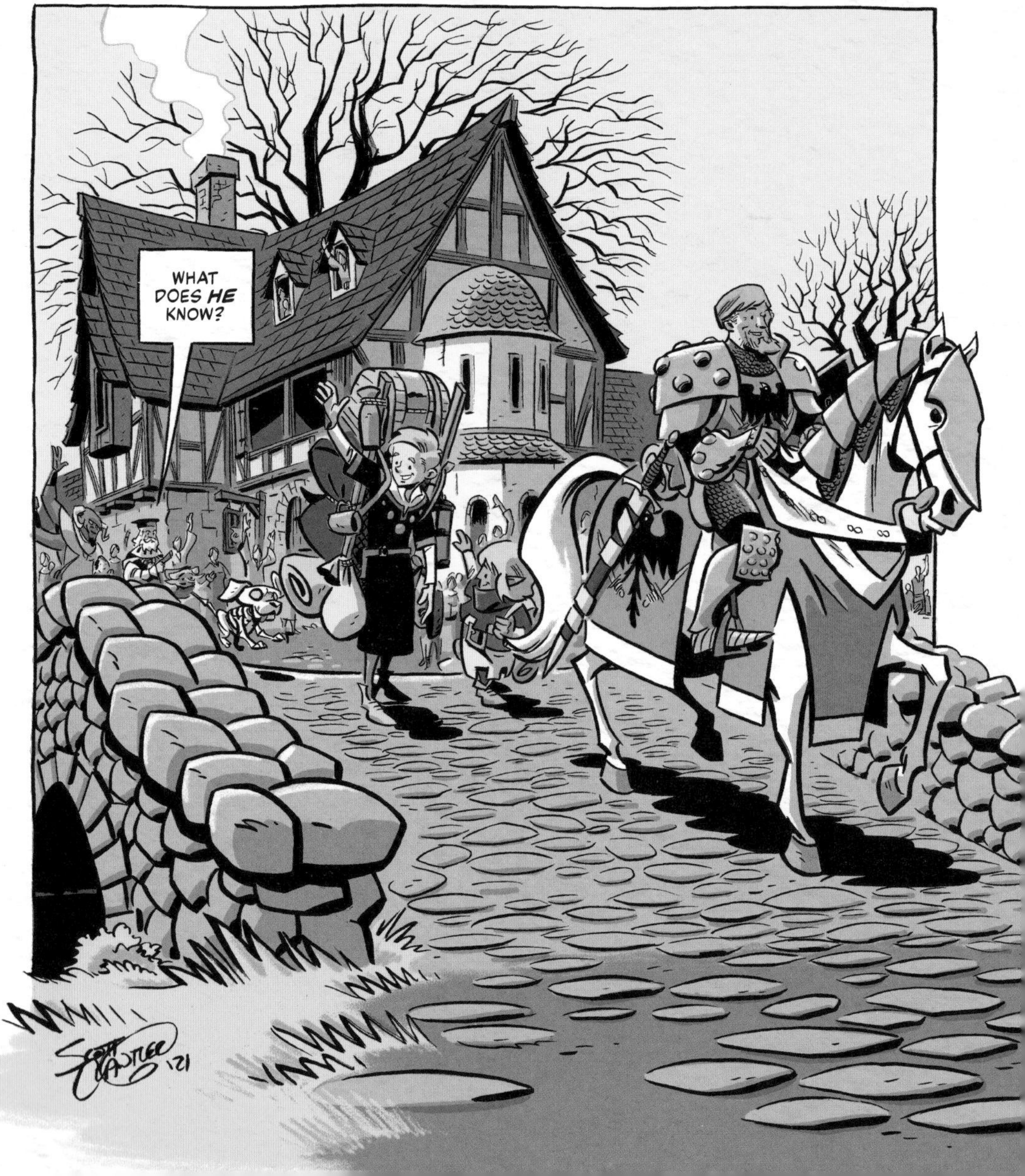
WHAT DOES **HE** KNOW?

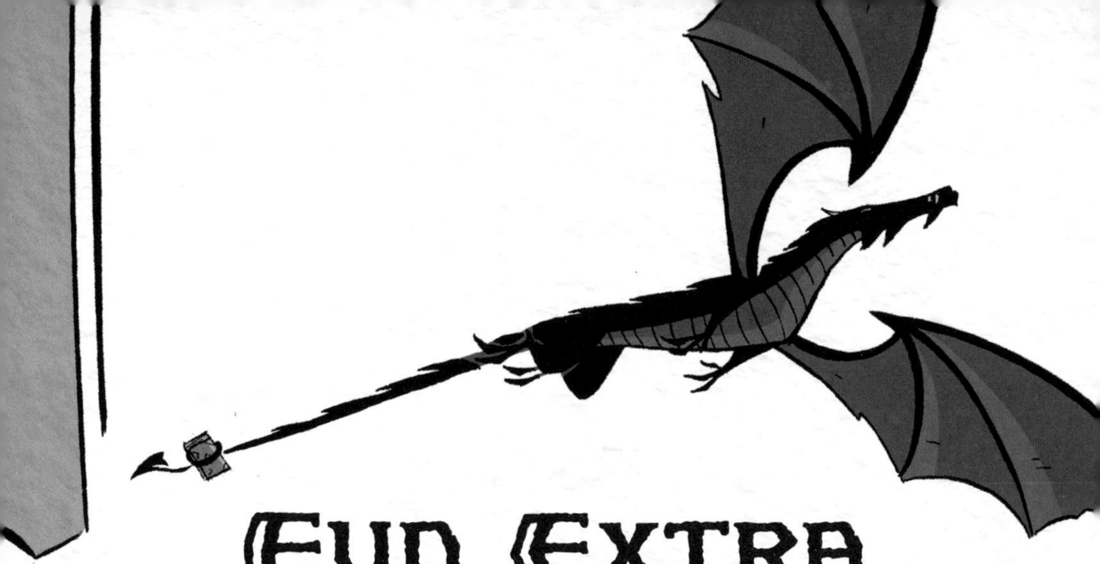

# Fun Extra Stuff

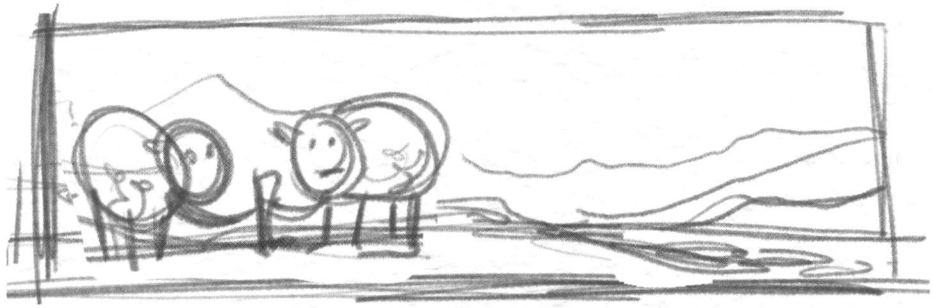

FOR YOU
PROCESS JUNKIES

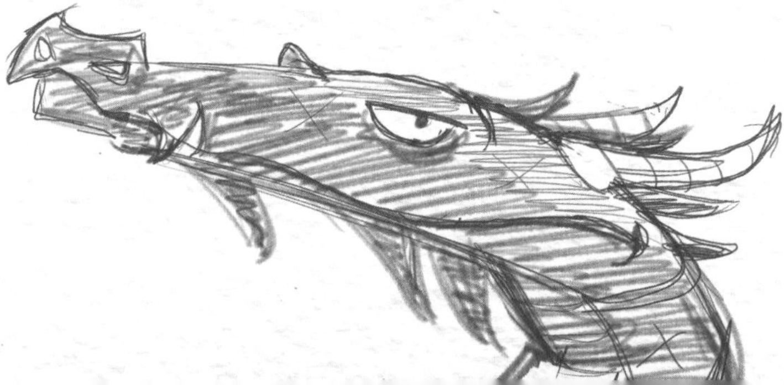

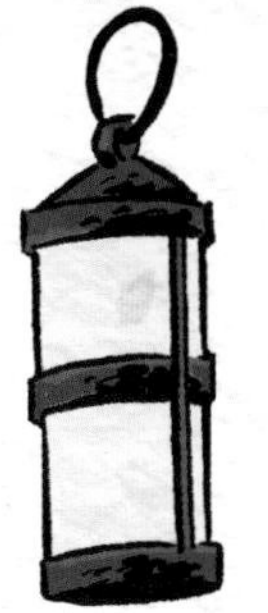

When I was a teenager, there was a British comedy film called *Without a Clue* (Thom Eberhardt, 1988) that starred Michael Caine and Ben Kingsley. It was a twist on *Sherlock Holmes* in which the sidekick, Dr. Watson, is the real genius, while Holmes is a clueless actor hired to take the credit in order to protect Watson's medical reputation.

The thing is, ***I don't think I've ever actually seen that movie.*** But the concept, which I've always thought was really clever, has stuck with me for decades. I love stories where heroes ***think*** their way out of problems, and also ones where arrogant blowhards are revealed to be...well, arrogant blowhards.

So I started to think about how those ideas might be applied to other genres. At the time, I was introducing my kids to another teenage interest of mine: Dungeons & Dragons. I created a short adventure for them in which a town was divided because the single bridge that joined the two halves had been distroyed. My kids lost interest before they ever solved the mystery of what happened to the bridge, but I gained a good idea for a book!

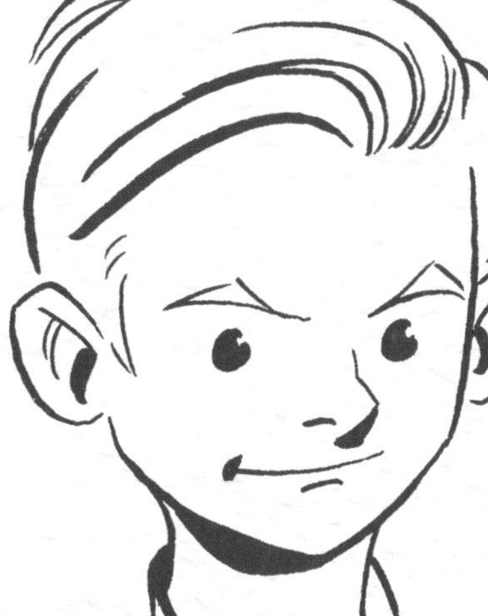

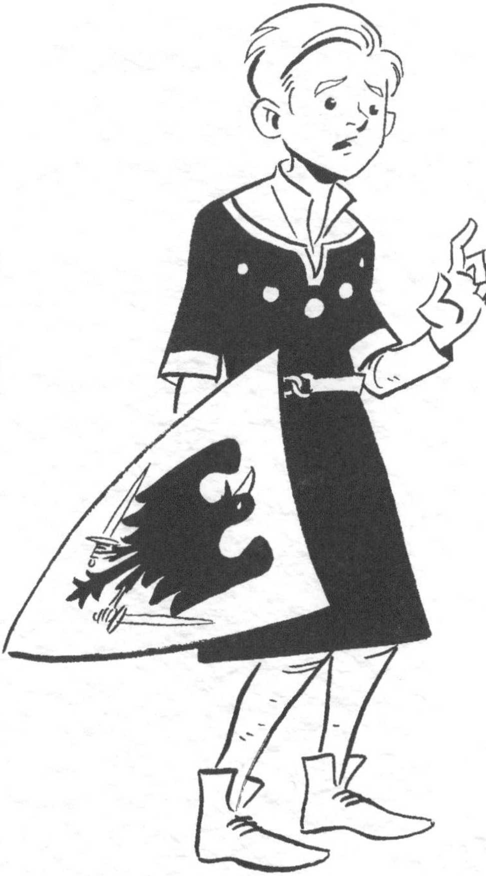

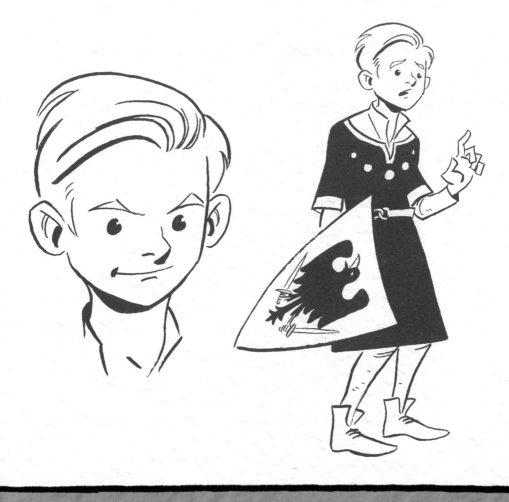

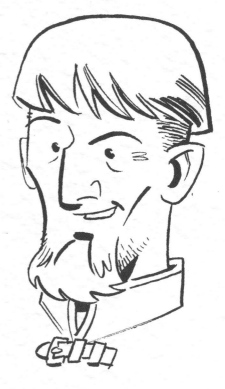

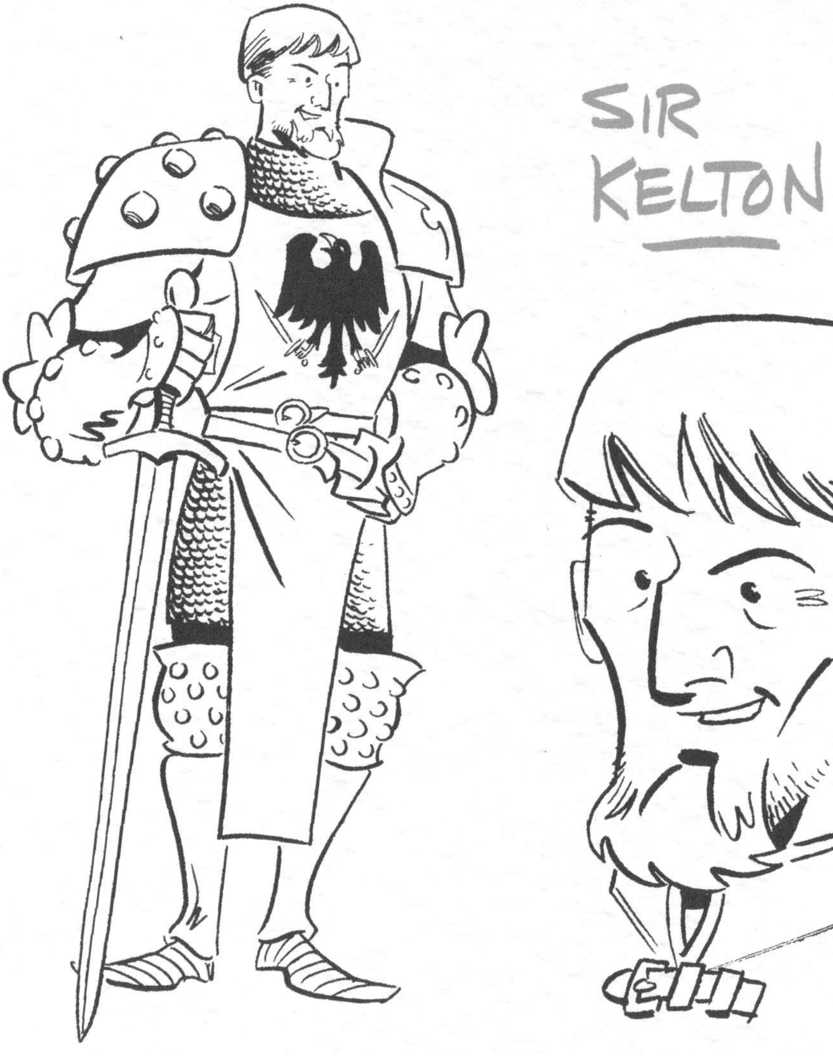
SIR KELTON

THE TITLE CHARACTERS WERE INSPIRED BY BRAINY, SENSITIVE "WART" AND HIS OVERBEARING BROTHER, SIR KAY, IN T. H. WHITE'S CLASSIC NOVEL *THE SWORD IN THE STONE*, YET ANOTHER CHILDHOOD FAVORITE.

IN FACT, MY ONE-LINE PITCH FOR *SQUIRE & KNIGHT* WAS "T. H. WHITE PLAYS DUNGEONS & DRAGONS WITH SIR ARTHUR CONAN DOYLE!"

SPEAKING OF THE PITCH, THE SQUIRE ***DID*** HAVE A NAME IN THE ORIGINAL OUTLINE. BUT BY THE TIME I STARTED WRITING THE SCRIPT, I DECIDED IT WOULD MAKE A GREAT (AND CHARACTER-DRIVEN!) JOKE IF SIR KELTON DIDN'T EVEN KNOW HIS SQUIRE'S NAME, REFERRING TO HIM SIMPLY AS "SQUIRE!" SO HE'S BEEN "THE SQUIRE" SINCE THEN. WILL WE ***EVER*** LEARN THE SQUIRE'S ACTUAL NAME? I'M NOT TELLING (AND HONESTLY, I DON'T KNOW YET)!

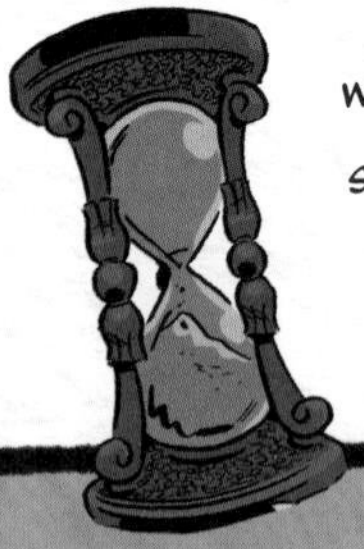

I ALMOST ALWAYS HAVE A GOOD IMAGE OF THE CHARACTERS IN MY HEAD ONCE I'VE BEEN WRITING THEM FOR A LITTLE WHILE, SO I CAN USUALLY NAIL DOWN THEIR LOOK IN A DRAWING OR TWO!

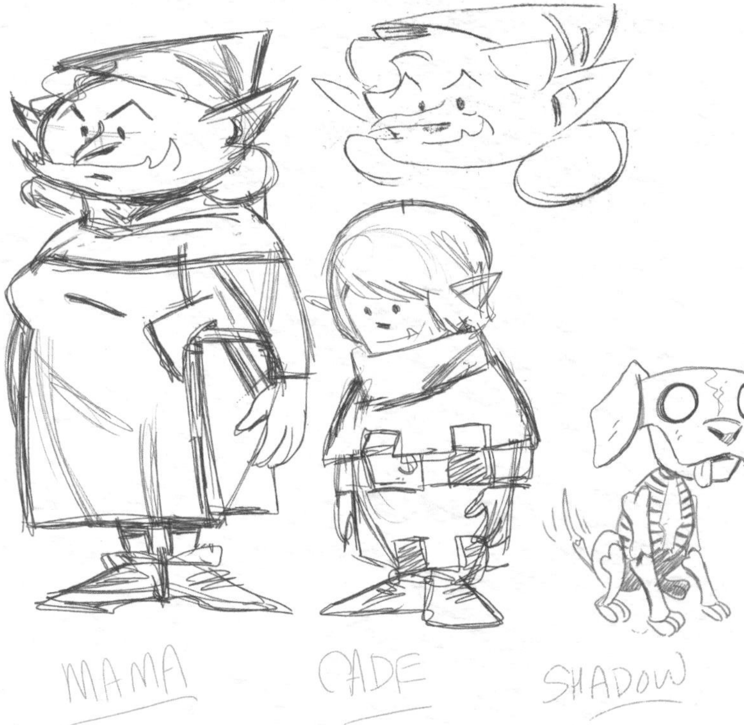

MAMA
CADE
SHADOW


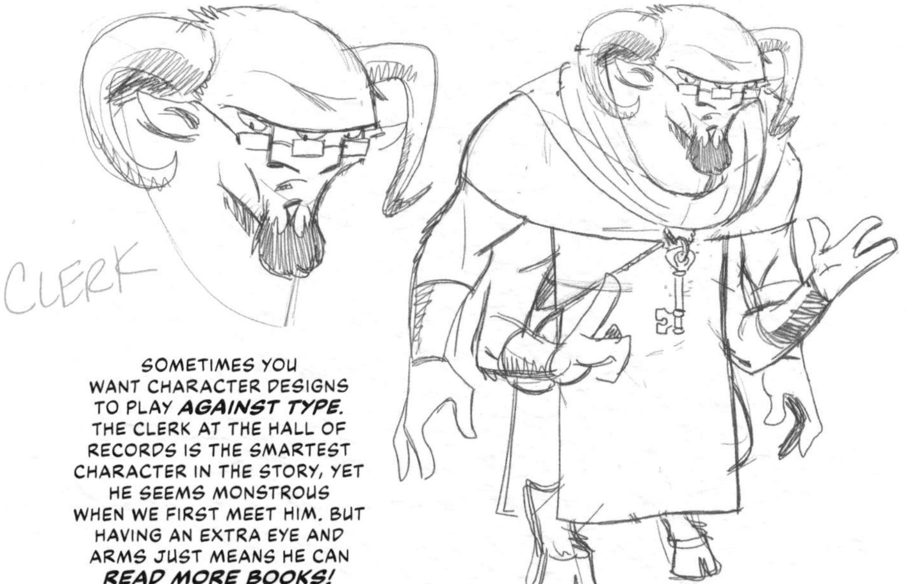

CLERK


SOMETIMES YOU WANT CHARACTER DESIGNS TO PLAY ***AGAINST TYPE.*** THE CLERK AT THE HALL OF RECORDS IS THE SMARTEST CHARACTER IN THE STORY, YET HE SEEMS MONSTROUS WHEN WE FIRST MEET HIM. BUT HAVING AN EXTRA EYE AND ARMS JUST MEANS HE CAN ***READ MORE BOOKS!***

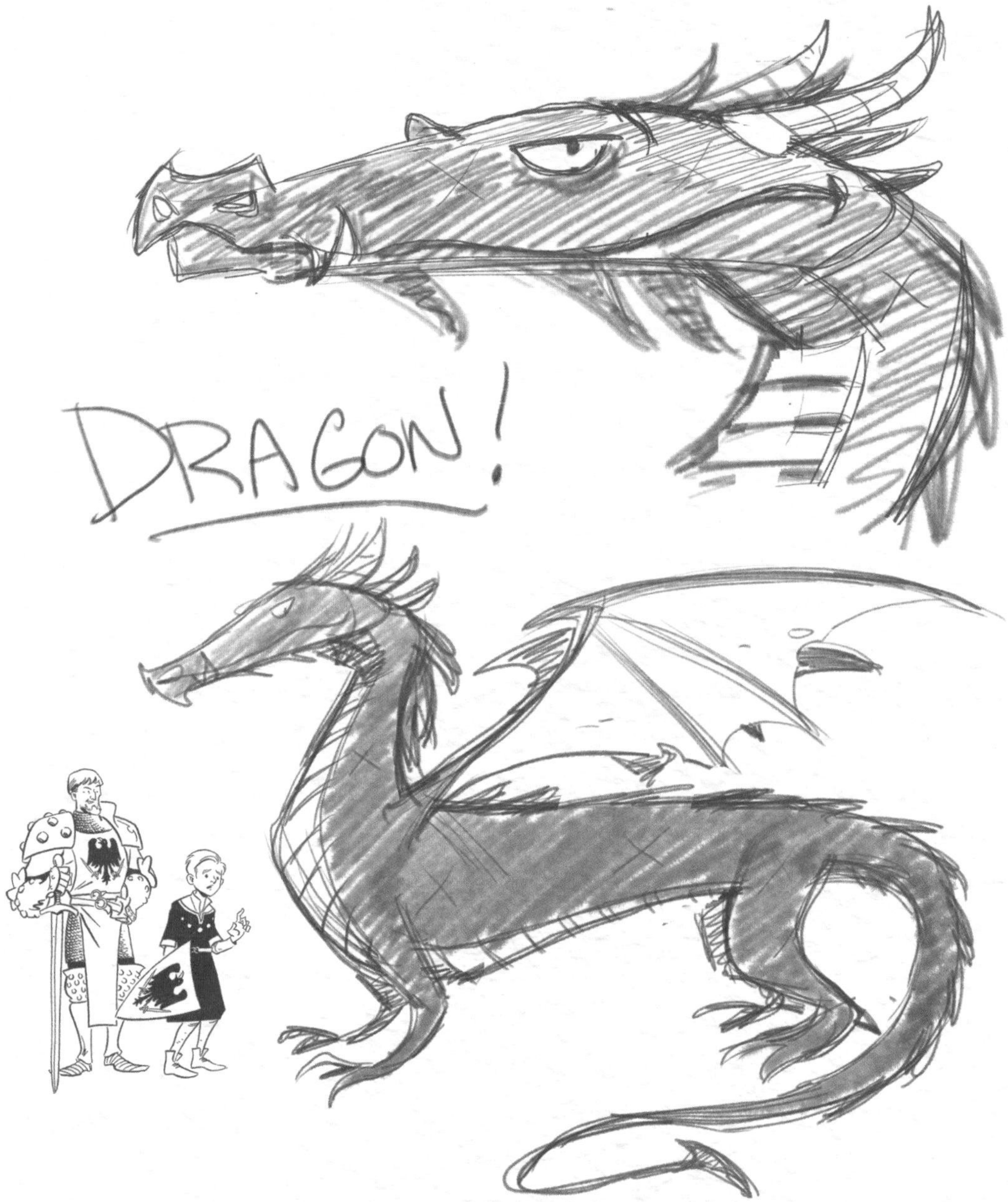
DRAGON!

DRAGONS HAVE BEEN A STAPLE OF FANTASY STORIES AND FANTASY ART FOR ***CENTURIES***, SO TRYING TO FIND A FRESH TAKE ON ONE WAS ***TOUGH!*** IT'S ALWAYS HELPFUL TO COMBINE SEEMINGLY DIFFERENT THINGS IN NEW WAYS TO SEE WHAT YOU GET, SO THE DRAGON I ENDED UP WITH IS A COMBINATION OF A ***BLACK CAIMAN*** ALLIGATOR, A ***KINGFISHER*** (WHICH HAS BUSHY FEATHERS SWEEPING AWAY FROM ITS HEAD), AND A SMUG, WISECRACKING COMEDIAN. THAT SEEMED TO CAPTURE WHAT I WANTED FROM YET ANOTHER CHARACTER WHO'S NOT QUITE WHAT YOU FIRST THINK!

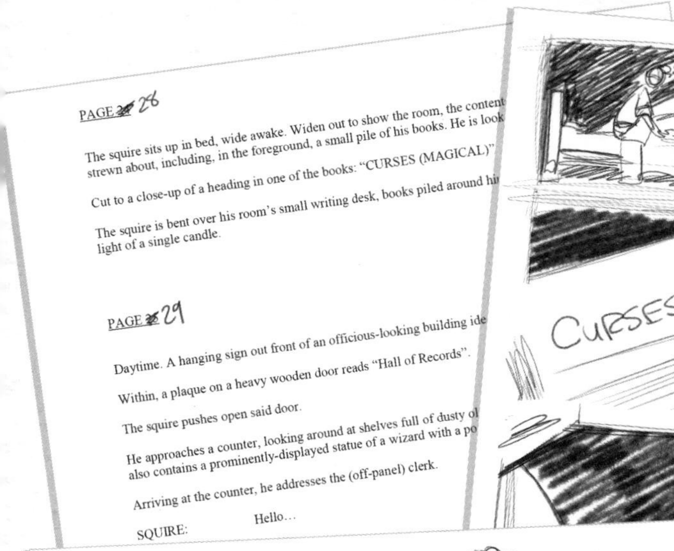
PAGE ~~27~~ 28

The squire sits up in bed, wide awake. Widen out to show the room, the content
strewn about, including, in the foreground, a small pile of his books. He is look

Cut to a close-up of a heading in one of the books: "CURSES (MAGICAL)"

The squire is bent over his room's small writing desk, books piled around hi
light of a single candle.

PAGE ~~28~~ 29

Daytime. A hanging sign out front of an officious-looking building ide

Within, a plaque on a heavy wooden door reads "Hall of Records".

The squire pushes open said door.

He approaches a counter, looking around at shelves full of dusty ol
also contains a prominently-displayed statue of a wizard with a po

Arriving at the counter, he addresses the (off-panel) clerk.

SQUIRE: Hello…

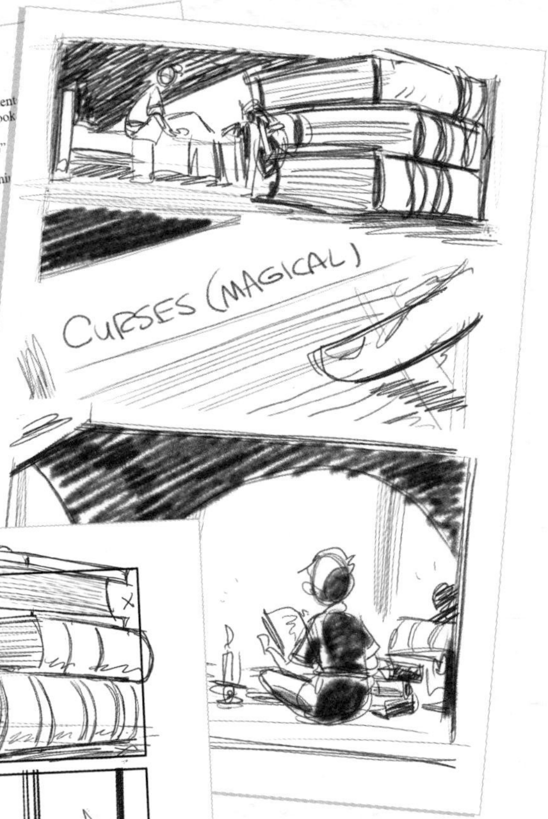

CURSES (MAGICAL)


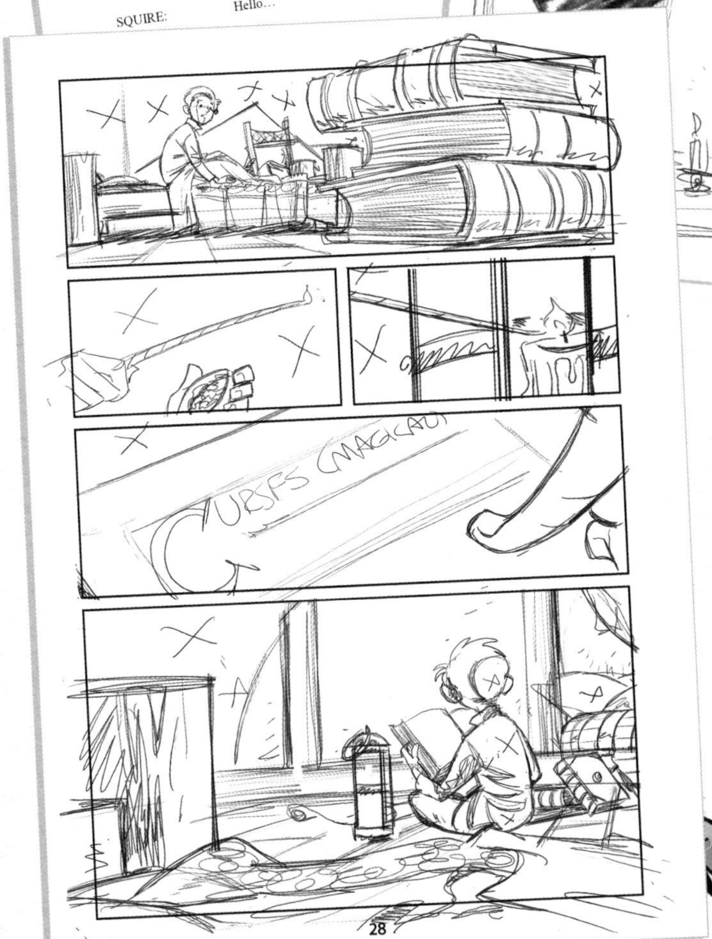

CURSES (MAGICAL)
28


COMICS MIGHT MAKE FOR RELATIVELY FAST READS, BUT THEY TAKE A ***LONG TIME*** TO MAKE! EACH PAGE GOES THROUGH A ***LOT*** OF STAGES, INCLUDING THE ***SCRIPT***, A ***THUMBNAIL ROUGH***, ***PENCILING***, ***INKING***, ***LETTERING***, AND ***COLORING!***

WHEW!

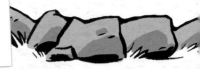

IT MAY SOUND LIKE A ***LOT OF WORK,*** AND IT ***IS!*** BUT EVERY STEP IS ANOTHER OPPORTUNITY TO ***REFINE THE STORY*** AND ***CLARIFY IT*** FOR THE READER.

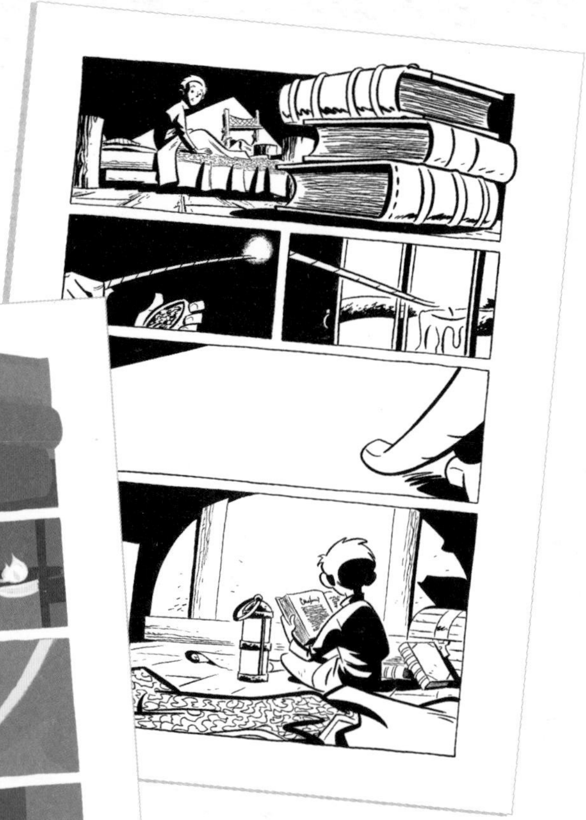

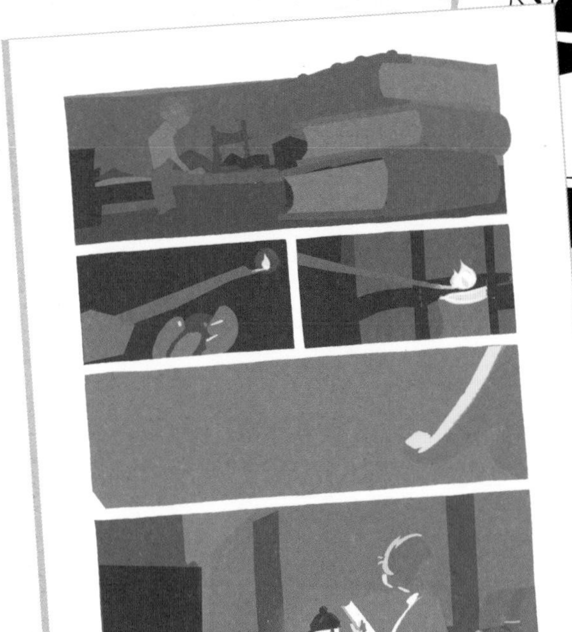

FOR INSTANCE: AT SOME POINT, I REALIZED WHAT AN IMPORTANT IMAGE THE ***LANTERN*** (AND LIGHT IN GENERAL...OR THE LACK OF IT) WAS GOING TO BE IN THIS BOOK.

SO I ADDED TWO PANELS TO PAGE 28 WHERE THAT LANTERN ***GETS LIT.*** IT SEEMS LIKE A SMALL THING, BUT IT TAKES AN EXTRA MOMENT OR TWO TO TELL THE AUDIENCE, "HEY, ***LOOK,*** THIS IS ***IMPORTANT!***"

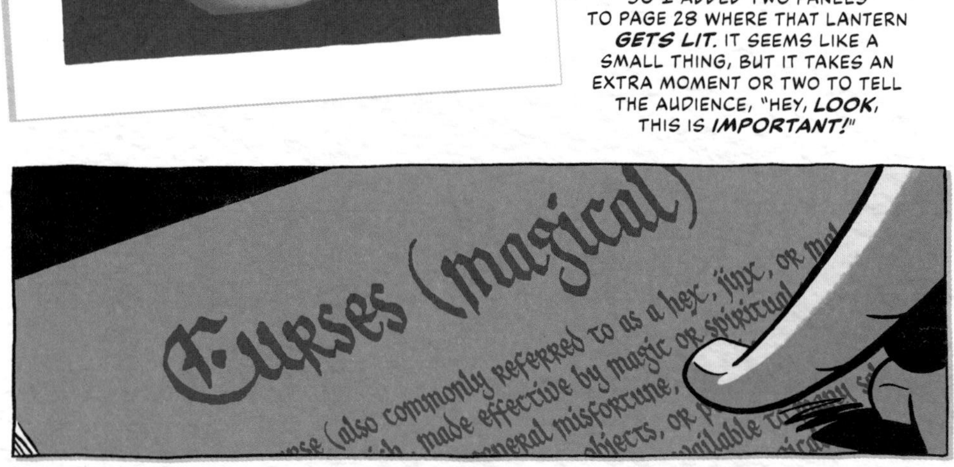
Curses (magical)
(also commonly referred to as a hex, jinx, or
made effective by magic or spiritual
general misfortune,
objects, or
available